LILAH STURGES · POLTERINK

# LUMBERJANES™

## THE SHAPE OF FRIENDSHIP

Ross Richie......................................................CEO & Founder
Joy Huffman.......................................................................CFO
Matt Gagnon..........................................Editor-in-Chief
Filip Sablik.........................President, Publishing & Marketing
Stephen Christy..............................President, Development
Lance Kreiter............Vice President, Licensing & Merchandising
Arune Singh ...................................Vice President, Marketing
Bryce Carlson.................Vice President, Editorial & Creative Strategy
Scott Newman ...............................Manager, Production Design
Kate Henning...................................Manager, Operations
Spencer Simpson ....................................Manager, Sales
Elyse Strandberg ..................................Manager, Finance
Sierra Hahn...........................................Executive Editor
Jeanine Schaefer.....................................Executive Editor
Dafna Pleban ..............................................Senior Editor
Shannon Watters ........................................Senior Editor
Eric Harburn ...............................................Senior Editor
Chris Rosa...........................................................Editor
Matthew Levine ...................................................Editor
Sophie Philips-Roberts........................Associate Editor
Amanda LaFranco....................................Associate Editor
Jonathan Manning...................................Associate Editor
Gavin Gronenthal ..................................Assistant Editor
Gwen Waller ...........................................Assistant Editor
Allyson Gronowitz...................................Assistant Editor
Jillian Crab.........................................Design Coordinator
Michelle Ankley...................................Design Coordinator
Kara Leopard ......................................Production Designer
Marie Krupina ....................................Production Designer
Grace Park ..........................................Production Designer
Chelsea Roberts................... Production Design Assistant
Samantha Knapp....................Production Design Assistant
José Meza ............................................. Live Events Lead
Stephanie Hocutt...........................Digital Marketing Lead
Esther Kim....................................Marketing Coordinator
Cat O'Grady .........................Digital Marketing Coordinator
Amanda Lawson .................................Marketing Assistant
Holly Aitchison ..............................Digital Sales Coordinator
Morgan Perry ..............................Retail Sales Coordinator
Megan Christopher...............................Operations Coordinator
Rodrigo Hernandez.................................Mailroom Assistant
Zipporah Smith......................................Operations Assistant
Sabrina Lesin.........................................Accounting Assistant
Breanna Sarpy...................................... Executive Assistant

# BOOM! BOX™

**LUMBERJANES: THE SHAPE OF FRIENDSHIP, November 2019.**
Published by BOOM! Box, a division of Boom Entertainment, Inc.
Lumberjanes is ™ & © 2019 Shannon Watters, Grace Ellis, Noelle
Stevenson & Brooklyn Allen. All rights reserved. BOOM! Box™ and
the BOOM! Box logo are trademarks of Boom Entertainment, Inc.,
registered in various countries and categories. All characters, events,
and institutions depicted herein are fictional. Any similarity between
any of the names, characters, persons, events, and/or institutions in
this publication to actual names, characters, and persons, whether
living or dead, events, and/or institutions is unintended and purely
coincidental. BOOM! Box does not read or accept unsolicited
submissions of ideas, stories, or artwork.

For information regarding the CPSIA on this printed material, call:
(203) 595-3636 and provide reference #RICH - 869599.

BOOM! Studios, 5670 Wilshire Boulevard, Suite 400, Los Angeles,
CA 90036-5679. Printed in USA. First Printing.

ISBN: 978-1-68415-451-7, eISBN: 978-1-64144-568-9

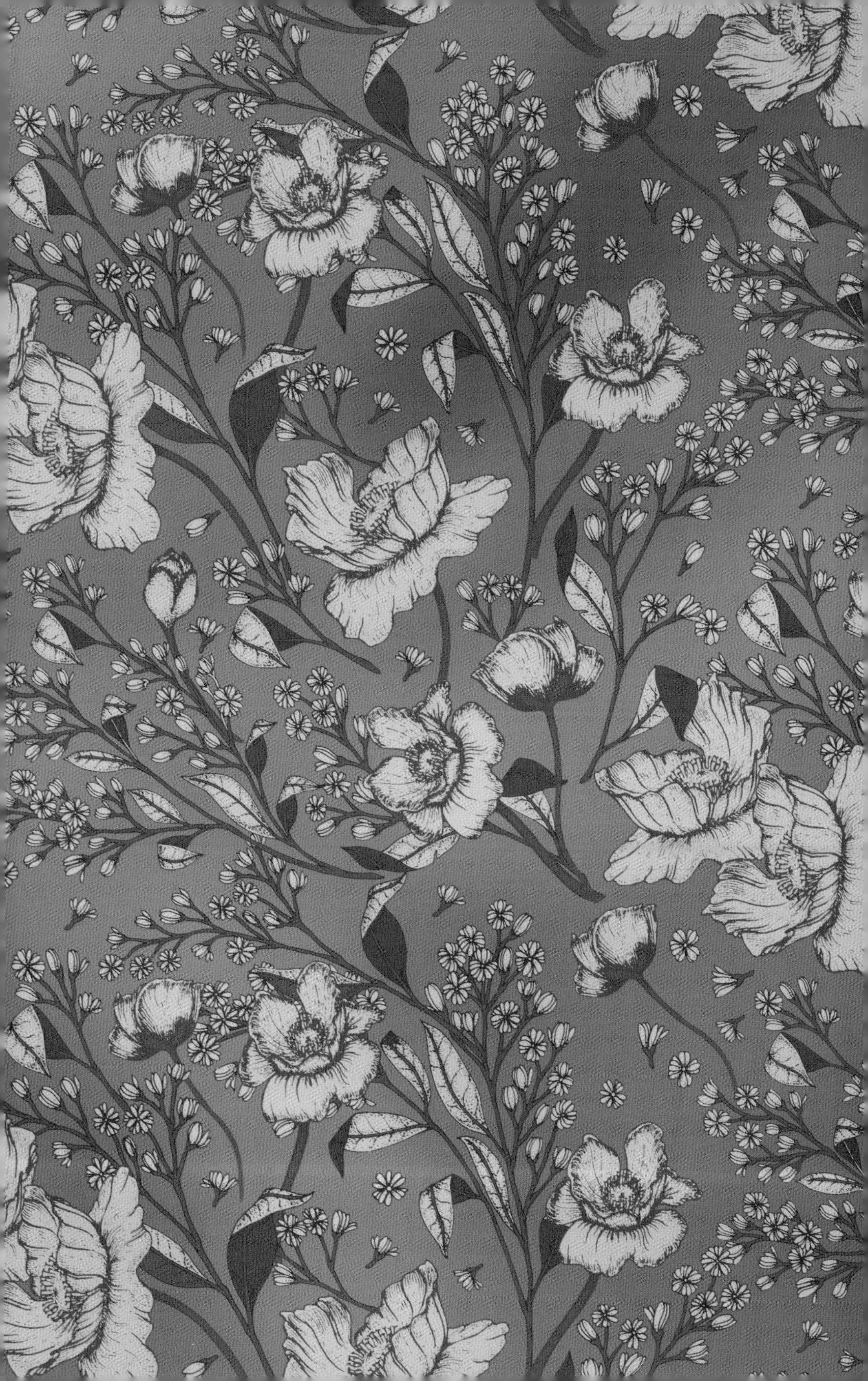

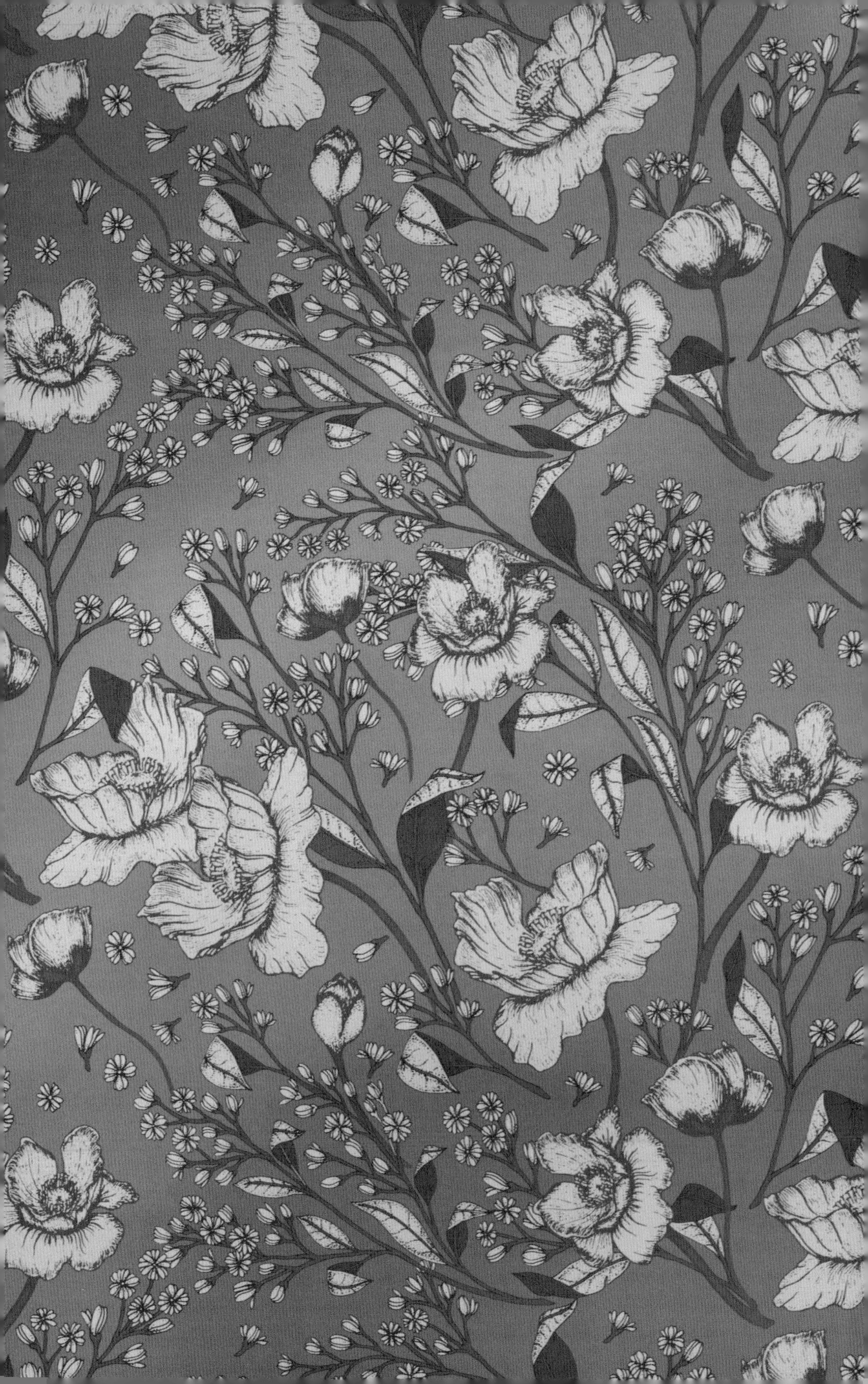

# LUMBERJANES™

## THE SHAPE OF FRIENDSHIP

Written by
## LILAH STURGES

Illustrated by
## POLTERINK

Lettered by
## JIM CAMPBELL

Cover by
## ALEXA SHARPE

Designer
**JILLIAN CRAB**

Associate Editor
**SOPHIE PHILIPS-ROBERTS**

Editor
**JEANINE SCHAEFER**

Special thanks to **Kelsey Pate** for giving the
Lumberjanes their name.

Created by
**SHANNON WATTERS, GRACE ELLIS,
NOELLE STEVENSON & BROOKLYN ALLEN**

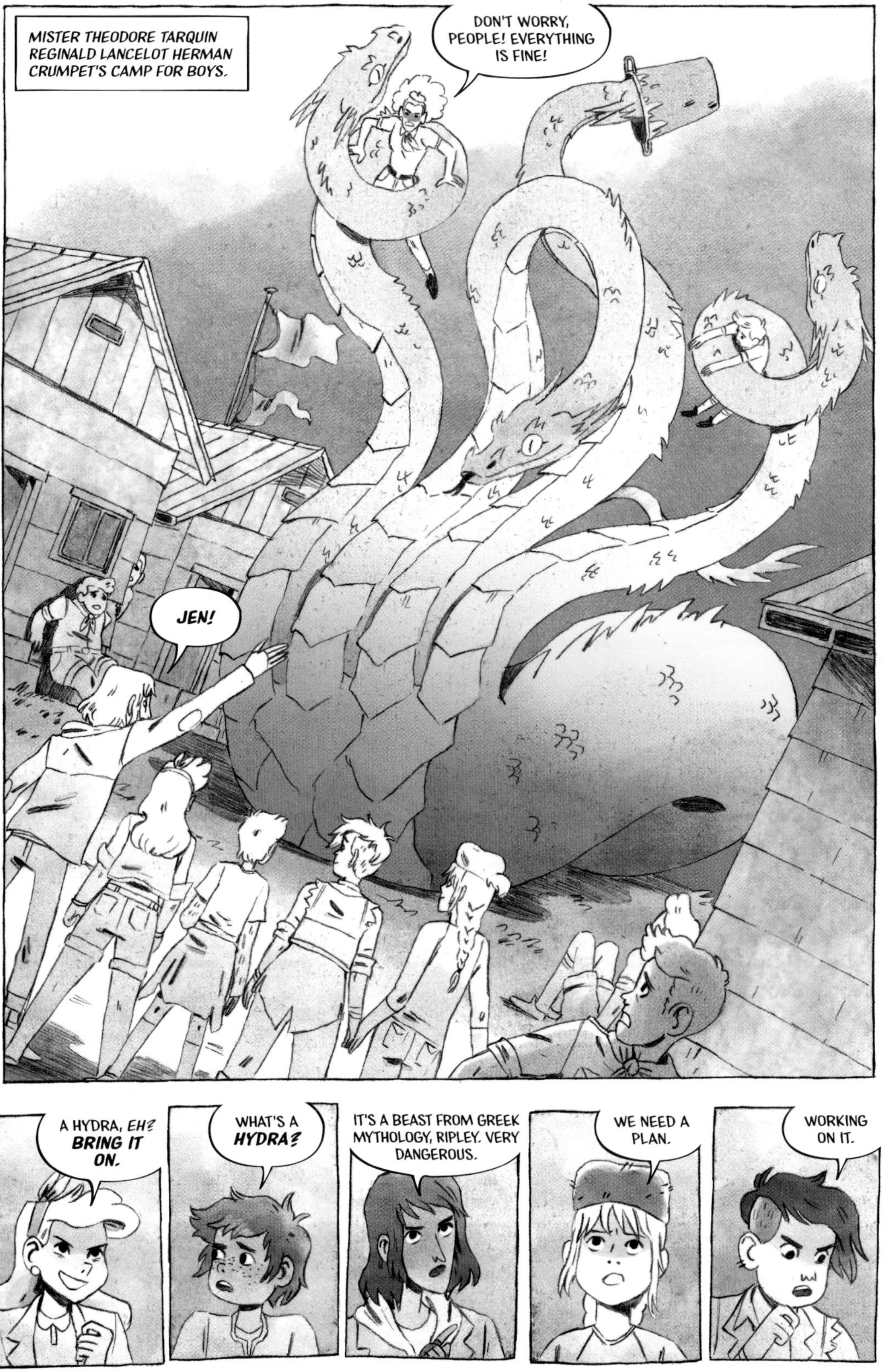

MISTER THEODORE TARQUIN REGINALD LANCELOT HERMAN CRUMPET'S CAMP FOR BOYS.
DON'T WORRY, PEOPLE! EVERYTHING IS FINE!
JEN!
A HYDRA, EH? BRING IT ON.
WHAT'S A HYDRA?
IT'S A BEAST FROM GREEK MYTHOLOGY, RIPLEY. VERY DANGEROUS.
WE NEED A PLAN.
WORKING ON IT.

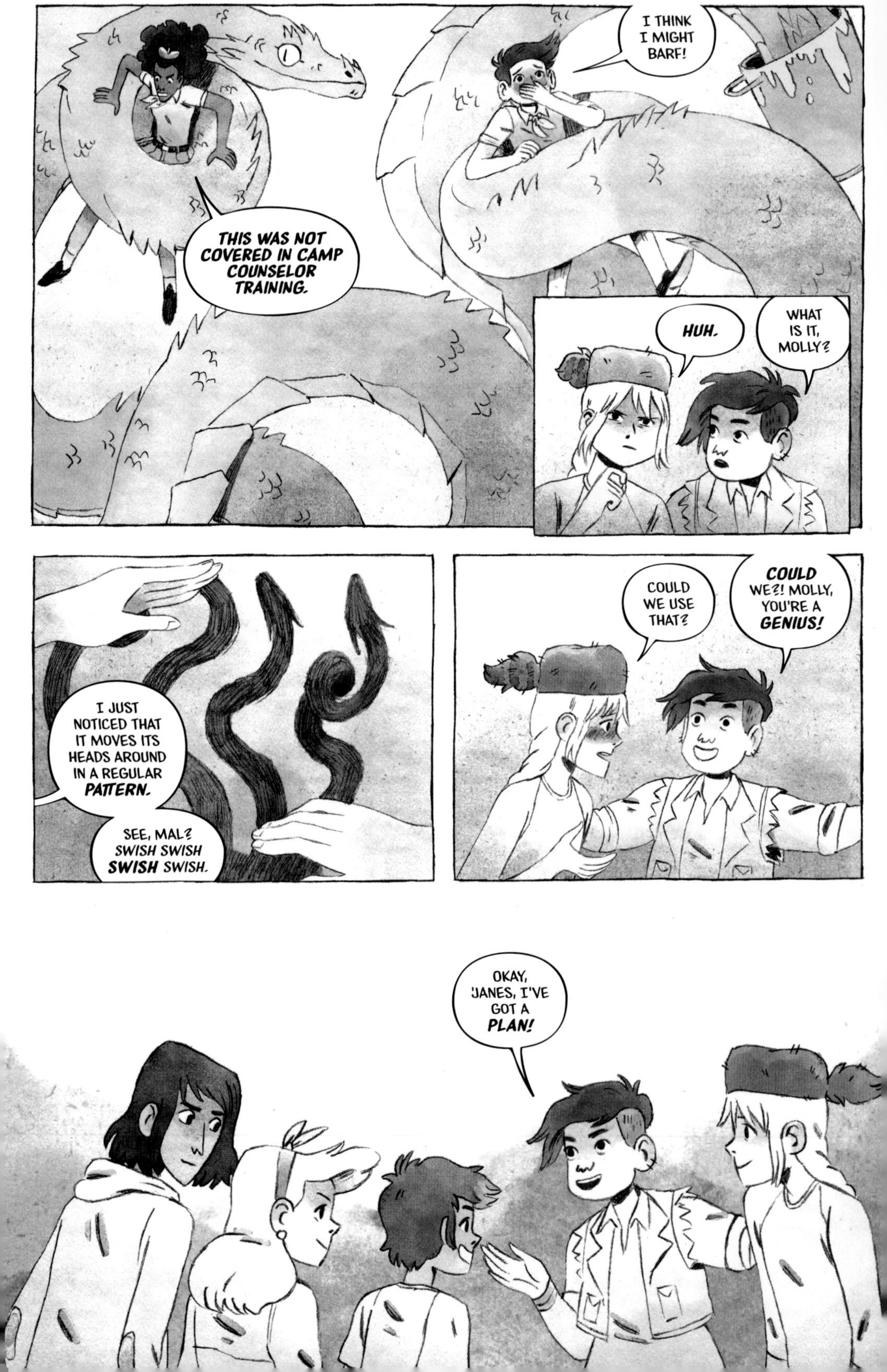
THIS WAS NOT COVERED IN CAMP COUNSELOR TRAINING.
I THINK I MIGHT BARF!
HUH.
WHAT IS IT, MOLLY?
I JUST NOTICED THAT IT MOVES ITS HEADS AROUND IN A REGULAR PATTERN.
SEE, MAL? SWISH SWISH SWISH SWISH.
COULD WE USE THAT?
COULD WE?! MOLLY, YOU'RE A GENIUS!
OKAY, JANES, I'VE GOT A PLAN!

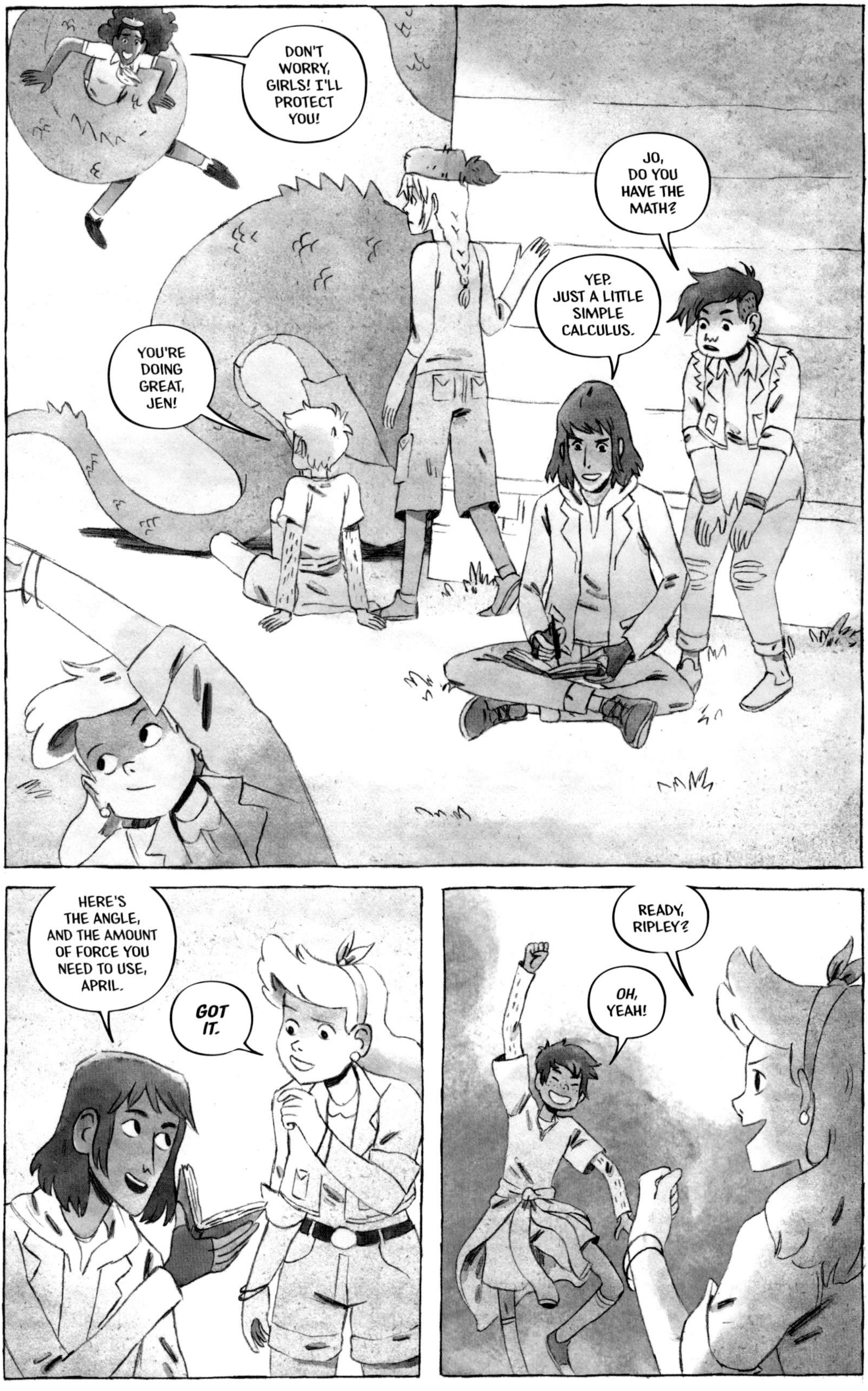
DON'T WORRY, GIRLS! I'LL PROTECT YOU!
JO, DO YOU HAVE THE MATH?
YEP. JUST A LITTLE SIMPLE CALCULUS.
YOU'RE DOING GREAT, JEN!
HERE'S THE ANGLE, AND THE AMOUNT OF FORCE YOU NEED TO USE, APRIL.
GOT IT.
READY, RIPLEY?
OH, YEAH!

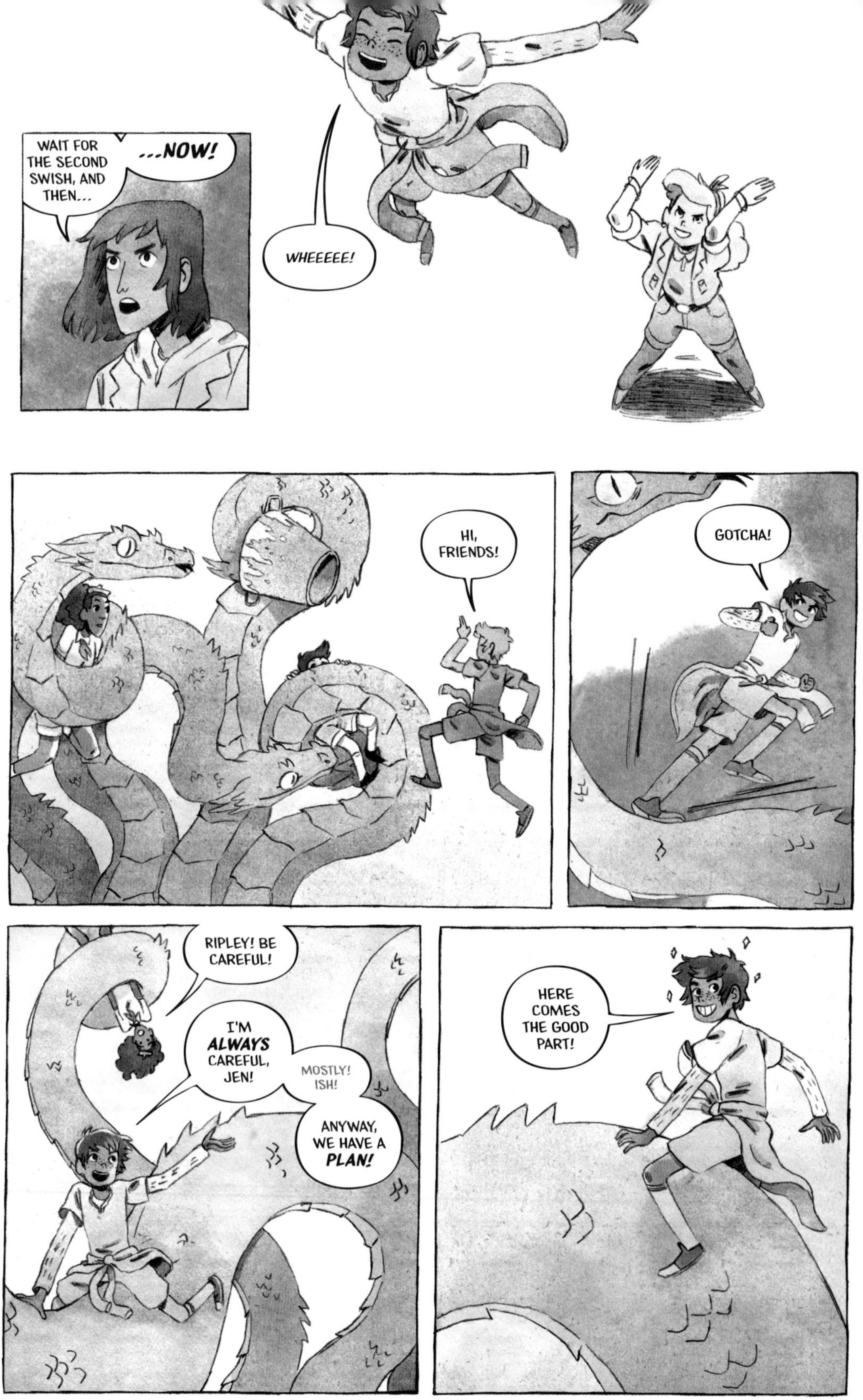
WAIT FOR THE SECOND SWISH, AND THEN...
...NOW!
WHEEEEE!
HI, FRIENDS!
GOTCHA!
RIPLEY! BE CAREFUL!
I'M ALWAYS CAREFUL, JEN!
MOSTLY! ISH!
ANYWAY, WE HAVE A PLAN!
HERE COMES THE GOOD PART!

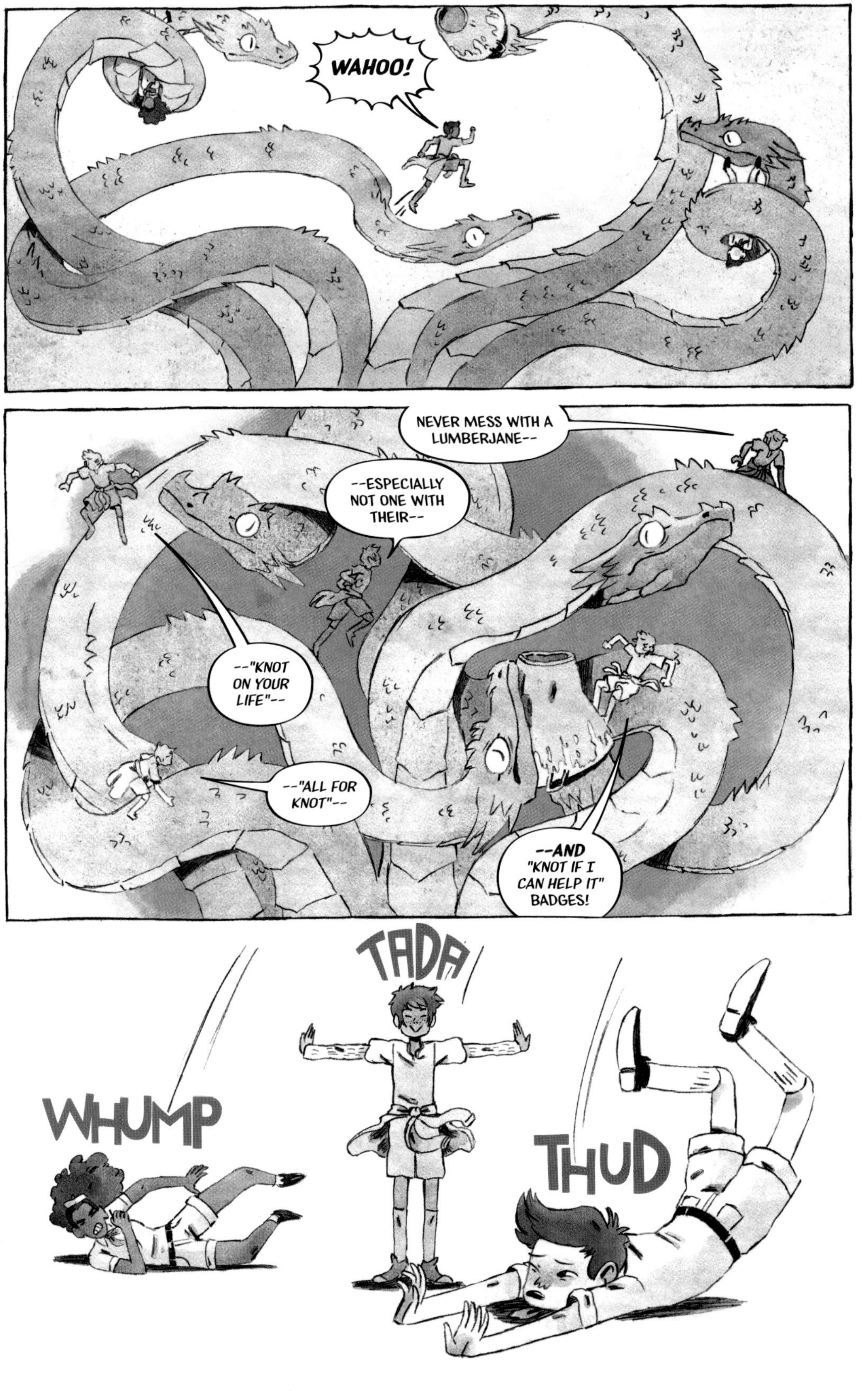
WAHOO!
NEVER MESS WITH A LUMBERJANE--
--ESPECIALLY NOT ONE WITH THEIR--
--"KNOT ON YOUR LIFE"--
--"ALL FOR KNOT"--
--AND "KNOT IF I CAN HELP IT" BADGES!
TADA
WHUMP
THUD

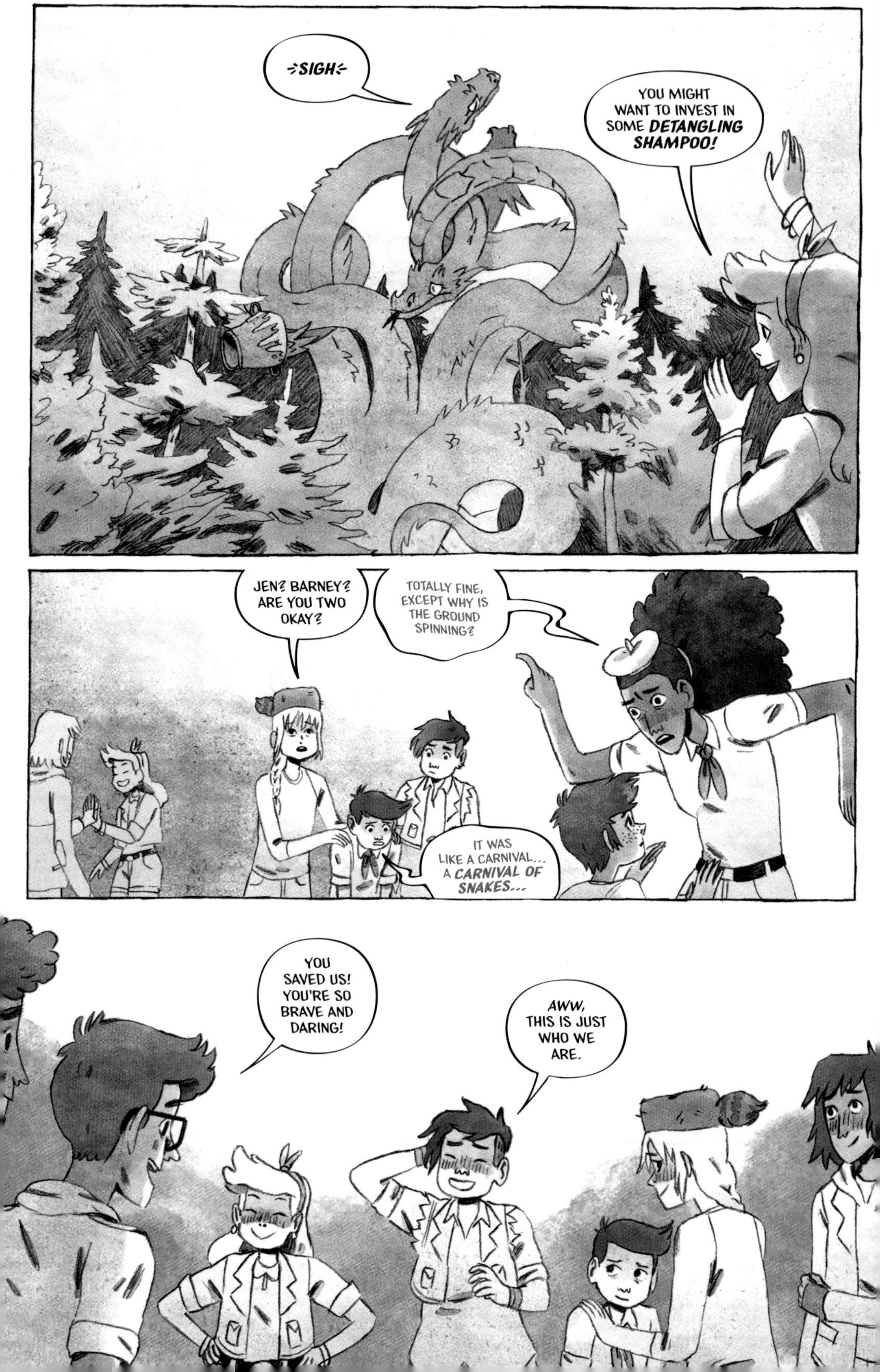

SIGH
YOU MIGHT WANT TO INVEST IN SOME DETANGLING SHAMPOO!
JEN? BARNEY? ARE YOU TWO OKAY?
TOTALLY FINE, EXCEPT WHY IS THE GROUND SPINNING?
IT WAS LIKE A CARNIVAL... A CARNIVAL OF SNAKES...
YOU SAVED US! YOU'RE SO BRAVE AND DARING!
AWW, THIS IS JUST WHO WE ARE.

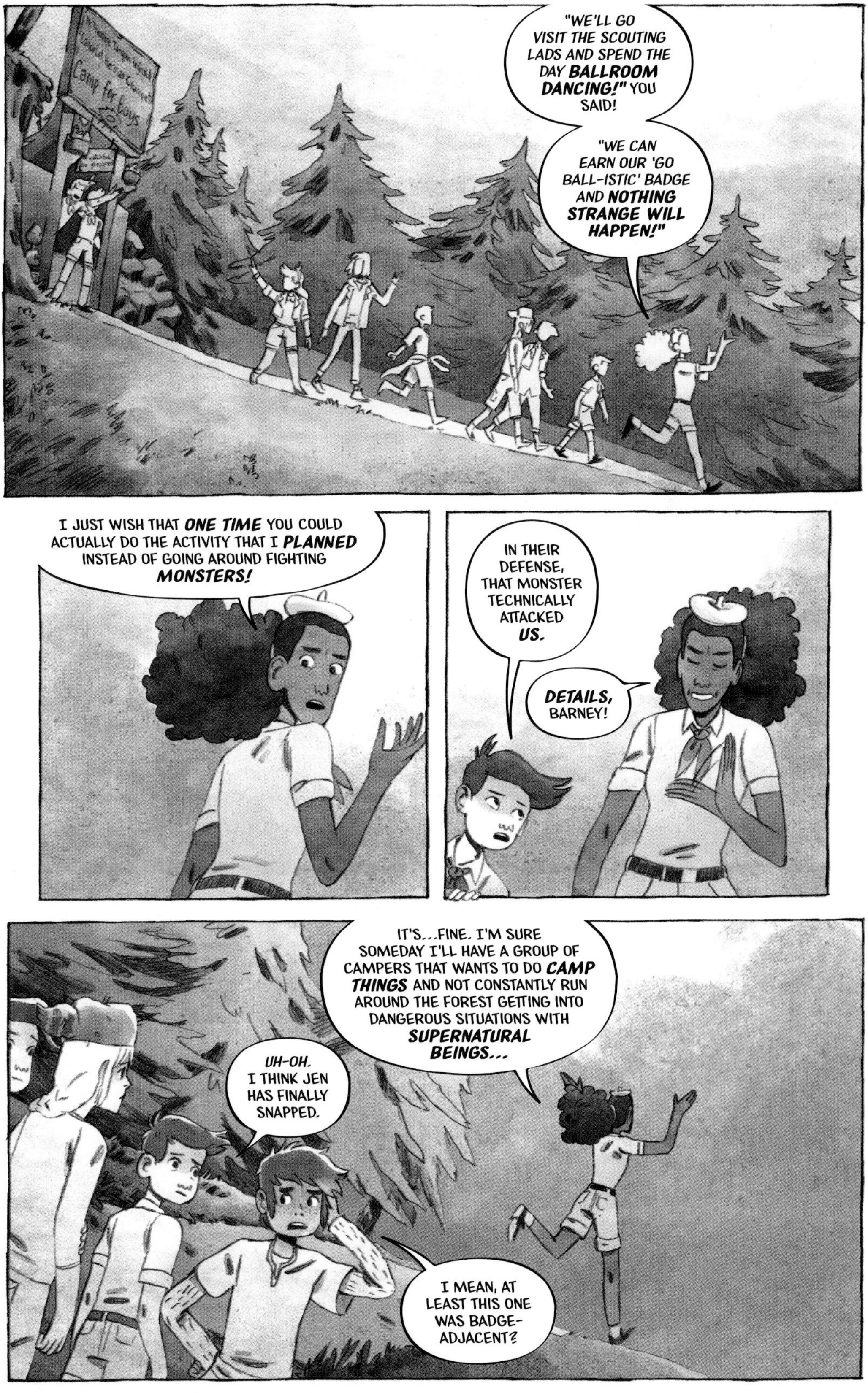
Camp for boys
"WE'LL GO VISIT THE SCOUTING LADS AND SPEND THE DAY **BALLROOM DANCING!"** YOU SAID!
"WE CAN EARN OUR 'GO BALL-ISTIC' BADGE AND **NOTHING STRANGE WILL HAPPEN!"**
I JUST WISH THAT ***ONE TIME*** YOU COULD ACTUALLY DO THE ACTIVITY THAT I ***PLANNED*** INSTEAD OF GOING AROUND FIGHTING ***MONSTERS!***
IN THEIR DEFENSE, THAT MONSTER TECHNICALLY ATTACKED ***US.***
***DETAILS,*** BARNEY!
IT'S...FINE. I'M SURE SOMEDAY I'LL HAVE A GROUP OF CAMPERS THAT WANTS TO DO ***CAMP THINGS*** AND NOT CONSTANTLY RUN AROUND THE FOREST GETTING INTO DANGEROUS SITUATIONS WITH ***SUPERNATURAL BEINGS...***
*UH-OH.* I THINK JEN HAS FINALLY SNAPPED.
I MEAN, AT LEAST THIS ONE WAS BADGE-ADJACENT?

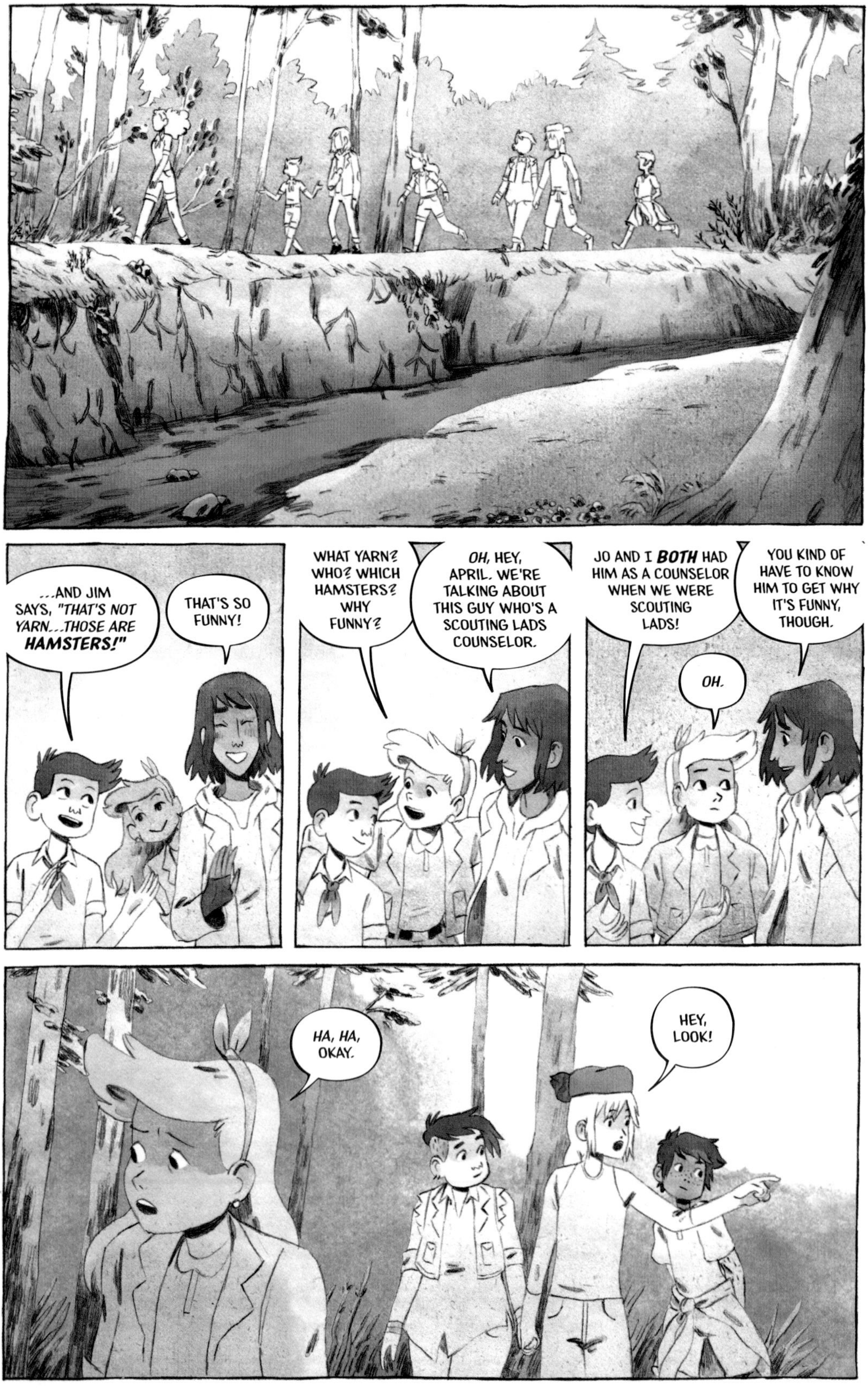
...AND JIM SAYS, "THAT'S NOT YARN...THOSE ARE **HAMSTERS!**"
THAT'S SO FUNNY!
WHAT YARN? WHO? WHICH HAMSTERS? WHY FUNNY?
*OH*, HEY, APRIL. WE'RE TALKING ABOUT THIS GUY WHO'S A SCOUTING LADS COUNSELOR.
JO AND I ***BOTH*** HAD HIM AS A COUNSELOR WHEN WE WERE SCOUTING LADS!
*OH.*
YOU KIND OF HAVE TO KNOW HIM TO GET WHY IT'S FUNNY, THOUGH.
HA, HA, OKAY.
HEY, LOOK!

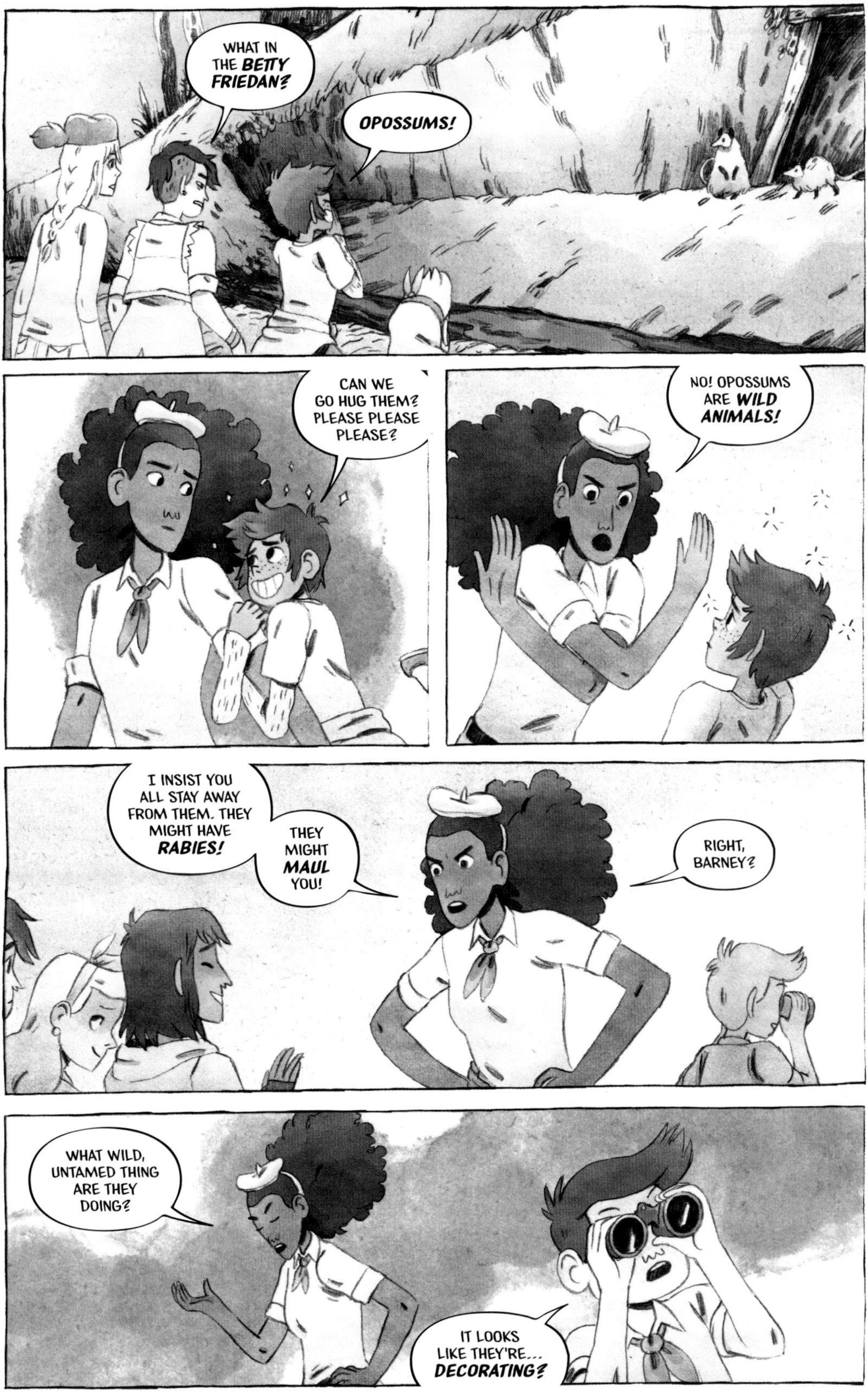
WHAT IN THE BETTY FRIEDAN?
OPOSSUMS!
CAN WE GO HUG THEM? PLEASE PLEASE PLEASE?
NO! OPOSSUMS ARE WILD ANIMALS!
I INSIST YOU ALL STAY AWAY FROM THEM. THEY MIGHT HAVE RABIES!
THEY MIGHT MAUL YOU!
RIGHT, BARNEY?
WHAT WILD, UNTAMED THING ARE THEY DOING?
IT LOOKS LIKE THEY'RE... DECORATING?

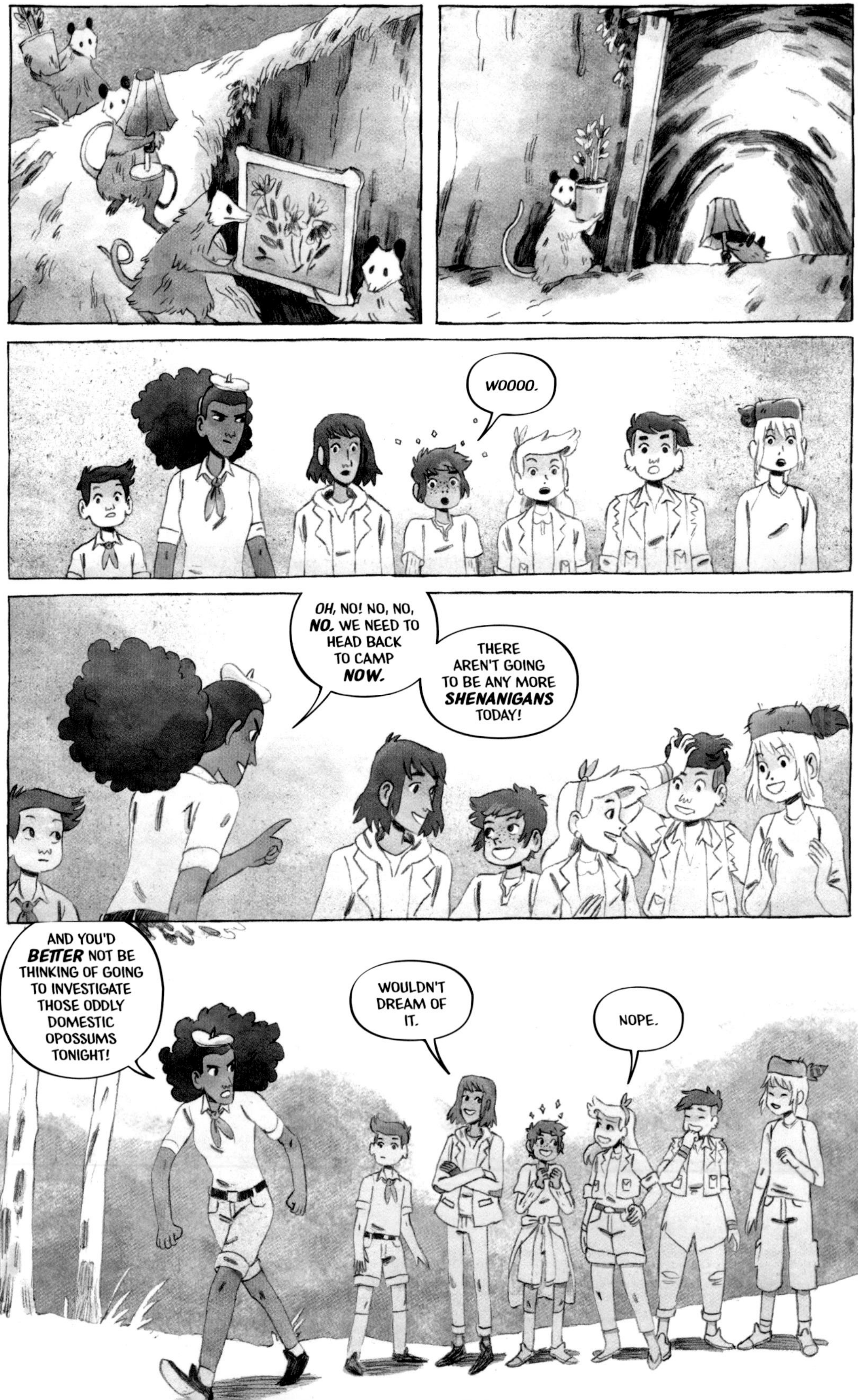
WOOOO.
OH, NO! NO, NO, NO. WE NEED TO HEAD BACK TO CAMP NOW.
THERE AREN'T GOING TO BE ANY MORE SHENANIGANS TODAY!
AND YOU'D BETTER NOT BE THINKING OF GOING TO INVESTIGATE THOSE ODDLY DOMESTIC OPOSSUMS TONIGHT!
WOULDN'T DREAM OF IT.
NOPE.

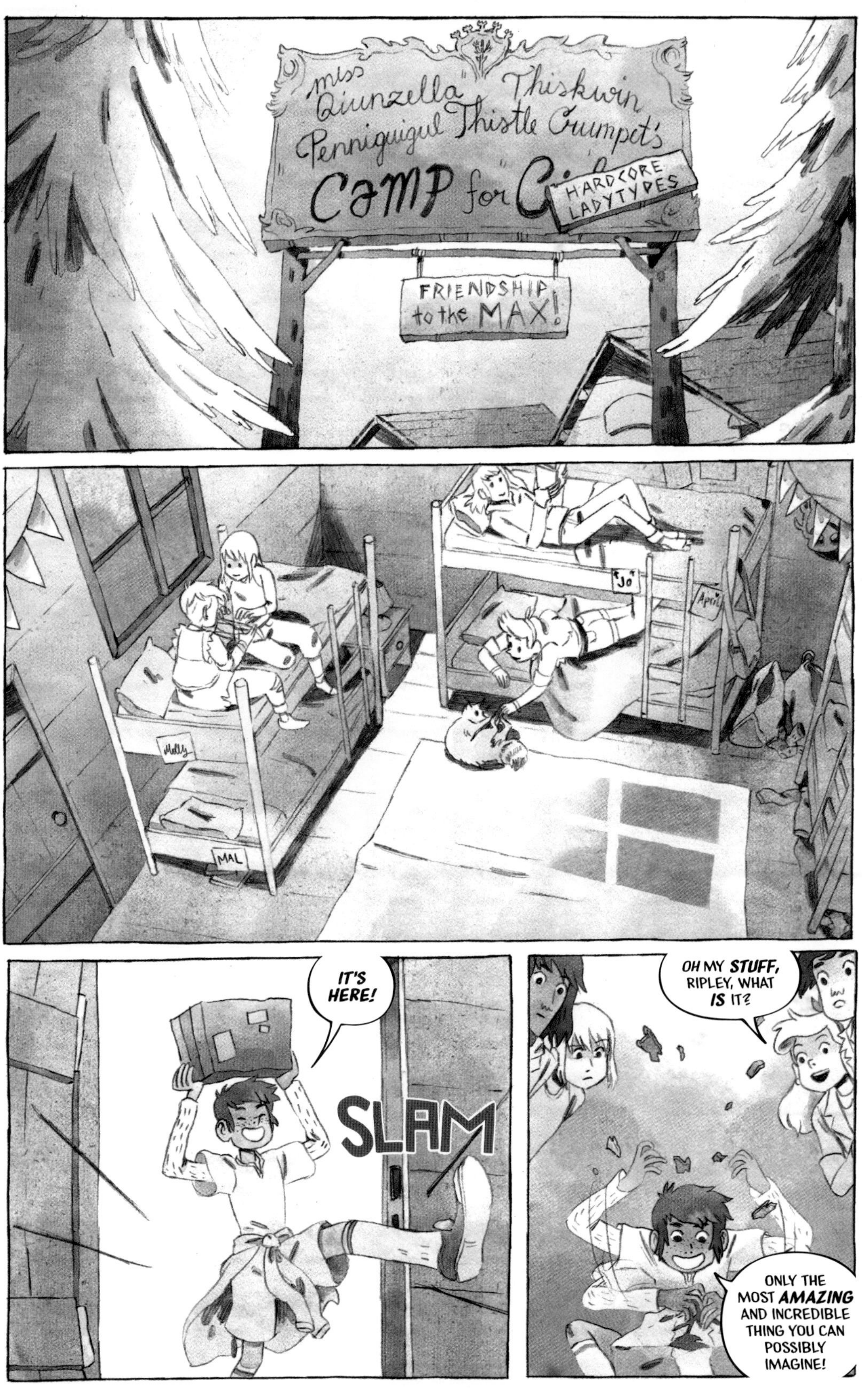

miss "Qiunzella" Thiskwin
Penniquiqul Thistle Crumpet's
CAMP for
HARDCORE LADYTYPES
FRIENDSHIP to the MAX!
Jo
April
Molly
MAL
IT'S HERE!
SLAM
OH MY **STUFF,** RIPLEY, WHAT **IS** IT?
ONLY THE MOST **AMAZING** AND INCREDIBLE THING YOU CAN POSSIBLY IMAGINE!

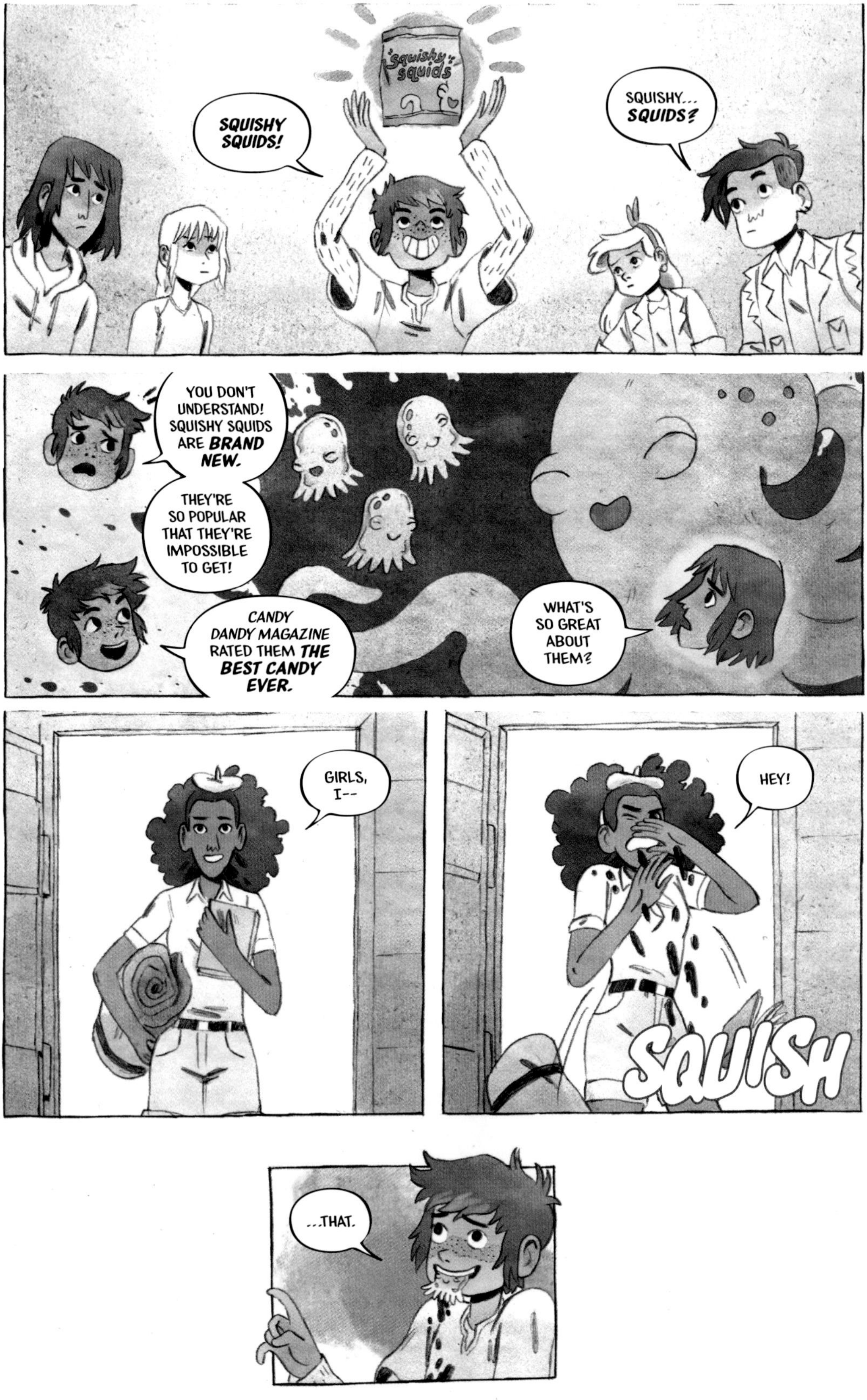

SQUISHY SQUIDS!
squishy squids
SQUISHY... SQUIDS?
YOU DON'T UNDERSTAND! SQUISHY SQUIDS ARE BRAND NEW.
THEY'RE SO POPULAR THAT THEY'RE IMPOSSIBLE TO GET!
CANDY DANDY MAGAZINE RATED THEM THE BEST CANDY EVER.
WHAT'S SO GREAT ABOUT THEM?
GIRLS, I--
HEY!
SQUISH
...THAT.

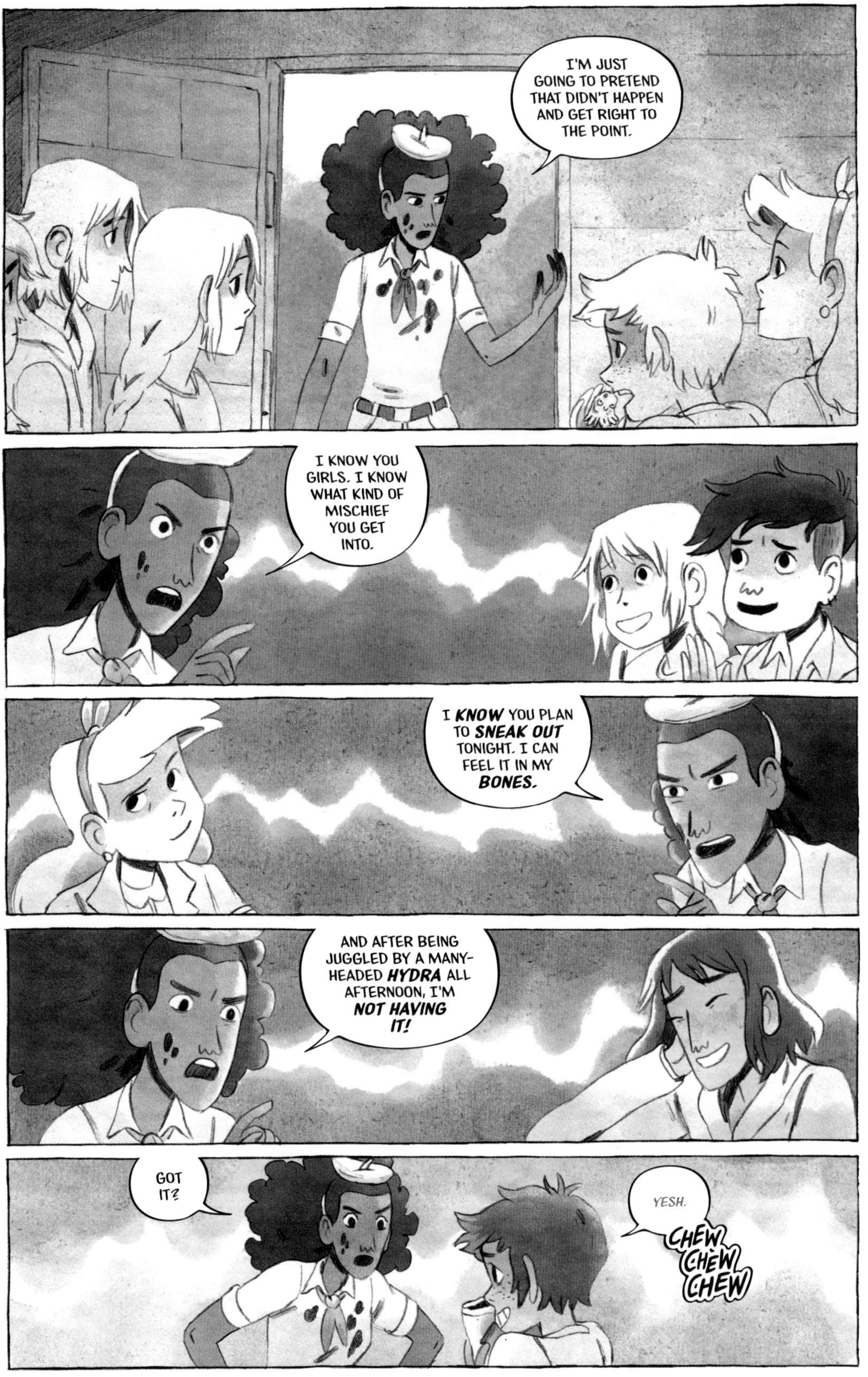
I'M JUST GOING TO PRETEND THAT DIDN'T HAPPEN AND GET RIGHT TO THE POINT.
I KNOW YOU GIRLS. I KNOW WHAT KIND OF MISCHIEF YOU GET INTO.
I KNOW YOU PLAN TO SNEAK OUT TONIGHT. I CAN FEEL IT IN MY BONES.
AND AFTER BEING JUGGLED BY A MANY-HEADED HYDRA ALL AFTERNOON, I'M NOT HAVING IT!
GOT IT?
YESH.
CHEW CHEW CHEW

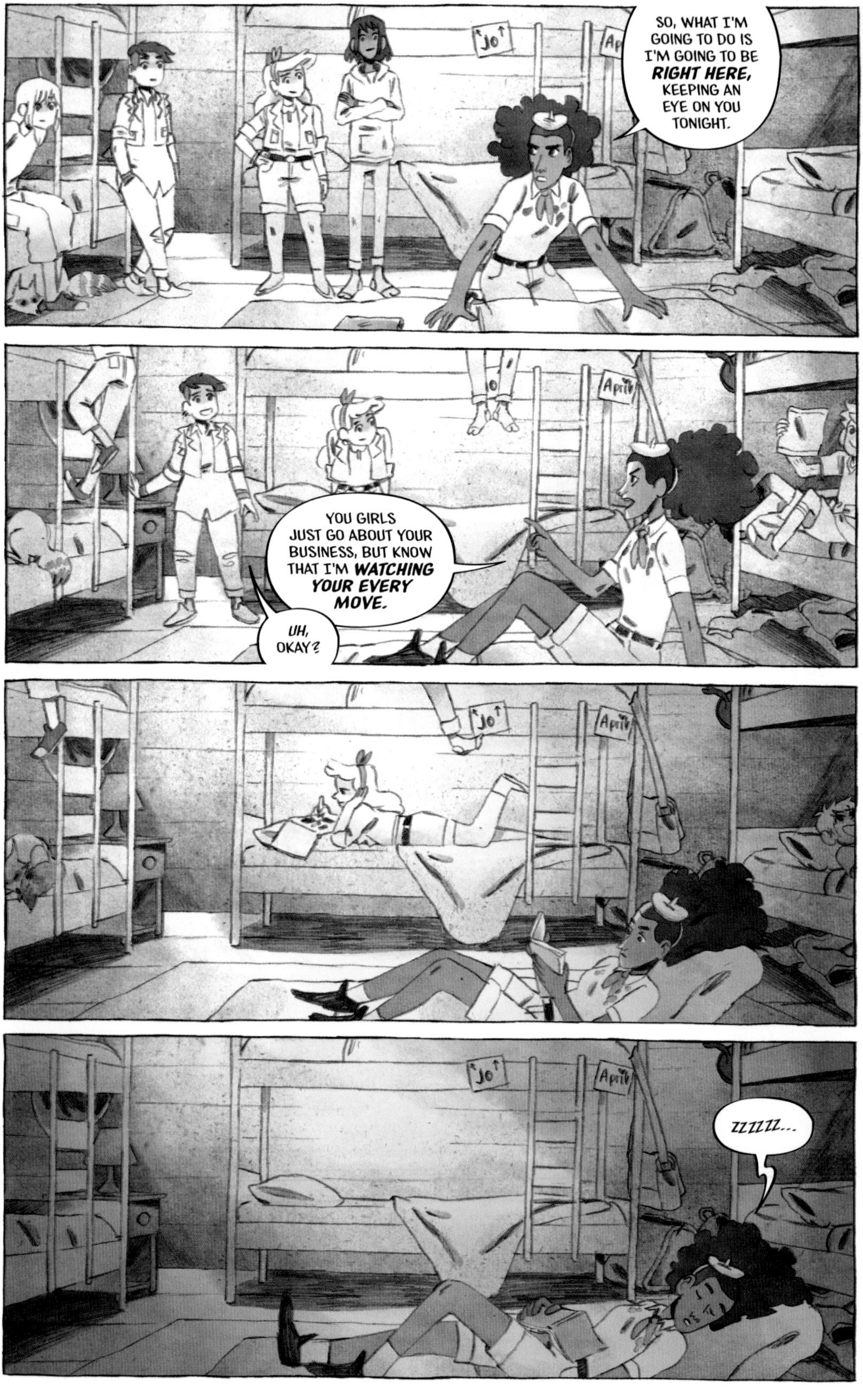

SO, WHAT I'M GOING TO DO IS I'M GOING TO BE RIGHT HERE, KEEPING AN EYE ON YOU TONIGHT.
Jo
April
YOU GIRLS JUST GO ABOUT YOUR BUSINESS, BUT KNOW THAT I'M WATCHING YOUR EVERY MOVE.
UH, OKAY?
ZZZZZZ...

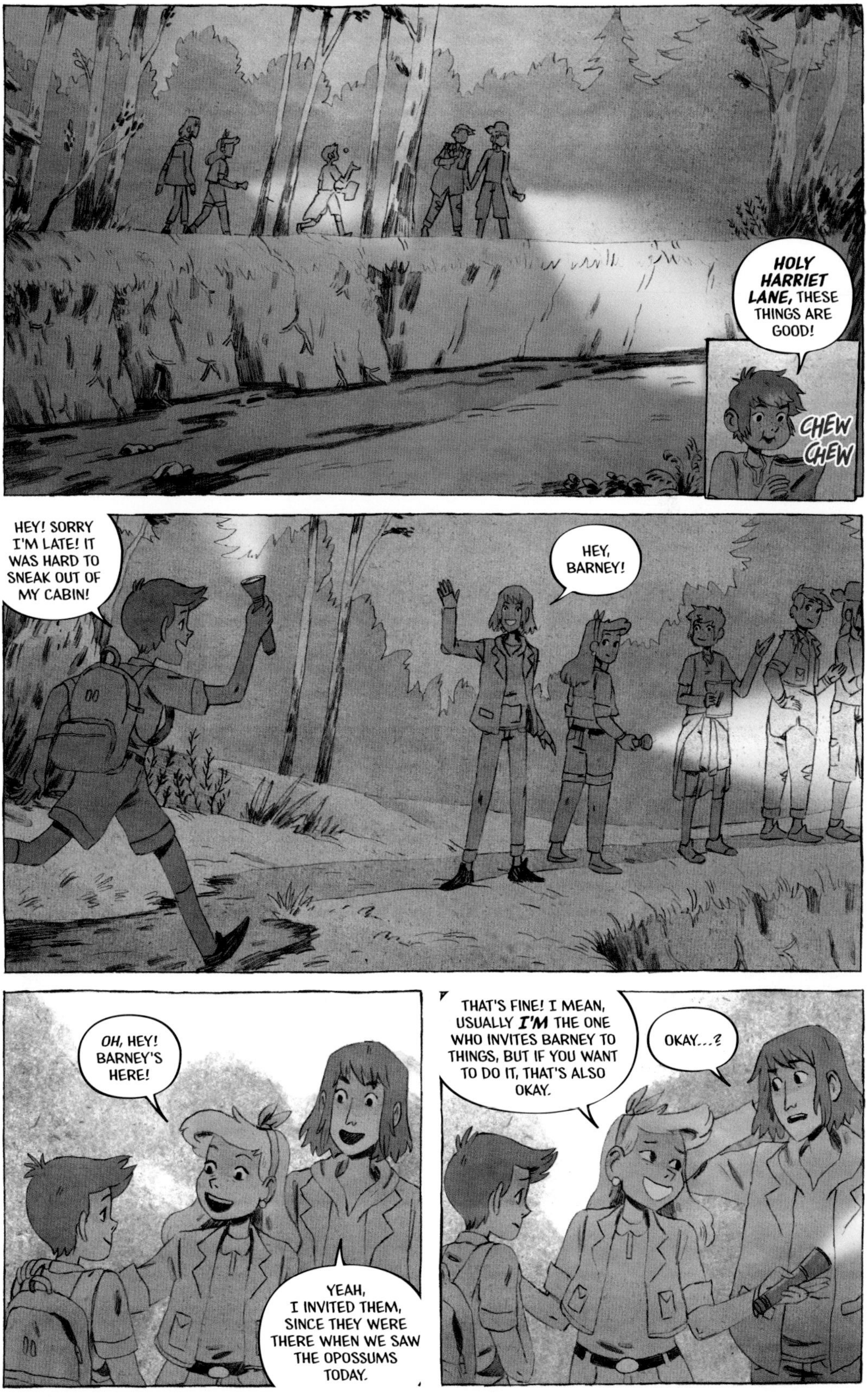

HOLY HARRIET LANE, THESE THINGS ARE GOOD!
CHEW CHEW
HEY! SORRY I'M LATE! IT WAS HARD TO SNEAK OUT OF MY CABIN!
HEY, BARNEY!
OH, HEY! BARNEY'S HERE!
YEAH, I INVITED THEM, SINCE THEY WERE THERE WHEN WE SAW THE OPOSSUMS TODAY.
THAT'S FINE! I MEAN, USUALLY I'M THE ONE WHO INVITES BARNEY TO THINGS, BUT IF YOU WANT TO DO IT, THAT'S ALSO OKAY.
OKAY...?

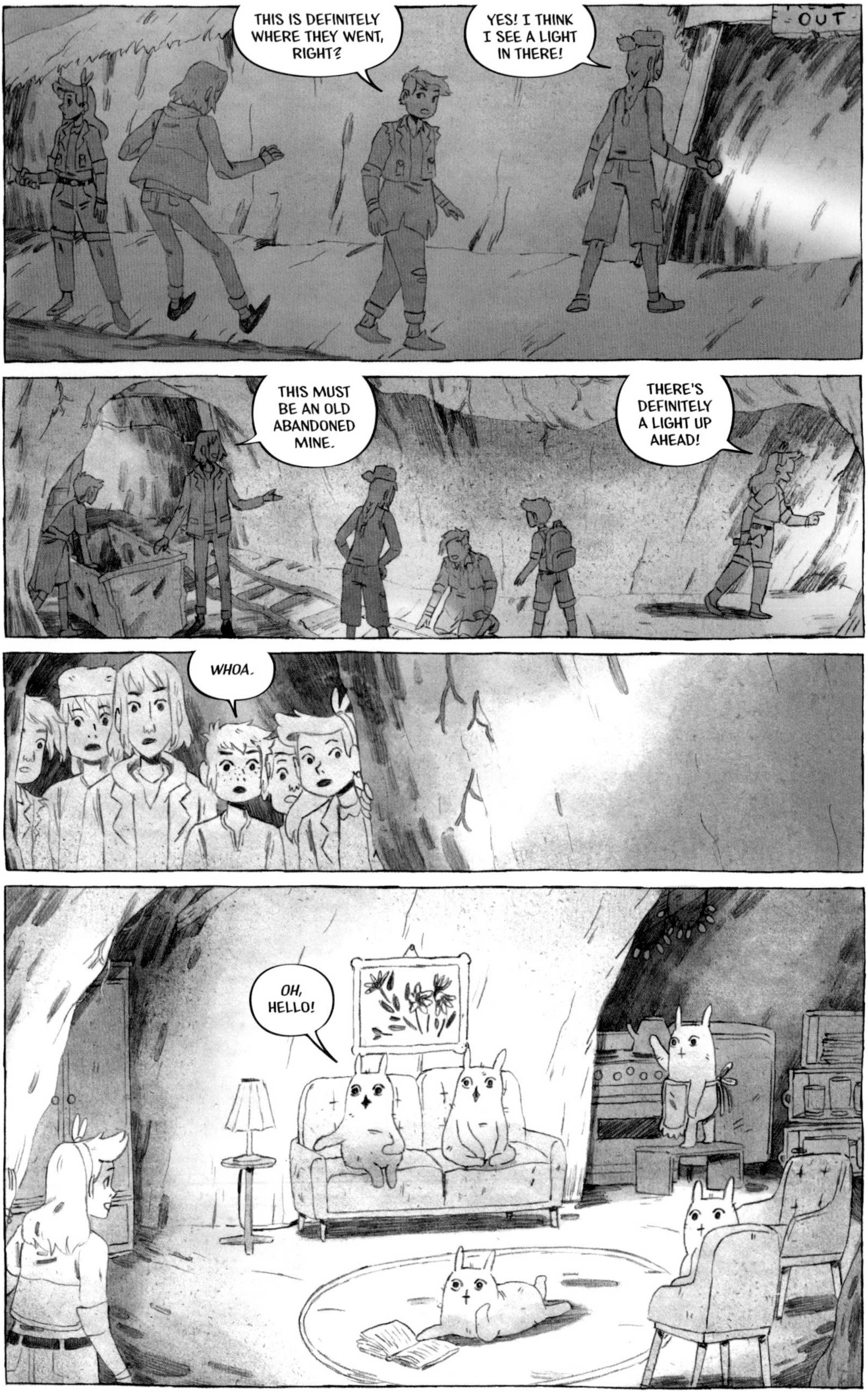
OUT
THIS IS DEFINITELY WHERE THEY WENT, RIGHT?
YES! I THINK I SEE A LIGHT IN THERE!
THIS MUST BE AN OLD ABANDONED MINE.
THERE'S DEFINITELY A LIGHT UP AHEAD!
WHOA.
OH, HELLO!

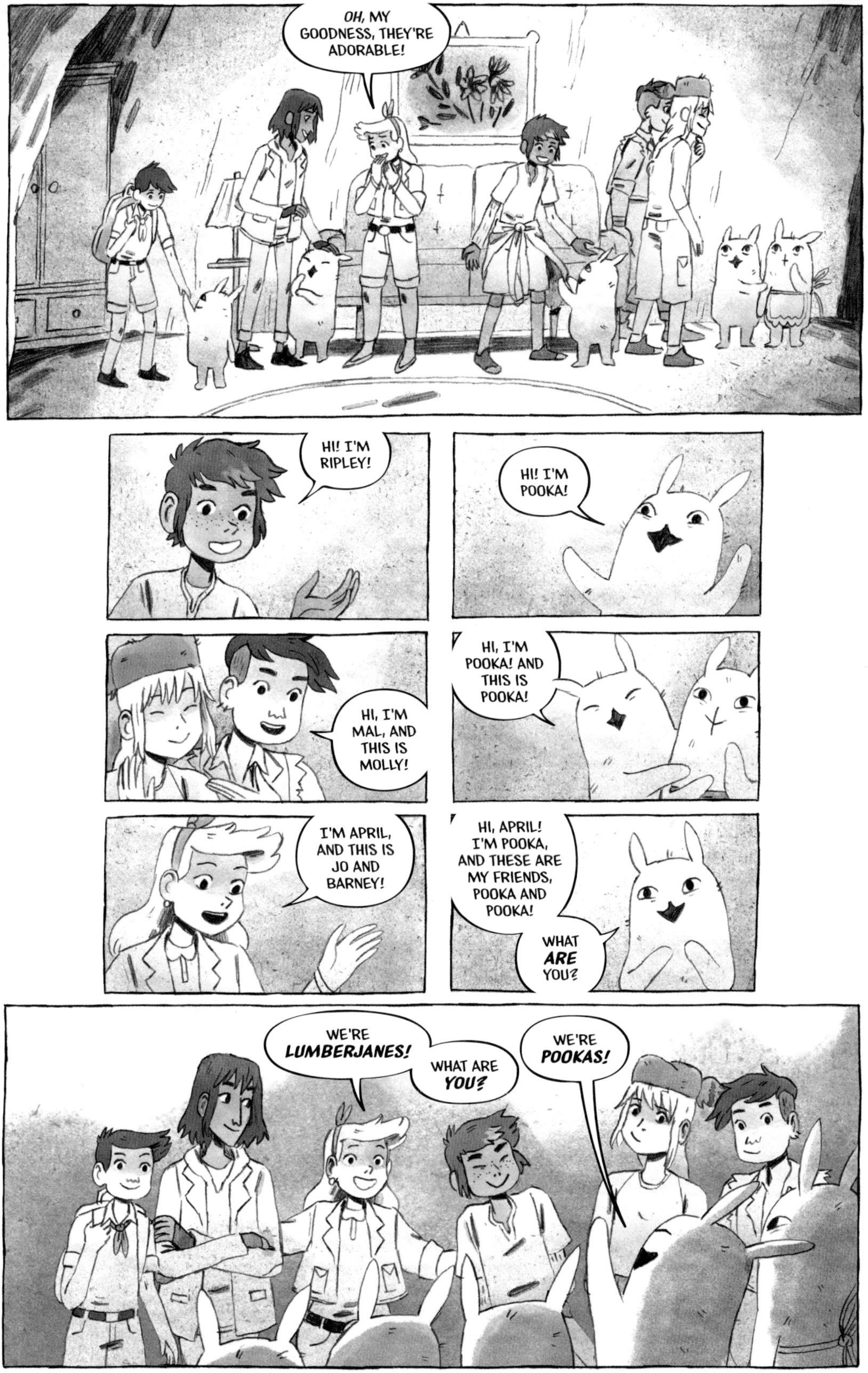
OH, MY GOODNESS, THEY'RE ADORABLE!
HI! I'M RIPLEY!
HI! I'M POOKA!
HI, I'M MAL, AND THIS IS MOLLY!
HI, I'M POOKA! AND THIS IS POOKA!
I'M APRIL, AND THIS IS JO AND BARNEY!
HI, APRIL! I'M POOKA, AND THESE ARE MY FRIENDS, POOKA AND POOKA!
WHAT ARE YOU?
WE'RE LUMBERJANES!
WHAT ARE YOU?
WE'RE POOKAS!

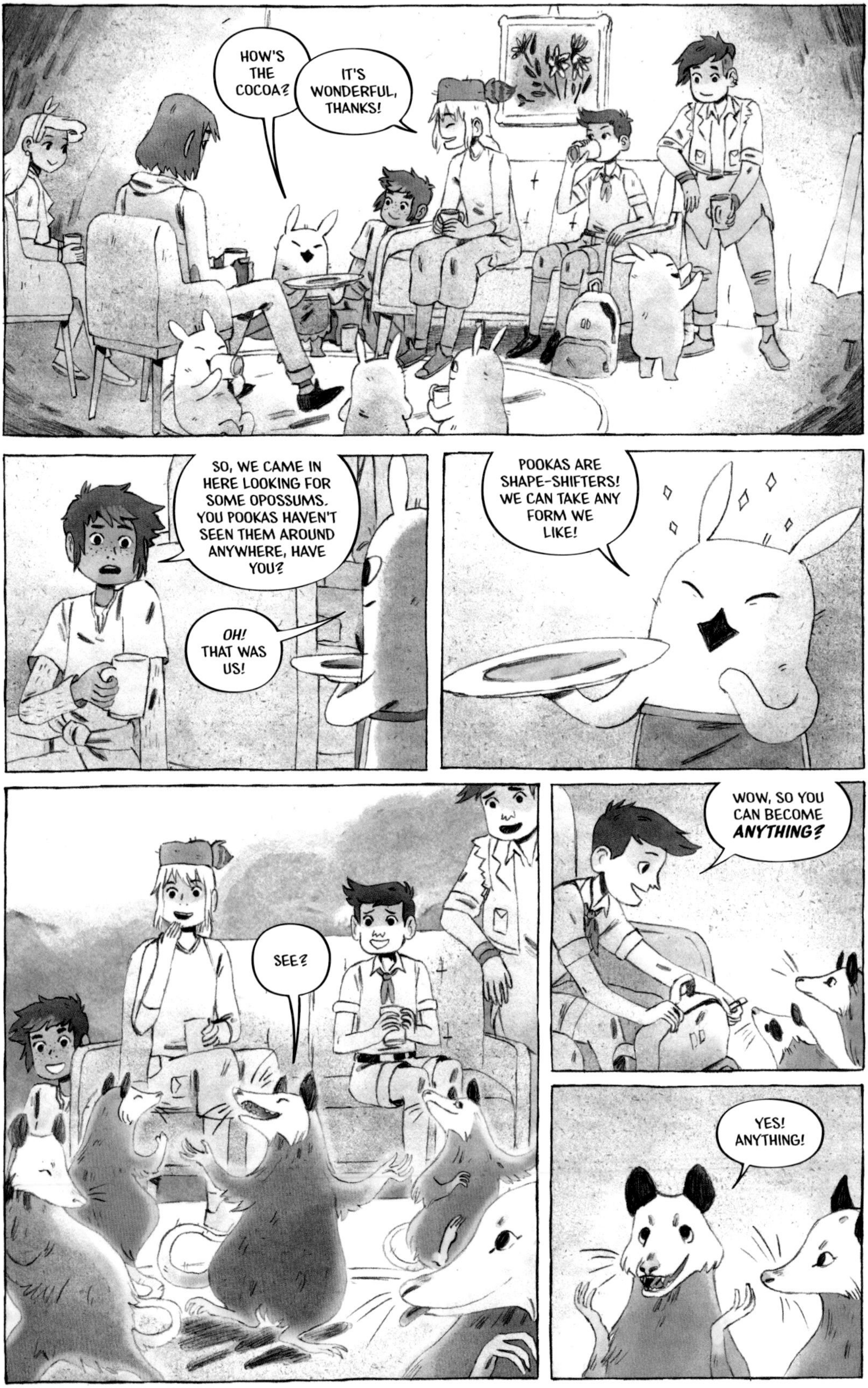
HOW'S THE COCOA?
IT'S WONDERFUL, THANKS!
SO, WE CAME IN HERE LOOKING FOR SOME OPOSSUMS. YOU POOKAS HAVEN'T SEEN THEM AROUND ANYWHERE, HAVE YOU?
OH! THAT WAS US!
POOKAS ARE SHAPE-SHIFTERS! WE CAN TAKE ANY FORM WE LIKE!
SEE?
WOW, SO YOU CAN BECOME ANYTHING?
YES! ANYTHING!

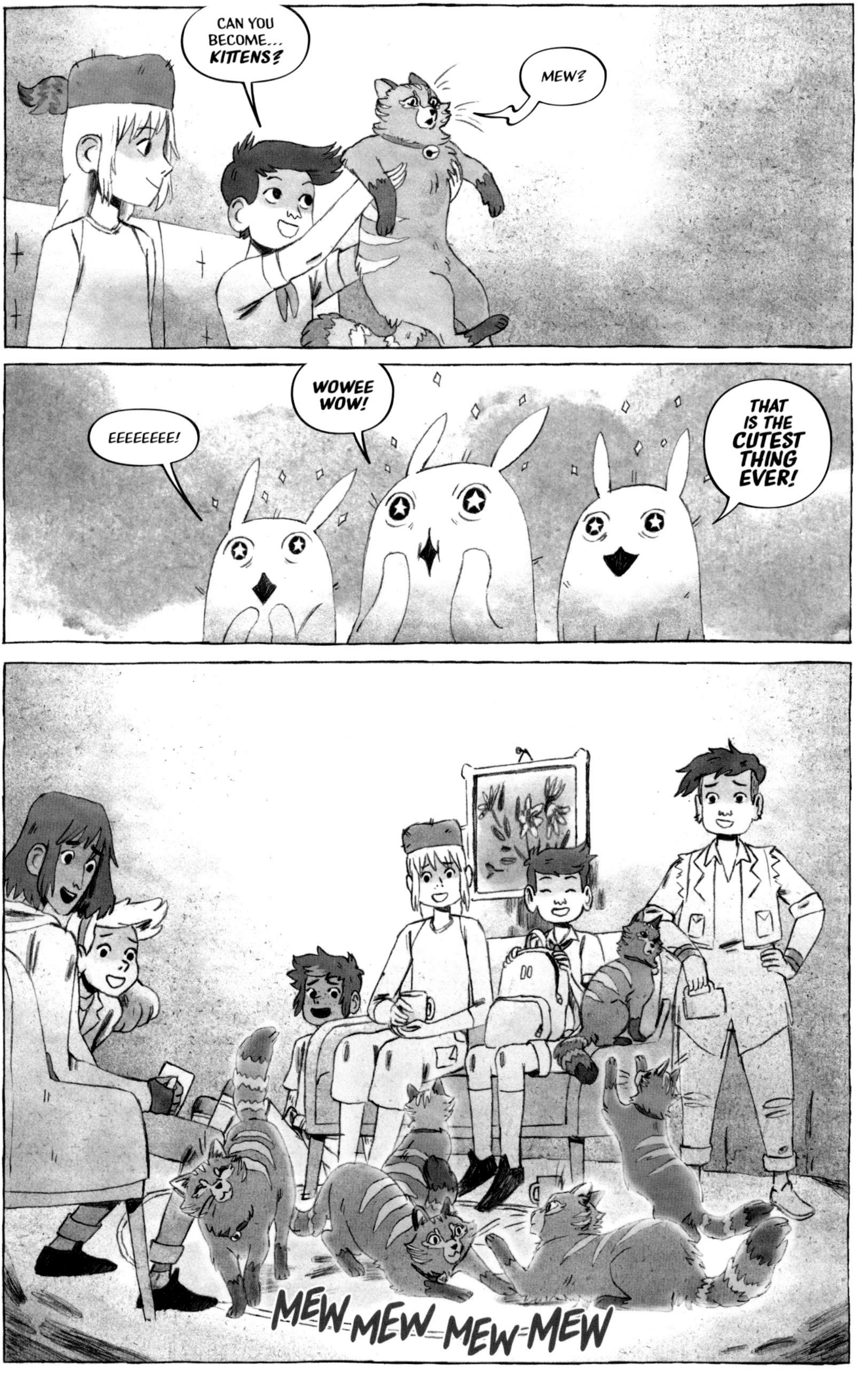
CAN YOU BECOME... KITTENS?
MEW?
EEEEEEEE!
WOWEE WOW!
THAT IS THE CUTEST THING EVER!
MEW MEW MEW MEW

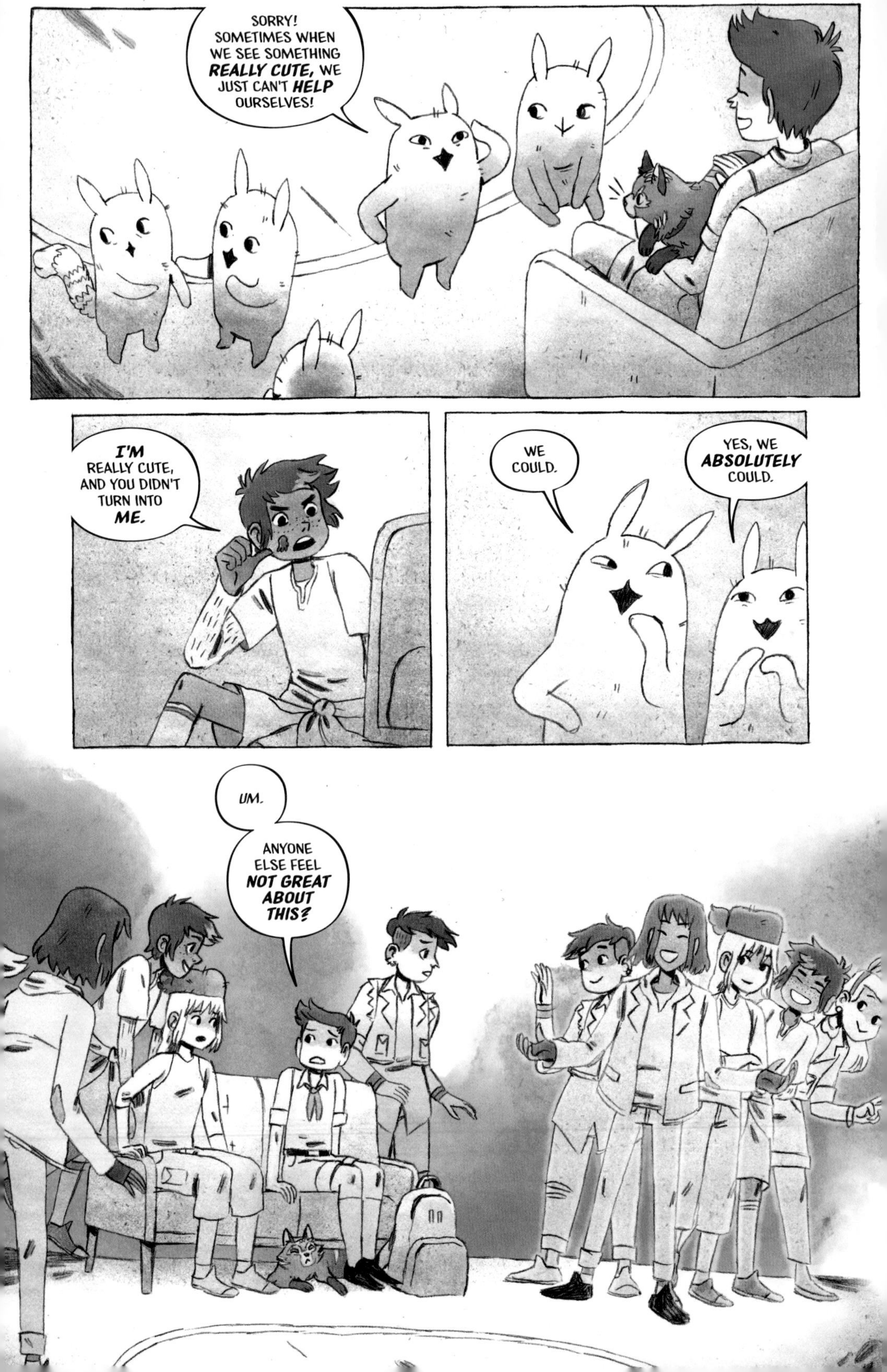
SORRY! SOMETIMES WHEN WE SEE SOMETHING REALLY CUTE, WE JUST CAN'T HELP OURSELVES!
I'M REALLY CUTE, AND YOU DIDN'T TURN INTO ME.
WE COULD.
YES, WE ABSOLUTELY COULD.
UM.
ANYONE ELSE FEEL NOT GREAT ABOUT THIS?

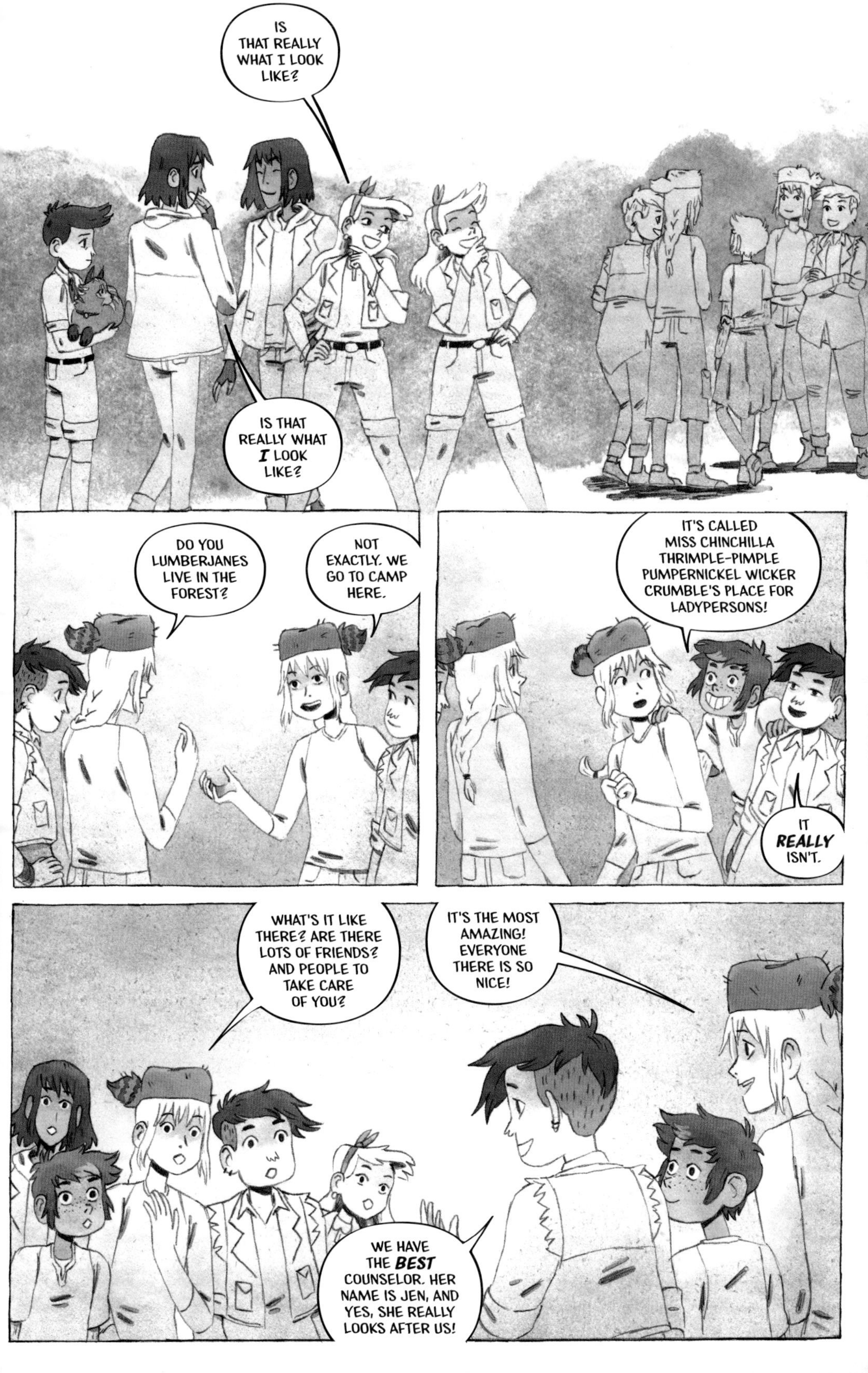
IS THAT REALLY WHAT I LOOK LIKE?
IS THAT REALLY WHAT *I* LOOK LIKE?
DO YOU LUMBERJANES LIVE IN THE FOREST?
NOT EXACTLY. WE GO TO CAMP HERE.
IT'S CALLED MISS CHINCHILLA THRIMPLE-PIMPLE PUMPERNICKEL WICKER CRUMBLE'S PLACE FOR LADYPERSONS!
IT *REALLY* ISN'T.
WHAT'S IT LIKE THERE? ARE THERE LOTS OF FRIENDS? AND PEOPLE TO TAKE CARE OF YOU?
IT'S THE MOST AMAZING! EVERYONE THERE IS SO NICE!
WE HAVE THE *BEST* COUNSELOR. HER NAME IS JEN, AND YES, SHE REALLY LOOKS AFTER US!

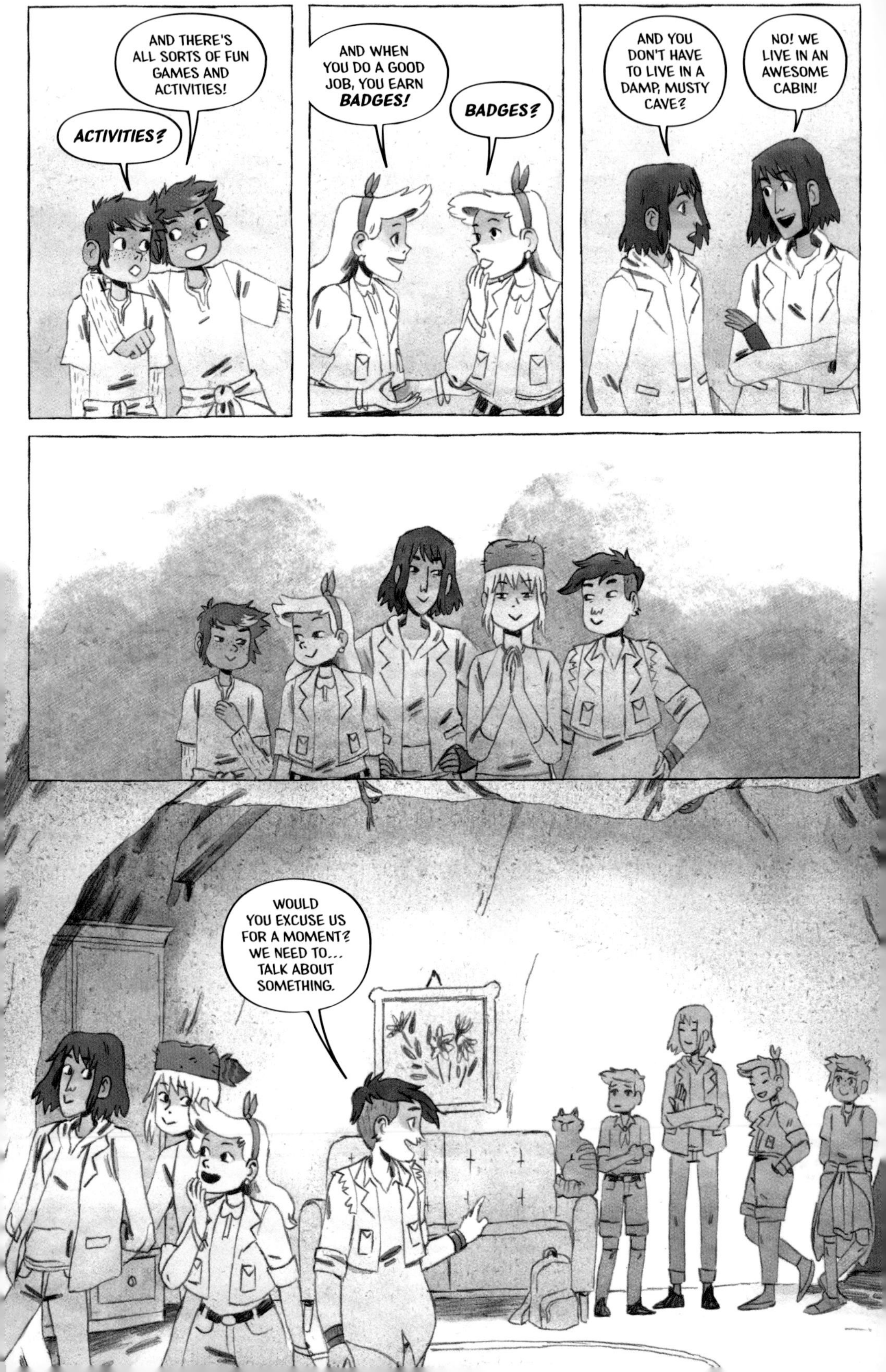
AND THERE'S ALL SORTS OF FUN GAMES AND ACTIVITIES!
ACTIVITIES?
AND WHEN YOU DO A GOOD JOB, YOU EARN BADGES!
BADGES?
AND YOU DON'T HAVE TO LIVE IN A DAMP, MUSTY CAVE?
NO! WE LIVE IN AN AWESOME CABIN!
WOULD YOU EXCUSE US FOR A MOMENT? WE NEED TO... TALK ABOUT SOMETHING.

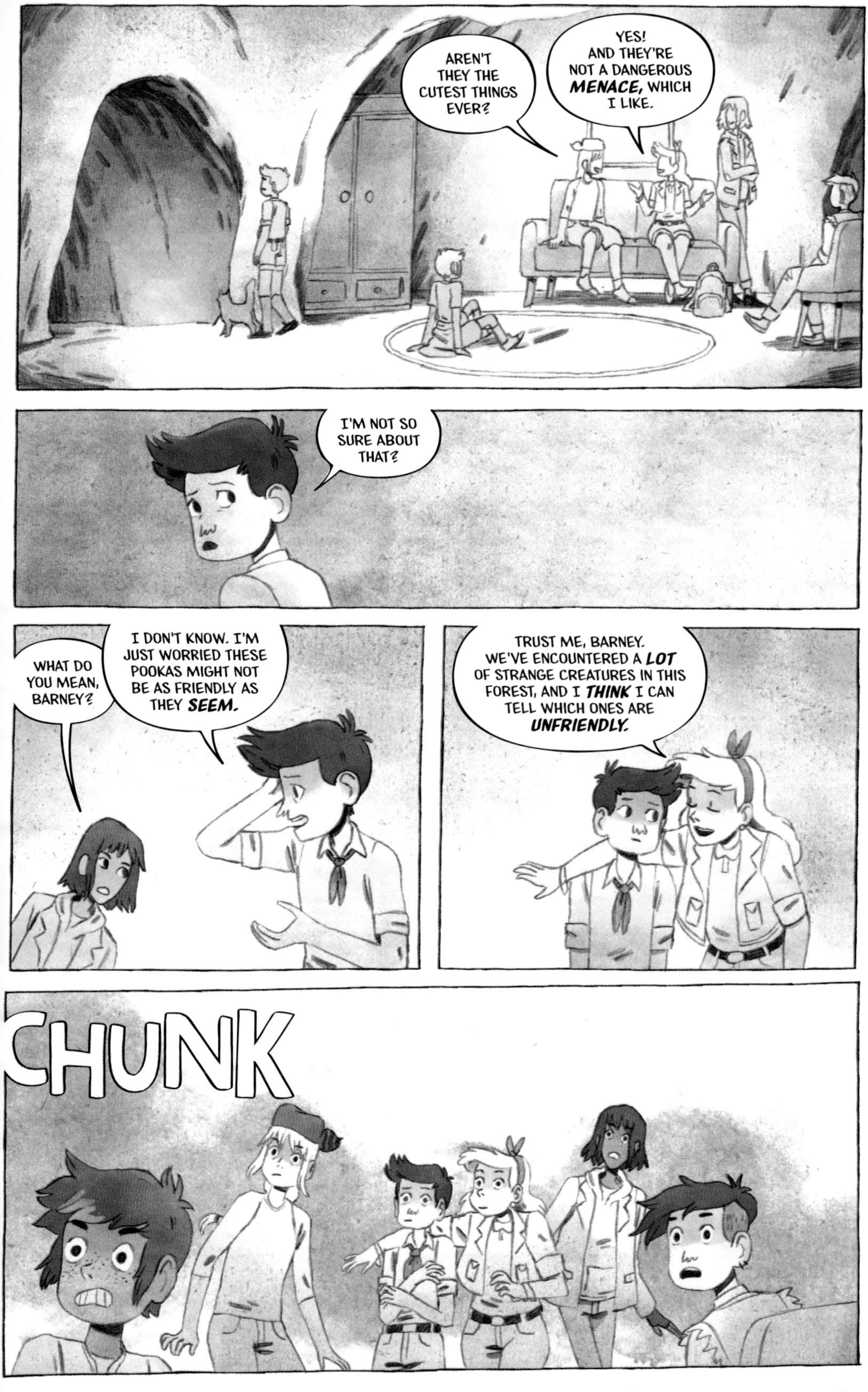
AREN'T THEY THE CUTEST THINGS EVER?
YES! AND THEY'RE NOT A DANGEROUS *MENACE,* WHICH I LIKE.
I'M NOT SO SURE ABOUT THAT?
WHAT DO YOU MEAN, BARNEY?
I DON'T KNOW. I'M JUST WORRIED THESE POOKAS MIGHT NOT BE AS FRIENDLY AS THEY *SEEM.*
TRUST ME, BARNEY. WE'VE ENCOUNTERED A *LOT* OF STRANGE CREATURES IN THIS FOREST, AND I *THINK* I CAN TELL WHICH ONES ARE *UNFRIENDLY.*
CHUNK

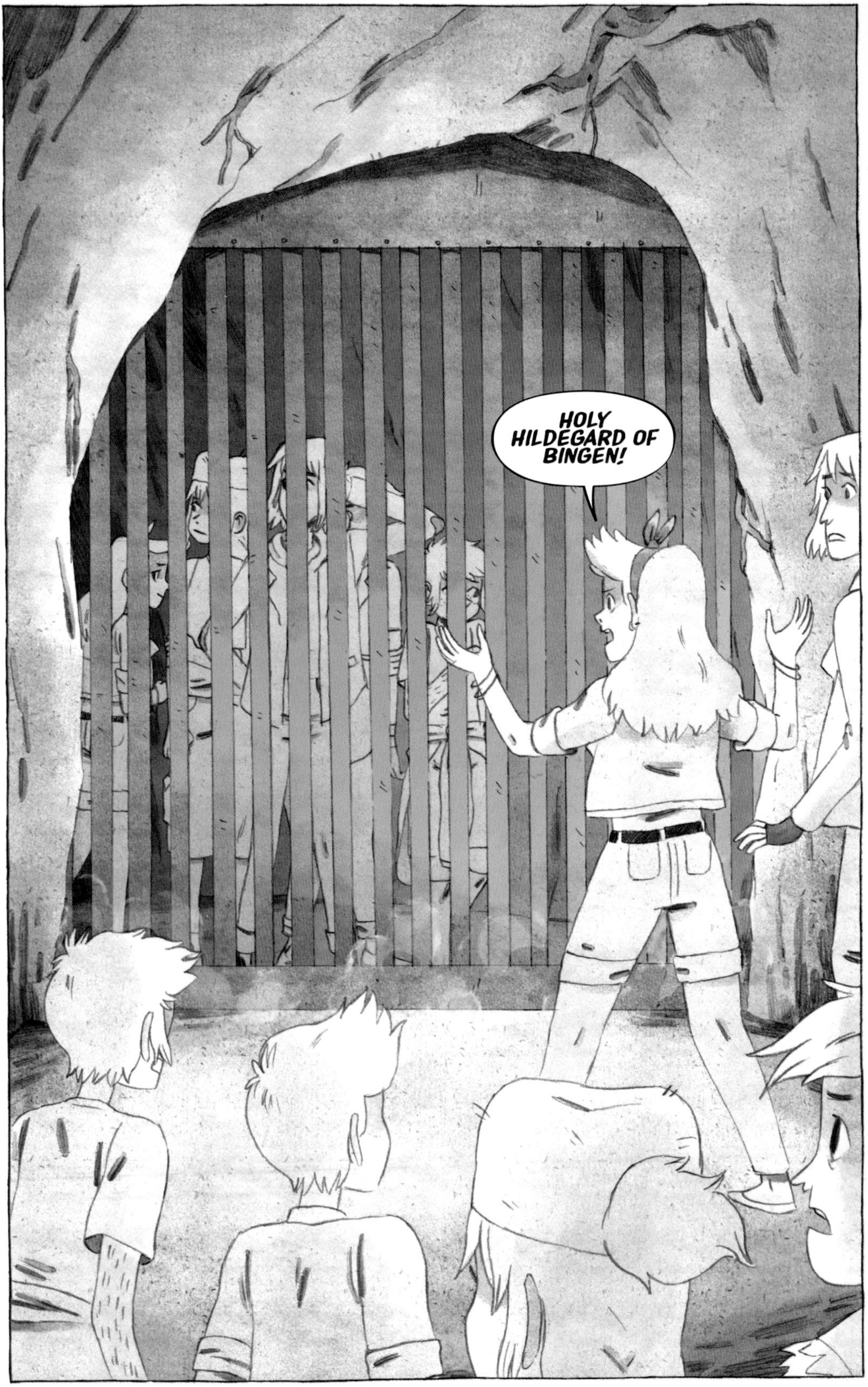
HOLY HILDEGARD OF BINGEN!

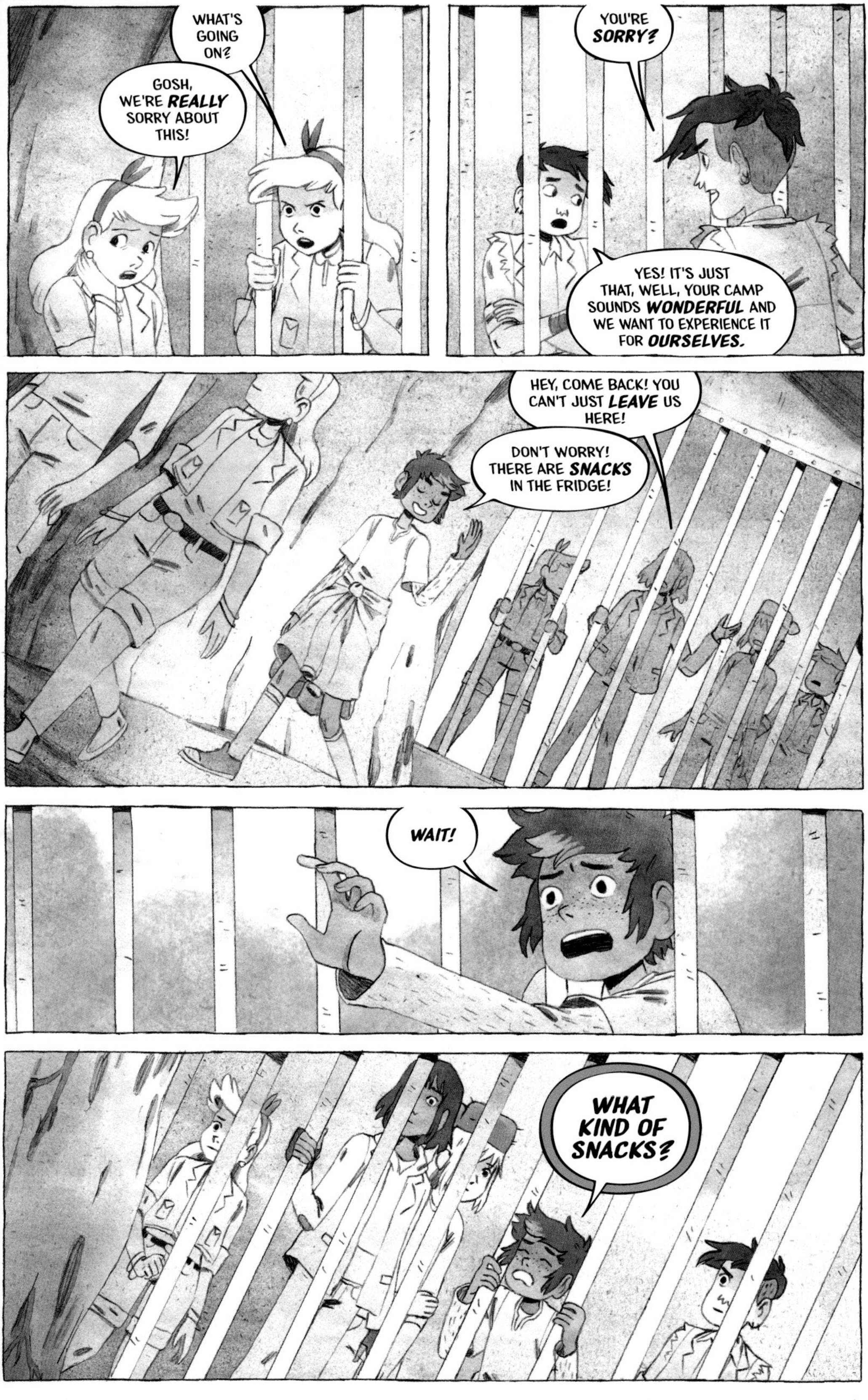
GOSH, WE'RE **REALLY** SORRY ABOUT THIS!
WHAT'S GOING ON?
YOU'RE **SORRY?**
YES! IT'S JUST THAT, WELL, YOUR CAMP SOUNDS **WONDERFUL** AND WE WANT TO EXPERIENCE IT FOR **OURSELVES.**
HEY, COME BACK! YOU CAN'T JUST **LEAVE** US HERE!
DON'T WORRY! THERE ARE **SNACKS** IN THE FRIDGE!
**WAIT!**
**WHAT KIND OF SNACKS?**

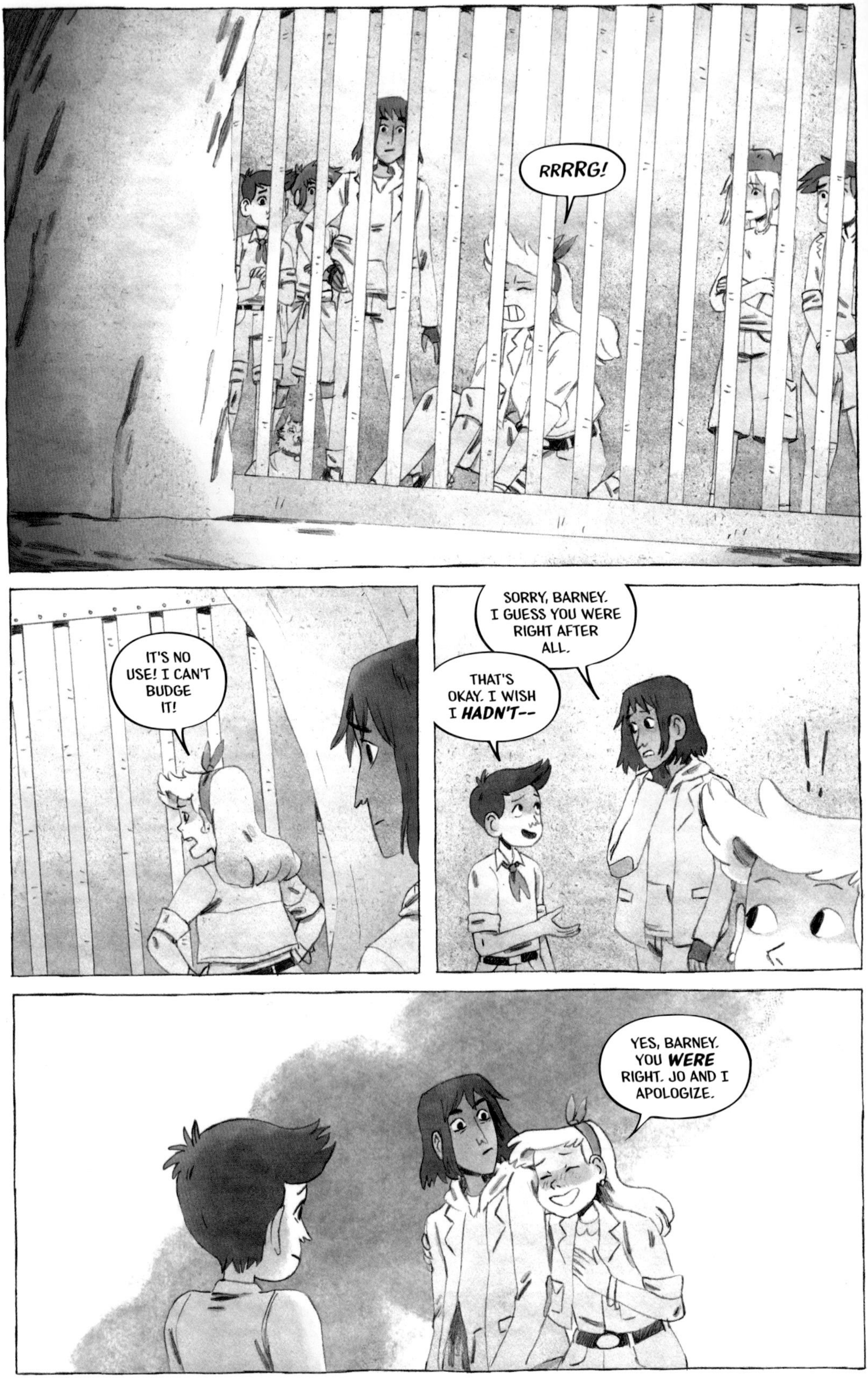
RRRRG!
IT'S NO USE! I CAN'T BUDGE IT!
SORRY, BARNEY. I GUESS YOU WERE RIGHT AFTER ALL.
THAT'S OKAY. I WISH I **HADN'T**--
!!
YES, BARNEY. YOU **WERE** RIGHT. JO AND I APOLOGIZE.

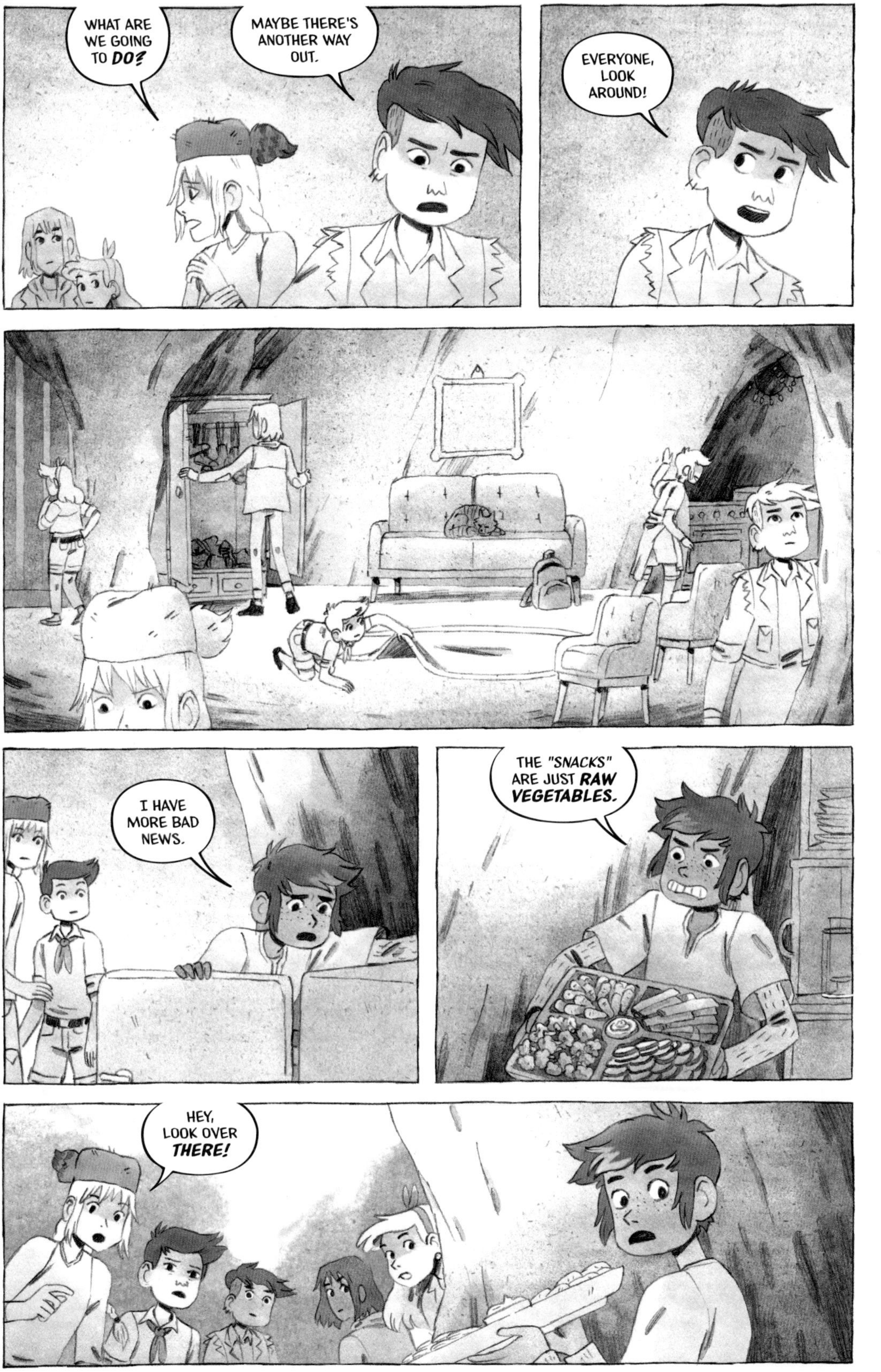
WHAT ARE WE GOING TO DO?
MAYBE THERE'S ANOTHER WAY OUT.
EVERYONE, LOOK AROUND!
I HAVE MORE BAD NEWS.
THE "SNACKS" ARE JUST RAW VEGETABLES.
HEY, LOOK OVER THERE!

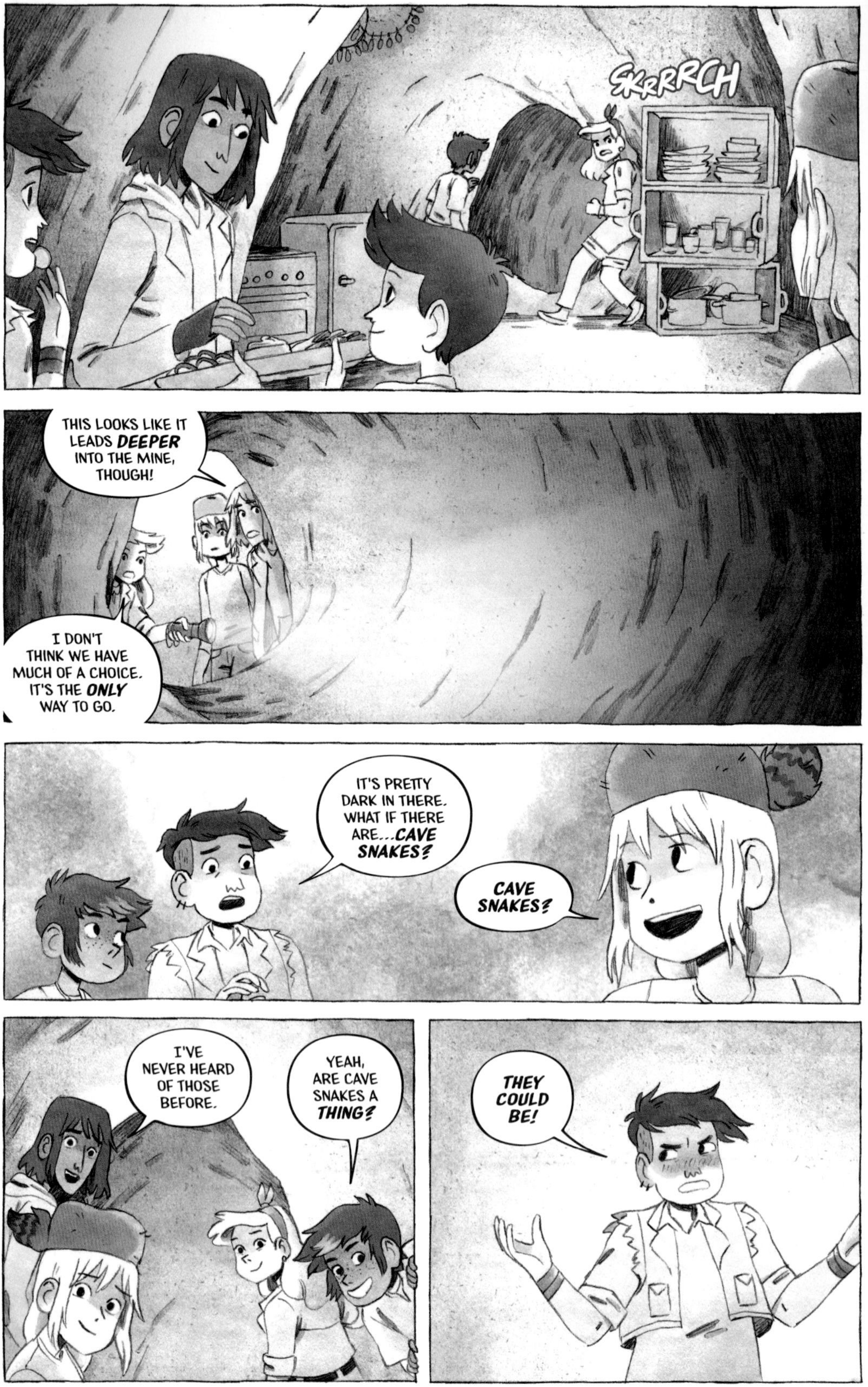
SKRRRCH
THIS LOOKS LIKE IT LEADS DEEPER INTO THE MINE, THOUGH!
I DON'T THINK WE HAVE MUCH OF A CHOICE. IT'S THE ONLY WAY TO GO.
IT'S PRETTY DARK IN THERE. WHAT IF THERE ARE...CAVE SNAKES?
CAVE SNAKES?
I'VE NEVER HEARD OF THOSE BEFORE.
YEAH, ARE CAVE SNAKES A THING?
THEY COULD BE!

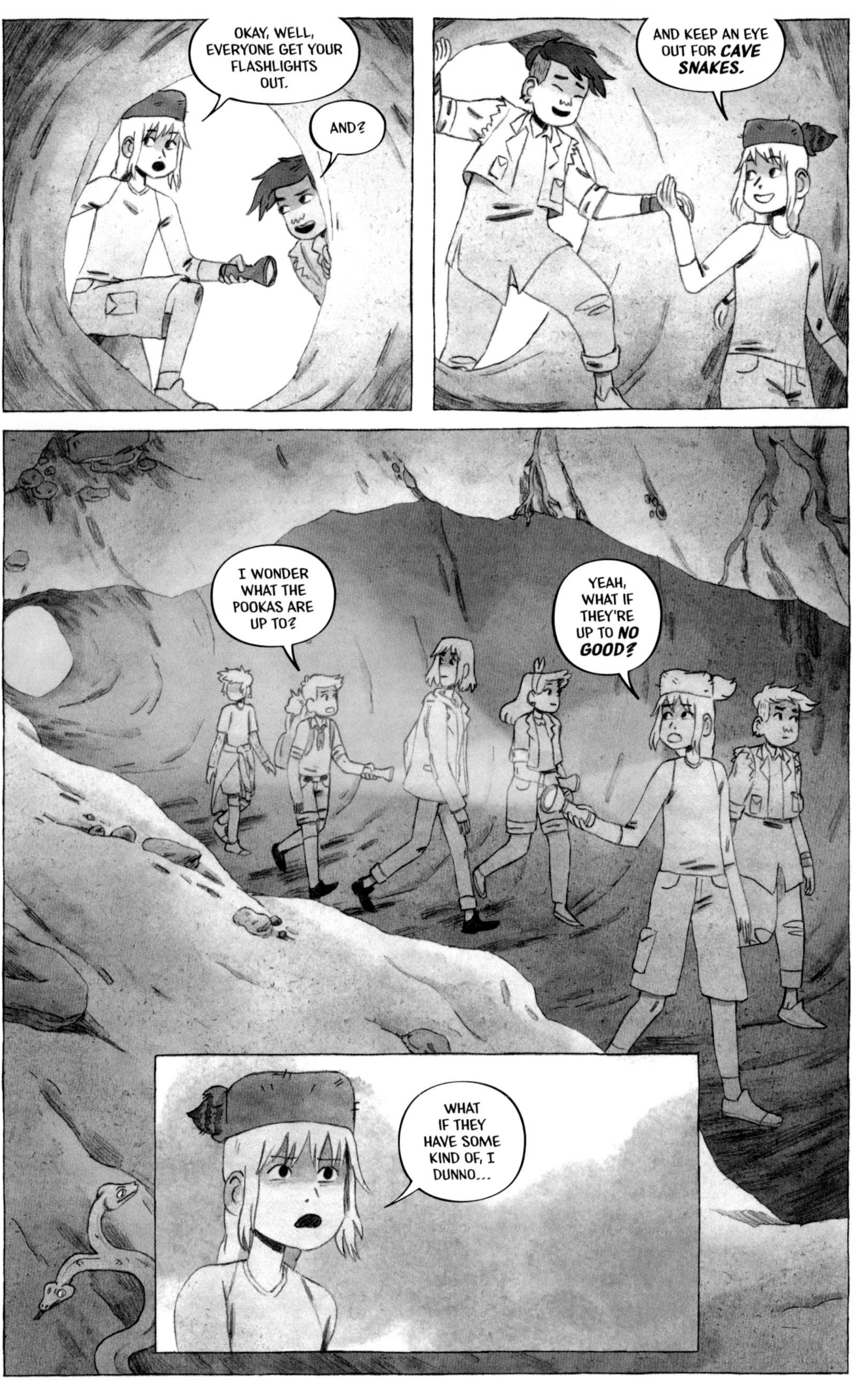
OKAY, WELL, EVERYONE GET YOUR FLASHLIGHTS OUT.
AND?
AND KEEP AN EYE OUT FOR CAVE SNAKES.
I WONDER WHAT THE POOKAS ARE UP TO?
YEAH, WHAT IF THEY'RE UP TO NO GOOD?
WHAT IF THEY HAVE SOME KIND OF, I DUNNO...

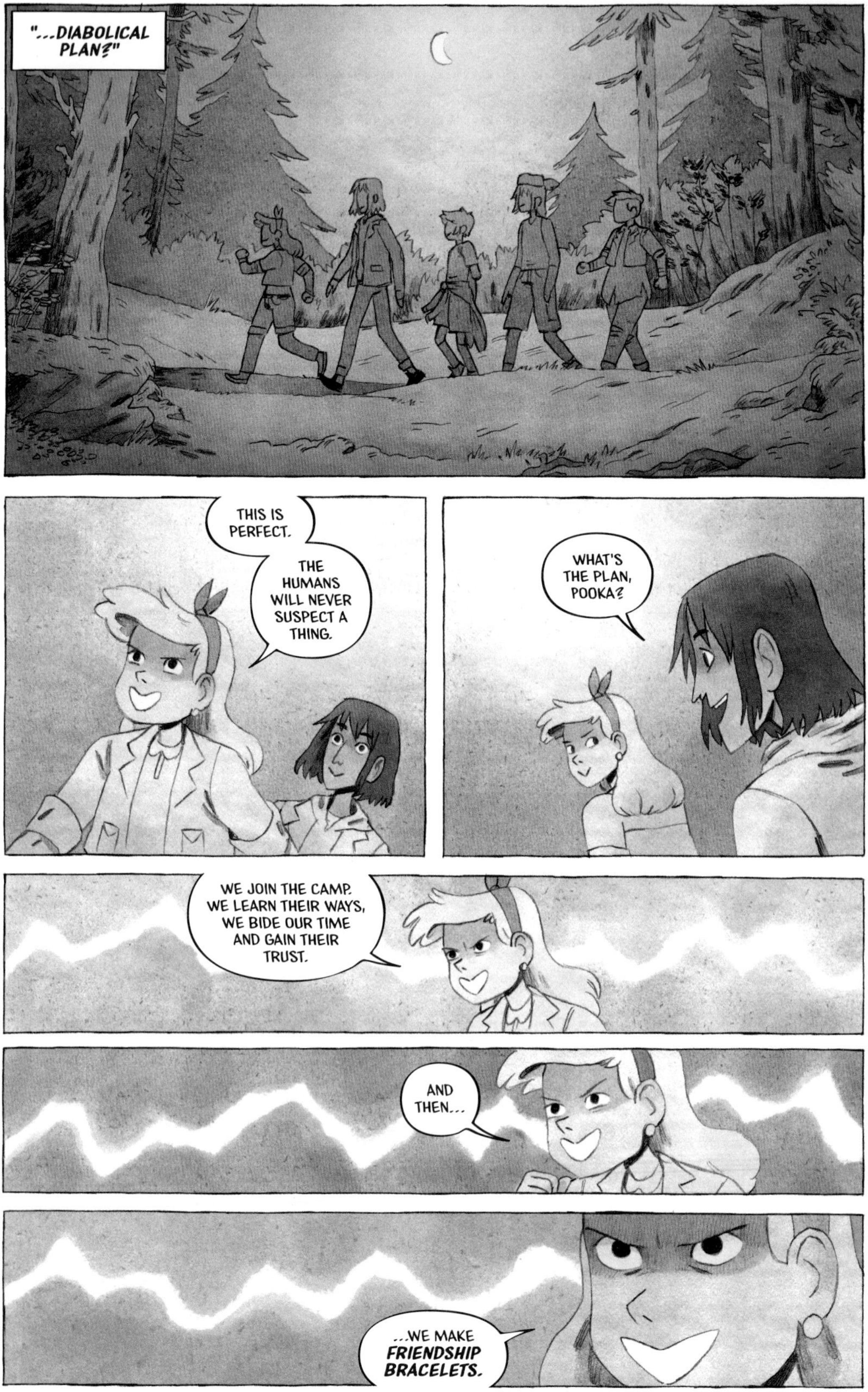
"...DIABOLICAL PLAN?"
THIS IS PERFECT.
THE HUMANS WILL NEVER SUSPECT A THING.
WHAT'S THE PLAN, POOKA?
WE JOIN THE CAMP. WE LEARN THEIR WAYS, WE BIDE OUR TIME AND GAIN THEIR TRUST.
AND THEN...
...WE MAKE FRIENDSHIP BRACELETS.

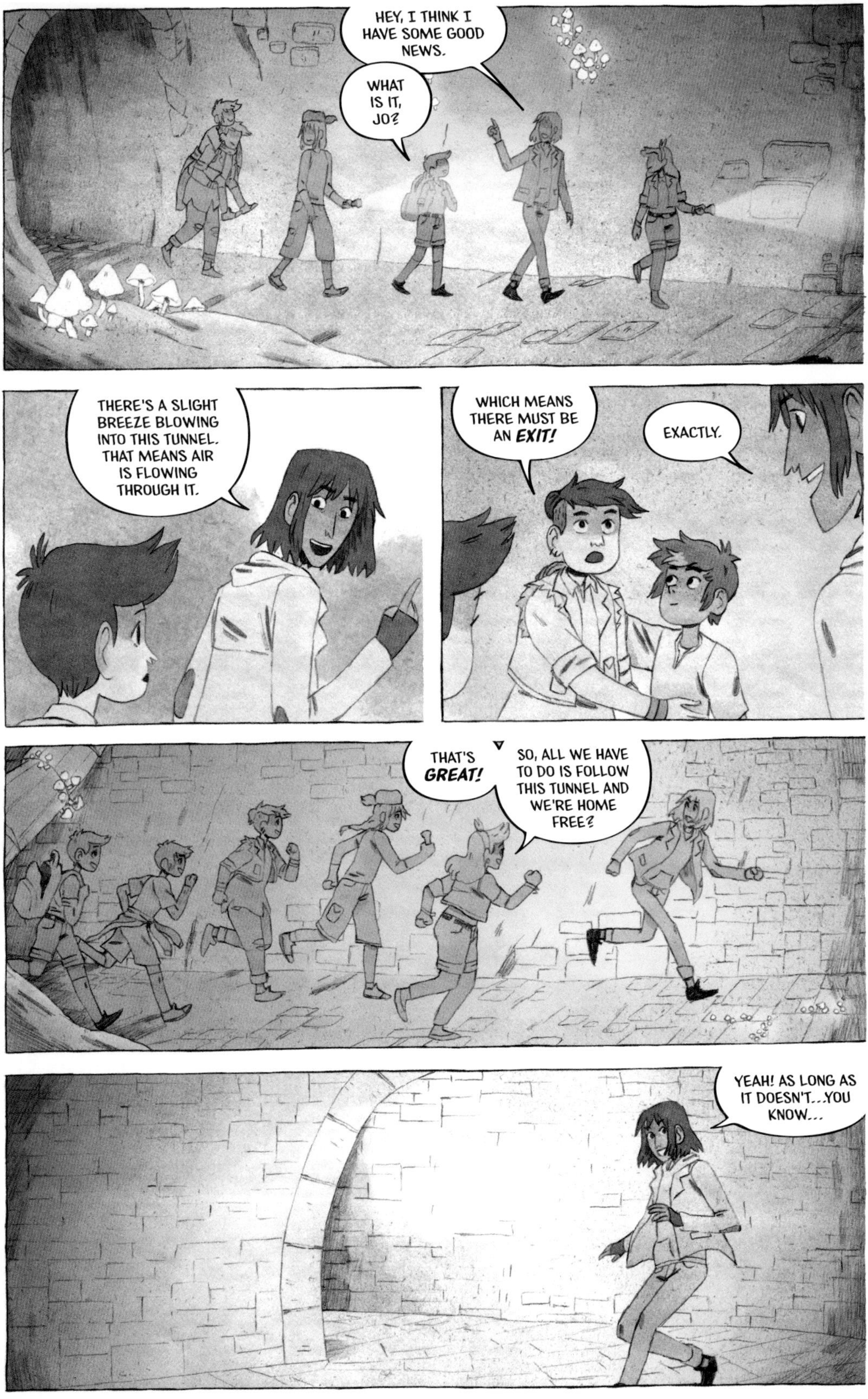
HEY, I THINK I HAVE SOME GOOD NEWS.
WHAT IS IT, JO?
THERE'S A SLIGHT BREEZE BLOWING INTO THIS TUNNEL. THAT MEANS AIR IS FLOWING THROUGH IT.
WHICH MEANS THERE MUST BE AN *EXIT!*
EXACTLY.
THAT'S *GREAT!*
SO, ALL WE HAVE TO DO IS FOLLOW THIS TUNNEL AND WE'RE HOME FREE?
YEAH! AS LONG AS IT DOESN'T...YOU KNOW...

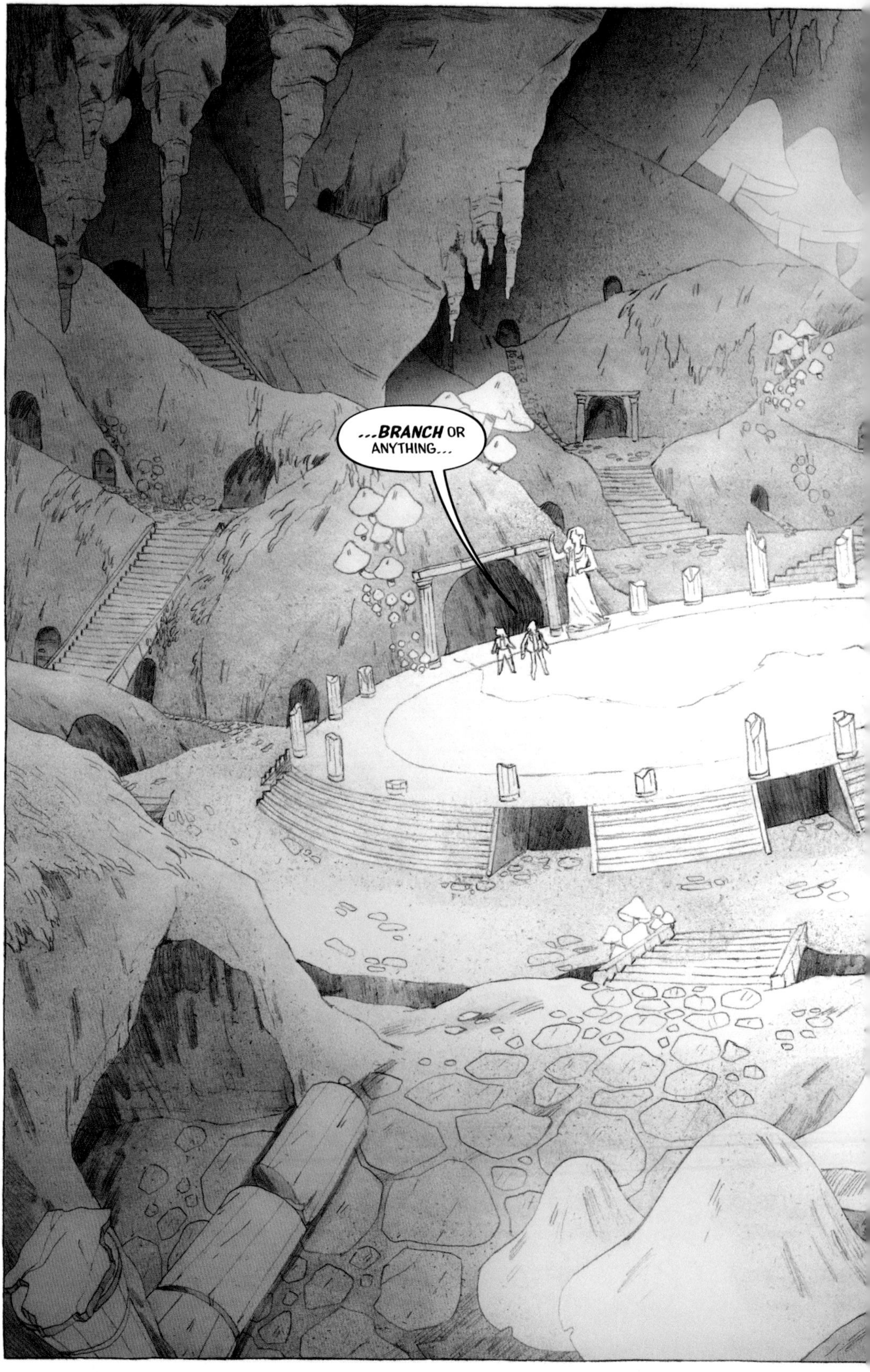
...BRANCH OR ANYTHING...

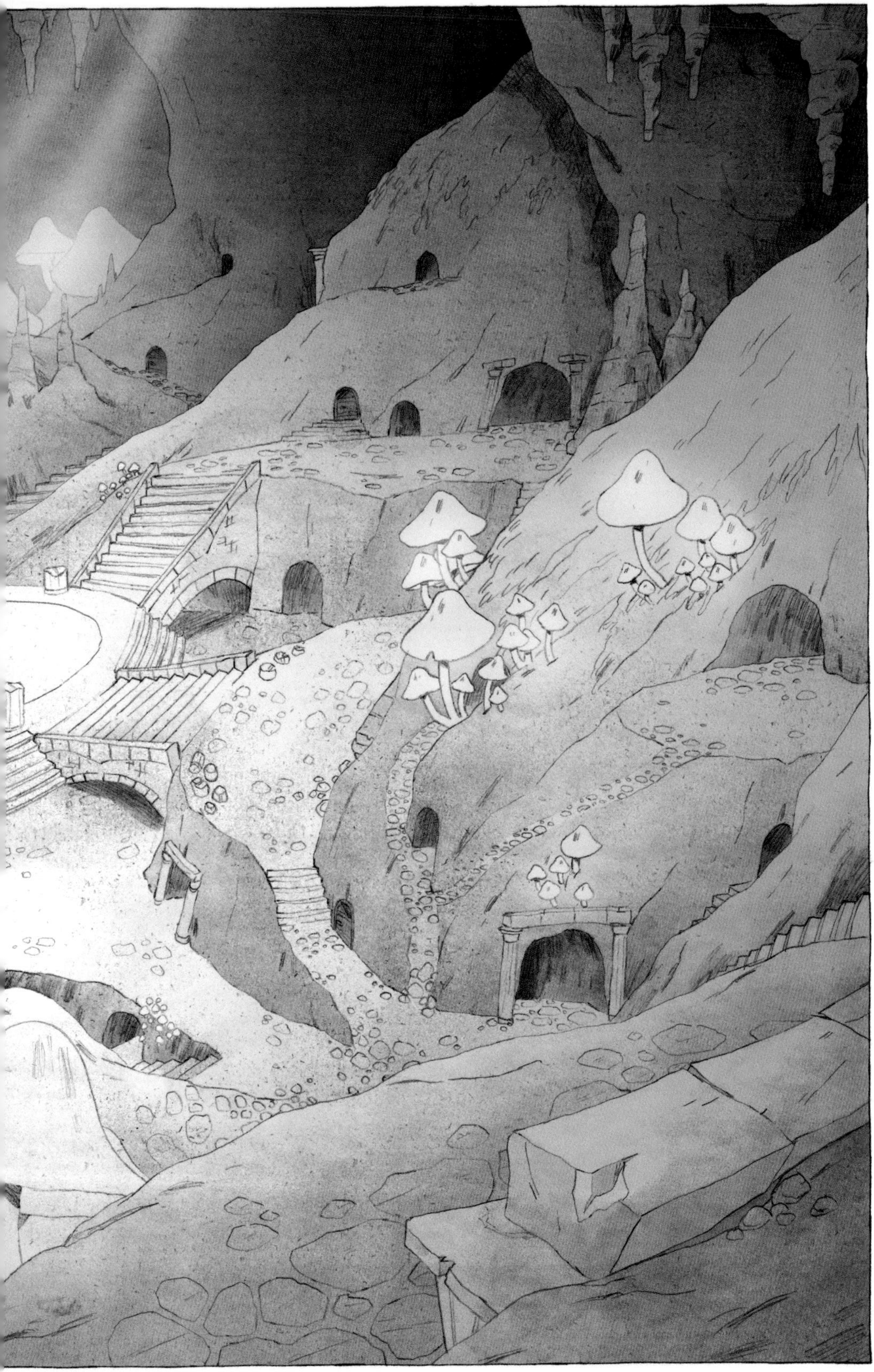

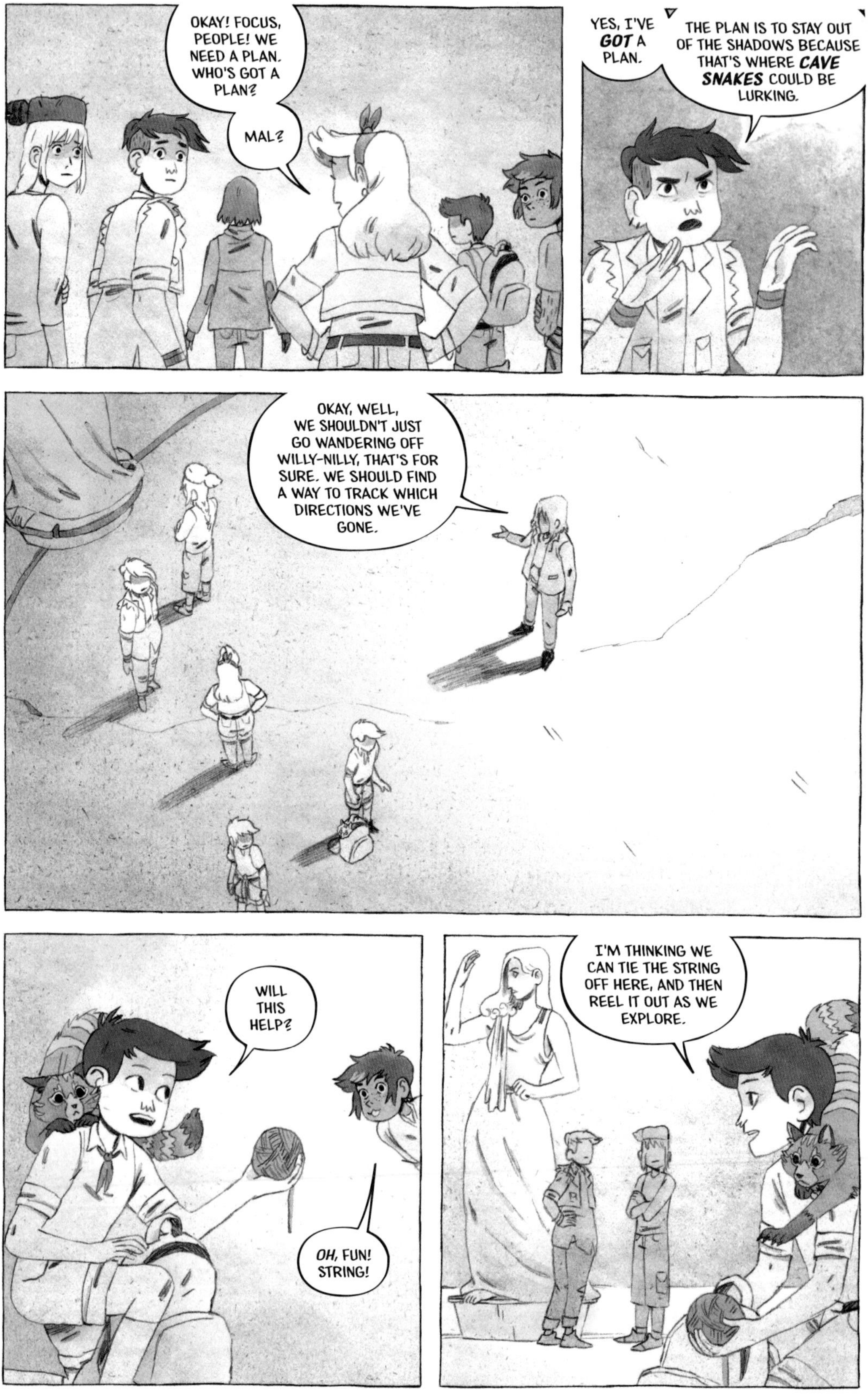
OKAY! FOCUS, PEOPLE! WE NEED A PLAN. WHO'S GOT A PLAN?
MAL?
YES, I'VE GOT A PLAN.
THE PLAN IS TO STAY OUT OF THE SHADOWS BECAUSE THAT'S WHERE CAVE SNAKES COULD BE LURKING.
OKAY, WELL, WE SHOULDN'T JUST GO WANDERING OFF WILLY-NILLY, THAT'S FOR SURE. WE SHOULD FIND A WAY TO TRACK WHICH DIRECTIONS WE'VE GONE.
WILL THIS HELP?
OH, FUN! STRING!
I'M THINKING WE CAN TIE THE STRING OFF HERE, AND THEN REEL IT OUT AS WE EXPLORE.

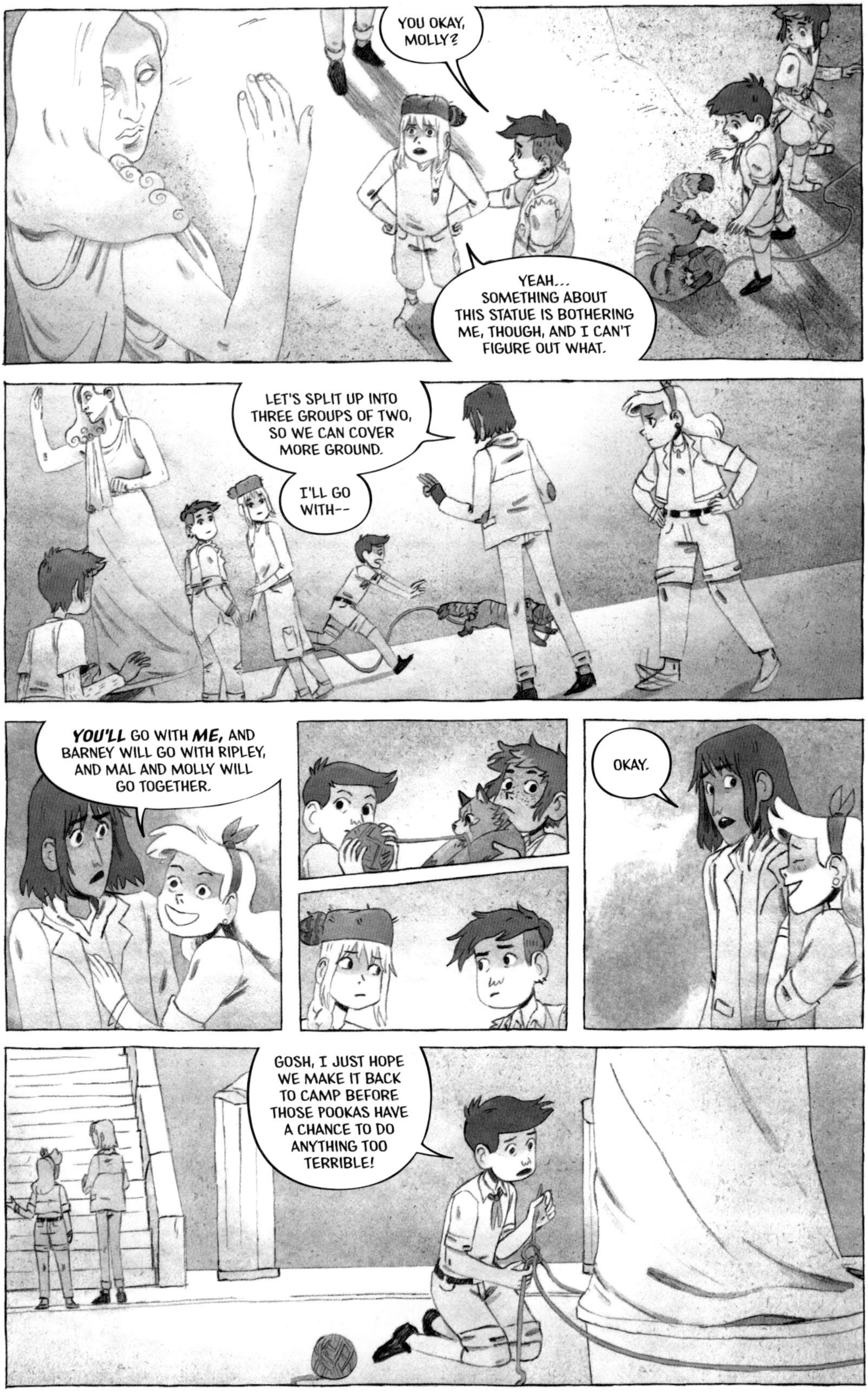
YOU OKAY, MOLLY?
YEAH... SOMETHING ABOUT THIS STATUE IS BOTHERING ME, THOUGH, AND I CAN'T FIGURE OUT WHAT.
LET'S SPLIT UP INTO THREE GROUPS OF TWO, SO WE CAN COVER MORE GROUND.
I'LL GO WITH--
YOU'LL GO WITH ME, AND BARNEY WILL GO WITH RIPLEY, AND MAL AND MOLLY WILL GO TOGETHER.
OKAY.
GOSH, I JUST HOPE WE MAKE IT BACK TO CAMP BEFORE THOSE POOKAS HAVE A CHANCE TO DO ANYTHING TOO TERRIBLE!

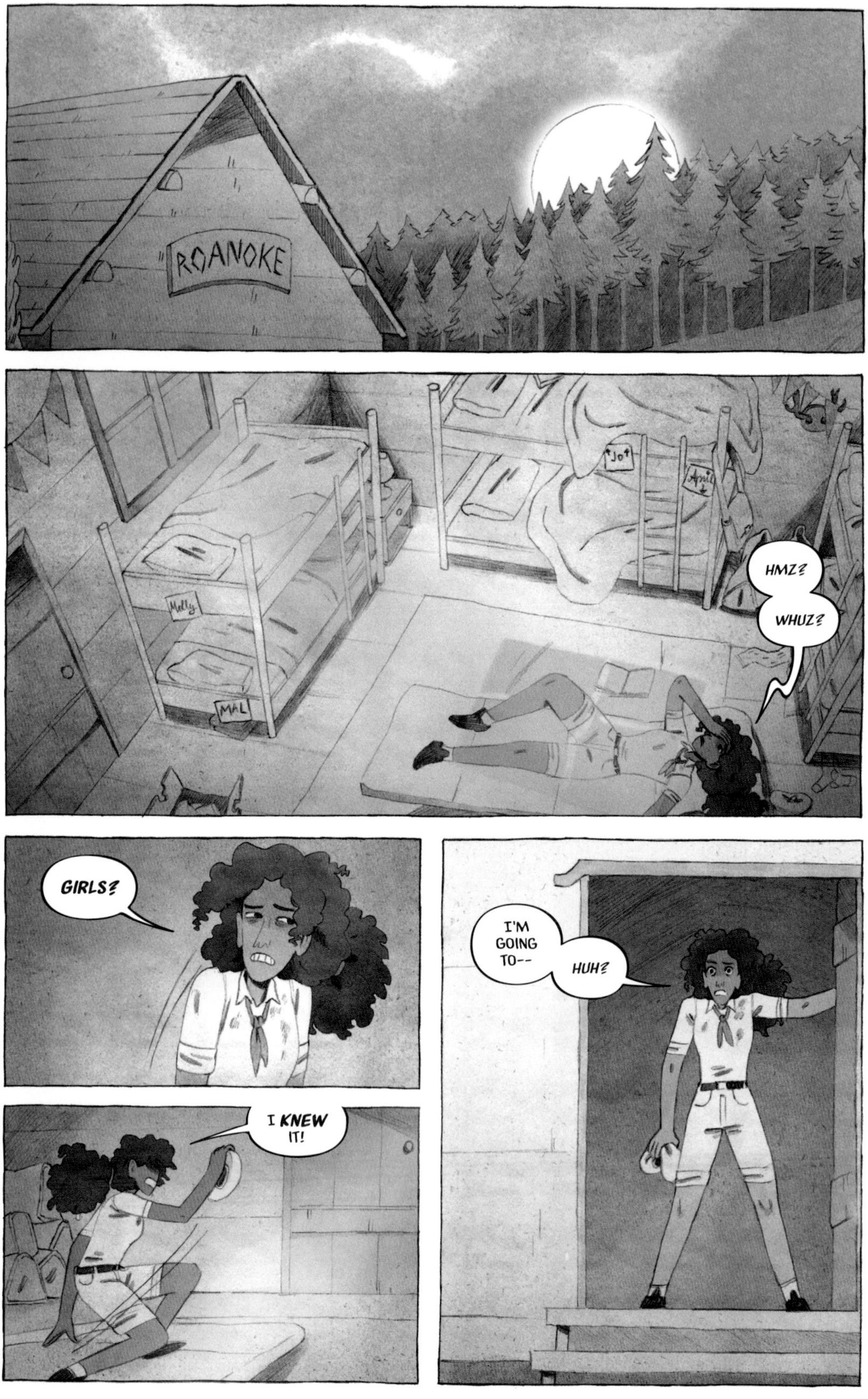
ROANOKE
Jo
April
Molly
MAL
HMZ?
WHUZ?
GIRLS?
I'M GOING TO--
HUH?
I KNEW IT!

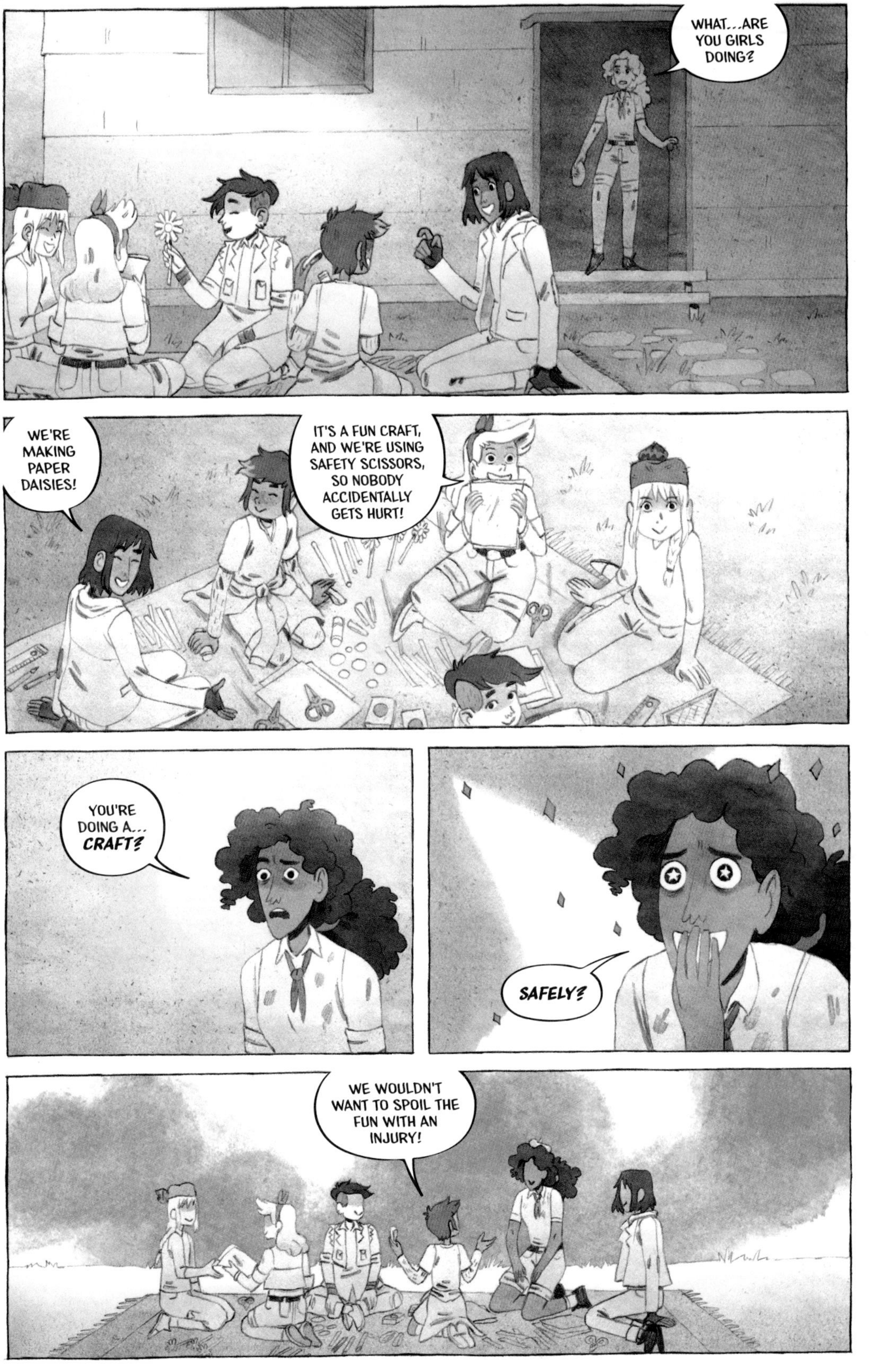
WHAT...ARE YOU GIRLS DOING?
WE'RE MAKING PAPER DAISIES!
IT'S A FUN CRAFT, AND WE'RE USING SAFETY SCISSORS, SO NOBODY ACCIDENTALLY GETS HURT!
YOU'RE DOING A... CRAFT?
SAFELY?
WE WOULDN'T WANT TO SPOIL THE FUN WITH AN INJURY!

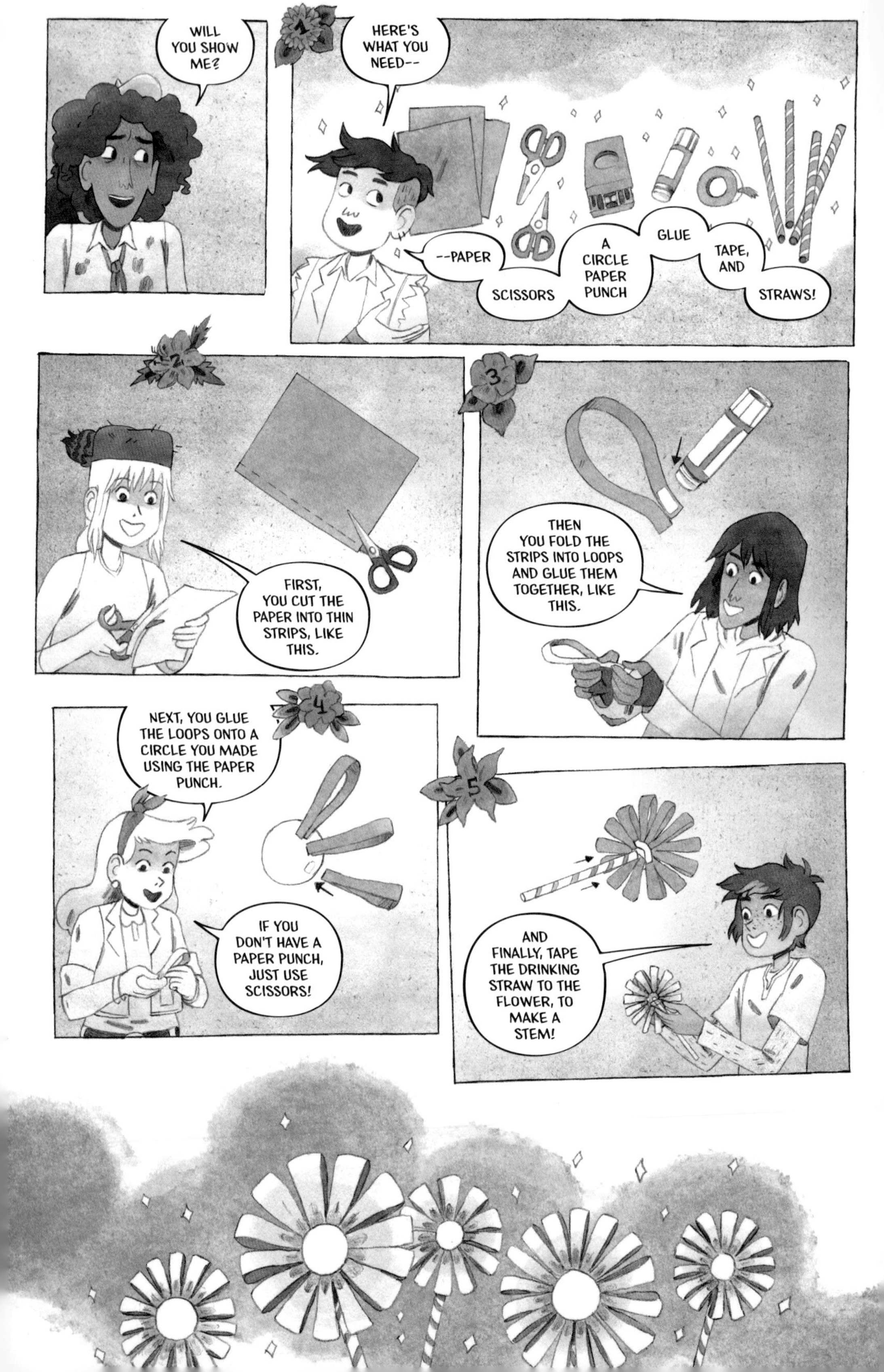
WILL YOU SHOW ME?
HERE'S WHAT YOU NEED--
--PAPER
SCISSORS
A CIRCLE PAPER PUNCH
GLUE
TAPE, AND
STRAWS!
FIRST, YOU CUT THE PAPER INTO THIN STRIPS, LIKE THIS.
THEN YOU FOLD THE STRIPS INTO LOOPS AND GLUE THEM TOGETHER, LIKE THIS.
NEXT, YOU GLUE THE LOOPS ONTO A CIRCLE YOU MADE USING THE PAPER PUNCH.
IF YOU DON'T HAVE A PAPER PUNCH, JUST USE SCISSORS!
AND FINALLY, TAPE THE DRINKING STRAW TO THE FLOWER, TO MAKE A STEM!

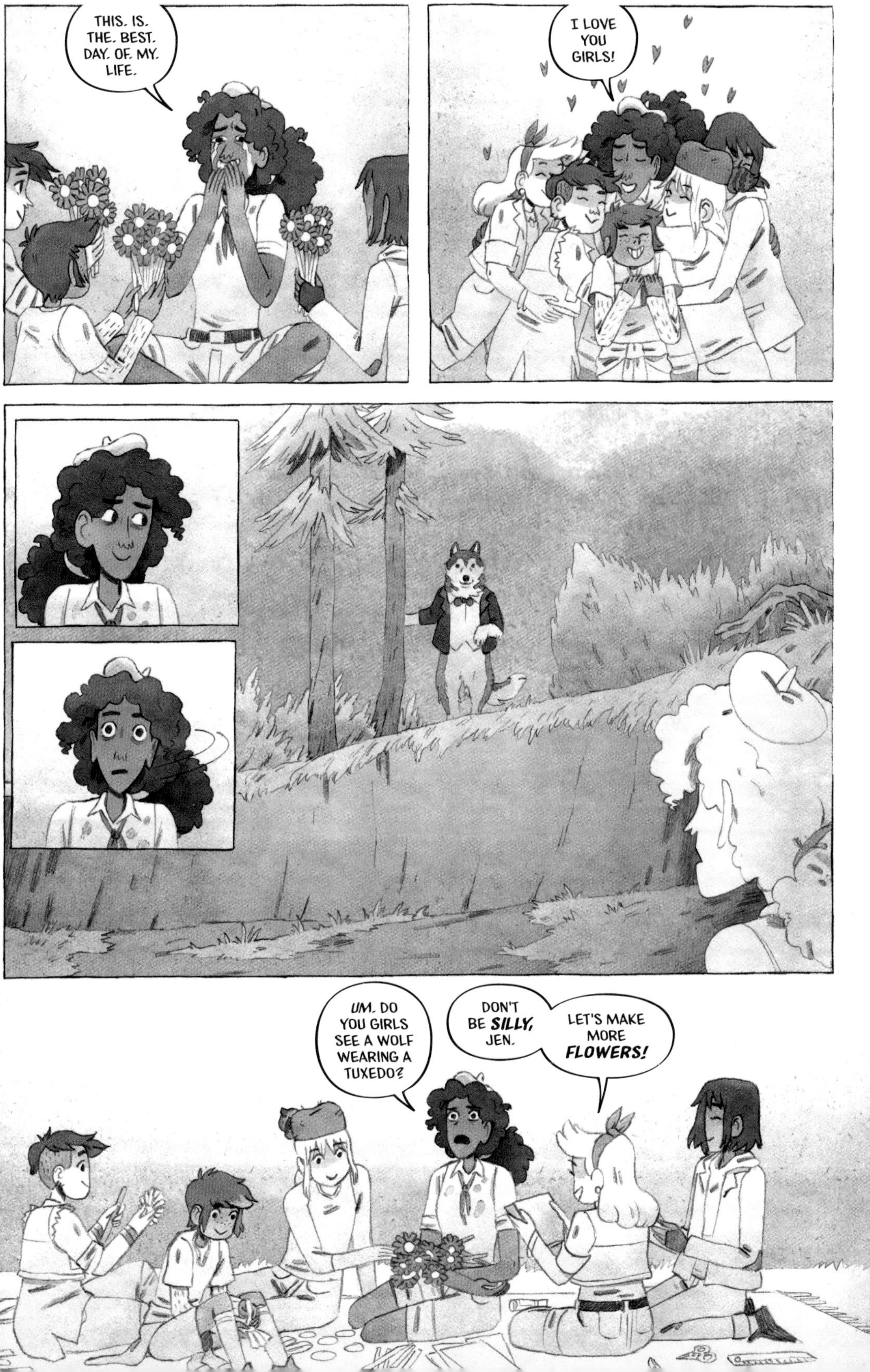
THIS. IS. THE. BEST. DAY. OF. MY. LIFE.
I LOVE YOU GIRLS!
UM. DO YOU GIRLS SEE A WOLF WEARING A TUXEDO?
DON'T BE SILLY, JEN.
LET'S MAKE MORE FLOWERS!

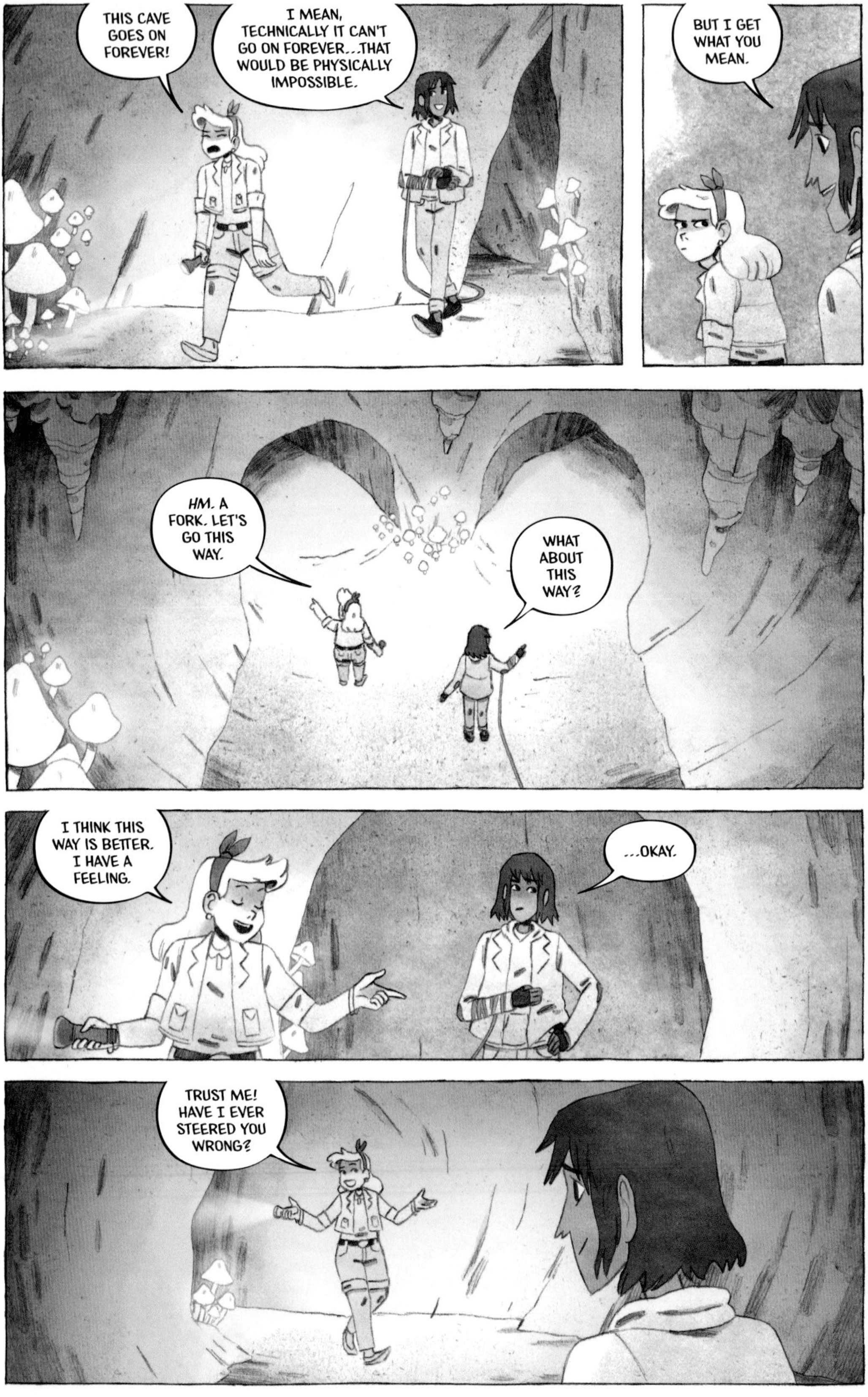
THIS CAVE GOES ON FOREVER!
I MEAN, TECHNICALLY IT CAN'T GO ON FOREVER...THAT WOULD BE PHYSICALLY IMPOSSIBLE.
BUT I GET WHAT YOU MEAN.
HM. A FORK. LET'S GO THIS WAY.
WHAT ABOUT THIS WAY?
I THINK THIS WAY IS BETTER. I HAVE A FEELING.
...OKAY.
TRUST ME! HAVE I EVER STEERED YOU WRONG?

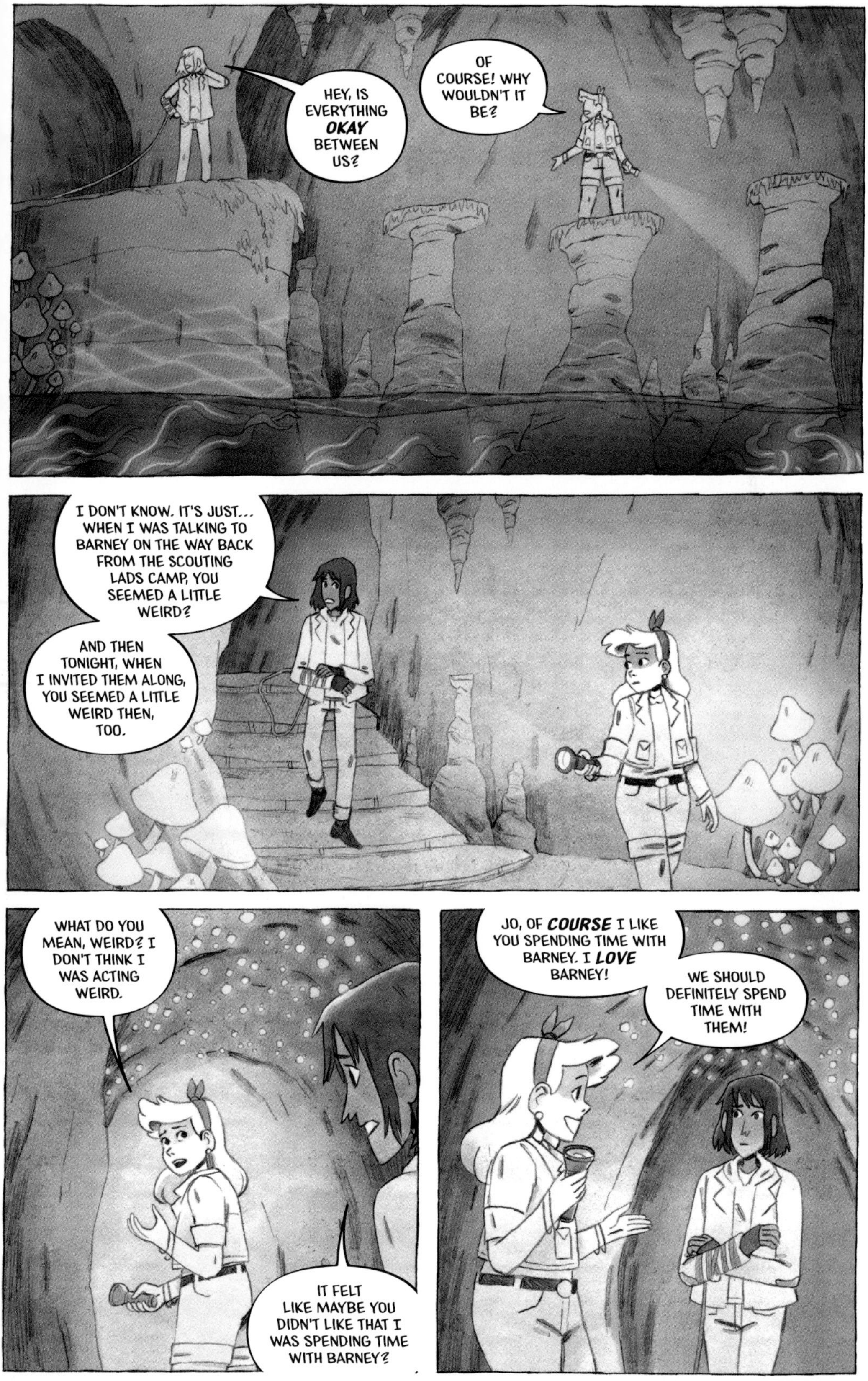
HEY, IS EVERYTHING OKAY BETWEEN US?
OF COURSE! WHY WOULDN'T IT BE?
I DON'T KNOW. IT'S JUST... WHEN I WAS TALKING TO BARNEY ON THE WAY BACK FROM THE SCOUTING LADS CAMP, YOU SEEMED A LITTLE WEIRD?
AND THEN TONIGHT, WHEN I INVITED THEM ALONG, YOU SEEMED A LITTLE WEIRD THEN, TOO.
WHAT DO YOU MEAN, WEIRD? I DON'T THINK I WAS ACTING WEIRD.
IT FELT LIKE MAYBE YOU DIDN'T LIKE THAT I WAS SPENDING TIME WITH BARNEY?
JO, OF COURSE I LIKE YOU SPENDING TIME WITH BARNEY. I LOVE BARNEY!
WE SHOULD DEFINITELY SPEND TIME WITH THEM!

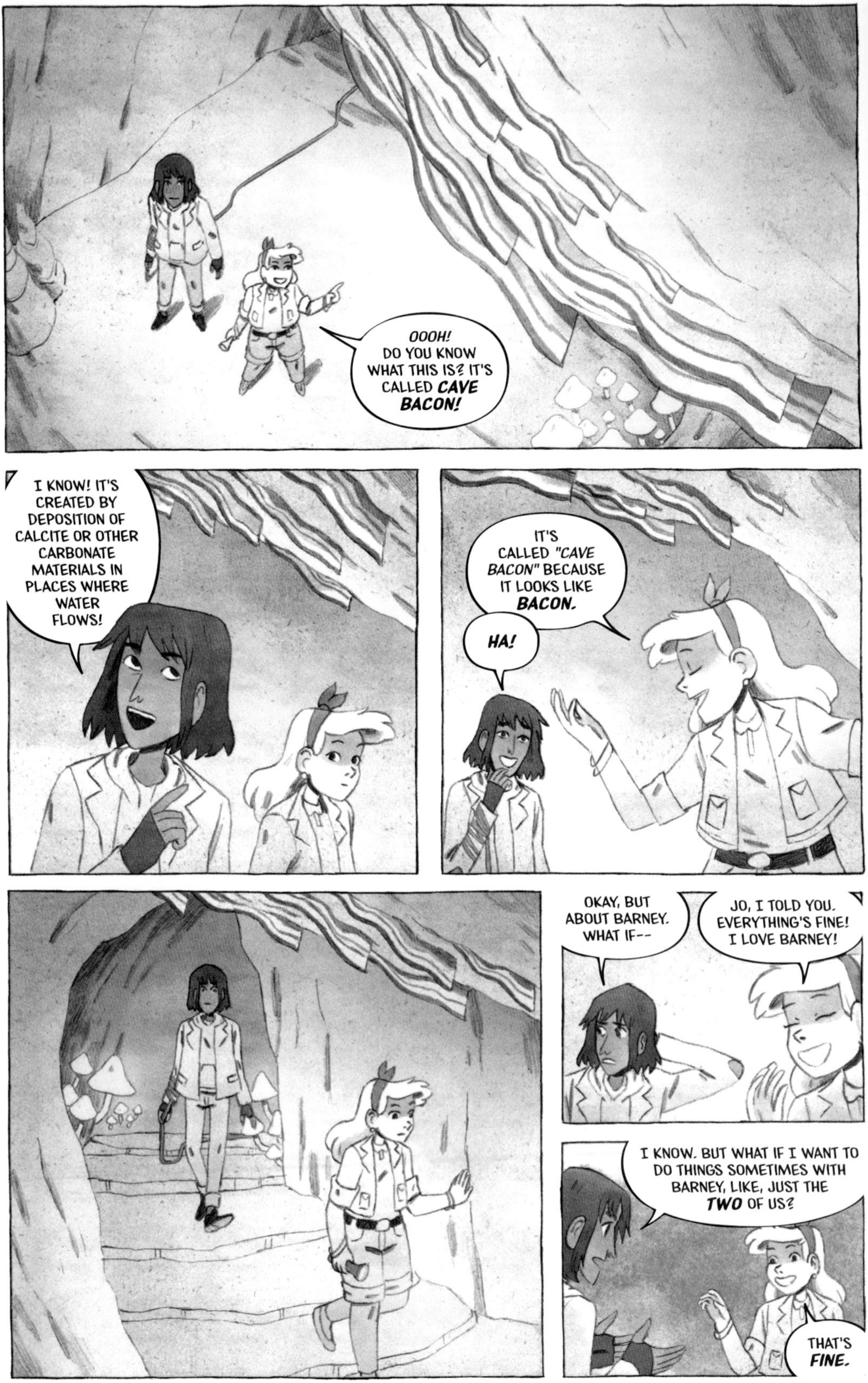

OOOH! DO YOU KNOW WHAT THIS IS? IT'S CALLED *CAVE BACON!*
I KNOW! IT'S CREATED BY DEPOSITION OF CALCITE OR OTHER CARBONATE MATERIALS IN PLACES WHERE WATER FLOWS!
IT'S CALLED "CAVE BACON" BECAUSE IT LOOKS LIKE **BACON.**
**HA!**
OKAY, BUT ABOUT BARNEY. WHAT IF--
JO, I TOLD YOU. EVERYTHING'S FINE! I LOVE BARNEY!
I KNOW. BUT WHAT IF I WANT TO DO THINGS SOMETIMES WITH BARNEY, LIKE, JUST THE **TWO** OF US?
THAT'S **FINE.**

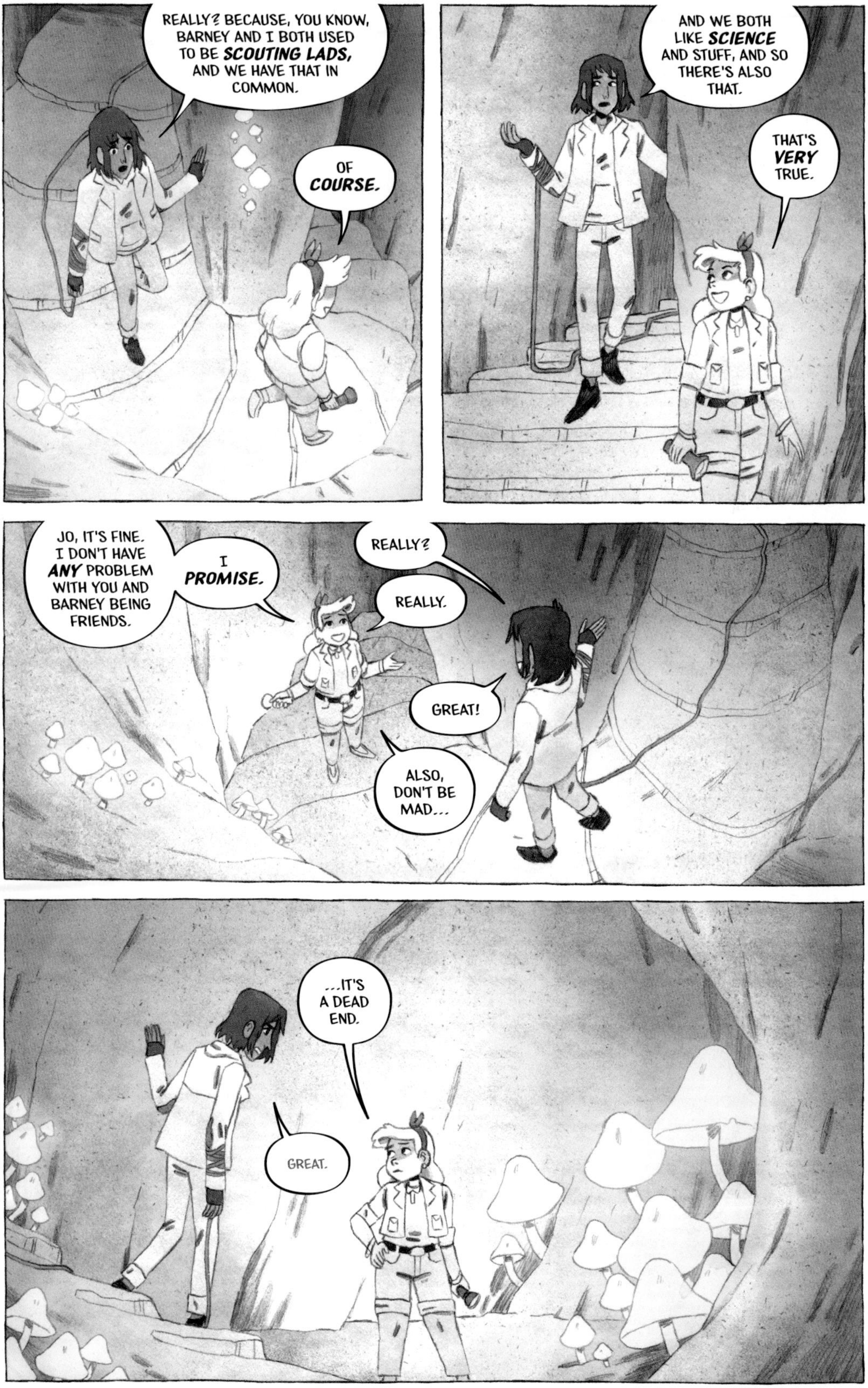
REALLY? BECAUSE, YOU KNOW, BARNEY AND I BOTH USED TO BE **SCOUTING LADS,** AND WE HAVE THAT IN COMMON.
OF **COURSE.**
AND WE BOTH LIKE **SCIENCE** AND STUFF, AND SO THERE'S ALSO THAT.
THAT'S **VERY** TRUE.
JO, IT'S FINE. I DON'T HAVE **ANY** PROBLEM WITH YOU AND BARNEY BEING FRIENDS.
I **PROMISE.**
REALLY?
REALLY.
GREAT!
ALSO, DON'T BE MAD...
...IT'S A DEAD END.
GREAT.

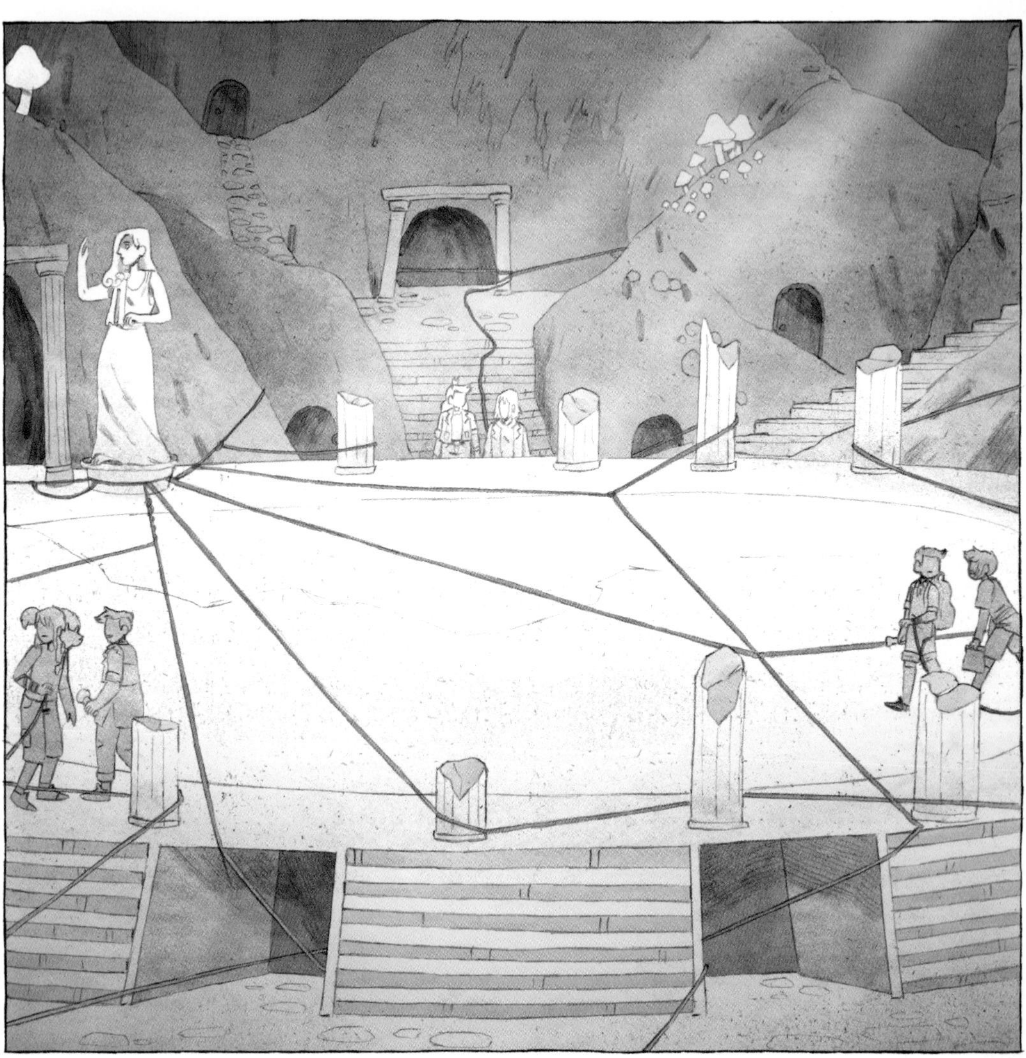

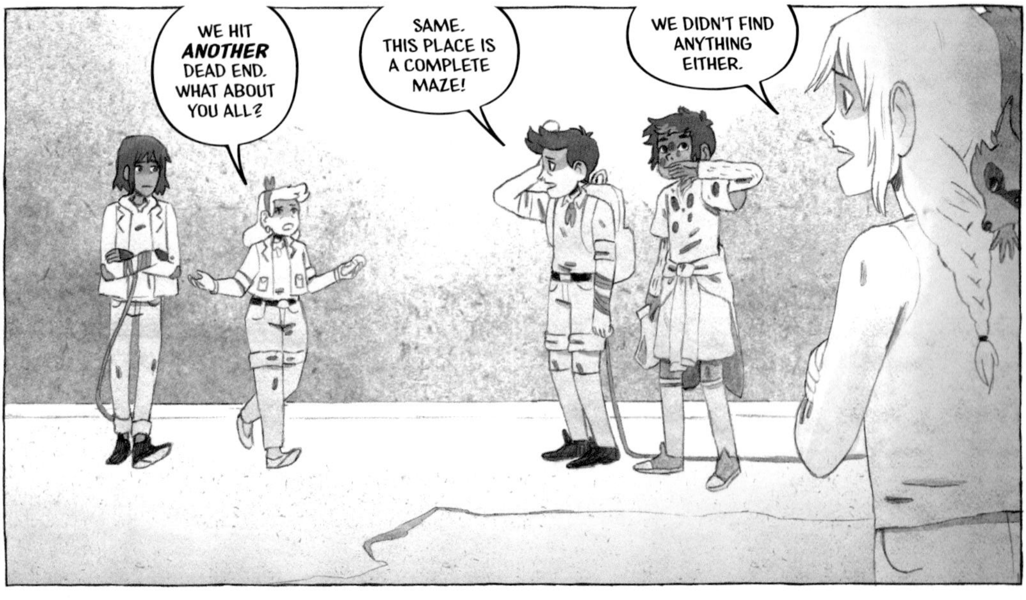
WE HIT ANOTHER DEAD END. WHAT ABOUT YOU ALL?
SAME. THIS PLACE IS A COMPLETE MAZE!
WE DIDN'T FIND ANYTHING EITHER.

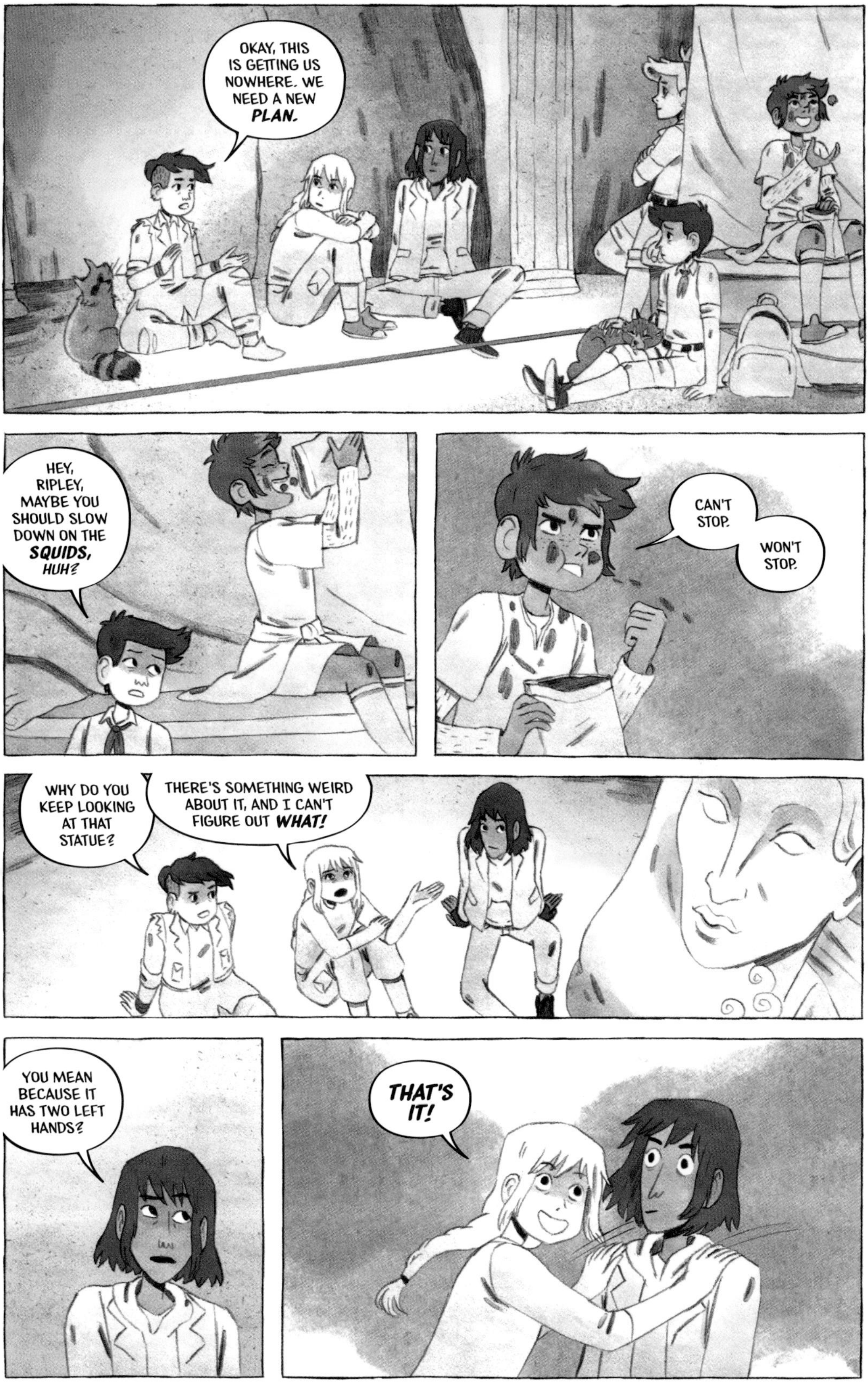

OKAY, THIS IS GETTING US NOWHERE. WE NEED A NEW *PLAN.*
HEY, RIPLEY, MAYBE YOU SHOULD SLOW DOWN ON THE *SQUIDS,* HUH?
CAN'T STOP.
WON'T STOP.
WHY DO YOU KEEP LOOKING AT THAT STATUE?
THERE'S SOMETHING WEIRD ABOUT IT, AND I CAN'T FIGURE OUT *WHAT!*
YOU MEAN BECAUSE IT HAS TWO LEFT HANDS?
*THAT'S IT!*

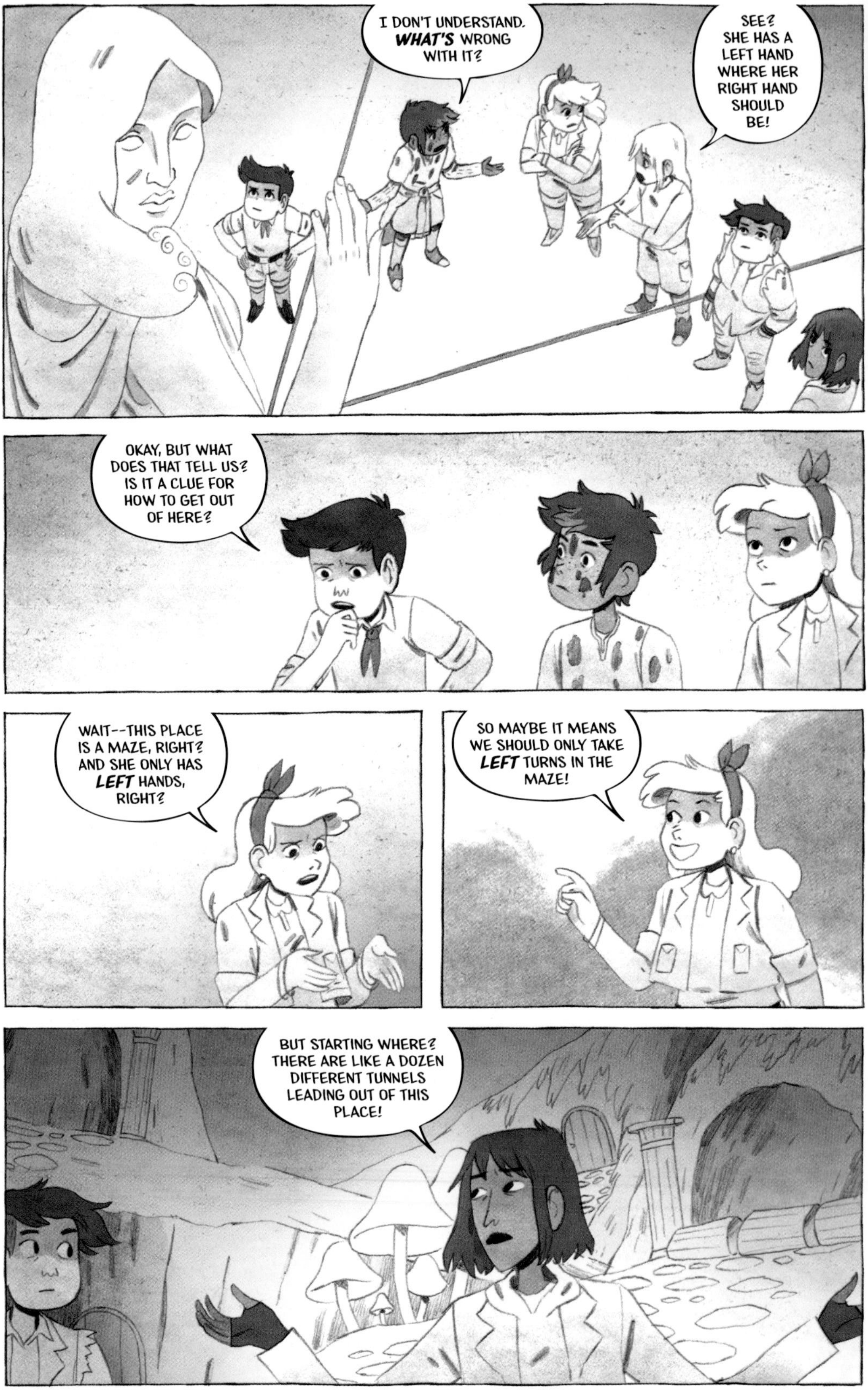
I DON'T UNDERSTAND. WHAT'S WRONG WITH IT?
SEE? SHE HAS A LEFT HAND WHERE HER RIGHT HAND SHOULD BE!
OKAY, BUT WHAT DOES THAT TELL US? IS IT A CLUE FOR HOW TO GET OUT OF HERE?
WAIT--THIS PLACE IS A MAZE, RIGHT? AND SHE ONLY HAS LEFT HANDS, RIGHT?
SO MAYBE IT MEANS WE SHOULD ONLY TAKE LEFT TURNS IN THE MAZE!
BUT STARTING WHERE? THERE ARE LIKE A DOZEN DIFFERENT TUNNELS LEADING OUT OF THIS PLACE!

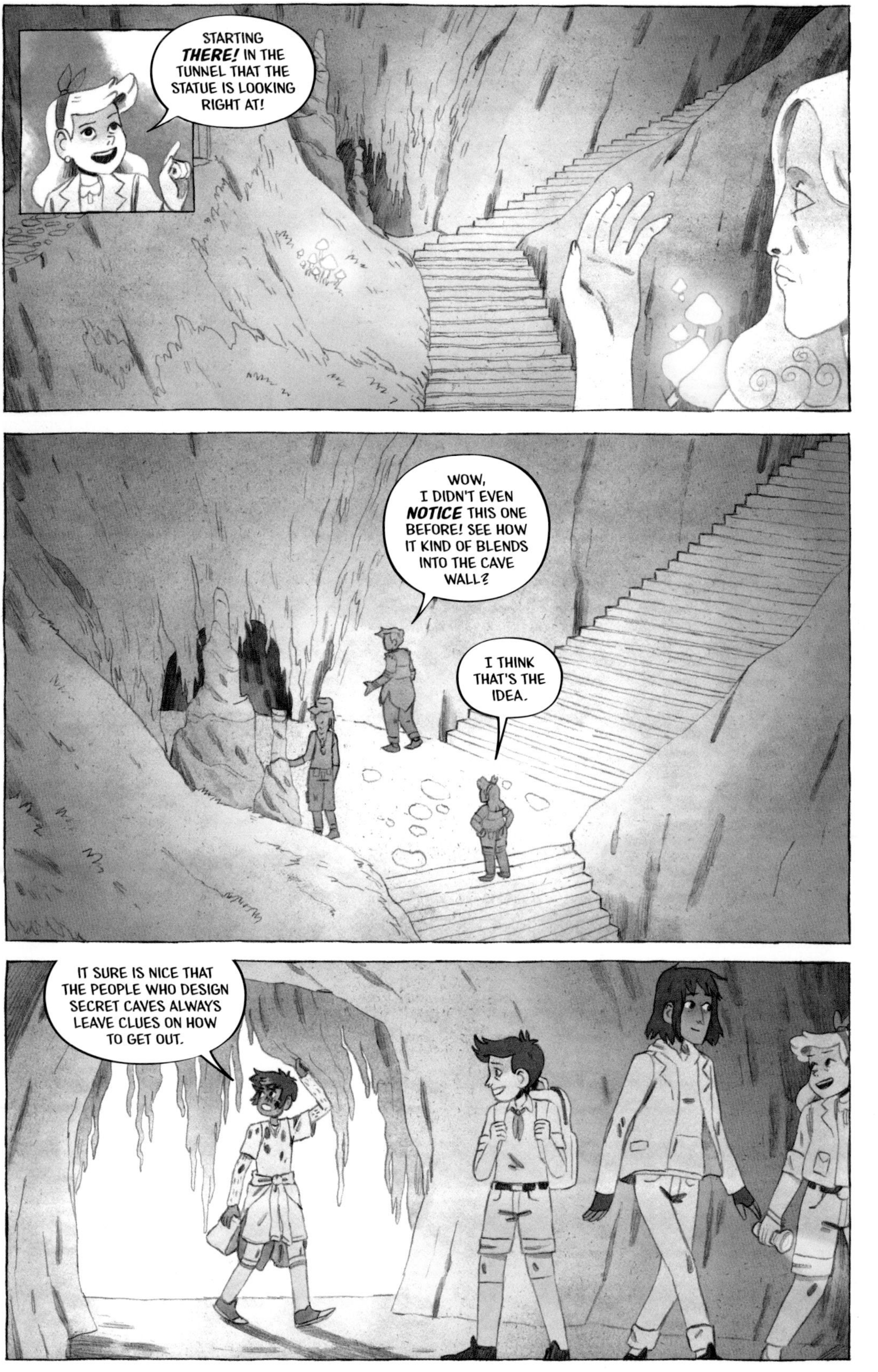
STARTING *THERE!* IN THE TUNNEL THAT THE STATUE IS LOOKING RIGHT AT!
WOW, I DIDN'T EVEN *NOTICE* THIS ONE BEFORE! SEE HOW IT KIND OF BLENDS INTO THE CAVE WALL?
I THINK THAT'S THE IDEA.
IT SURE IS NICE THAT THE PEOPLE WHO DESIGN SECRET CAVES ALWAYS LEAVE CLUES ON HOW TO GET OUT.

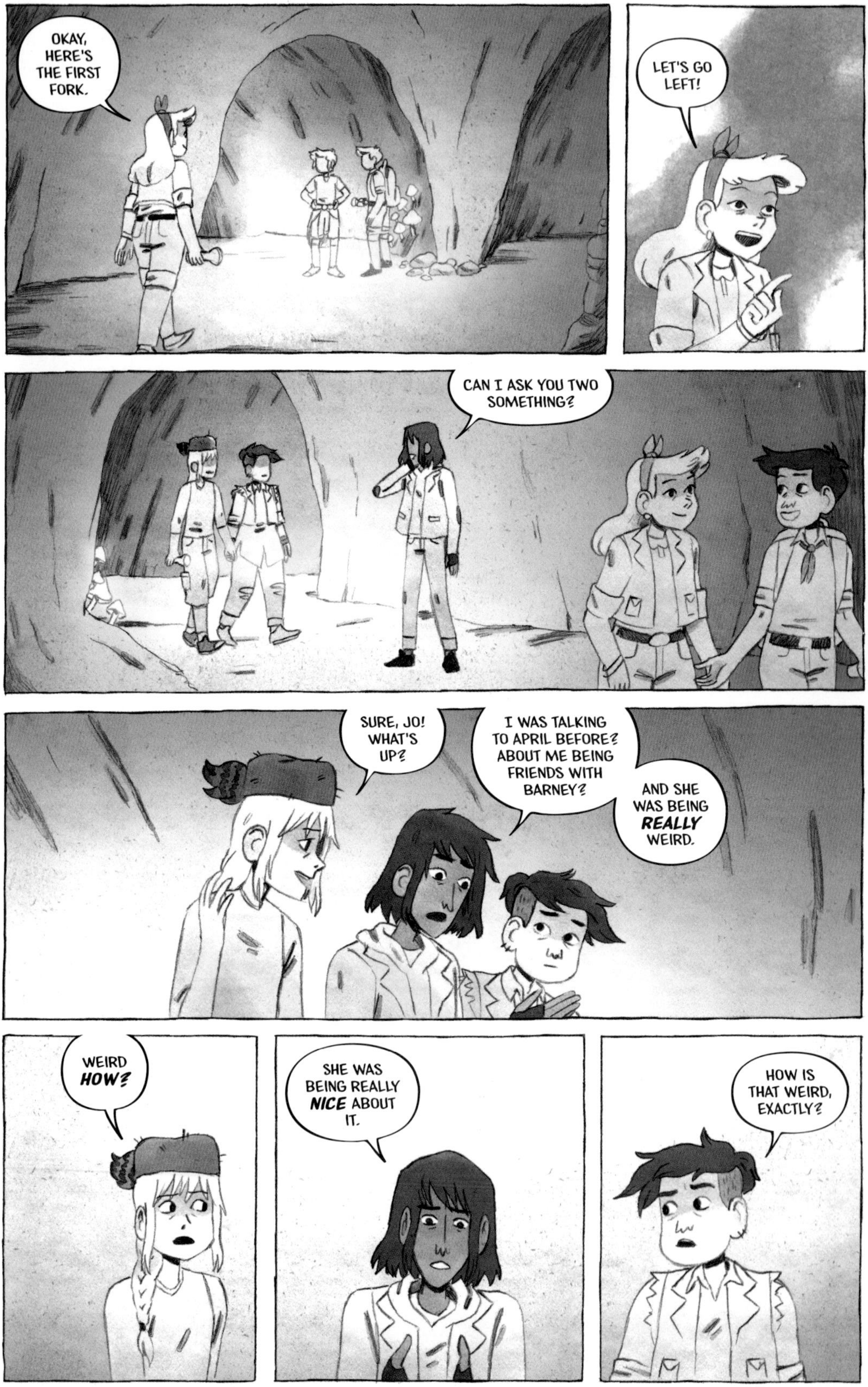
OKAY, HERE'S THE FIRST FORK.
LET'S GO LEFT!
CAN I ASK YOU TWO SOMETHING?
SURE, JO! WHAT'S UP?
I WAS TALKING TO APRIL BEFORE? ABOUT ME BEING FRIENDS WITH BARNEY?
AND SHE WAS BEING REALLY WEIRD.
WEIRD HOW?
SHE WAS BEING REALLY NICE ABOUT IT.
HOW IS THAT WEIRD, EXACTLY?

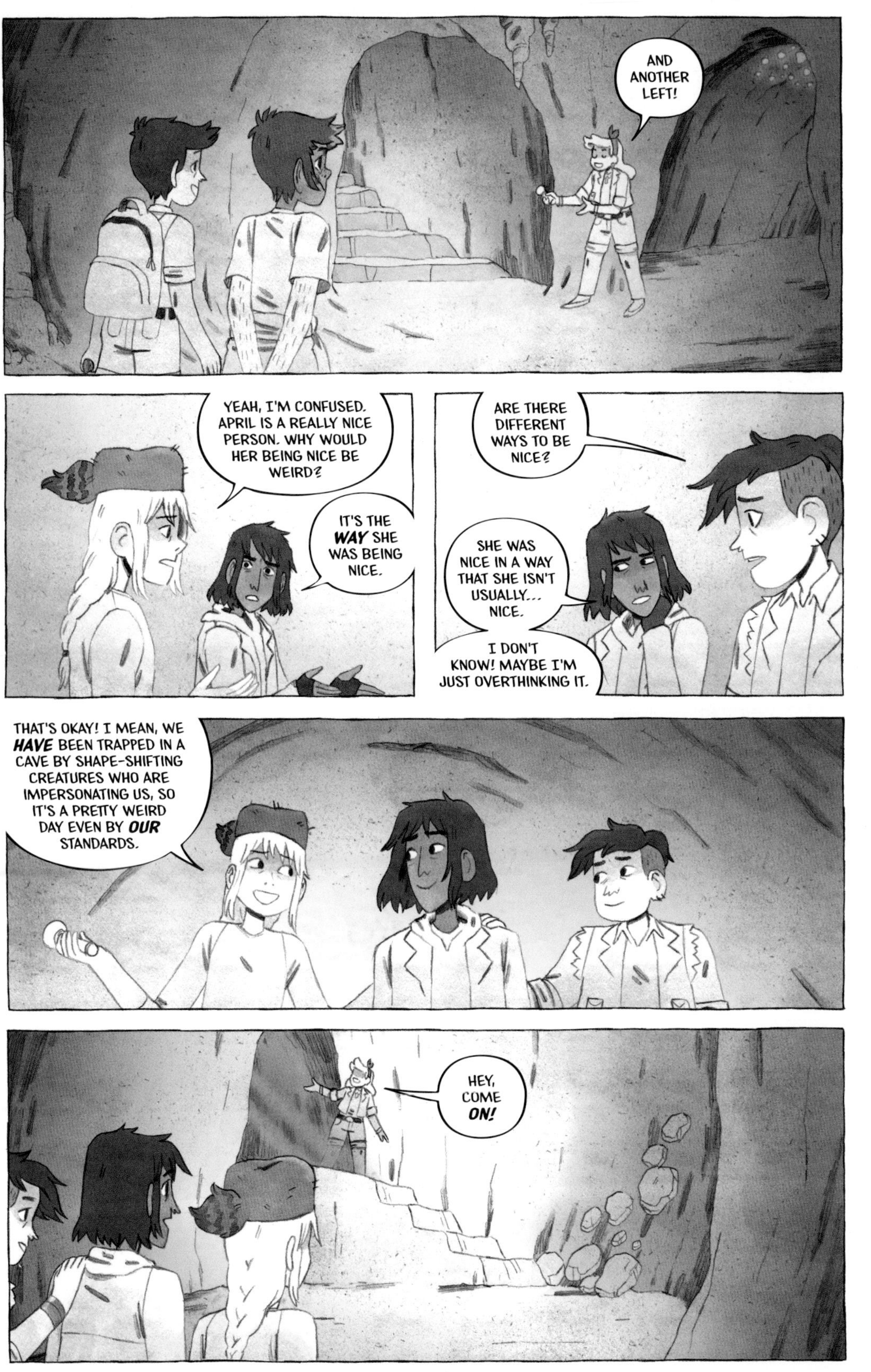
AND ANOTHER LEFT!
YEAH, I'M CONFUSED. APRIL IS A REALLY NICE PERSON. WHY WOULD HER BEING NICE BE WEIRD?
IT'S THE WAY SHE WAS BEING NICE.
ARE THERE DIFFERENT WAYS TO BE NICE?
SHE WAS NICE IN A WAY THAT SHE ISN'T USUALLY... NICE.
I DON'T KNOW! MAYBE I'M JUST OVERTHINKING IT.
THAT'S OKAY! I MEAN, WE HAVE BEEN TRAPPED IN A CAVE BY SHAPE-SHIFTING CREATURES WHO ARE IMPERSONATING US, SO IT'S A PRETTY WEIRD DAY EVEN BY OUR STANDARDS.
HEY, COME ON!

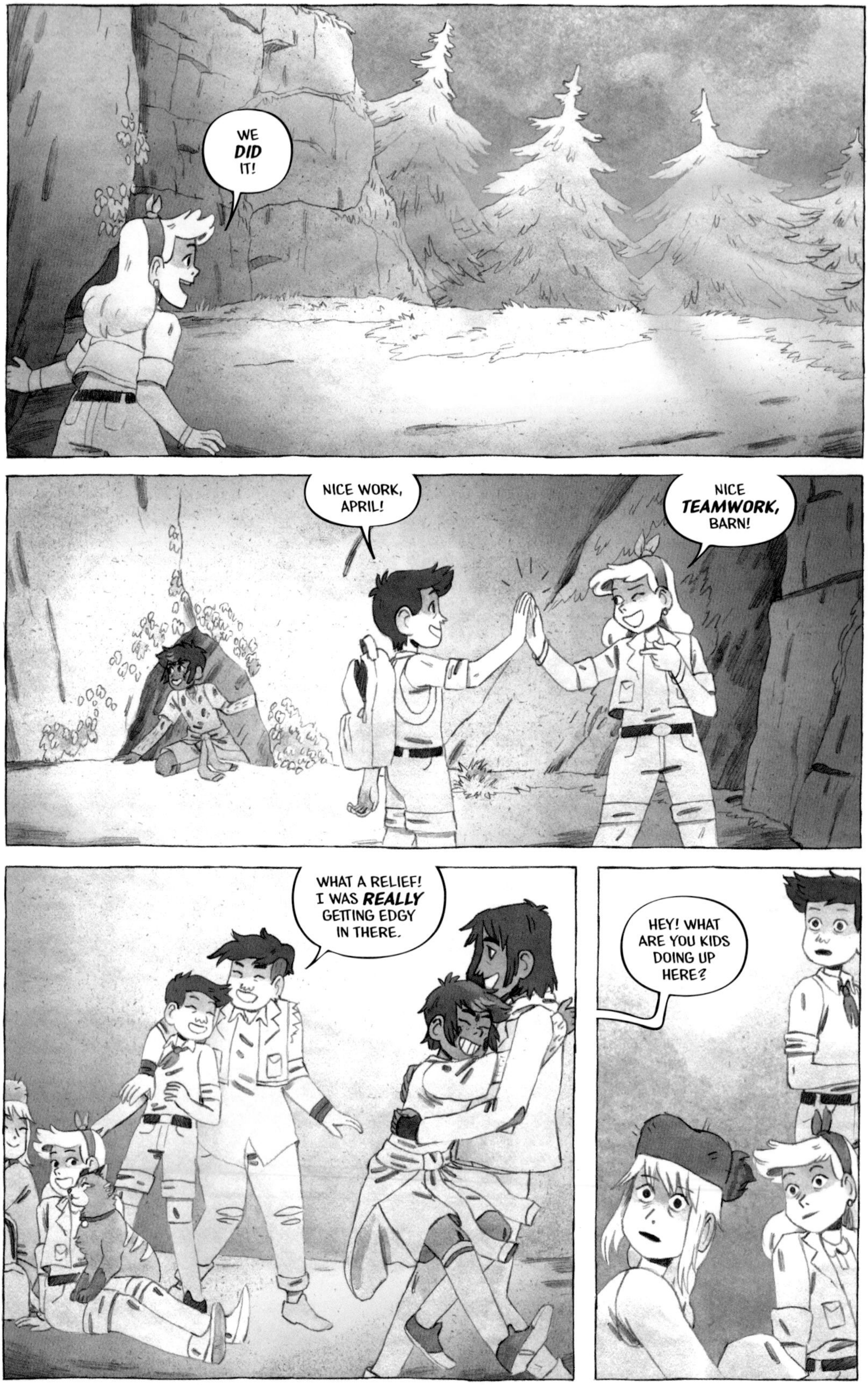
WE DID IT!
NICE WORK, APRIL!
NICE TEAMWORK, BARN!
WHAT A RELIEF! I WAS REALLY GETTING EDGY IN THERE.
HEY! WHAT ARE YOU KIDS DOING UP HERE?

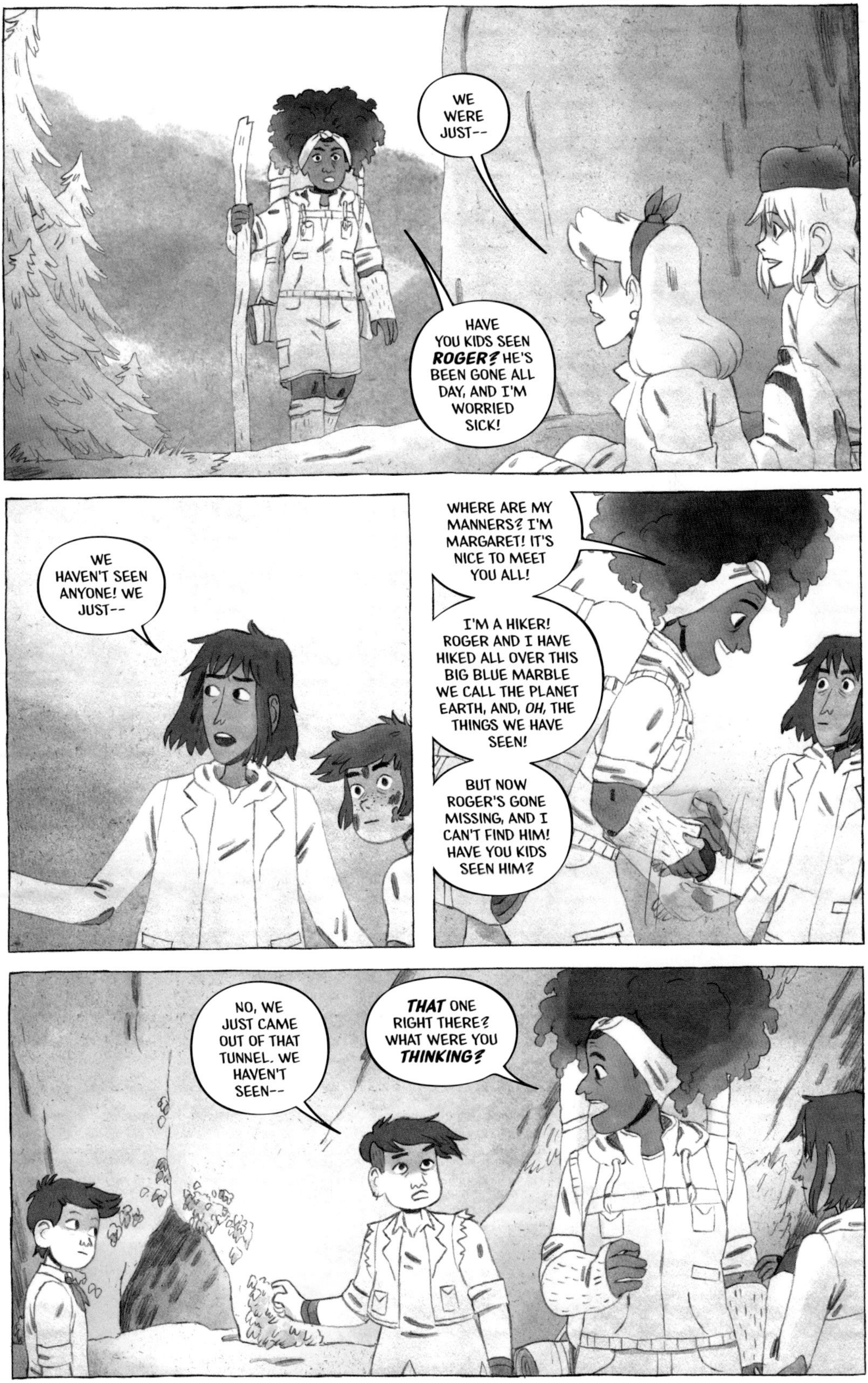

WE WERE JUST--
HAVE YOU KIDS SEEN ***ROGER?*** HE'S BEEN GONE ALL DAY, AND I'M WORRIED SICK!
WE HAVEN'T SEEN ANYONE! WE JUST--
WHERE ARE MY MANNERS? I'M MARGARET! IT'S NICE TO MEET YOU ALL!
I'M A HIKER! ROGER AND I HAVE HIKED ALL OVER THIS BIG BLUE MARBLE WE CALL THE PLANET EARTH, AND, *OH*, THE THINGS WE HAVE SEEN!
BUT NOW ROGER'S GONE MISSING, AND I CAN'T FIND HIM! HAVE YOU KIDS SEEN HIM?
NO, WE JUST CAME OUT OF THAT TUNNEL. WE HAVEN'T SEEN--
***THAT*** ONE RIGHT THERE? WHAT WERE YOU ***THINKING?***

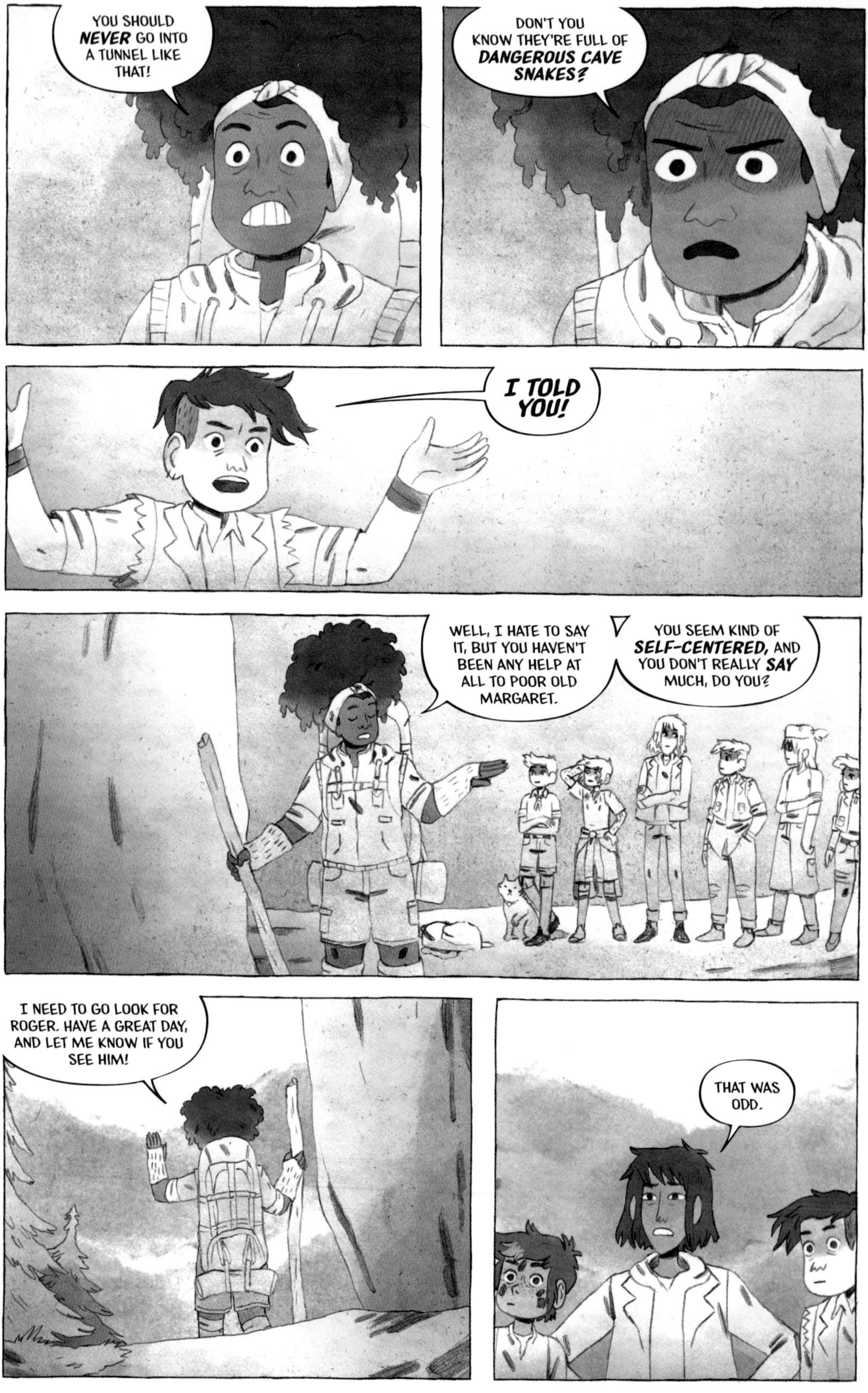
YOU SHOULD NEVER GO INTO A TUNNEL LIKE THAT!
DON'T YOU KNOW THEY'RE FULL OF DANGEROUS CAVE SNAKES?
I TOLD YOU!
WELL, I HATE TO SAY IT, BUT YOU HAVEN'T BEEN ANY HELP AT ALL TO POOR OLD MARGARET.
YOU SEEM KIND OF SELF-CENTERED, AND YOU DON'T REALLY SAY MUCH, DO YOU?
I NEED TO GO LOOK FOR ROGER. HAVE A GREAT DAY, AND LET ME KNOW IF YOU SEE HIM!
THAT WAS ODD.

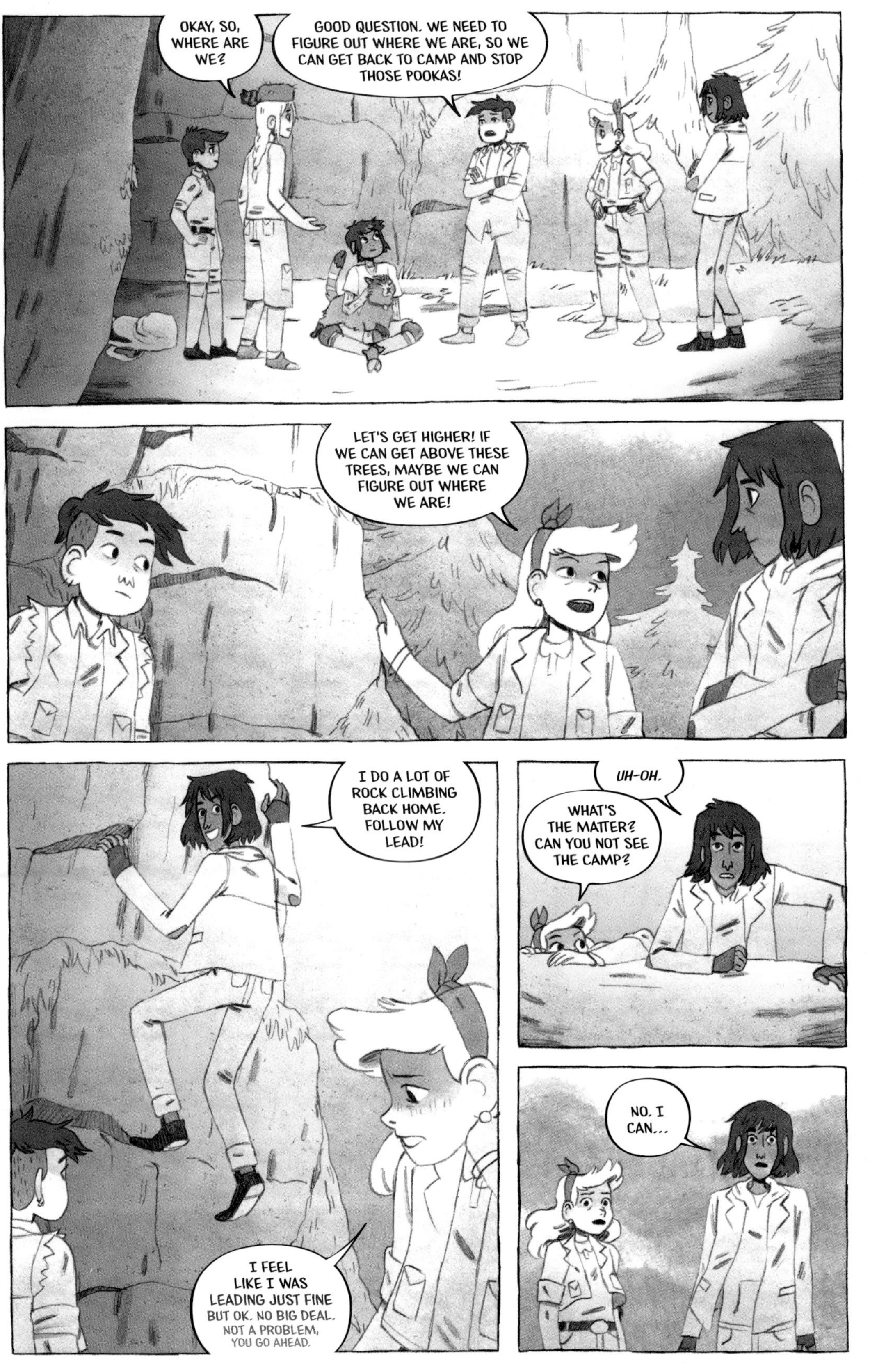

OKAY, SO, WHERE ARE WE?
GOOD QUESTION. WE NEED TO FIGURE OUT WHERE WE ARE, SO WE CAN GET BACK TO CAMP AND STOP THOSE POOKAS!
LET'S GET HIGHER! IF WE CAN GET ABOVE THESE TREES, MAYBE WE CAN FIGURE OUT WHERE WE ARE!
I DO A LOT OF ROCK CLIMBING BACK HOME. FOLLOW MY LEAD!
I FEEL LIKE I WAS LEADING JUST FINE BUT OK. NO BIG DEAL. NOT A PROBLEM, YOU GO AHEAD.
UH-OH.
WHAT'S THE MATTER? CAN YOU NOT SEE THE CAMP?
NO. I CAN...

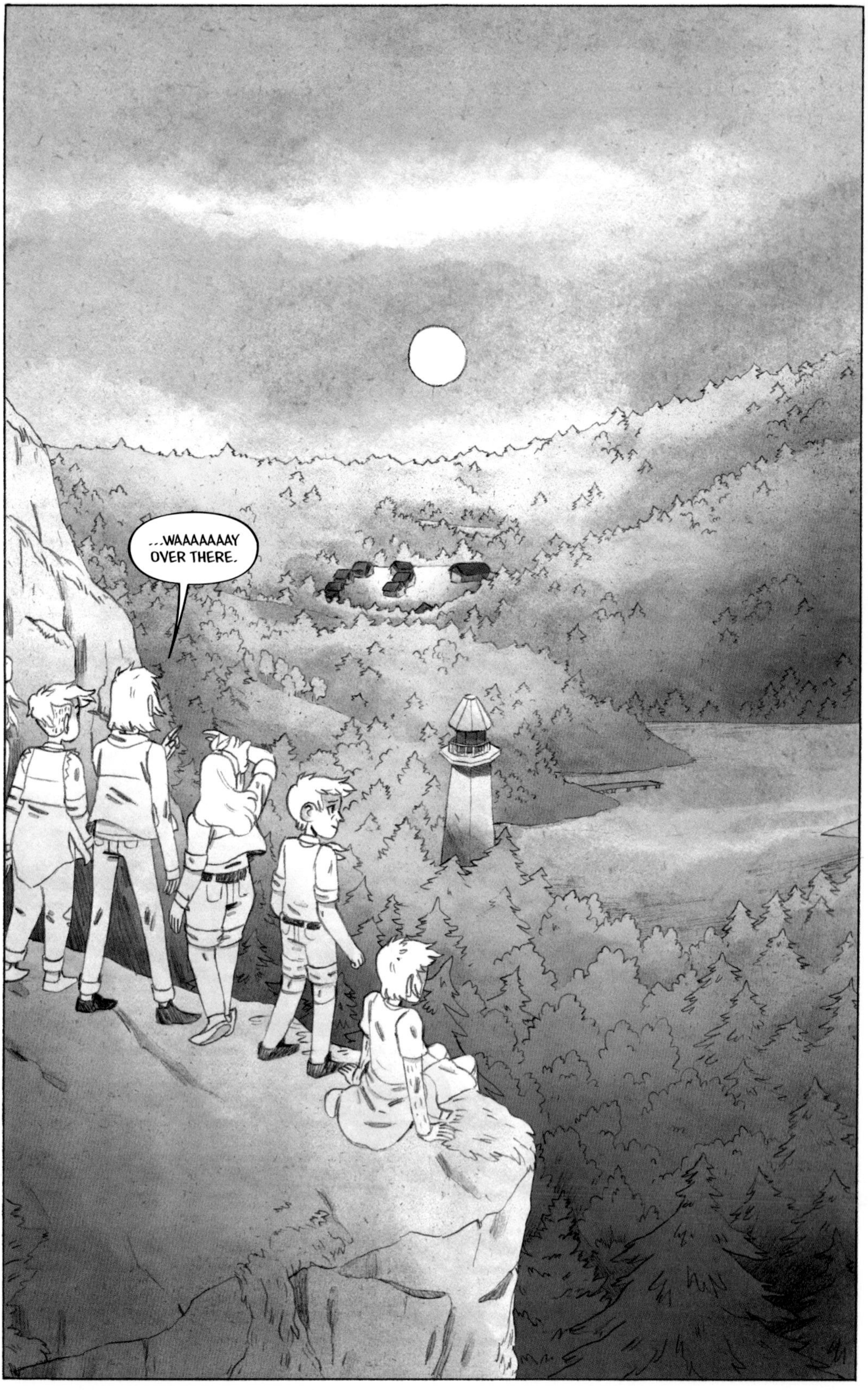
...WAAAAAAAY OVER THERE.

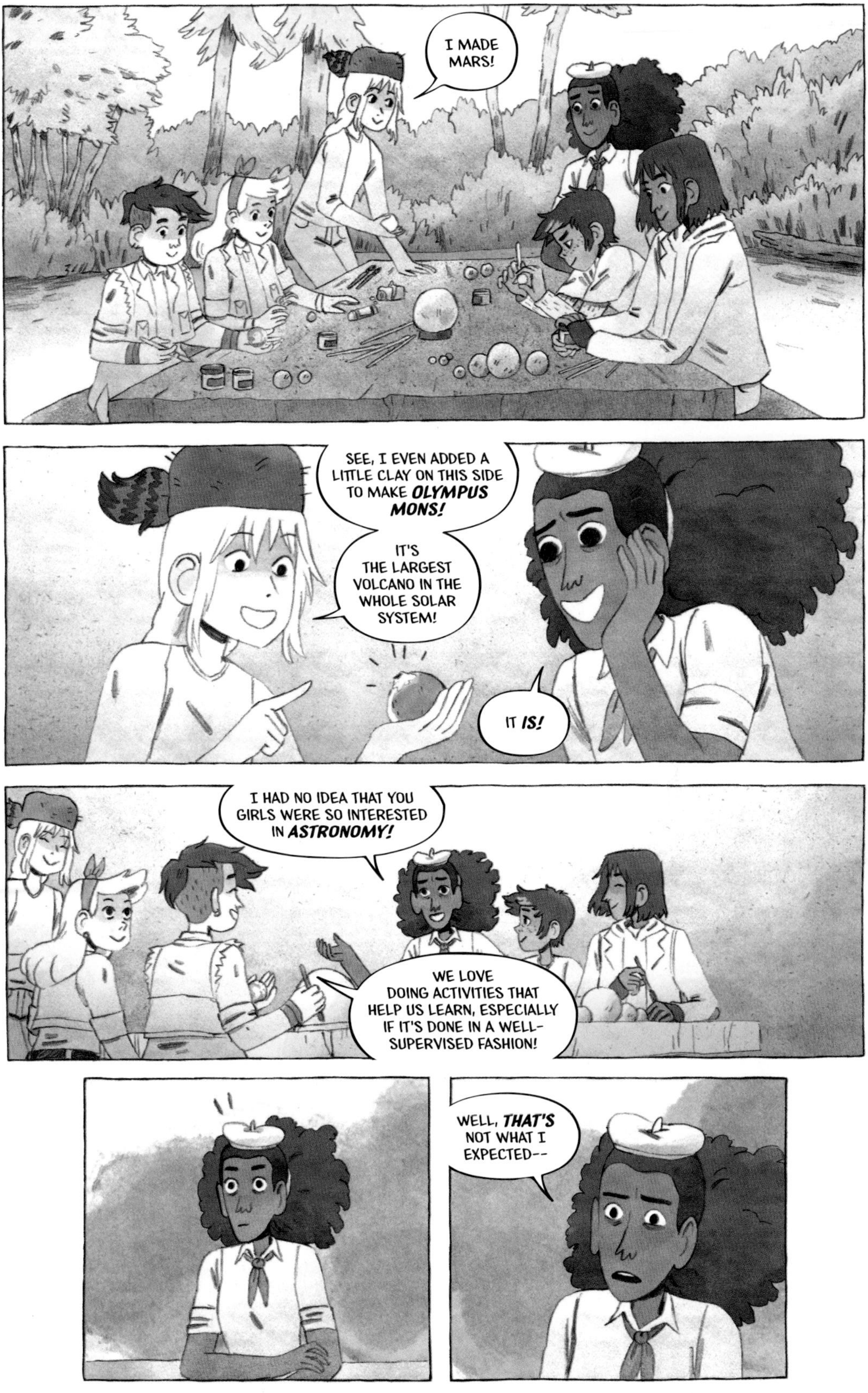
I MADE MARS!
SEE, I EVEN ADDED A LITTLE CLAY ON THIS SIDE TO MAKE OLYMPUS MONS!
IT'S THE LARGEST VOLCANO IN THE WHOLE SOLAR SYSTEM!
IT IS!
I HAD NO IDEA THAT YOU GIRLS WERE SO INTERESTED IN ASTRONOMY!
WE LOVE DOING ACTIVITIES THAT HELP US LEARN, ESPECIALLY IF IT'S DONE IN A WELL-SUPERVISED FASHION!
WELL, THAT'S NOT WHAT I EXPECTED--

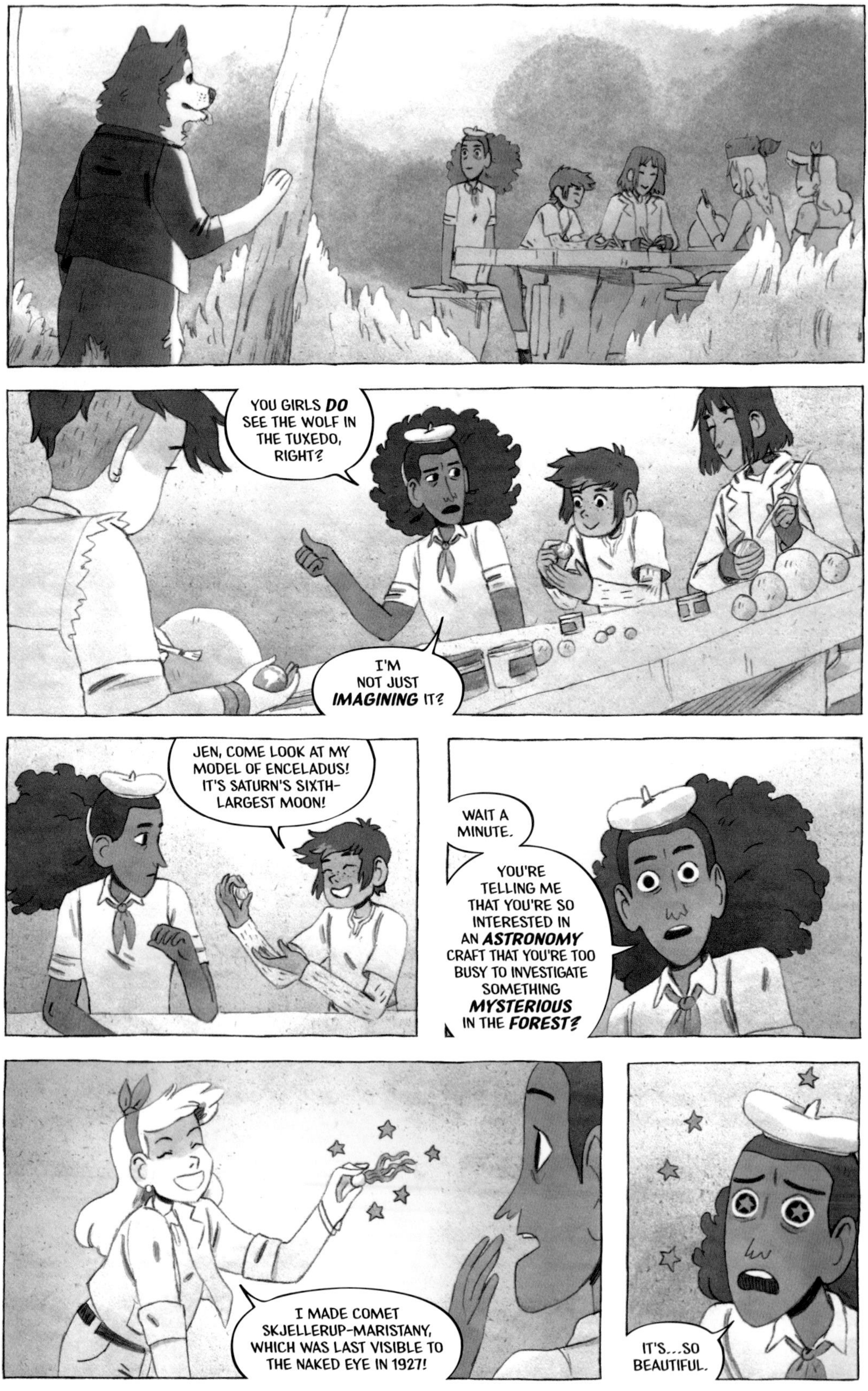
YOU GIRLS DO SEE THE WOLF IN THE TUXEDO, RIGHT?
I'M NOT JUST IMAGINING IT?
JEN, COME LOOK AT MY MODEL OF ENCELADUS! IT'S SATURN'S SIXTH-LARGEST MOON!
WAIT A MINUTE.
YOU'RE TELLING ME THAT YOU'RE SO INTERESTED IN AN ASTRONOMY CRAFT THAT YOU'RE TOO BUSY TO INVESTIGATE SOMETHING MYSTERIOUS IN THE FOREST?
I MADE COMET SKJELLERUP-MARISTANY, WHICH WAS LAST VISIBLE TO THE NAKED EYE IN 1927!
IT'S...SO BEAUTIFUL.

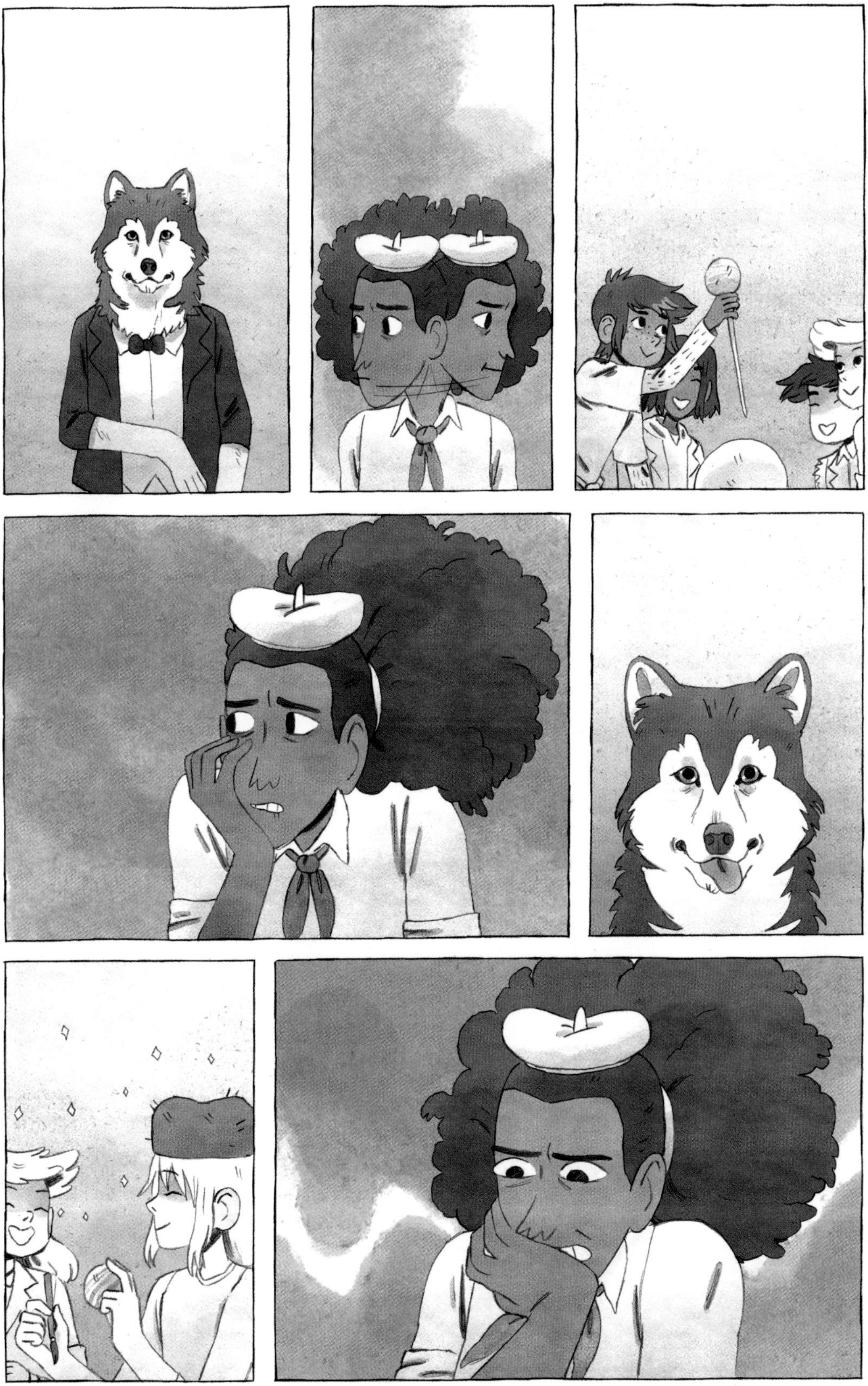

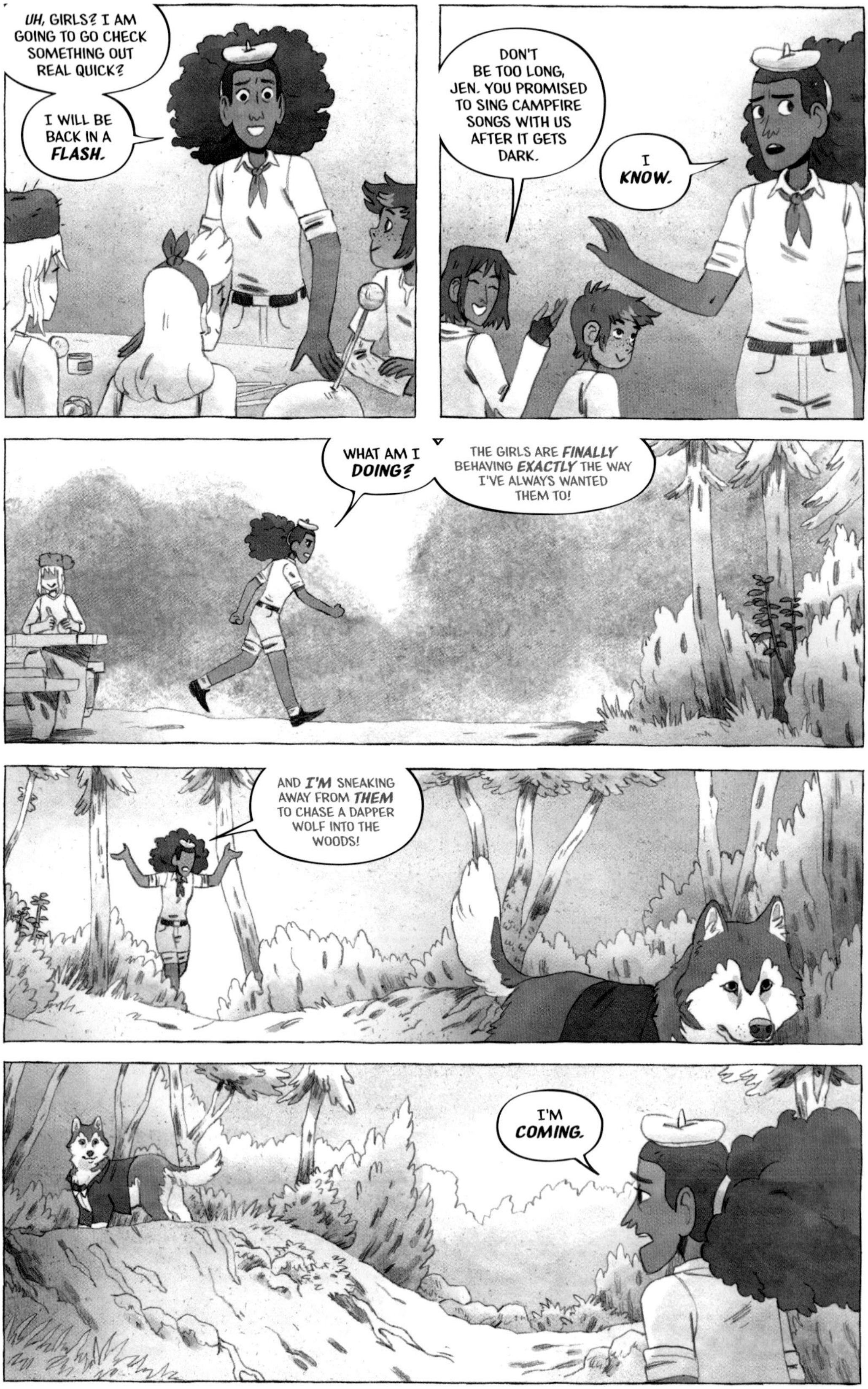
UH, GIRLS? I AM GOING TO GO CHECK SOMETHING OUT REAL QUICK?
I WILL BE BACK IN A FLASH.
DON'T BE TOO LONG, JEN. YOU PROMISED TO SING CAMPFIRE SONGS WITH US AFTER IT GETS DARK.
I KNOW.
WHAT AM I DOING?
THE GIRLS ARE FINALLY BEHAVING EXACTLY THE WAY I'VE ALWAYS WANTED THEM TO!
AND I'M SNEAKING AWAY FROM THEM TO CHASE A DAPPER WOLF INTO THE WOODS!
I'M COMING.

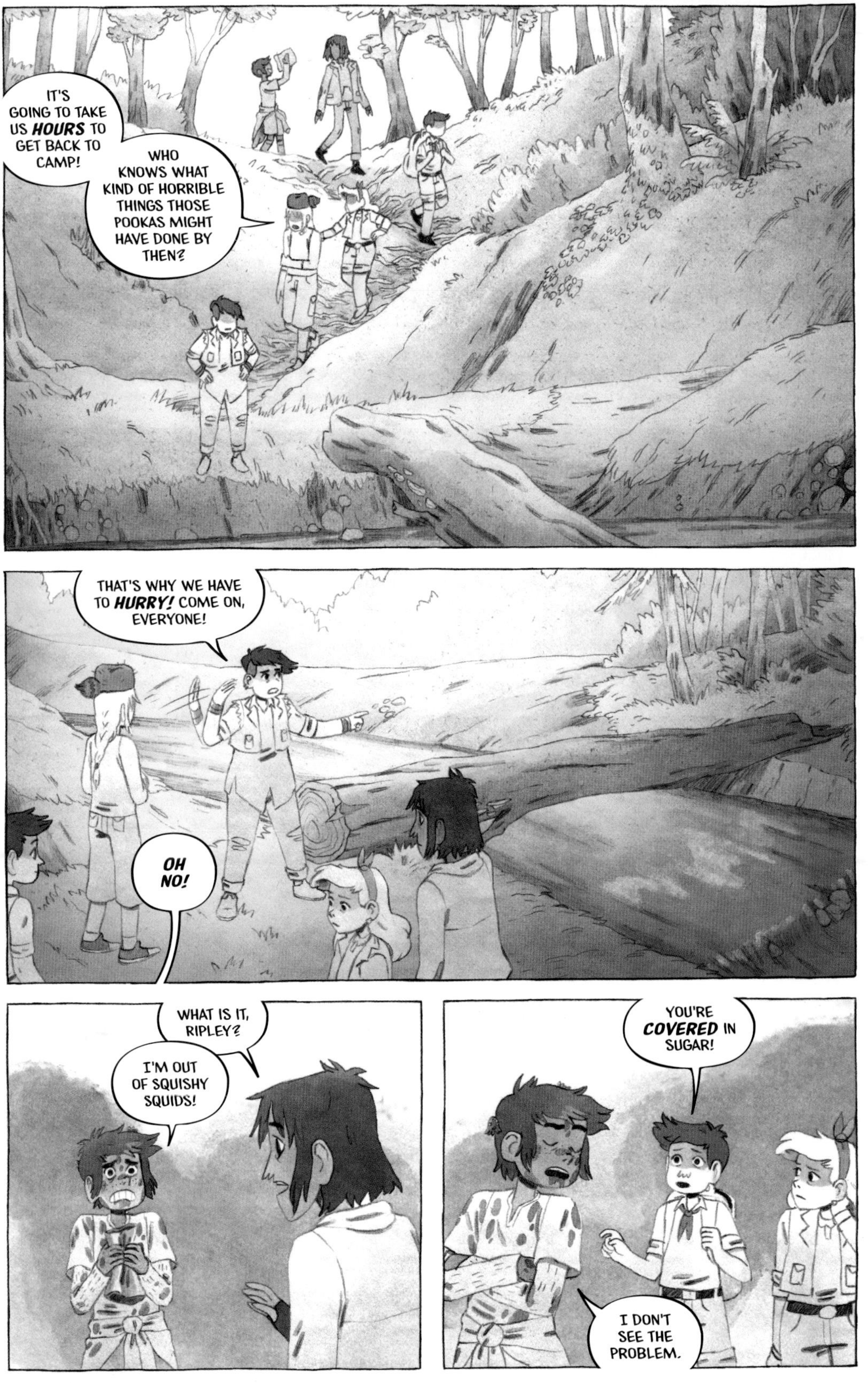
IT'S GOING TO TAKE US HOURS TO GET BACK TO CAMP!
WHO KNOWS WHAT KIND OF HORRIBLE THINGS THOSE POOKAS MIGHT HAVE DONE BY THEN?
THAT'S WHY WE HAVE TO HURRY! COME ON, EVERYONE!
OH NO!
WHAT IS IT, RIPLEY?
I'M OUT OF SQUISHY SQUIDS!
YOU'RE COVERED IN SUGAR!
I DON'T SEE THE PROBLEM.

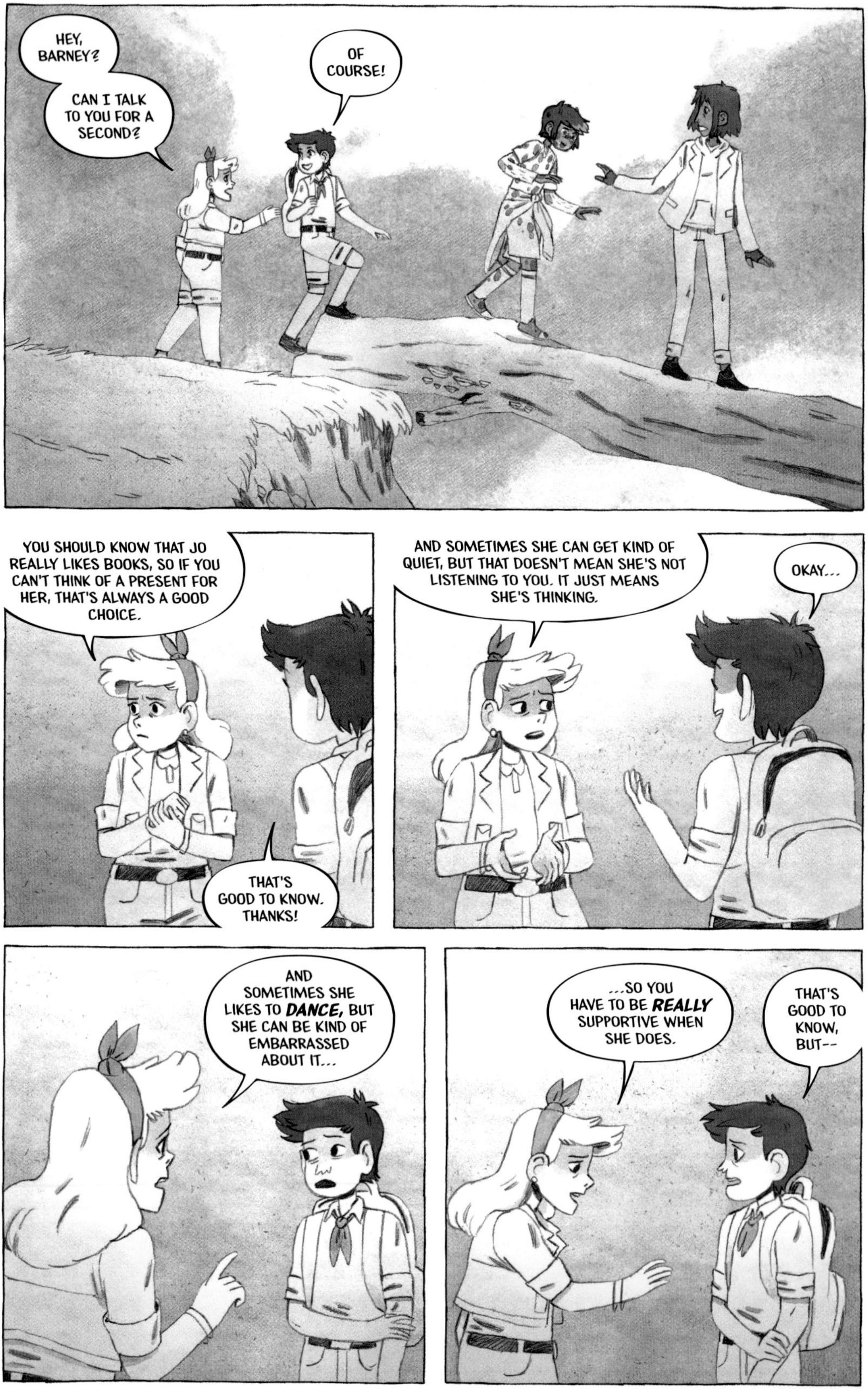
HEY, BARNEY?
CAN I TALK TO YOU FOR A SECOND?
OF COURSE!
YOU SHOULD KNOW THAT JO REALLY LIKES BOOKS, SO IF YOU CAN'T THINK OF A PRESENT FOR HER, THAT'S ALWAYS A GOOD CHOICE.
THAT'S GOOD TO KNOW. THANKS!
AND SOMETIMES SHE CAN GET KIND OF QUIET, BUT THAT DOESN'T MEAN SHE'S NOT LISTENING TO YOU. IT JUST MEANS SHE'S THINKING.
OKAY...
AND SOMETIMES SHE LIKES TO DANCE, BUT SHE CAN BE KIND OF EMBARRASSED ABOUT IT...
...SO YOU HAVE TO BE REALLY SUPPORTIVE WHEN SHE DOES.
THAT'S GOOD TO KNOW, BUT--

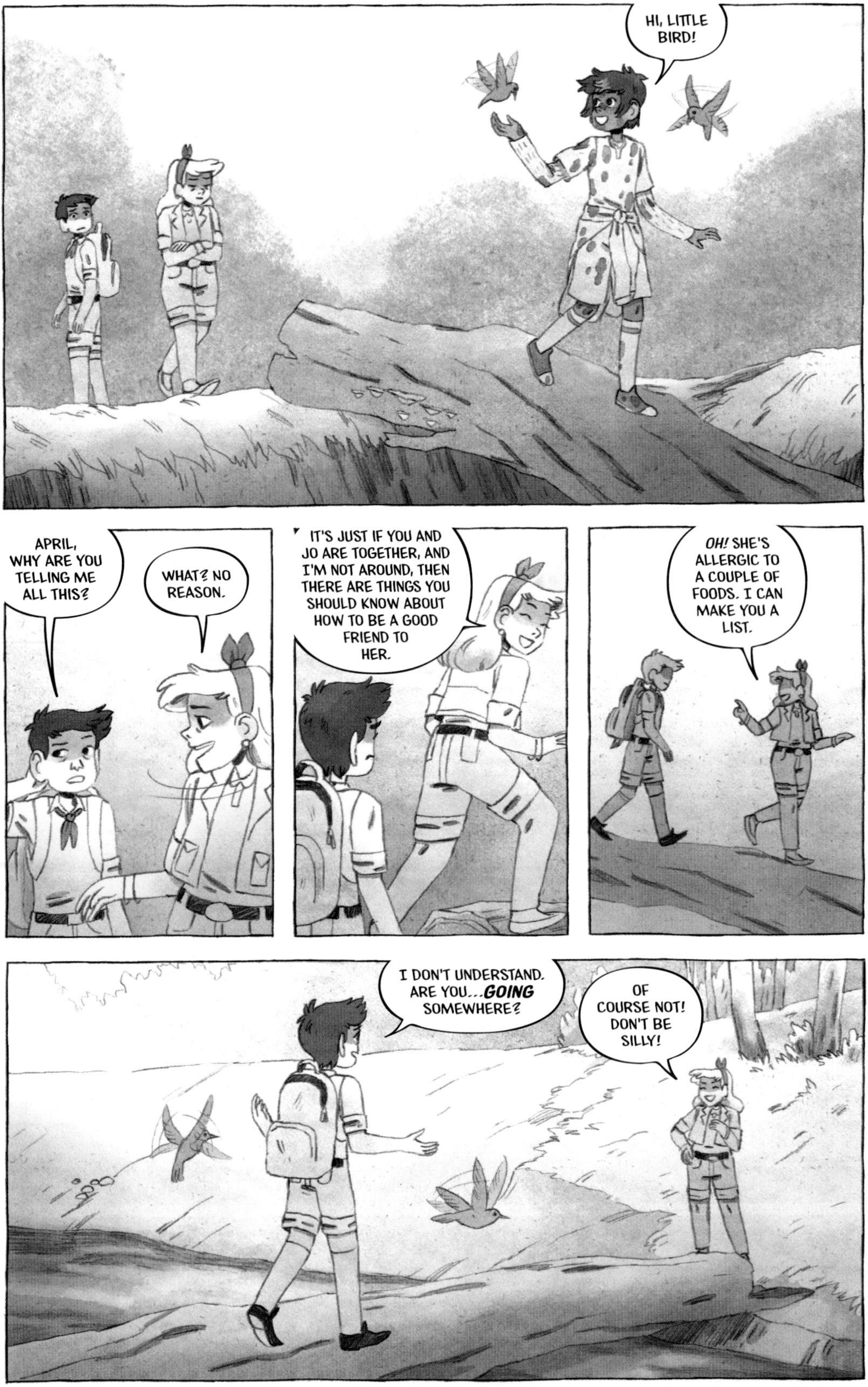
HI, LITTLE BIRD!
APRIL, WHY ARE YOU TELLING ME ALL THIS?
WHAT? NO REASON.
IT'S JUST IF YOU AND JO ARE TOGETHER, AND I'M NOT AROUND, THEN THERE ARE THINGS YOU SHOULD KNOW ABOUT HOW TO BE A GOOD FRIEND TO HER.
OH! SHE'S ALLERGIC TO A COUPLE OF FOODS. I CAN MAKE YOU A LIST.
I DON'T UNDERSTAND. ARE YOU...GOING SOMEWHERE?
OF COURSE NOT! DON'T BE SILLY!

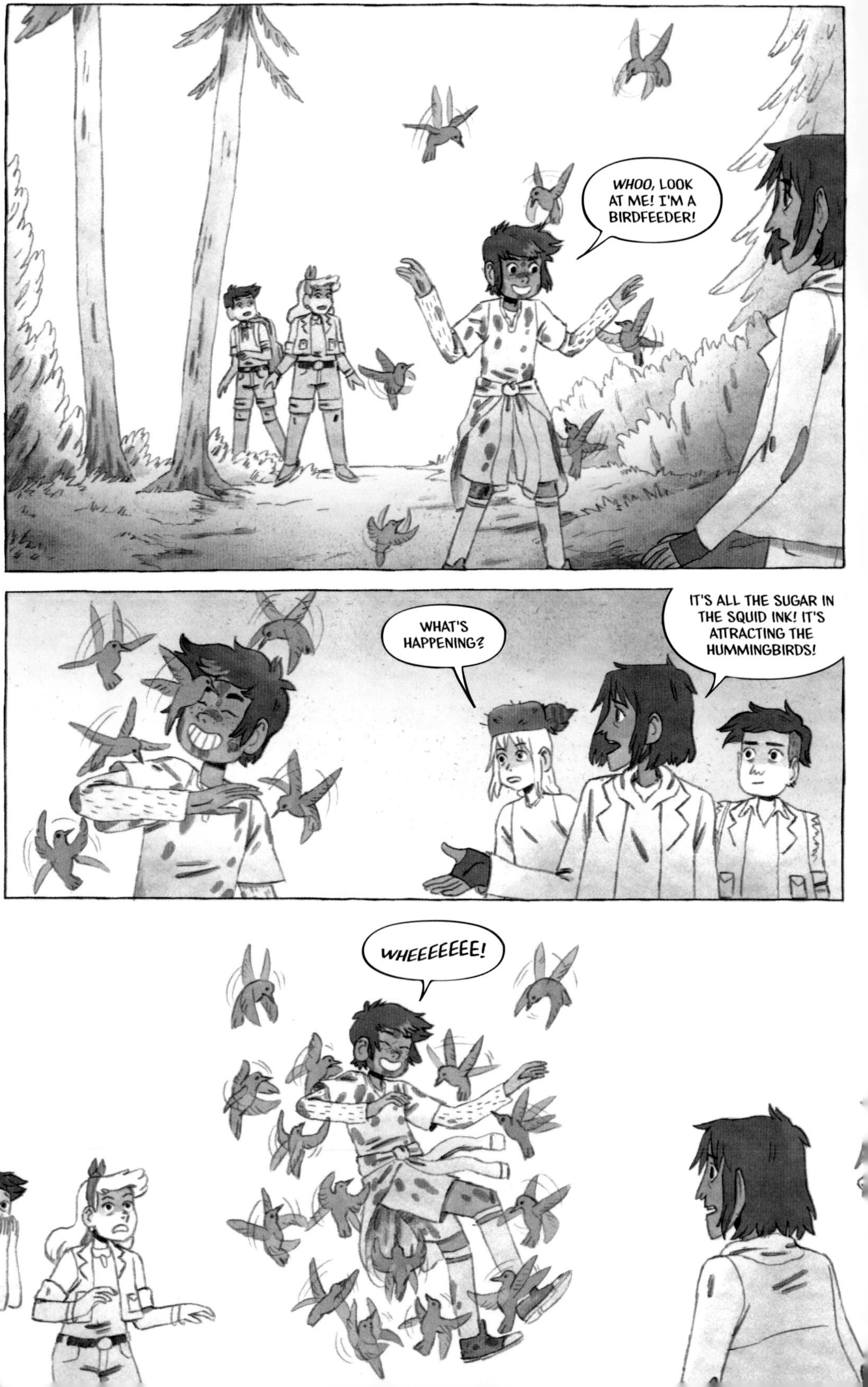
WHOO, LOOK AT ME! I'M A BIRDFEEDER!
WHAT'S HAPPENING?
IT'S ALL THE SUGAR IN THE SQUID INK! IT'S ATTRACTING THE HUMMINGBIRDS!
WHEEEEEEE!

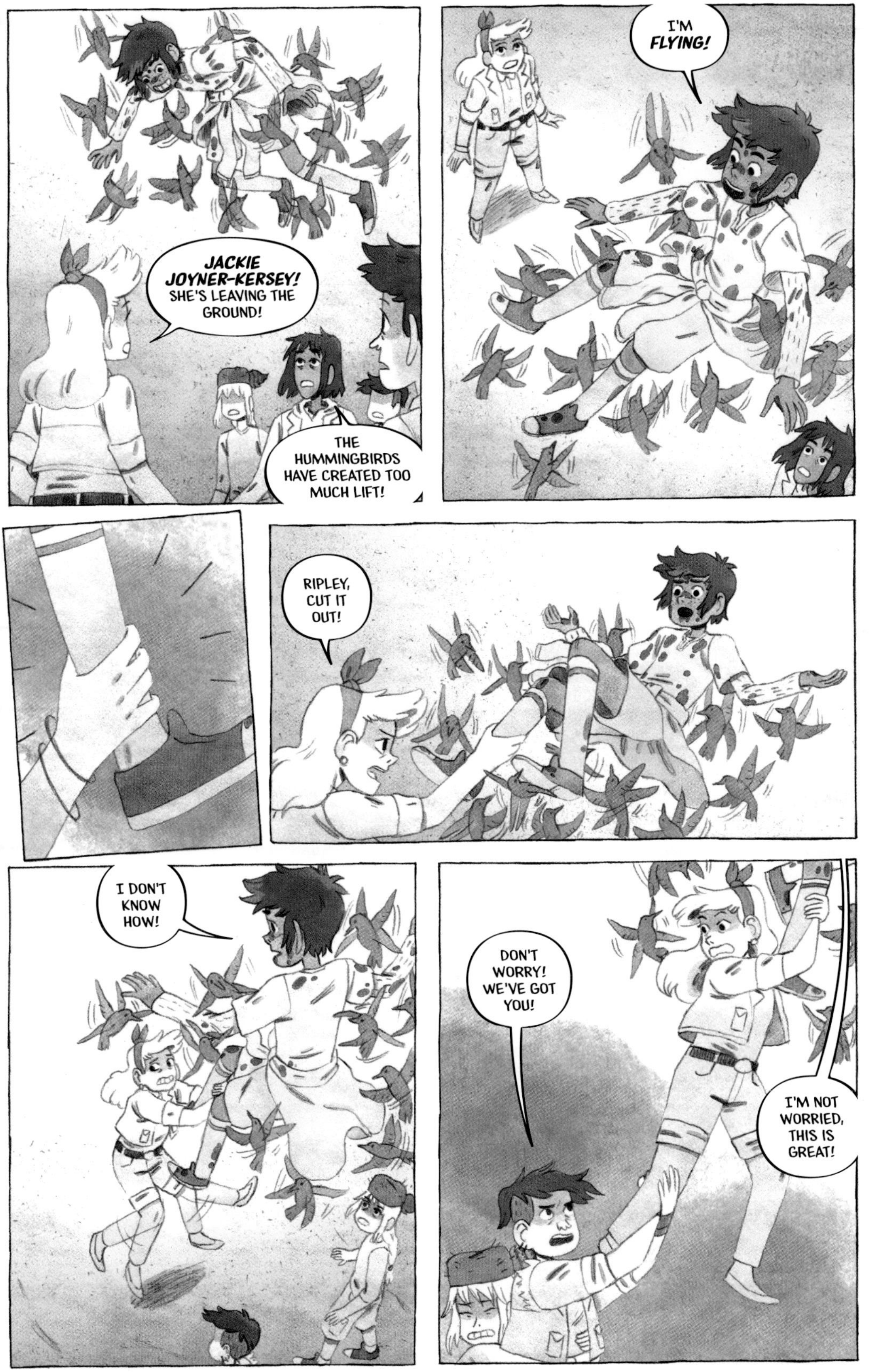
JACKIE JOYNER-KERSEY! SHE'S LEAVING THE GROUND!
THE HUMMINGBIRDS HAVE CREATED TOO MUCH LIFT!
I'M FLYING!
RIPLEY, CUT IT OUT!
I DON'T KNOW HOW!
DON'T WORRY! WE'VE GOT YOU!
I'M NOT WORRIED, THIS IS GREAT!

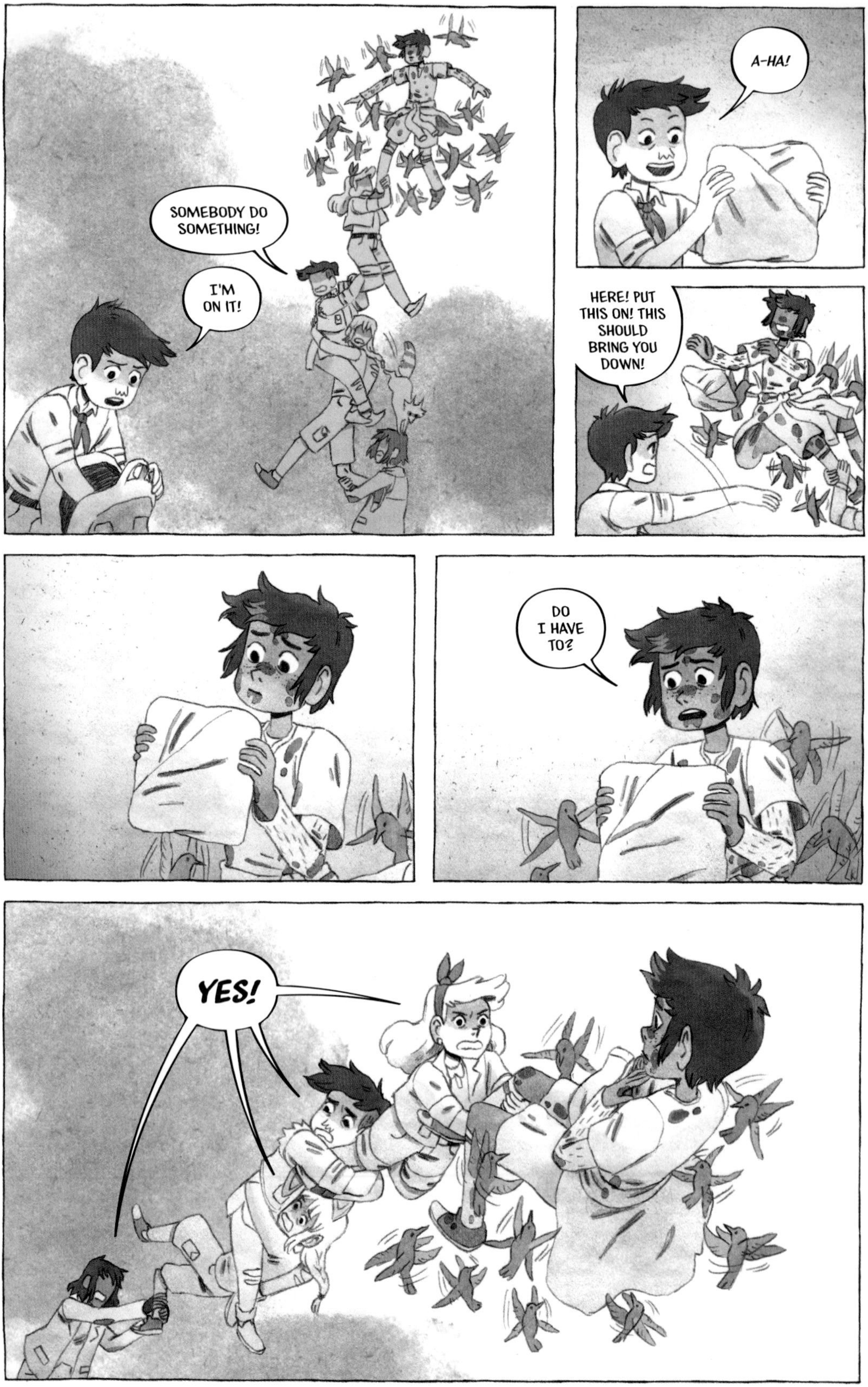
A-HA!
SOMEBODY DO SOMETHING!
I'M ON IT!
HERE! PUT THIS ON! THIS SHOULD BRING YOU DOWN!
DO I HAVE TO?
YES!

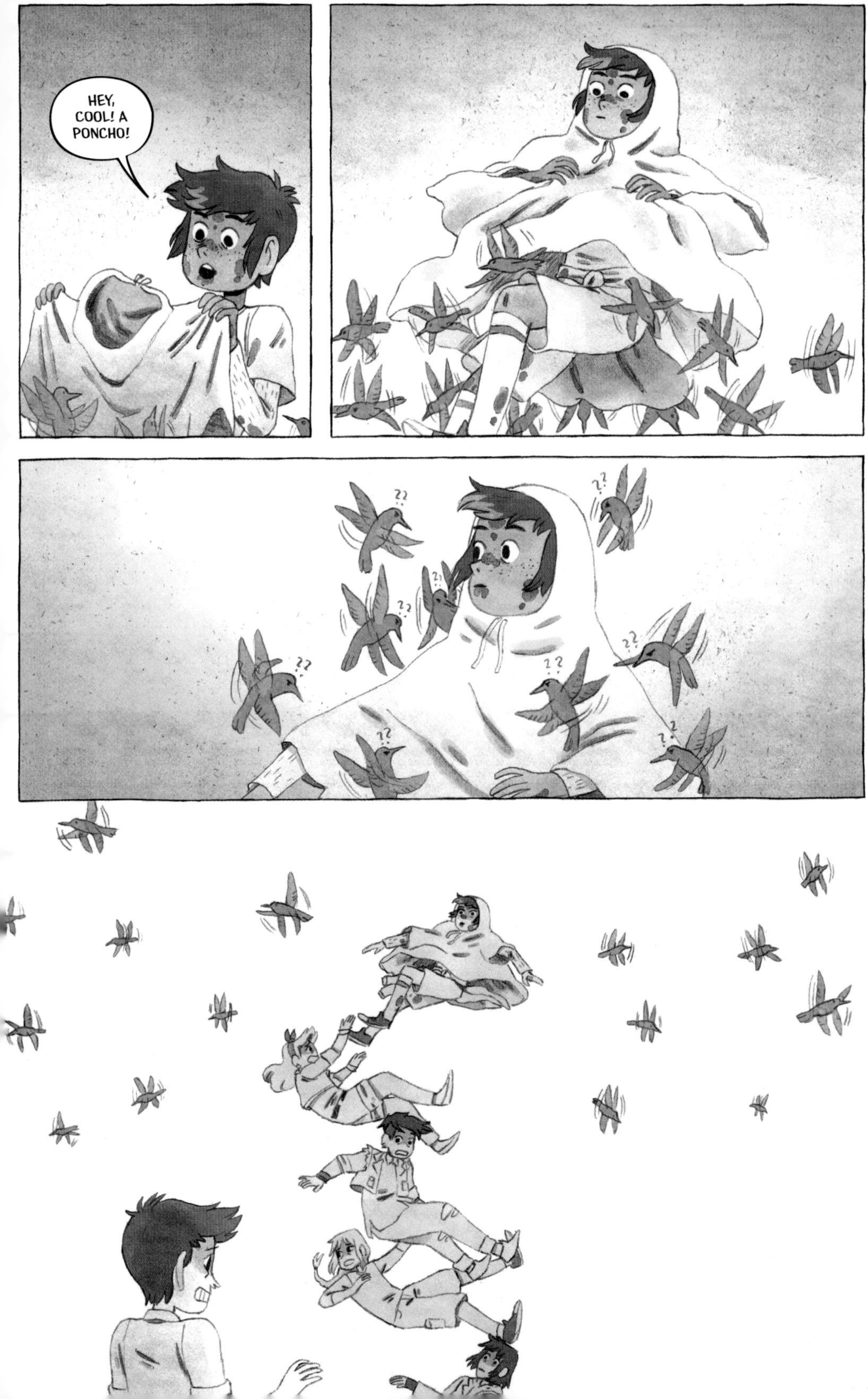
HEY, COOL! A PONCHO!

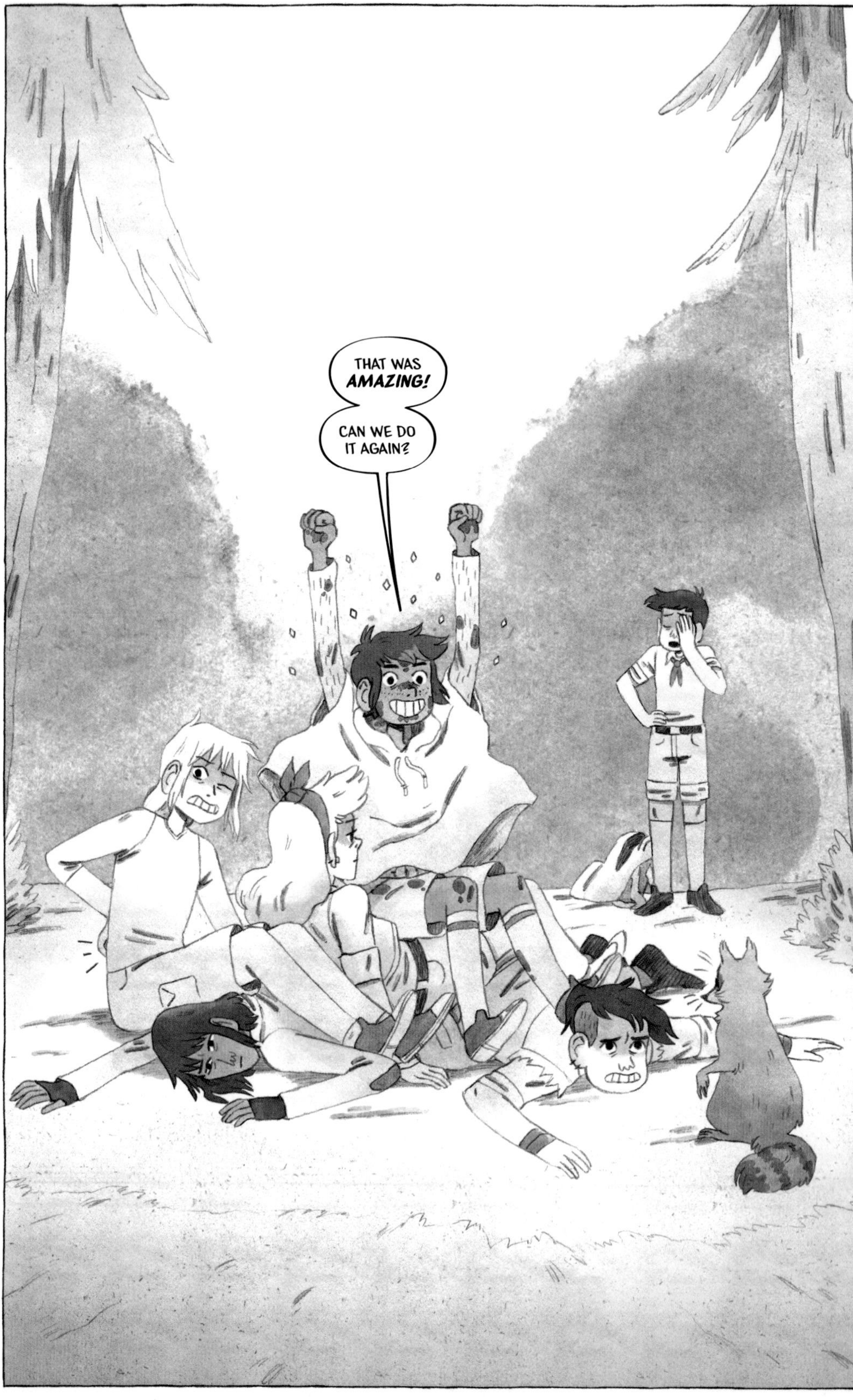
THAT WAS AMAZING!
CAN WE DO IT AGAIN?

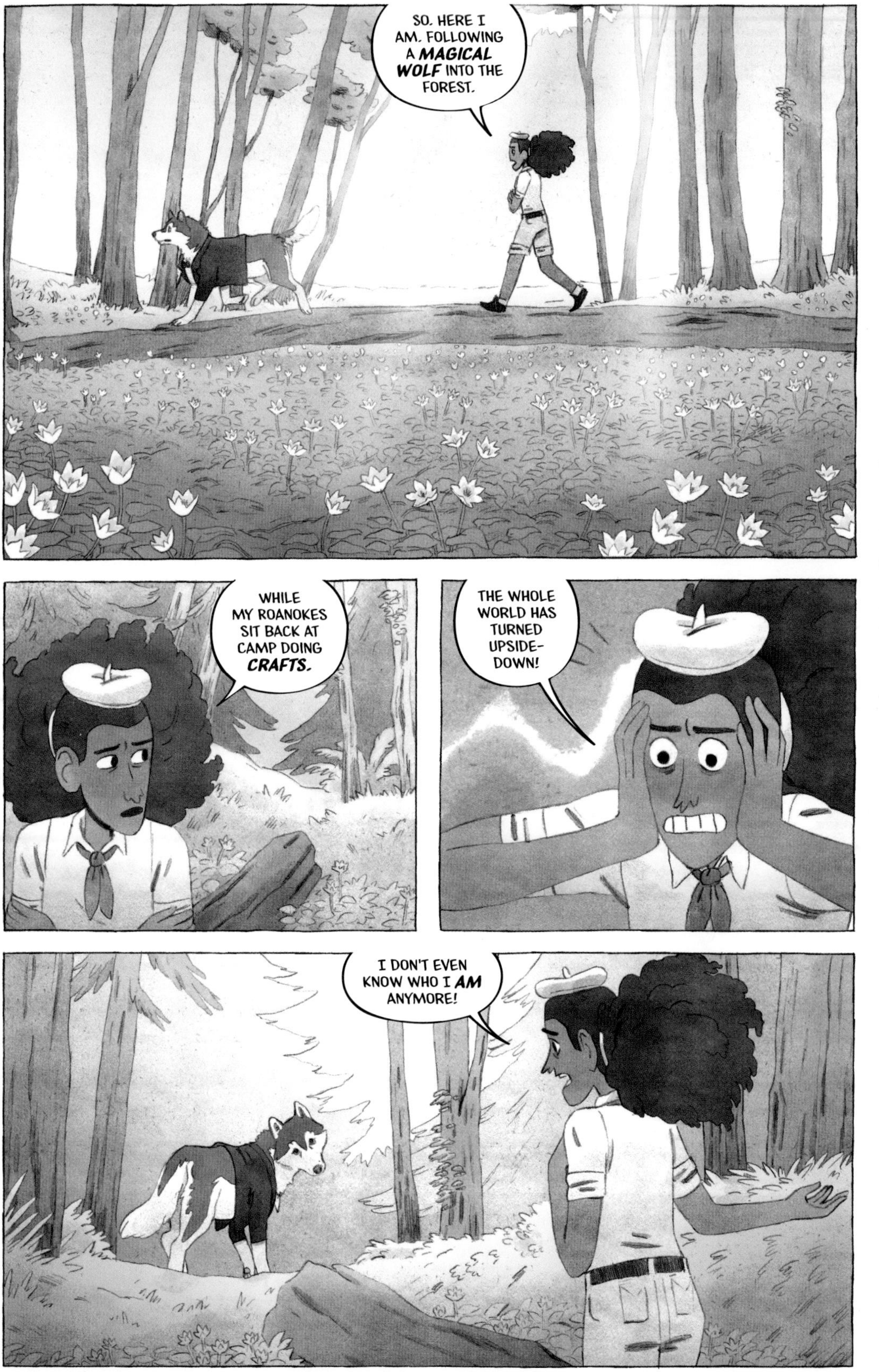
SO. HERE I AM. FOLLOWING A **MAGICAL WOLF** INTO THE FOREST.
WHILE MY ROANOKES SIT BACK AT CAMP DOING **CRAFTS.**
THE WHOLE WORLD HAS TURNED UPSIDE-DOWN!
I DON'T EVEN KNOW WHO I **AM** ANYMORE!

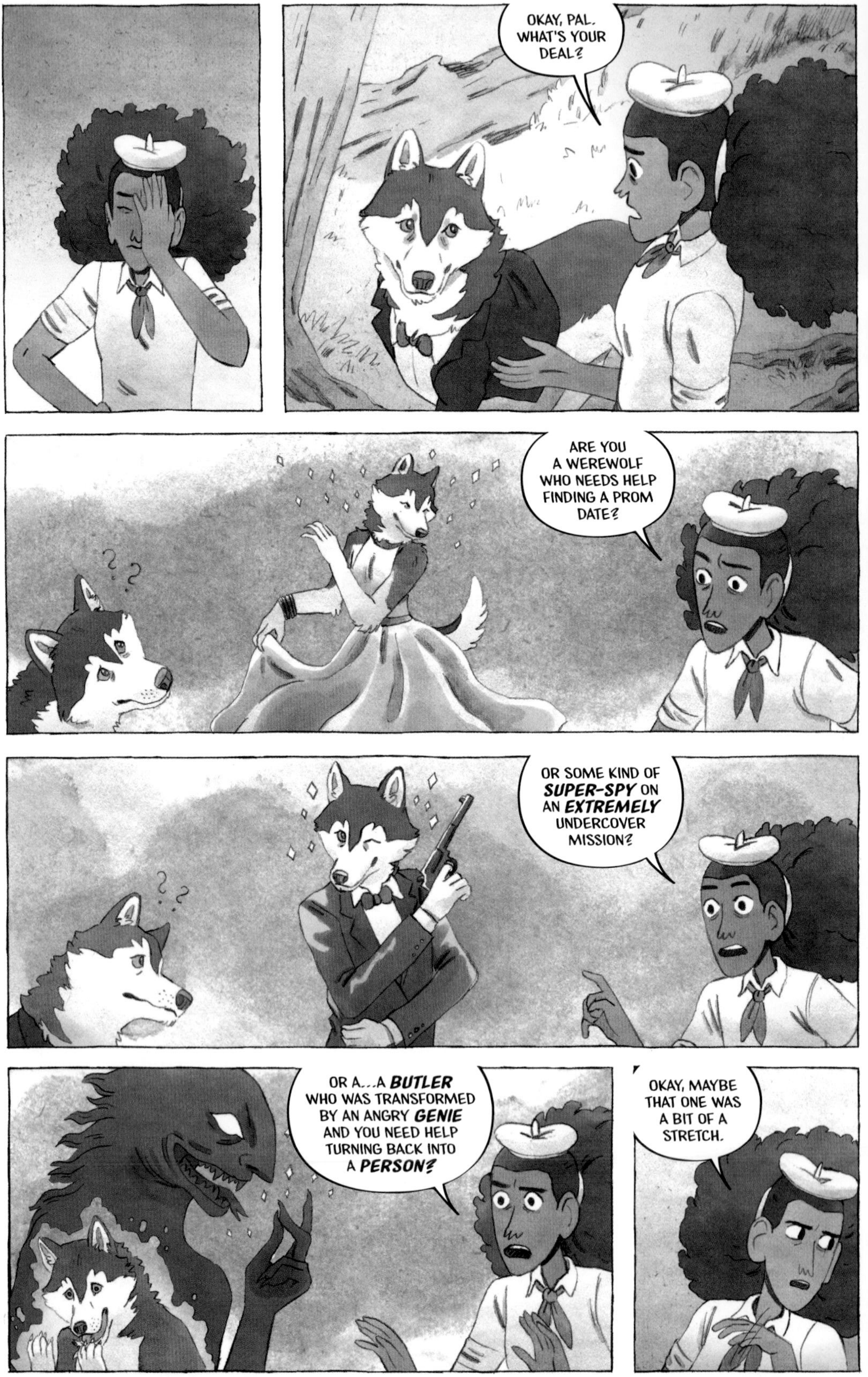
OKAY, PAL. WHAT'S YOUR DEAL?
ARE YOU A WEREWOLF WHO NEEDS HELP FINDING A PROM DATE?
OR SOME KIND OF *SUPER-SPY* ON AN *EXTREMELY* UNDERCOVER MISSION?
OR A...A *BUTLER* WHO WAS TRANSFORMED BY AN ANGRY *GENIE* AND YOU NEED HELP TURNING BACK INTO A *PERSON?*
OKAY, MAYBE THAT ONE WAS A BIT OF A STRETCH.

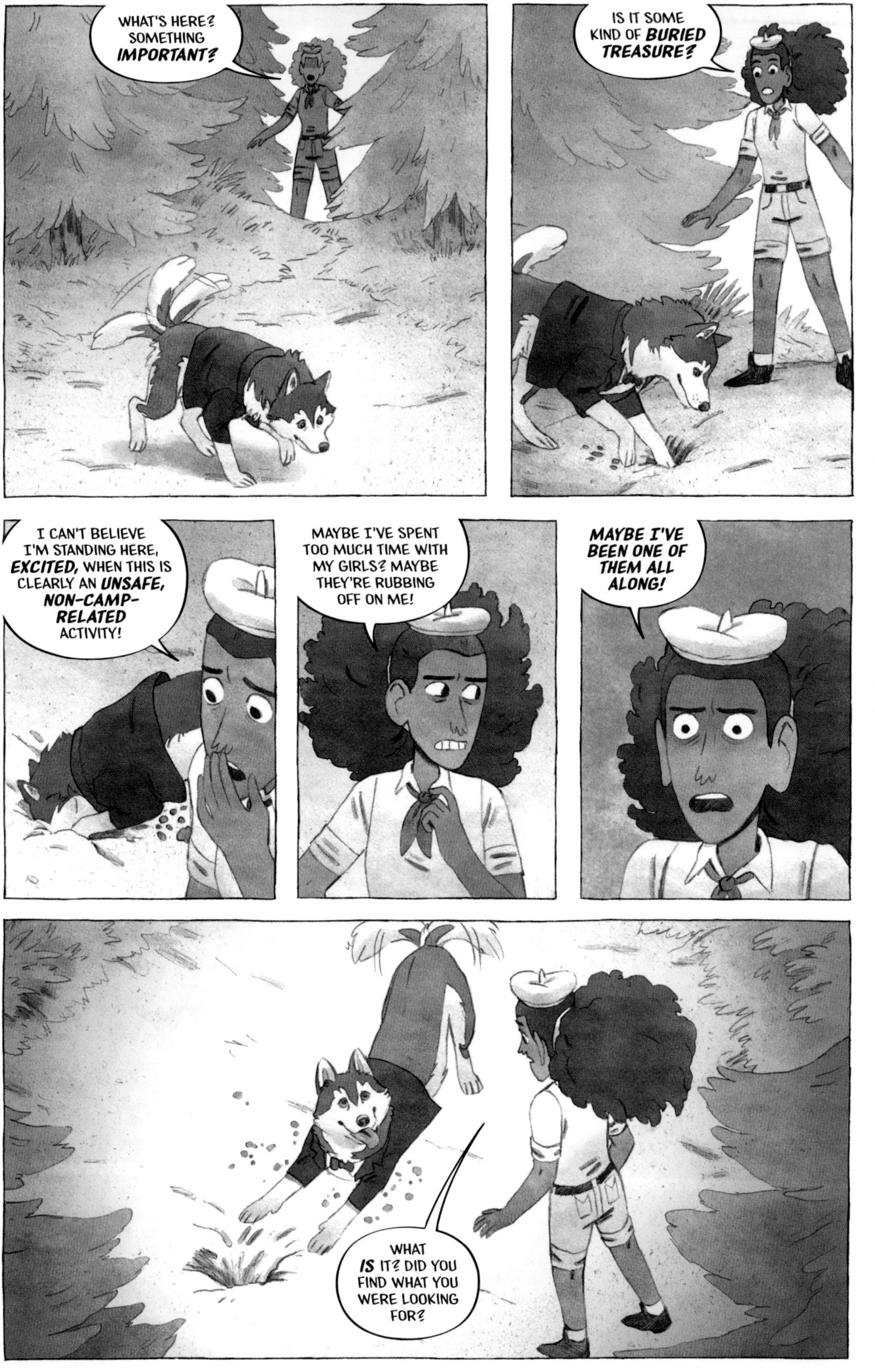
WHAT'S HERE? SOMETHING IMPORTANT?
IS IT SOME KIND OF BURIED TREASURE?
I CAN'T BELIEVE I'M STANDING HERE, EXCITED, WHEN THIS IS CLEARLY AN UNSAFE, NON-CAMP-RELATED ACTIVITY!
MAYBE I'VE SPENT TOO MUCH TIME WITH MY GIRLS? MAYBE THEY'RE RUBBING OFF ON ME!
MAYBE I'VE BEEN ONE OF THEM ALL ALONG!
WHAT IS IT? DID YOU FIND WHAT YOU WERE LOOKING FOR?

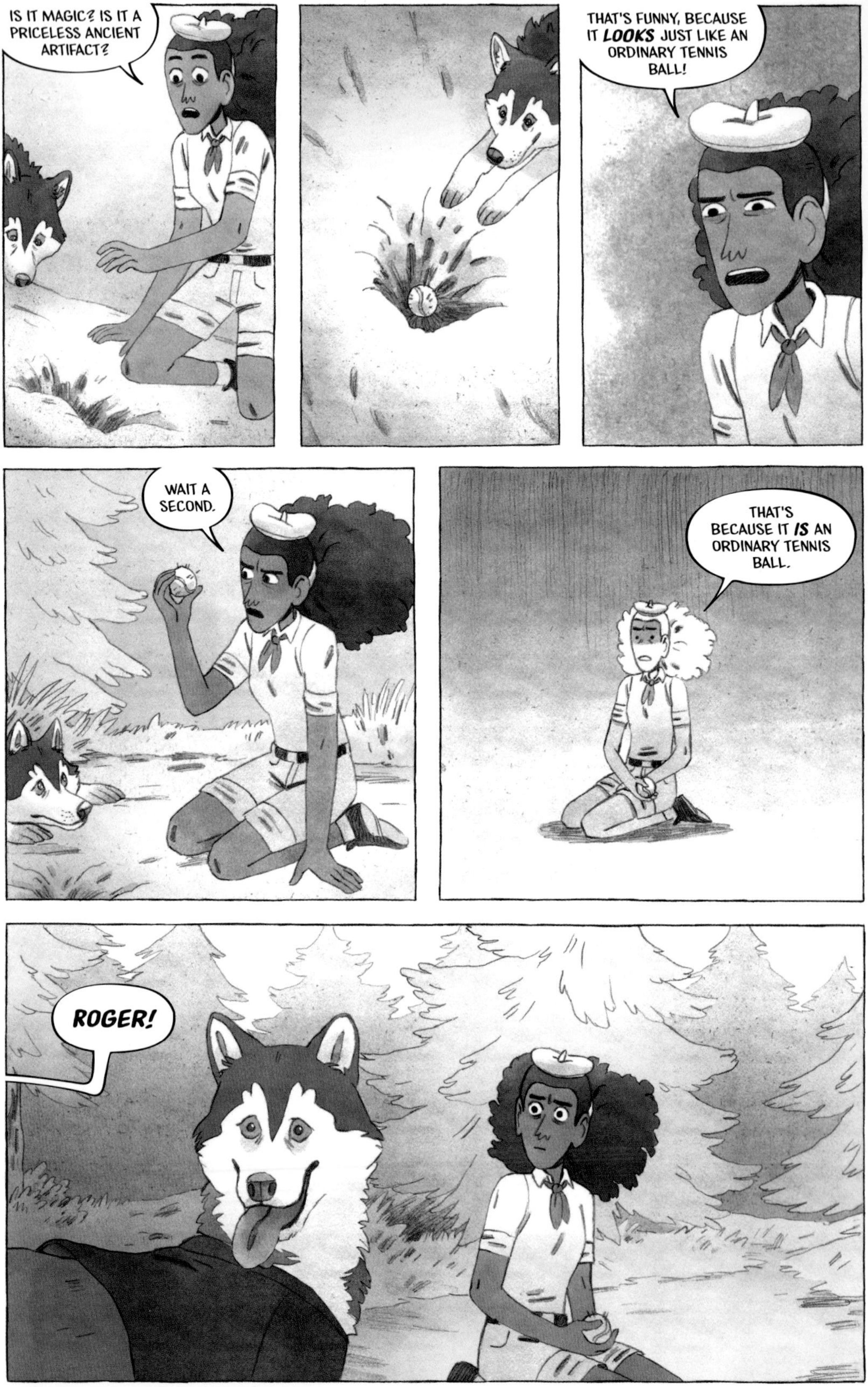
IS IT MAGIC? IS IT A PRICELESS ANCIENT ARTIFACT?
THAT'S FUNNY, BECAUSE IT LOOKS JUST LIKE AN ORDINARY TENNIS BALL!
WAIT A SECOND.
THAT'S BECAUSE IT IS AN ORDINARY TENNIS BALL.
ROGER!

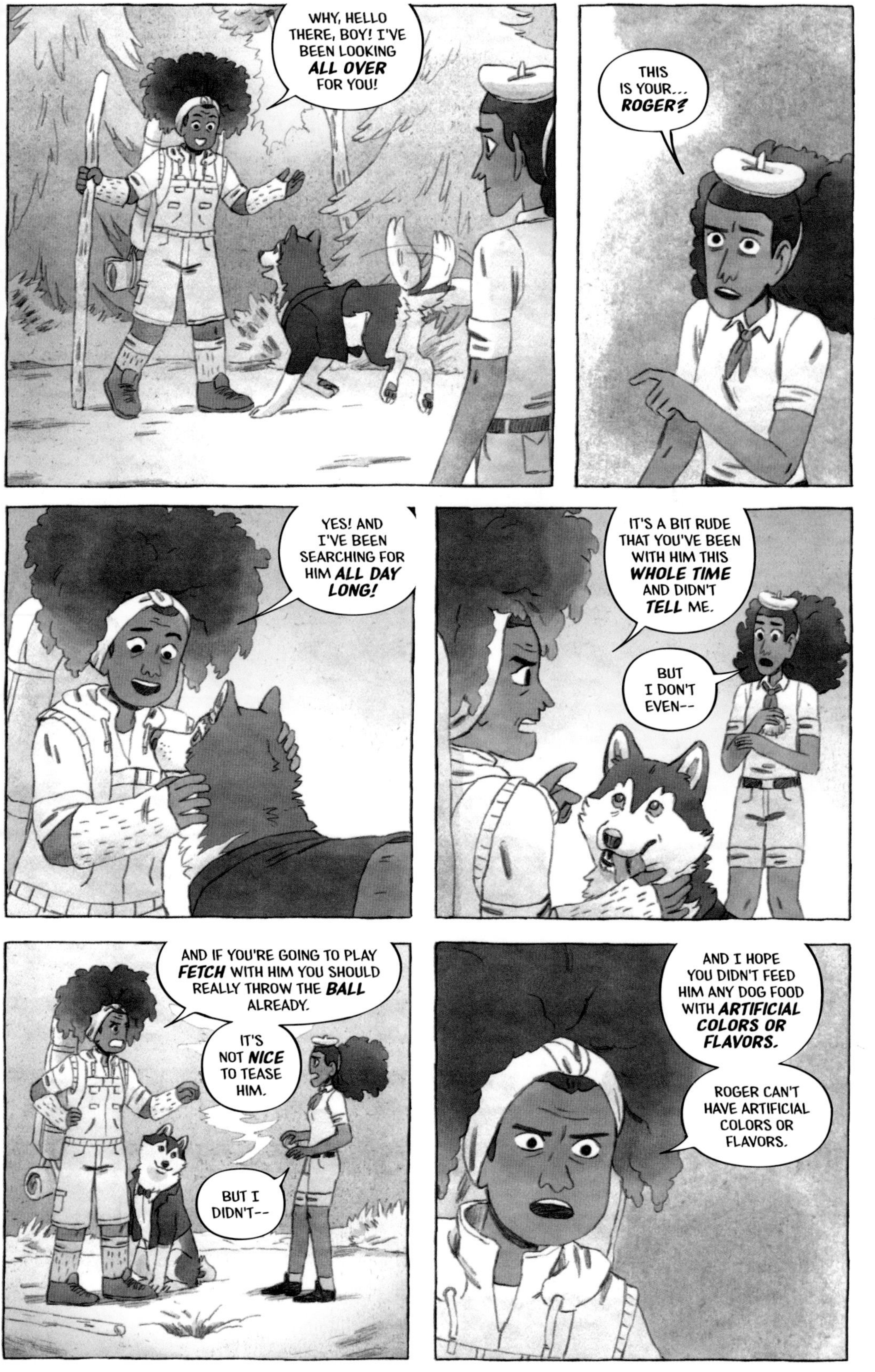
WHY, HELLO THERE, BOY! I'VE BEEN LOOKING ALL OVER FOR YOU!
THIS IS YOUR... ROGER?
YES! AND I'VE BEEN SEARCHING FOR HIM ALL DAY LONG!
IT'S A BIT RUDE THAT YOU'VE BEEN WITH HIM THIS WHOLE TIME AND DIDN'T TELL ME.
BUT I DON'T EVEN--
AND IF YOU'RE GOING TO PLAY FETCH WITH HIM YOU SHOULD REALLY THROW THE BALL ALREADY.
IT'S NOT NICE TO TEASE HIM.
BUT I DIDN'T--
AND I HOPE YOU DIDN'T FEED HIM ANY DOG FOOD WITH ARTIFICIAL COLORS OR FLAVORS.
ROGER CAN'T HAVE ARTIFICIAL COLORS OR FLAVORS.

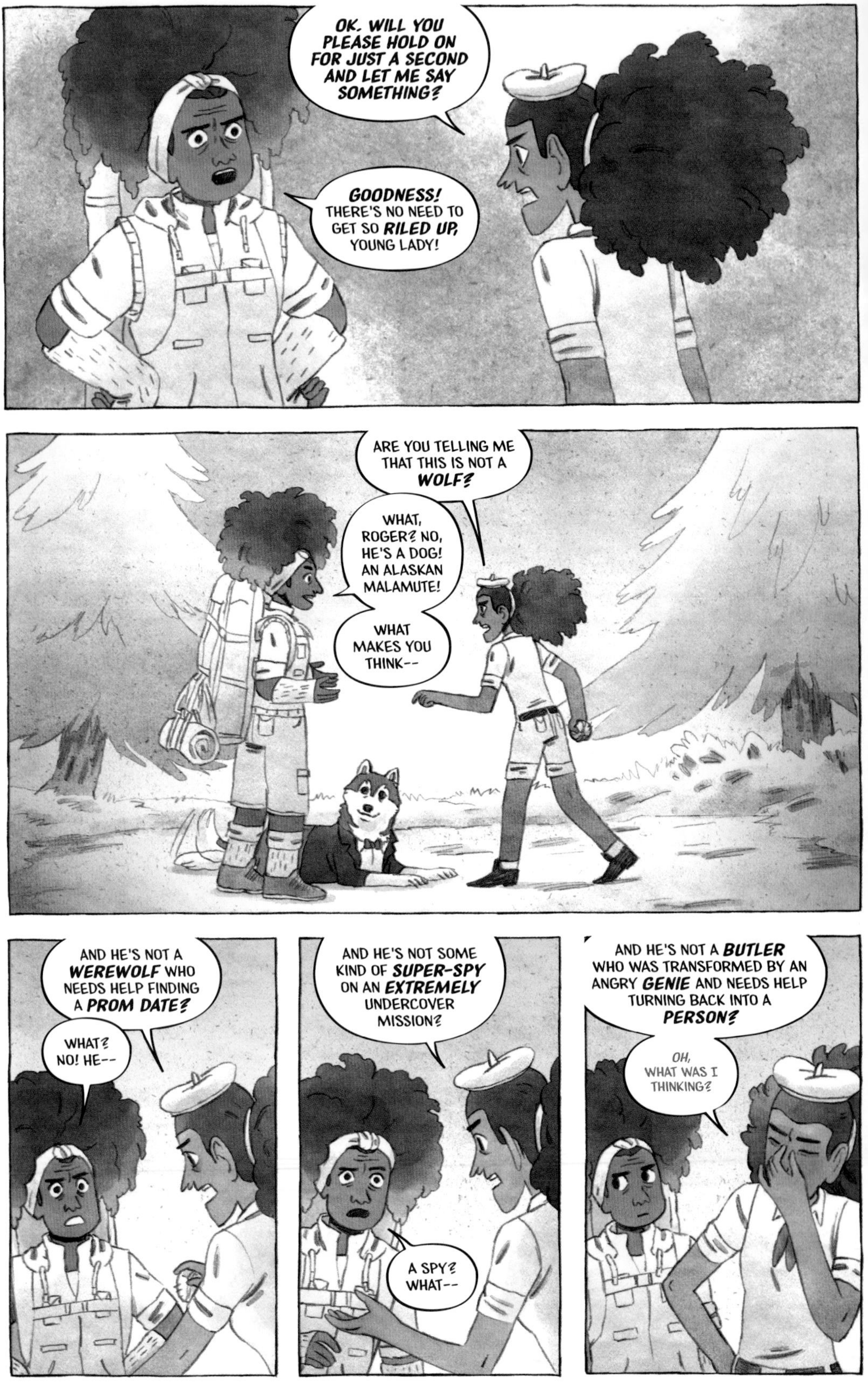
OK. WILL YOU PLEASE HOLD ON FOR JUST A SECOND AND LET ME SAY SOMETHING?
GOODNESS! THERE'S NO NEED TO GET SO RILED UP, YOUNG LADY!
ARE YOU TELLING ME THAT THIS IS NOT A WOLF?
WHAT, ROGER? NO, HE'S A DOG! AN ALASKAN MALAMUTE!
WHAT MAKES YOU THINK--
AND HE'S NOT A WEREWOLF WHO NEEDS HELP FINDING A PROM DATE?
WHAT? NO! HE--
AND HE'S NOT SOME KIND OF SUPER-SPY ON AN EXTREMELY UNDERCOVER MISSION?
A SPY? WHAT--
AND HE'S NOT A BUTLER WHO WAS TRANSFORMED BY AN ANGRY GENIE AND NEEDS HELP TURNING BACK INTO A PERSON?
OH, WHAT WAS I THINKING?

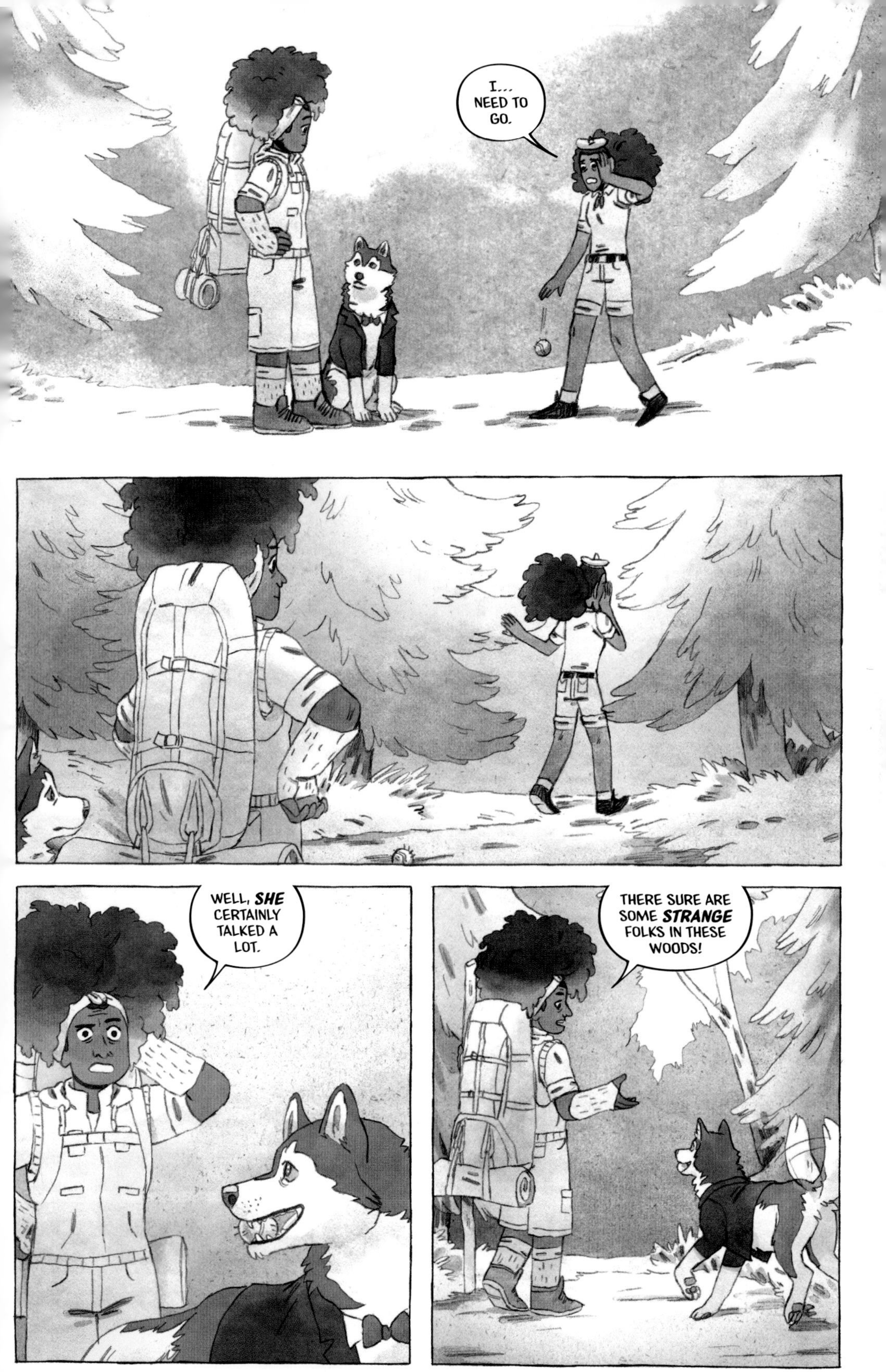
I... NEED TO GO.
WELL, *SHE* CERTAINLY TALKED A LOT.
THERE SURE ARE SOME *STRANGE* FOLKS IN THESE WOODS!

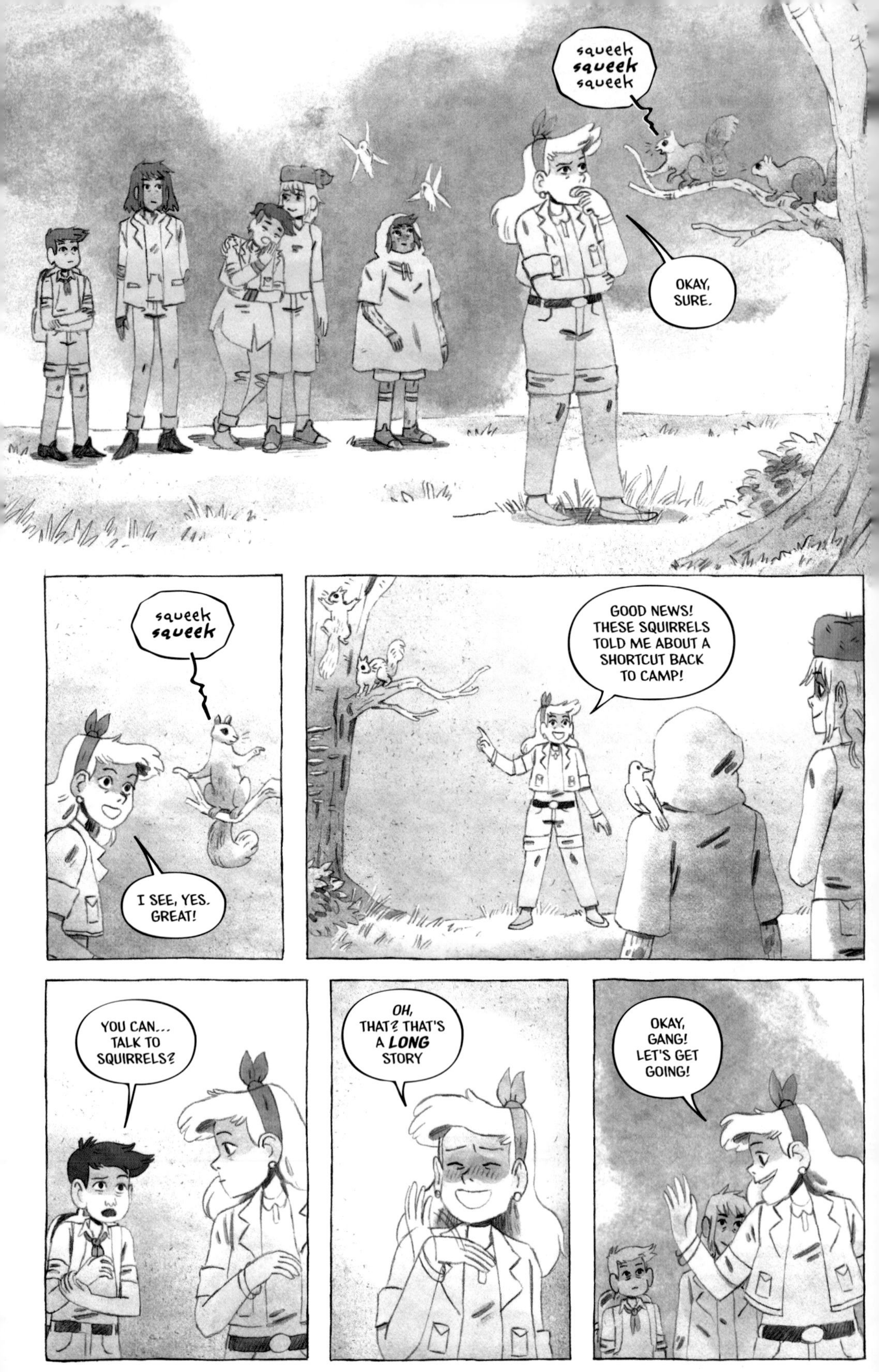
squeek squeek squeek
OKAY, SURE.
squeek squeek
I SEE, YES. GREAT!
GOOD NEWS! THESE SQUIRRELS TOLD ME ABOUT A SHORTCUT BACK TO CAMP!
YOU CAN... TALK TO SQUIRRELS?
OH, THAT? THAT'S A LONG STORY
OKAY, GANG! LET'S GET GOING!

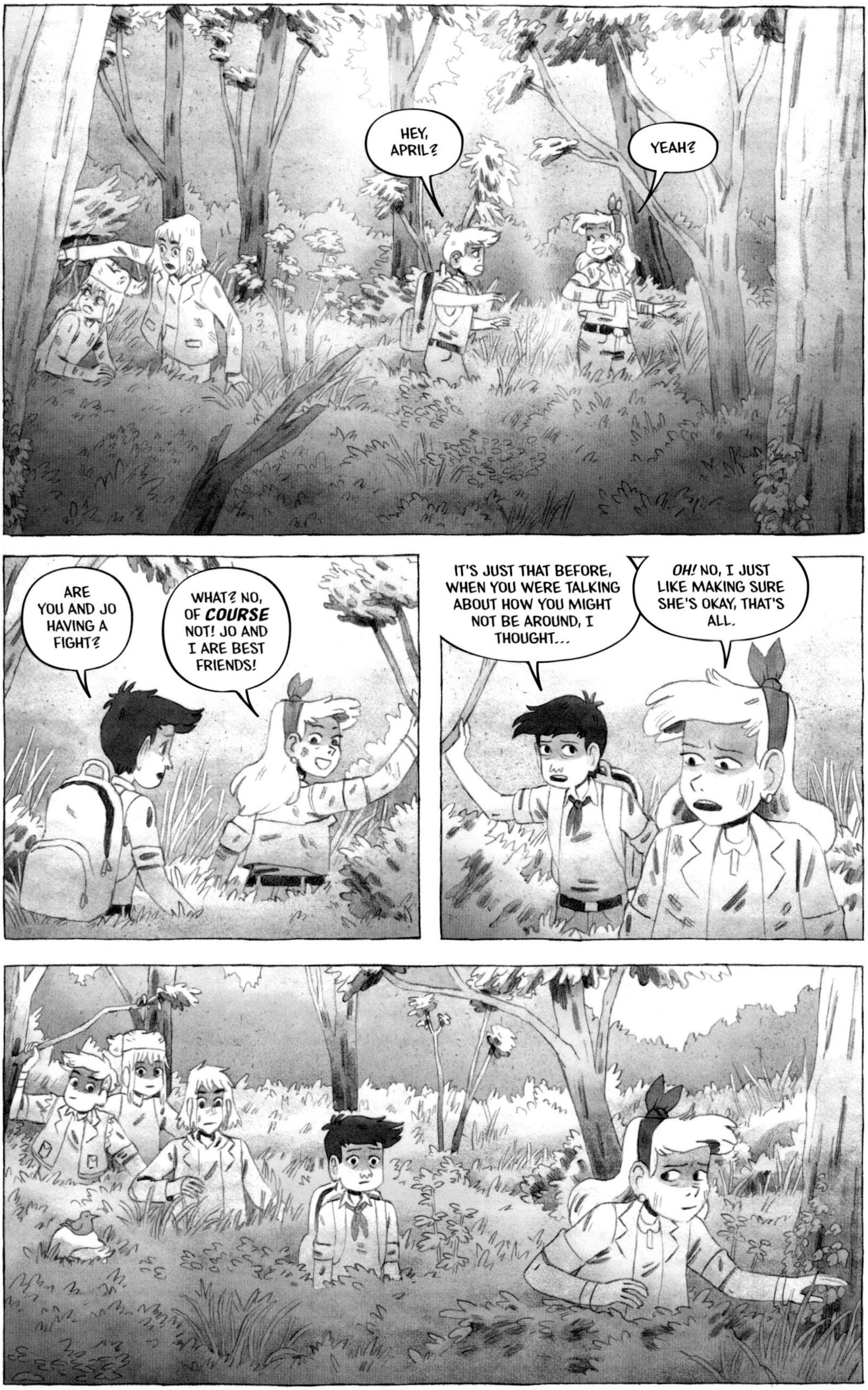
HEY, APRIL?
YEAH?
ARE YOU AND JO HAVING A FIGHT?
WHAT? NO, OF **COURSE** NOT! JO AND I ARE BEST FRIENDS!
IT'S JUST THAT BEFORE, WHEN YOU WERE TALKING ABOUT HOW YOU MIGHT NOT BE AROUND, I THOUGHT...
*OH!* NO, I JUST LIKE MAKING SURE SHE'S OKAY, THAT'S ALL.

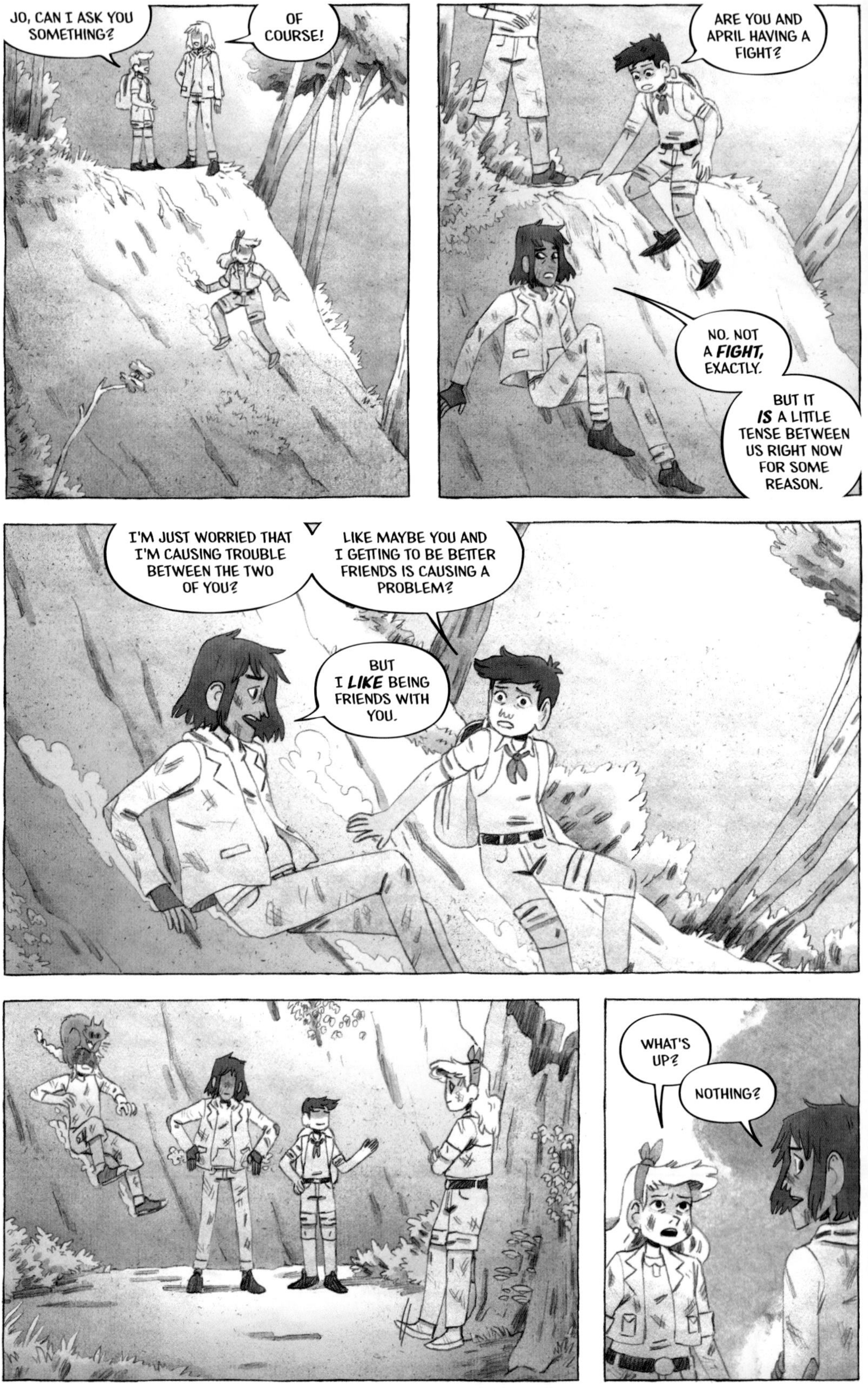
JO, CAN I ASK YOU SOMETHING?
OF COURSE!
ARE YOU AND APRIL HAVING A FIGHT?
NO. NOT A FIGHT, EXACTLY.
BUT IT IS A LITTLE TENSE BETWEEN US RIGHT NOW FOR SOME REASON.
I'M JUST WORRIED THAT I'M CAUSING TROUBLE BETWEEN THE TWO OF YOU?
LIKE MAYBE YOU AND I GETTING TO BE BETTER FRIENDS IS CAUSING A PROBLEM?
BUT I LIKE BEING FRIENDS WITH YOU.
WHAT'S UP?
NOTHING?

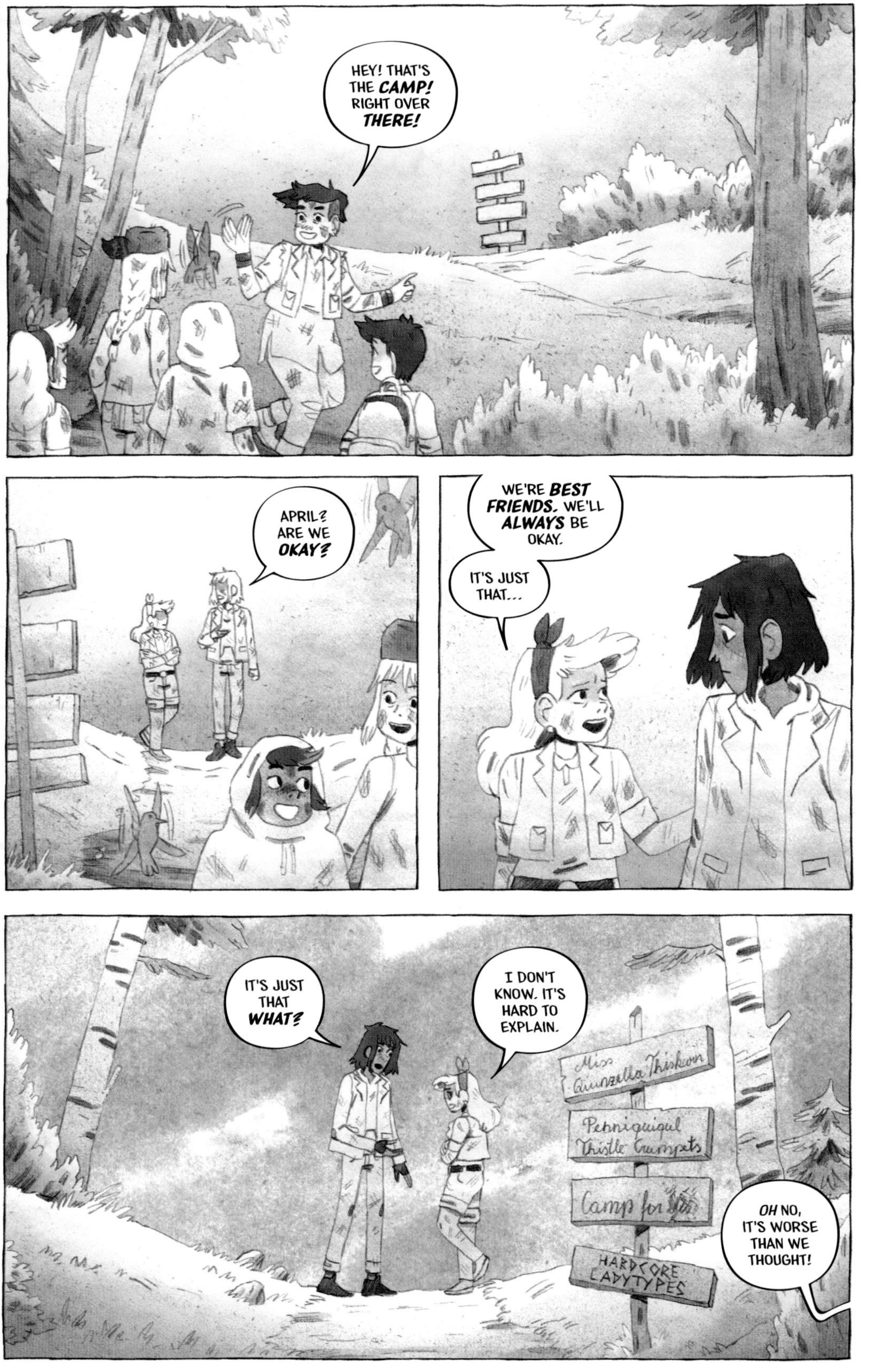
HEY! THAT'S THE CAMP! RIGHT OVER THERE!
APRIL? ARE WE OKAY?
WE'RE BEST FRIENDS. WE'LL ALWAYS BE OKAY.
IT'S JUST THAT...
IT'S JUST THAT WHAT?
I DON'T KNOW. IT'S HARD TO EXPLAIN.
Miss
Camp for
HARDCORE LADYTYPES
OH NO, IT'S WORSE THAN WE THOUGHT!

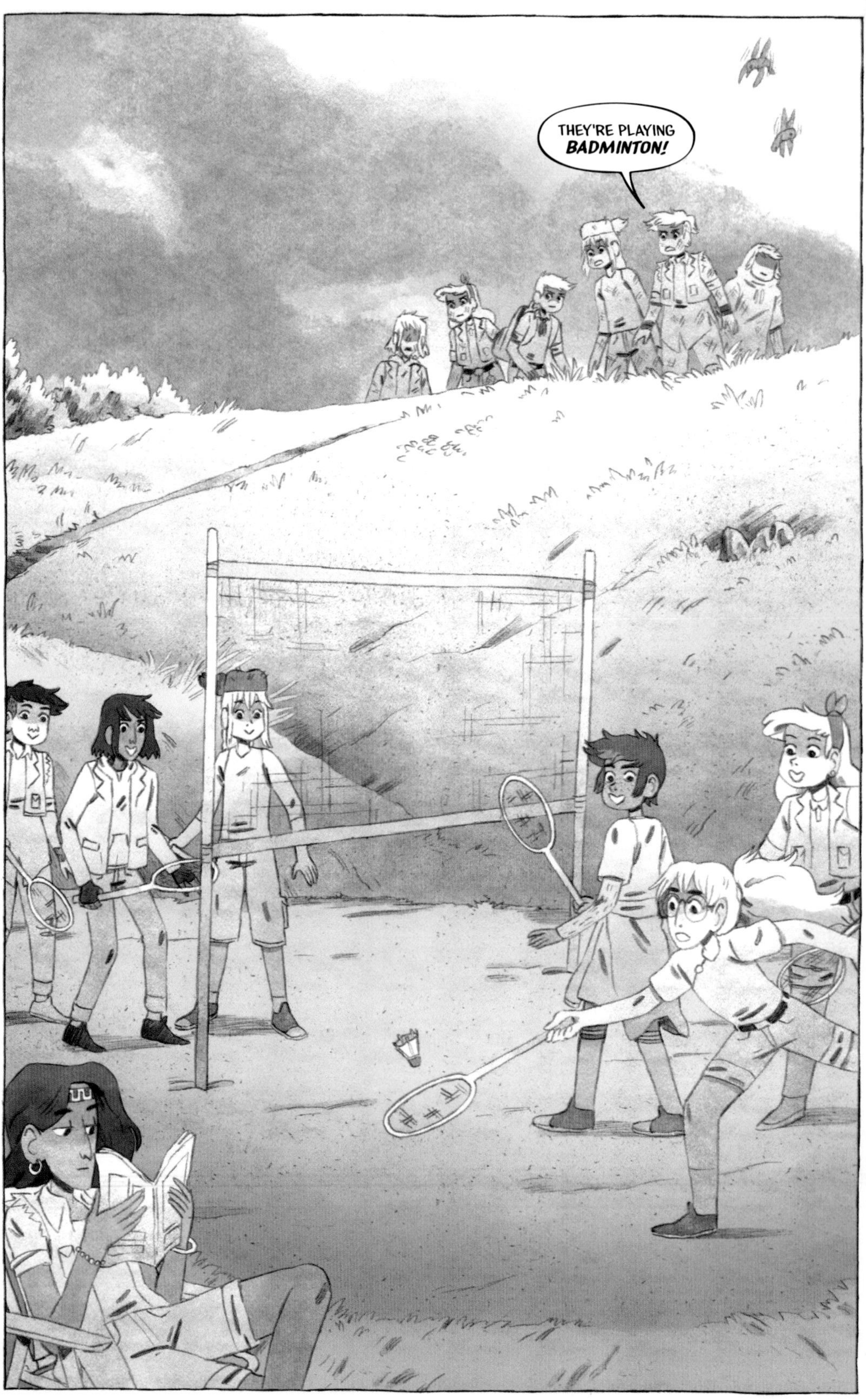
THEY'RE PLAYING BADMINTON!

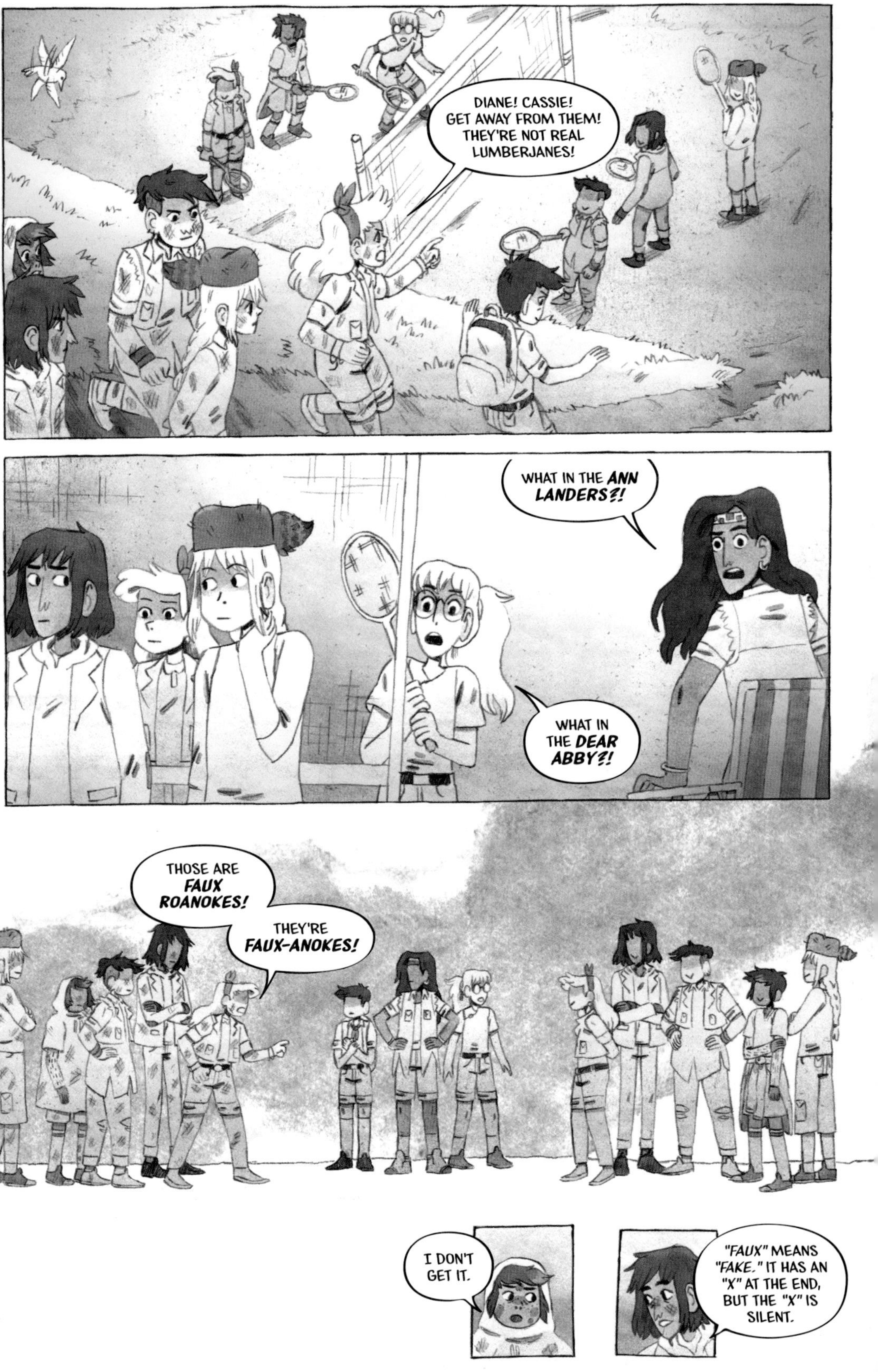
DIANE! CASSIE! GET AWAY FROM THEM! THEY'RE NOT REAL LUMBERJANES!
WHAT IN THE ANN LANDERS?!
WHAT IN THE DEAR ABBY?!
THOSE ARE FAUX ROANOKES!
THEY'RE FAUX-ANOKES!
I DON'T GET IT.
"FAUX" MEANS "FAKE." IT HAS AN "X" AT THE END, BUT THE "X" IS SILENT.

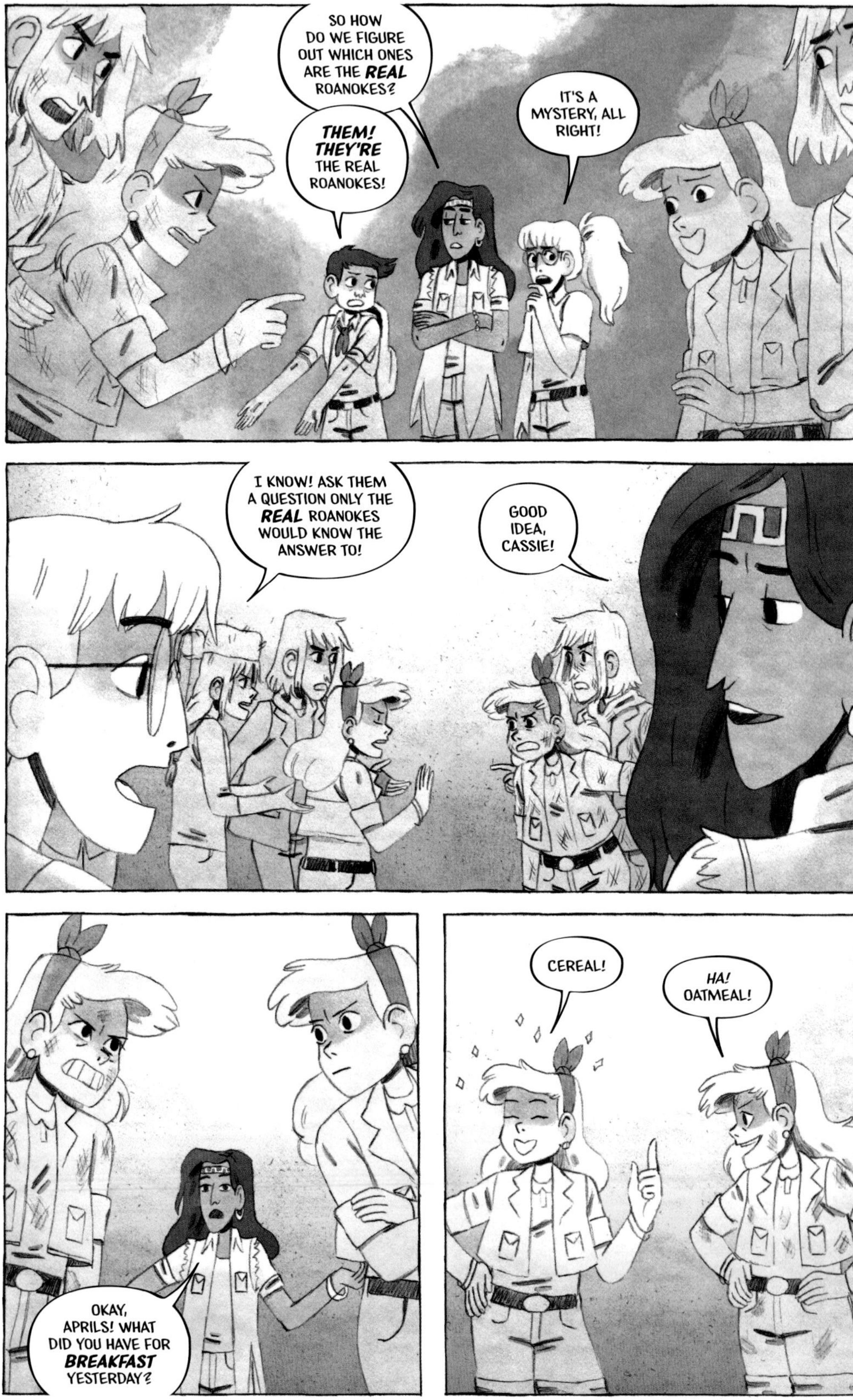
SO HOW DO WE FIGURE OUT WHICH ONES ARE THE *REAL* ROANOKES?
*THEM! THEY'RE* THE REAL ROANOKES!
IT'S A MYSTERY, ALL RIGHT!
I KNOW! ASK THEM A QUESTION ONLY THE *REAL* ROANOKES WOULD KNOW THE ANSWER TO!
GOOD IDEA, CASSIE!
OKAY, APRILS! WHAT DID YOU HAVE FOR *BREAKFAST* YESTERDAY?
CEREAL!
*HA!* OATMEAL!

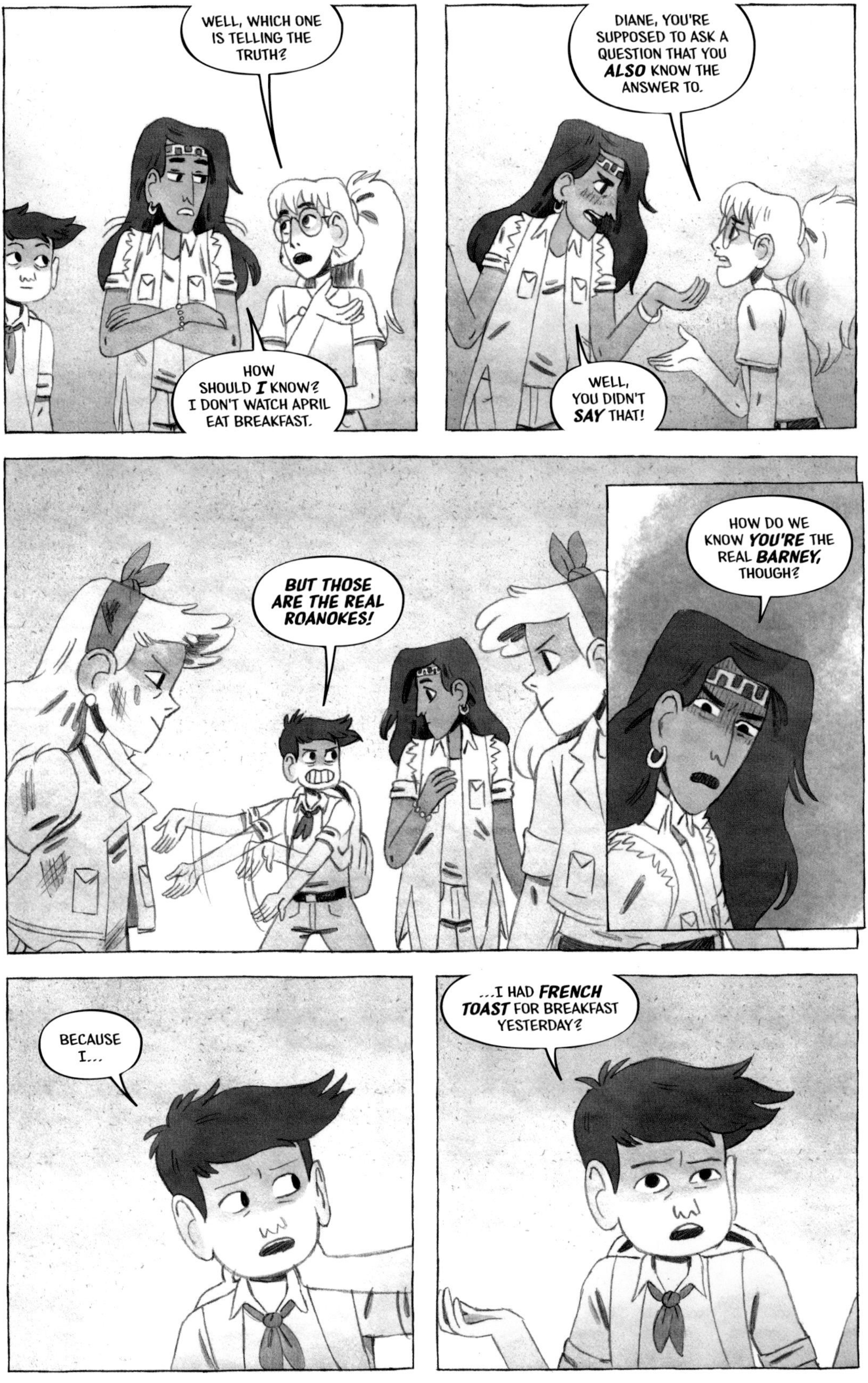
WELL, WHICH ONE IS TELLING THE TRUTH?
HOW SHOULD I KNOW? I DON'T WATCH APRIL EAT BREAKFAST.
DIANE, YOU'RE SUPPOSED TO ASK A QUESTION THAT YOU ALSO KNOW THE ANSWER TO.
WELL, YOU DIDN'T SAY THAT!
BUT THOSE ARE THE REAL ROANOKES!
HOW DO WE KNOW YOU'RE THE REAL BARNEY, THOUGH?
BECAUSE I...
...I HAD FRENCH TOAST FOR BREAKFAST YESTERDAY?

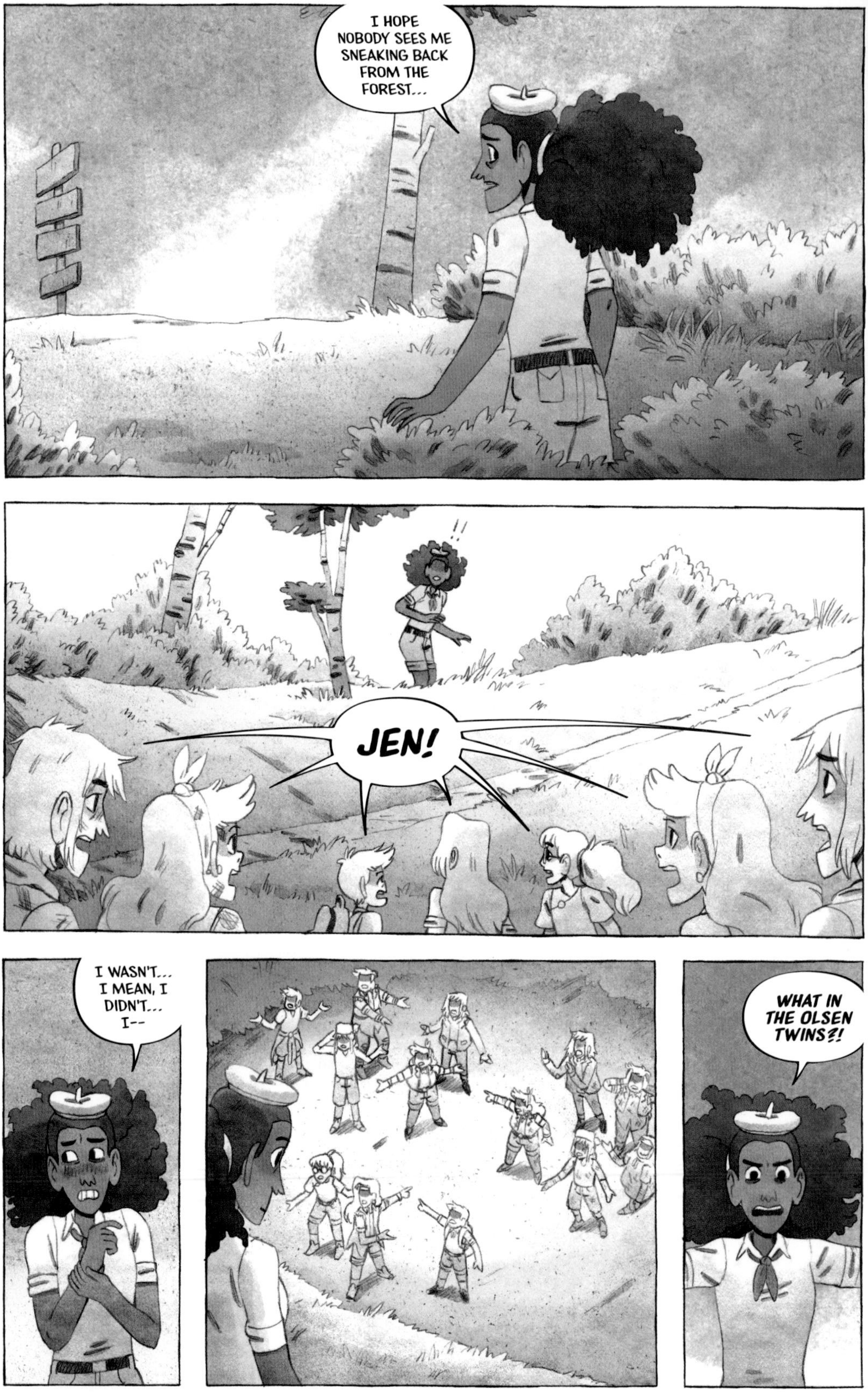
I HOPE NOBODY SEES ME SNEAKING BACK FROM THE FOREST...
!!
JEN!
I WASN'T... I MEAN, I DIDN'T... I--
WHAT IN THE OLSEN TWINS?!

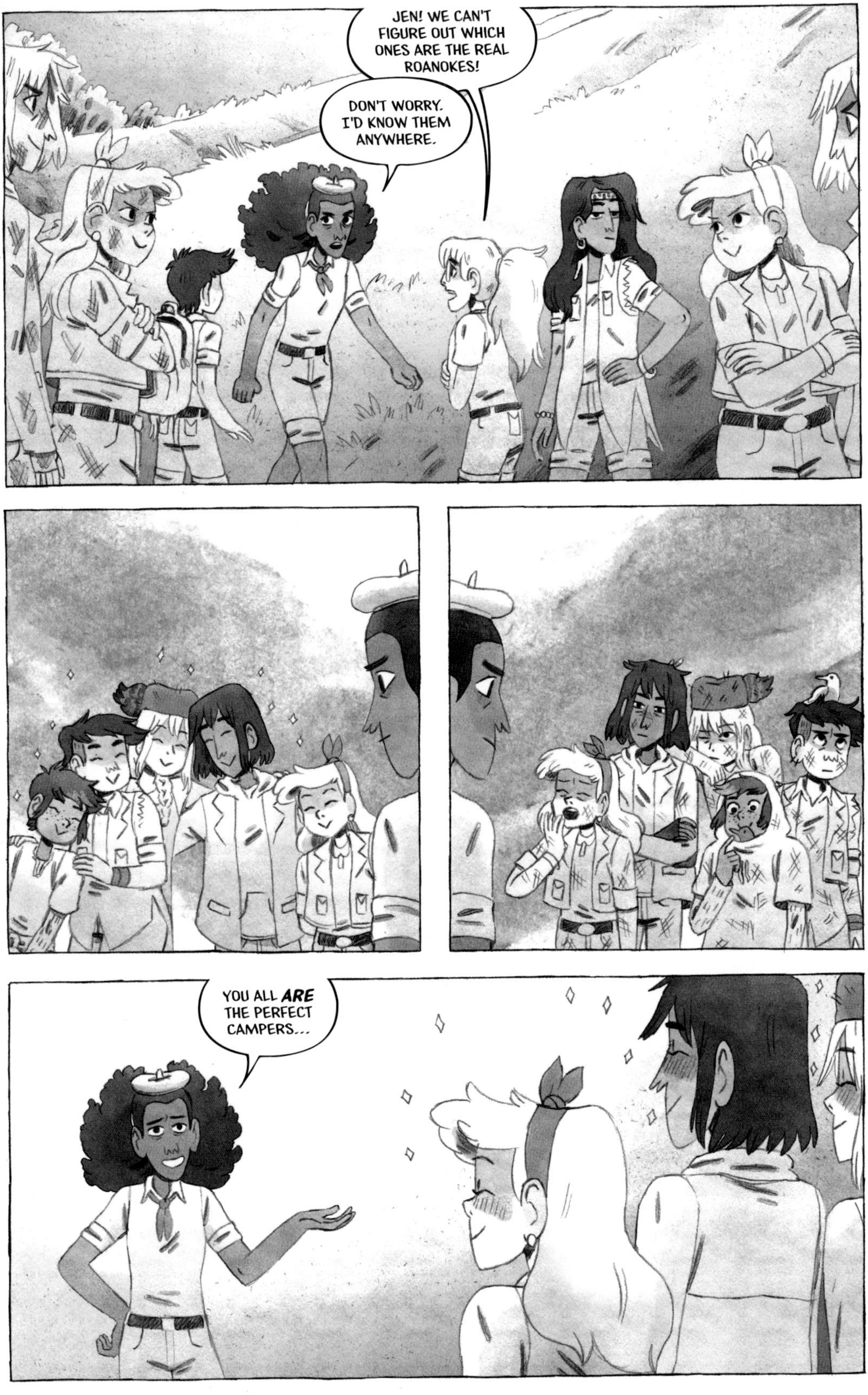
JEN! WE CAN'T FIGURE OUT WHICH ONES ARE THE REAL ROANOKES!
DON'T WORRY. I'D KNOW THEM ANYWHERE.
YOU ALL **ARE** THE PERFECT CAMPERS...

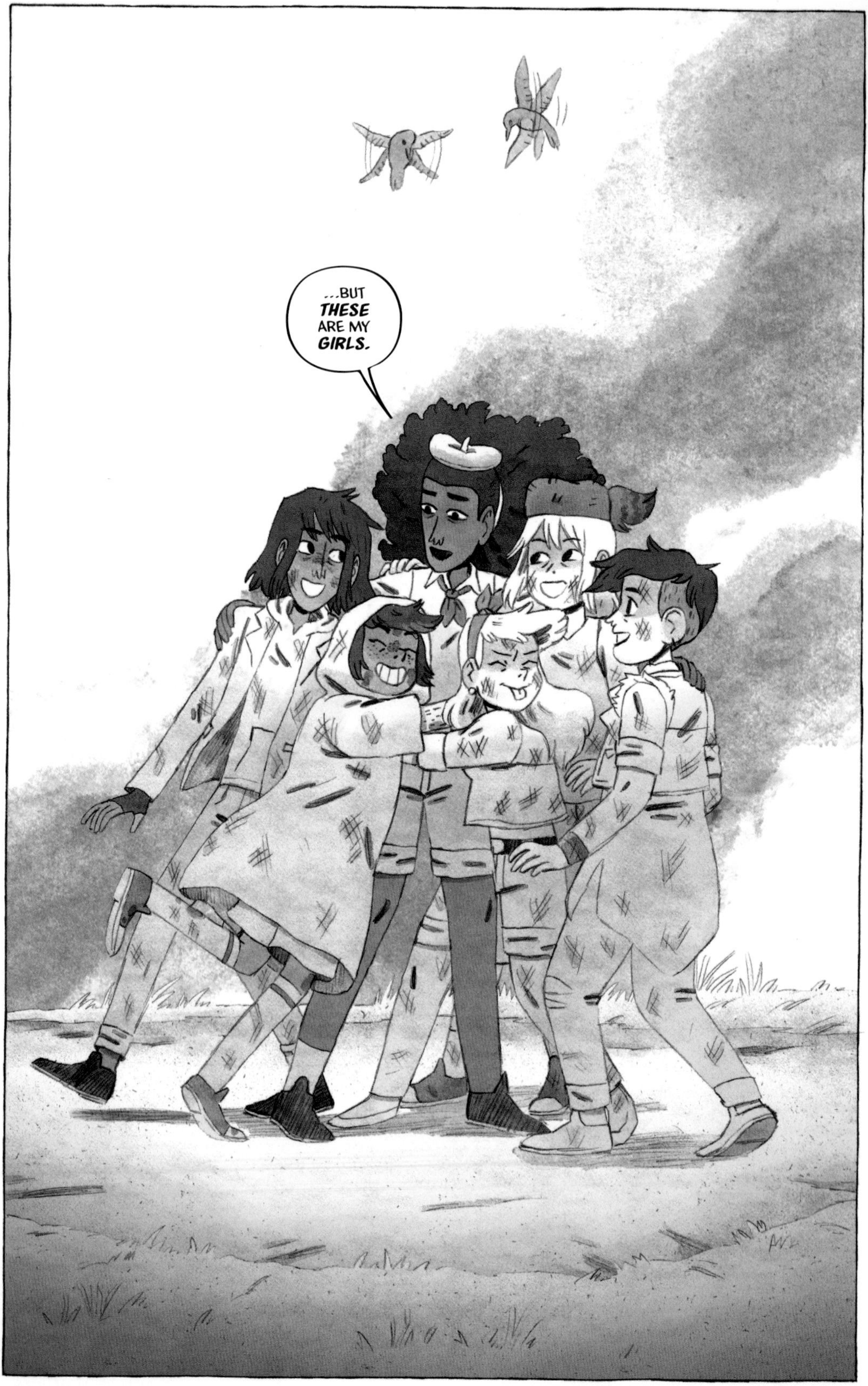
...BUT THESE ARE MY GIRLS.

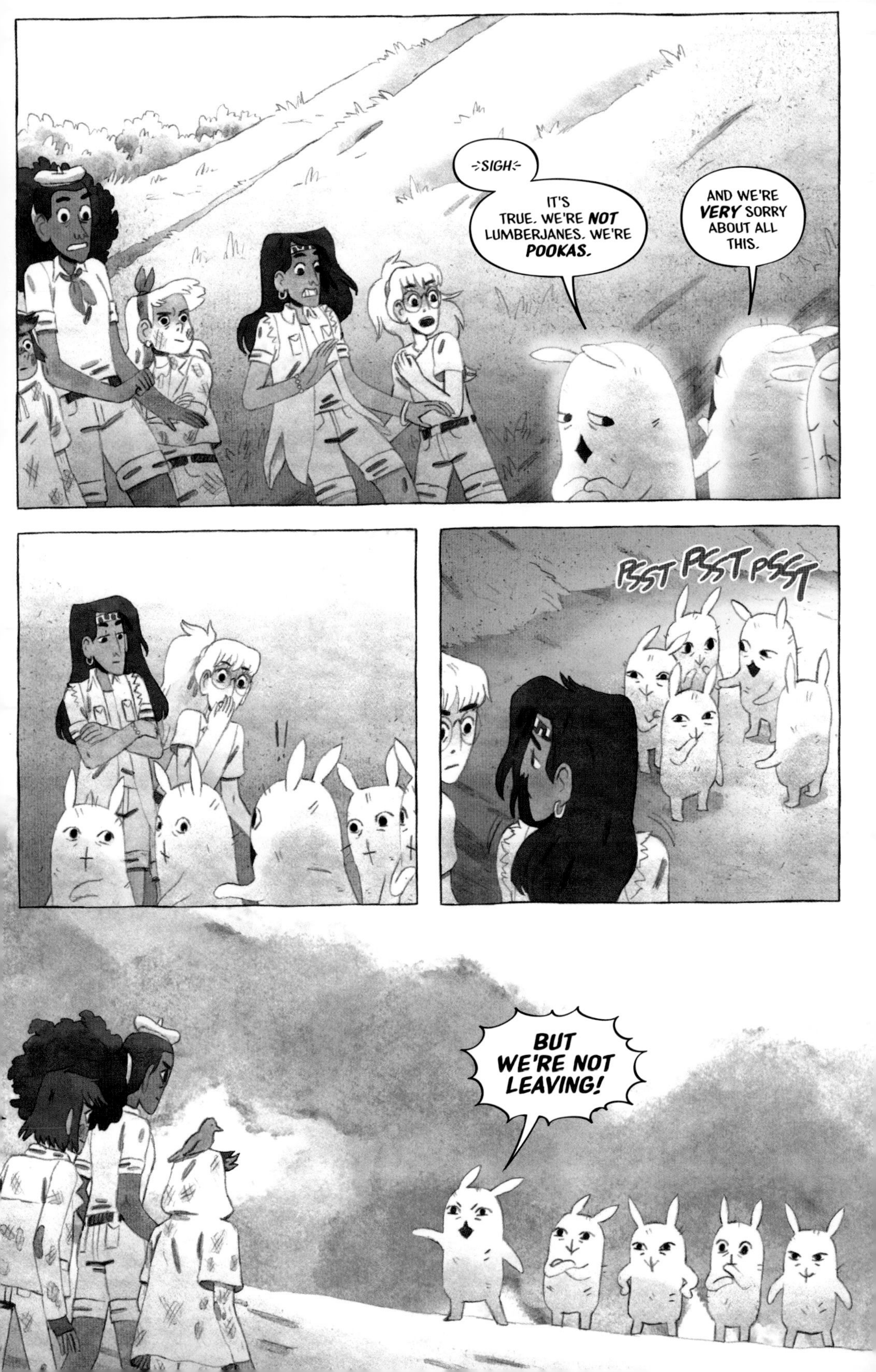

-SIGH-
IT'S TRUE. WE'RE NOT LUMBERJANES. WE'RE POOKAS.
AND WE'RE VERY SORRY ABOUT ALL THIS.
!!
PSST PSST PSST
BUT WE'RE NOT LEAVING!

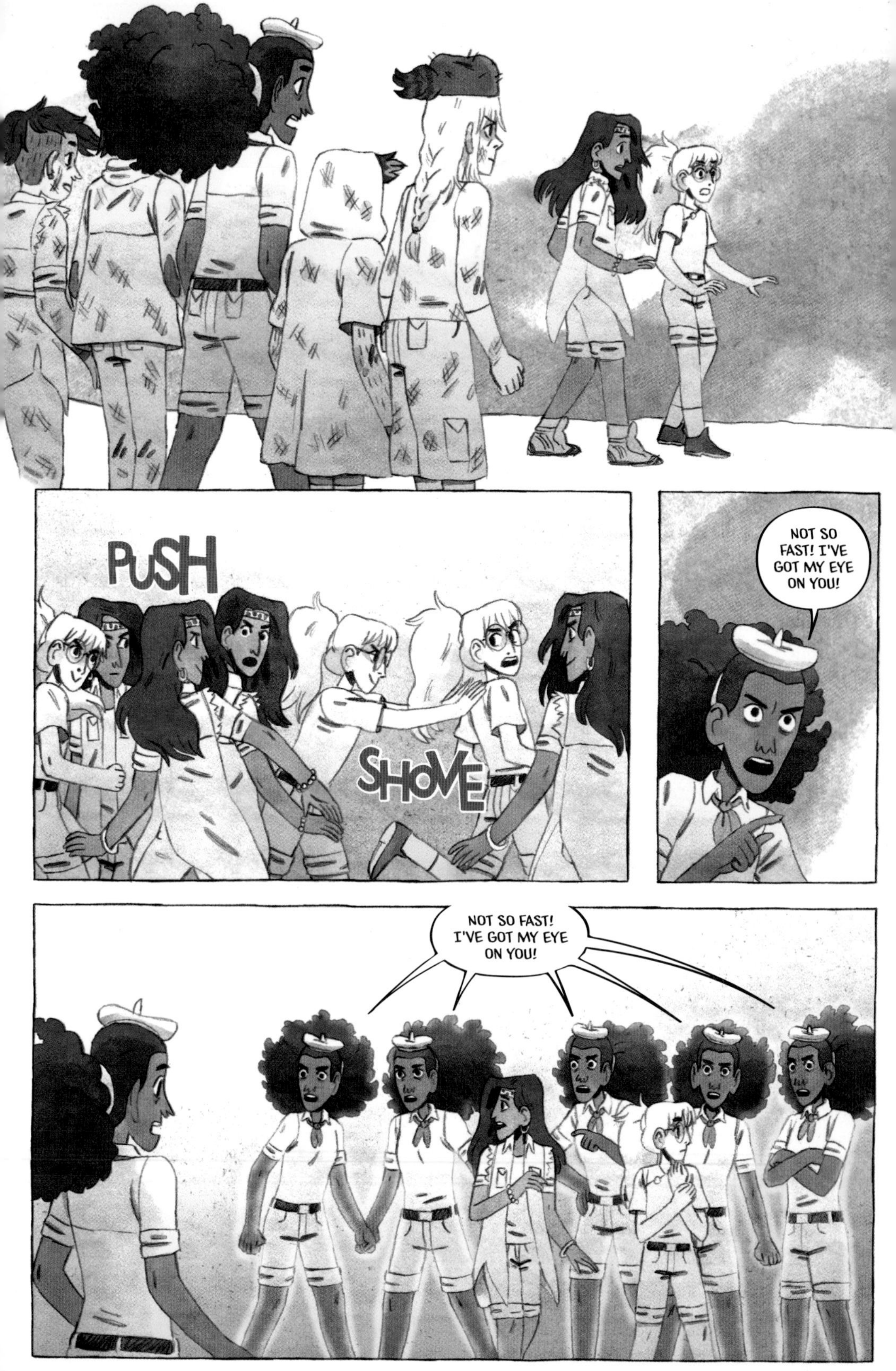
PUSH
SHOVE
NOT SO FAST! I'VE GOT MY EYE ON YOU!
NOT SO FAST! I'VE GOT MY EYE ON YOU!

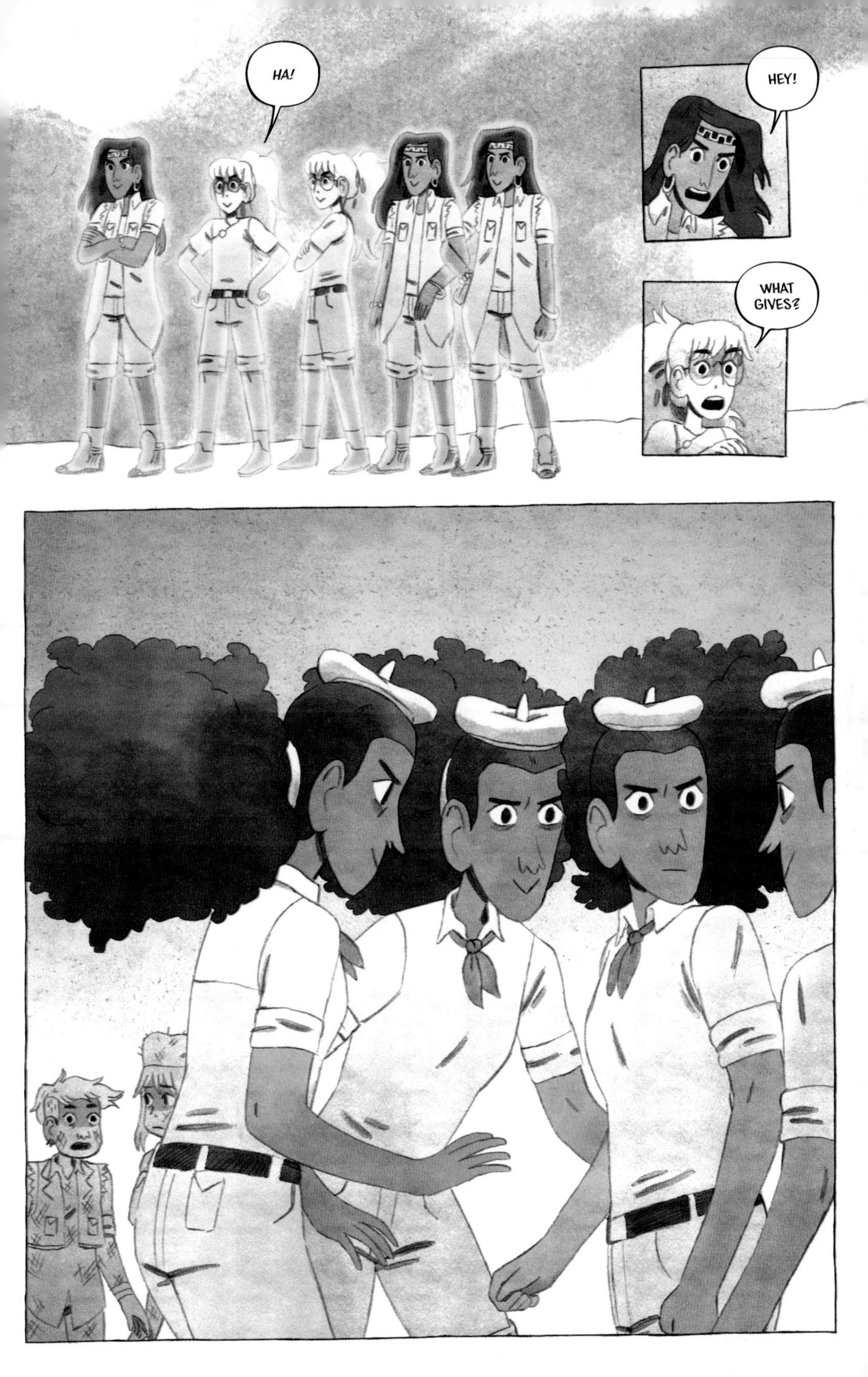
HA!
HEY!
WHAT GIVES?

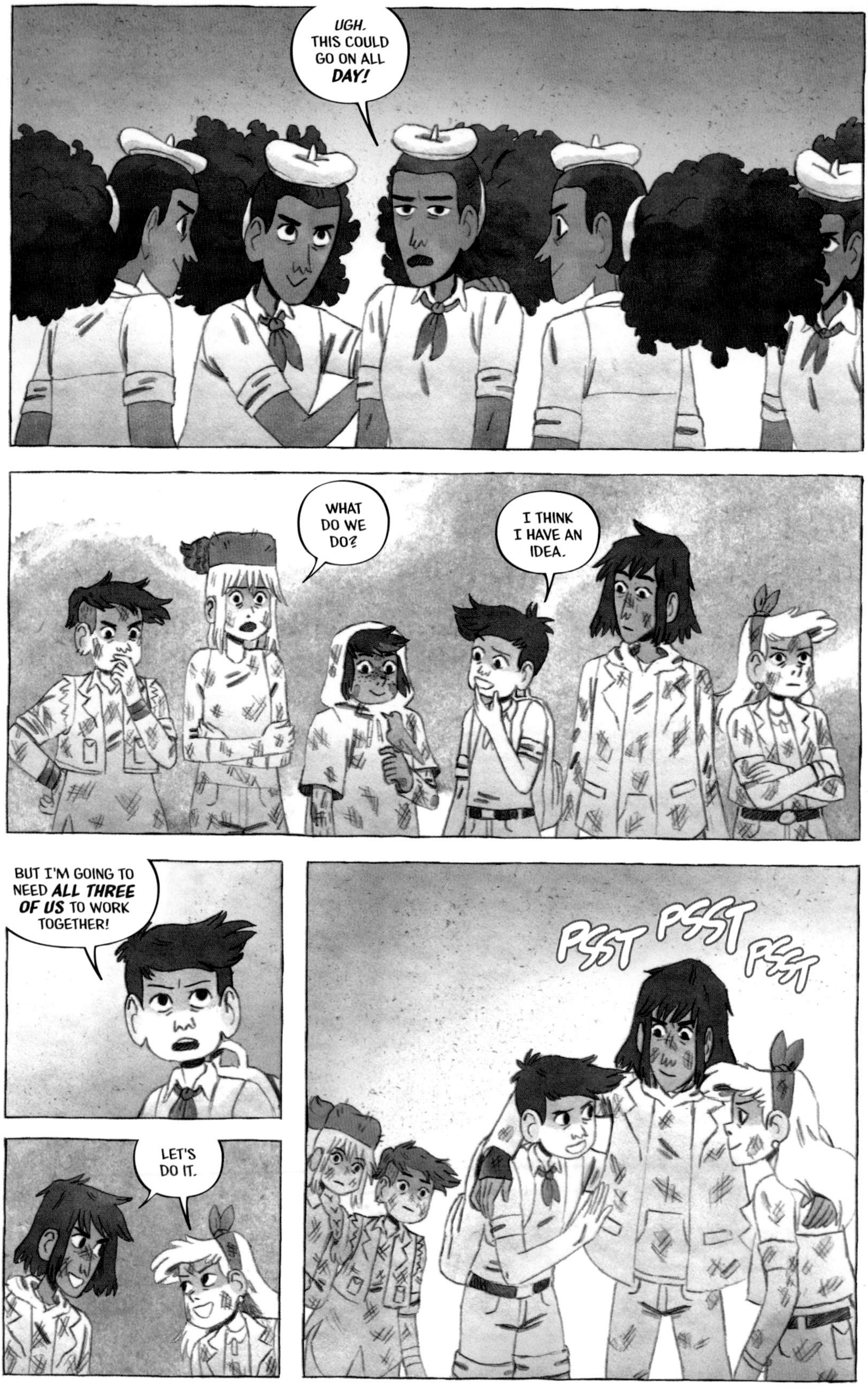
UGH. THIS COULD GO ON ALL DAY!
WHAT DO WE DO?
I THINK I HAVE AN IDEA.
BUT I'M GOING TO NEED ALL THREE OF US TO WORK TOGETHER!
LET'S DO IT.
PSST PSST PSST

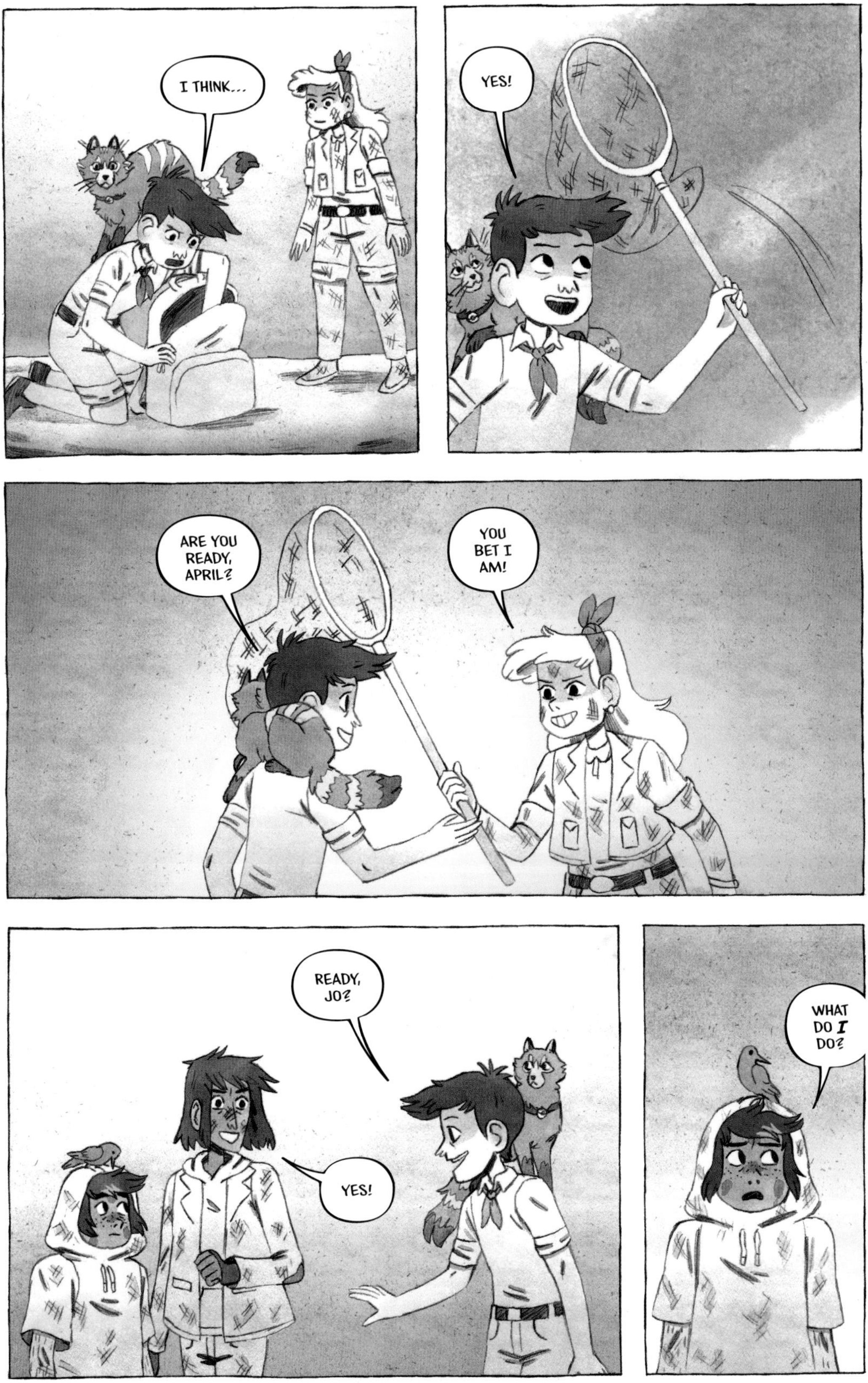
I THINK...
YES!
ARE YOU READY, APRIL?
YOU BET I AM!
READY, JO?
YES!
WHAT DO I DO?

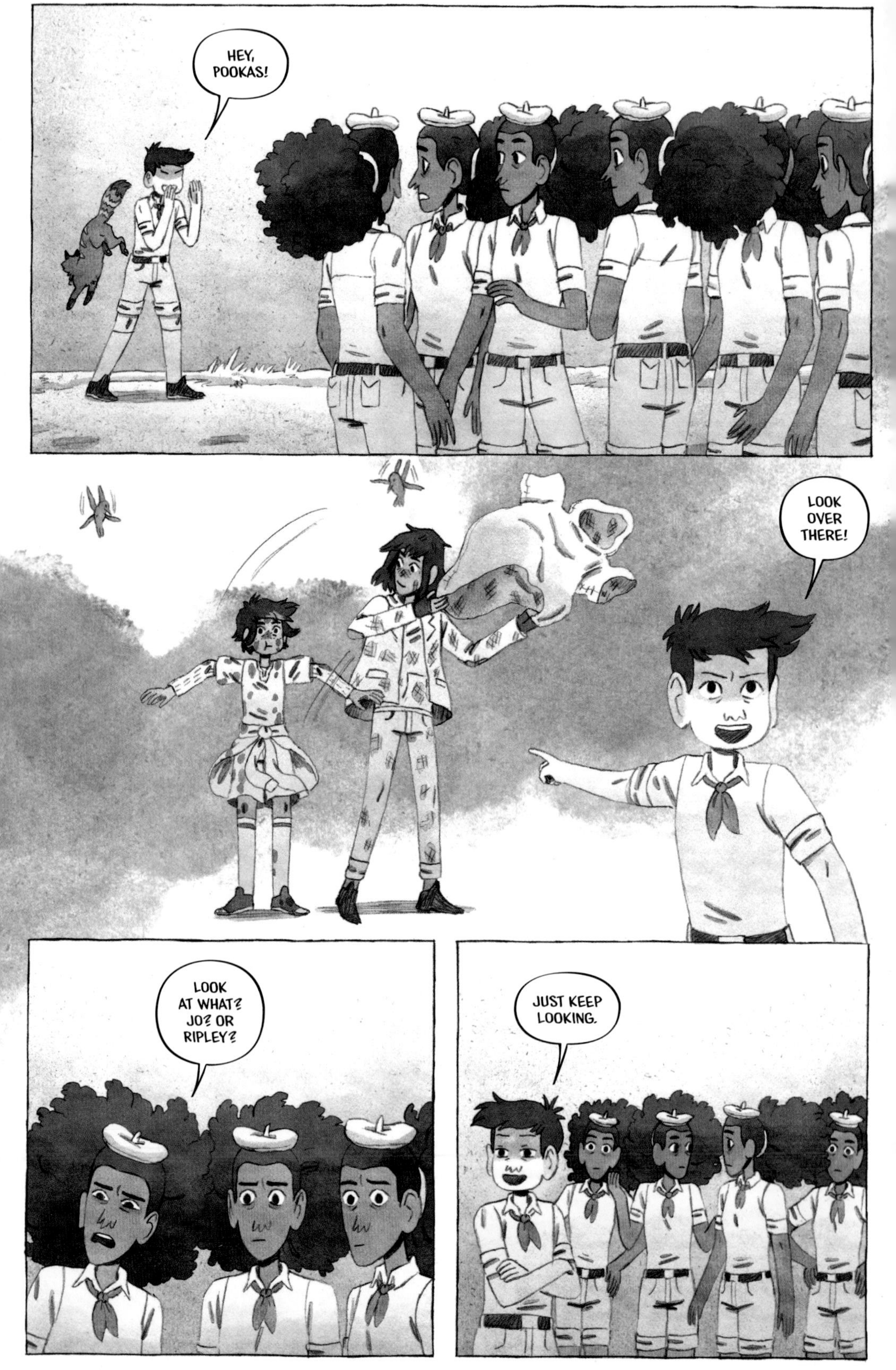
HEY, POOKAS!
LOOK OVER THERE!
LOOK AT WHAT? JO? OR RIPLEY?
JUST KEEP LOOKING.

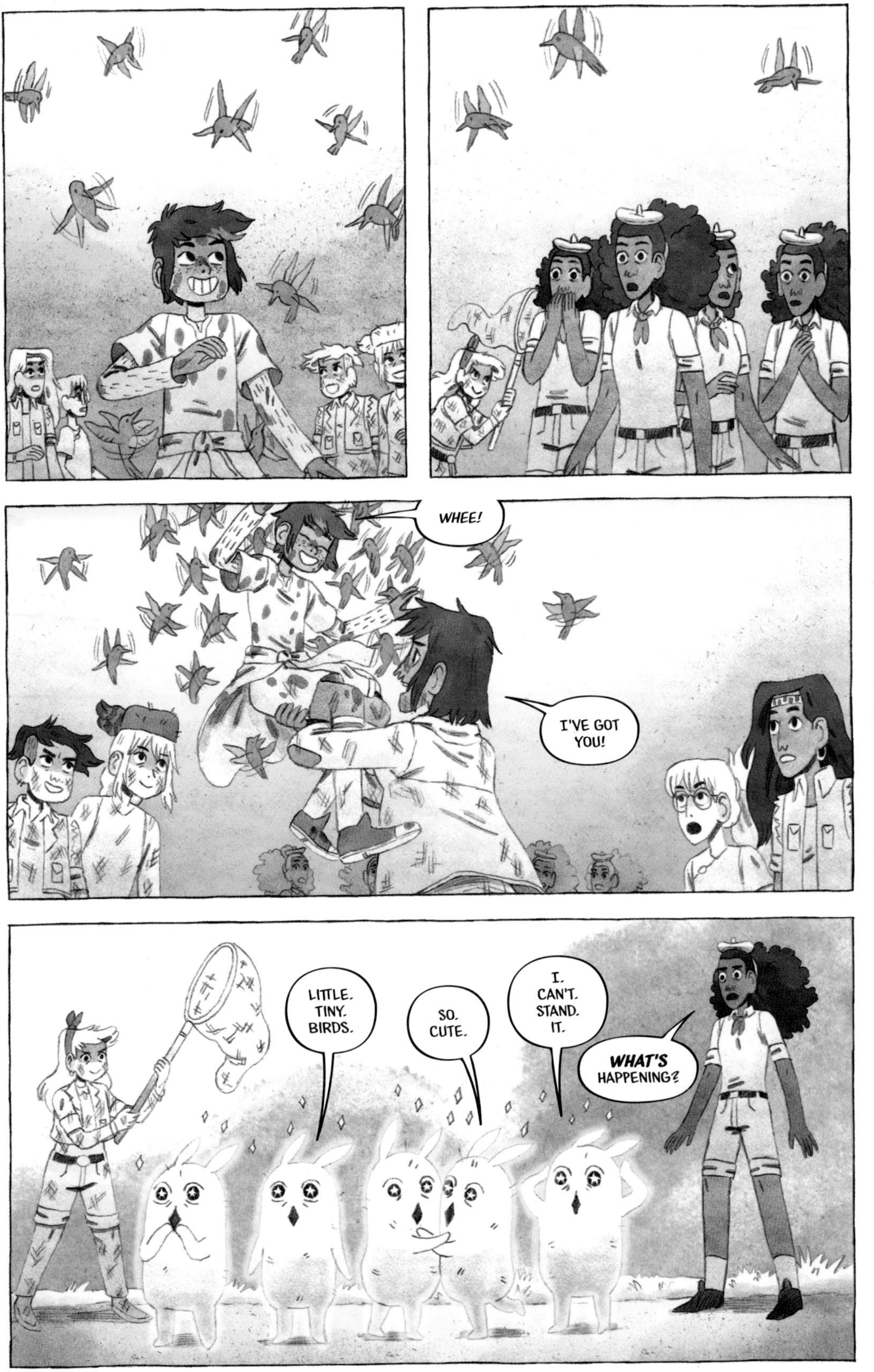
WHEE!
I'VE GOT YOU!
LITTLE. TINY. BIRDS.
SO. CUTE.
I. CAN'T. STAND. IT.
WHAT'S HAPPENING?

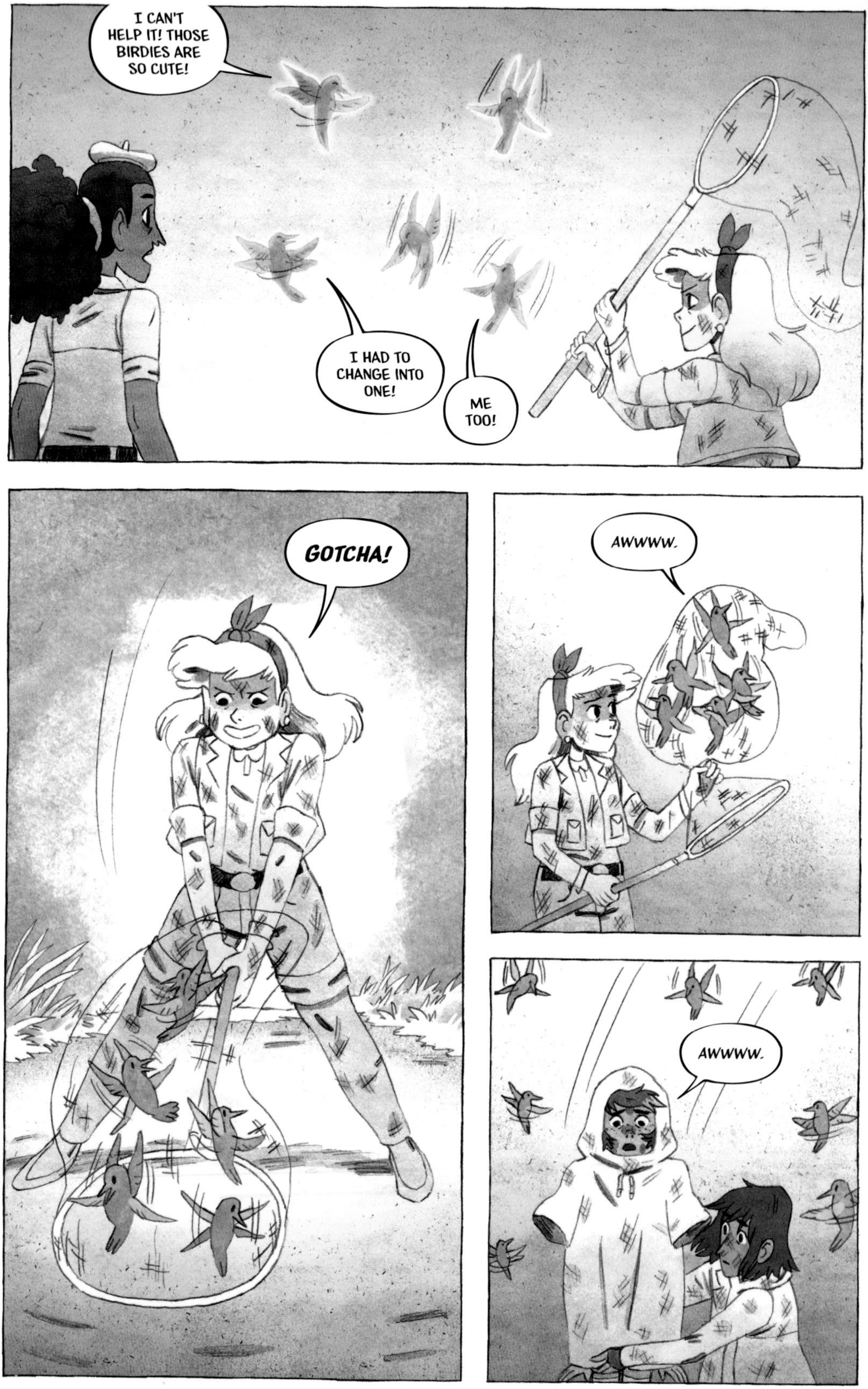
I CAN'T HELP IT! THOSE BIRDIES ARE SO CUTE!
I HAD TO CHANGE INTO ONE!
ME TOO!
GOTCHA!
AWWWW.
AWWWW.

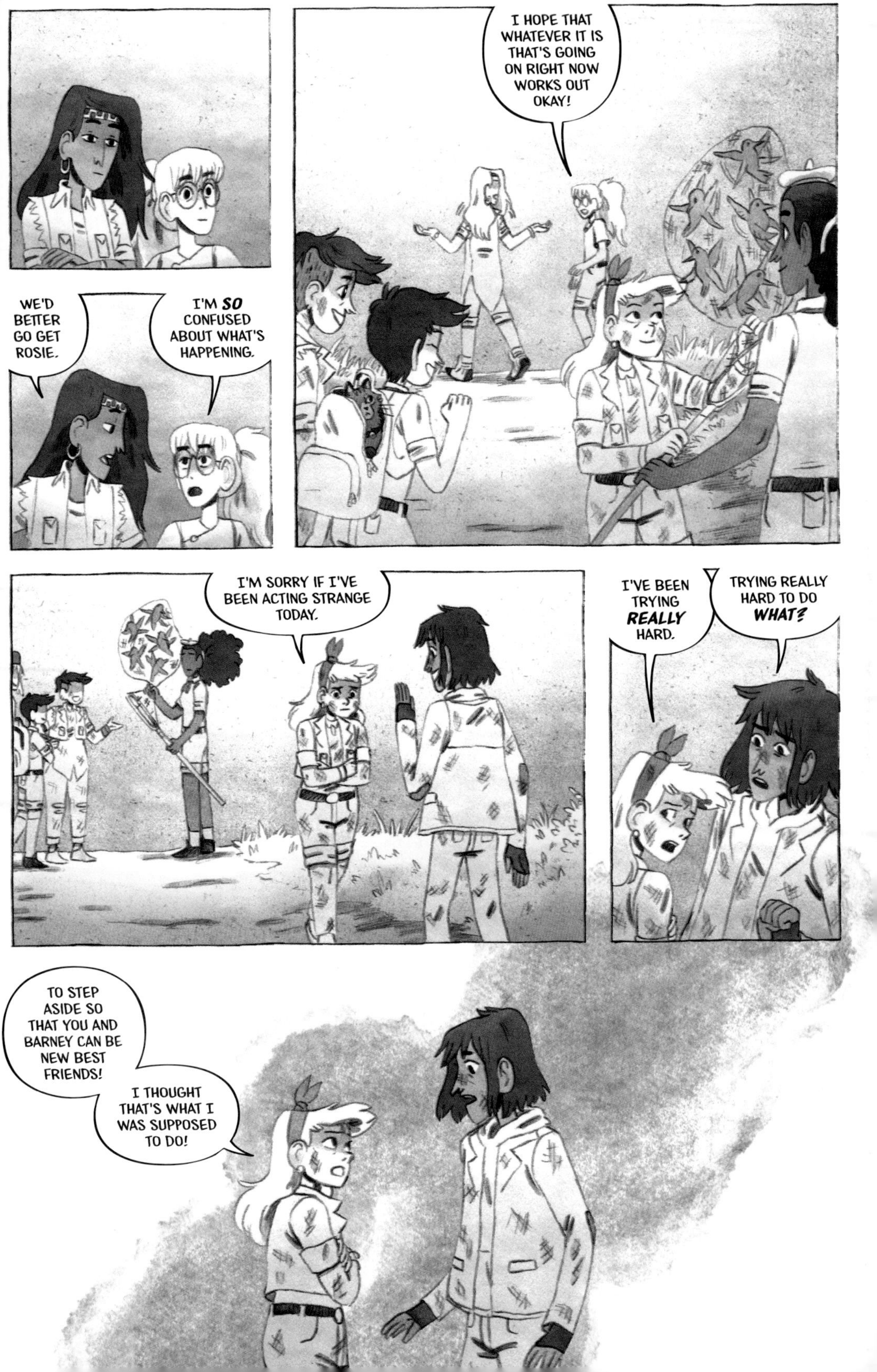
WE'D BETTER GO GET ROSIE.
I'M **SO** CONFUSED ABOUT WHAT'S HAPPENING.
I HOPE THAT WHATEVER IT IS THAT'S GOING ON RIGHT NOW WORKS OUT OKAY!
I'M SORRY IF I'VE BEEN ACTING STRANGE TODAY.
I'VE BEEN TRYING ***REALLY*** HARD.
TRYING REALLY HARD TO DO ***WHAT?***
TO STEP ASIDE SO THAT YOU AND BARNEY CAN BE NEW BEST FRIENDS!
I THOUGHT THAT'S WHAT I WAS SUPPOSED TO DO!

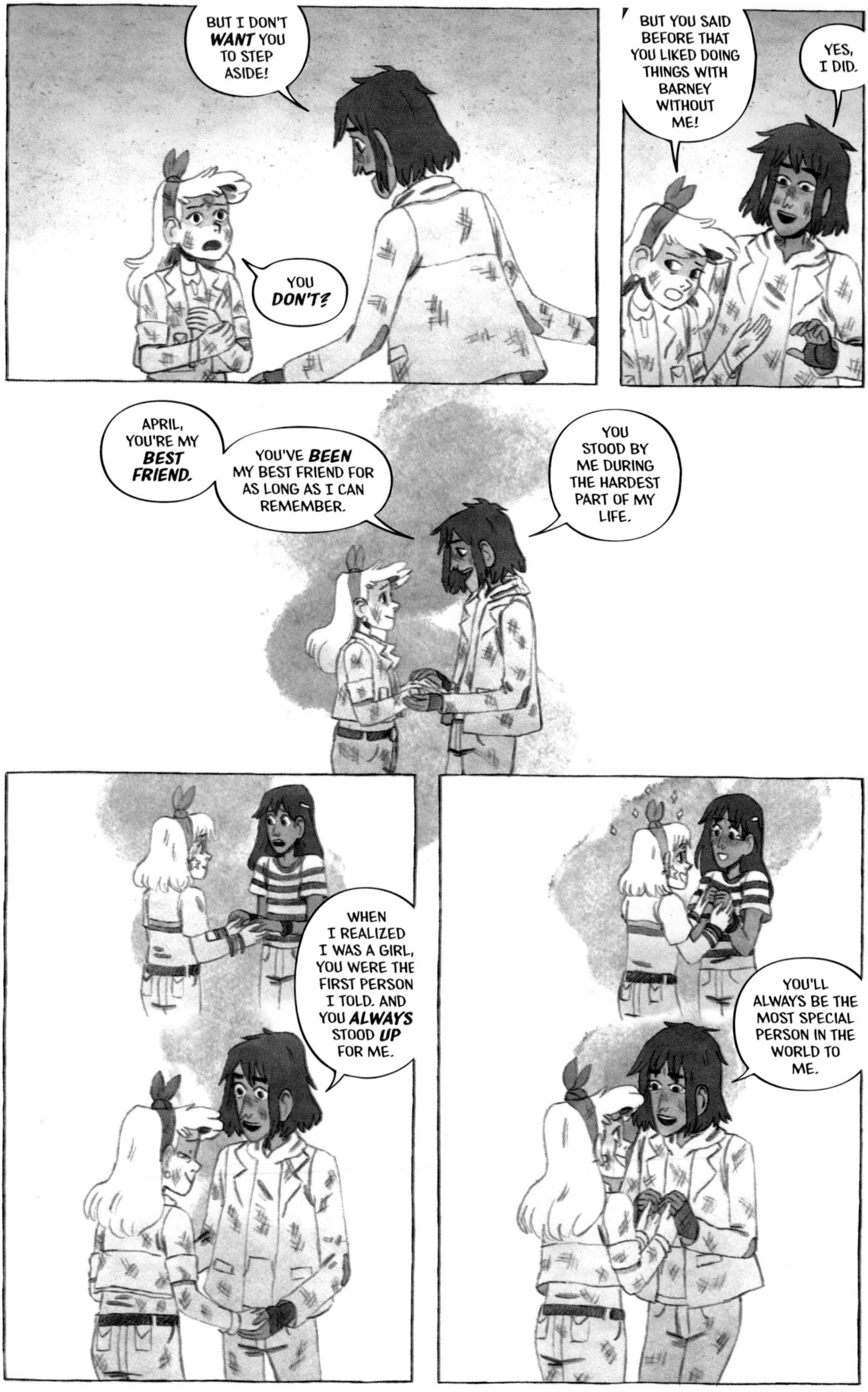
BUT I DON'T WANT YOU TO STEP ASIDE!
YOU DON'T?
BUT YOU SAID BEFORE THAT YOU LIKED DOING THINGS WITH BARNEY WITHOUT ME!
YES, I DID.
APRIL, YOU'RE MY BEST FRIEND.
YOU'VE BEEN MY BEST FRIEND FOR AS LONG AS I CAN REMEMBER.
YOU STOOD BY ME DURING THE HARDEST PART OF MY LIFE.
WHEN I REALIZED I WAS A GIRL, YOU WERE THE FIRST PERSON I TOLD. AND YOU ALWAYS STOOD UP FOR ME.
YOU'LL ALWAYS BE THE MOST SPECIAL PERSON IN THE WORLD TO ME.

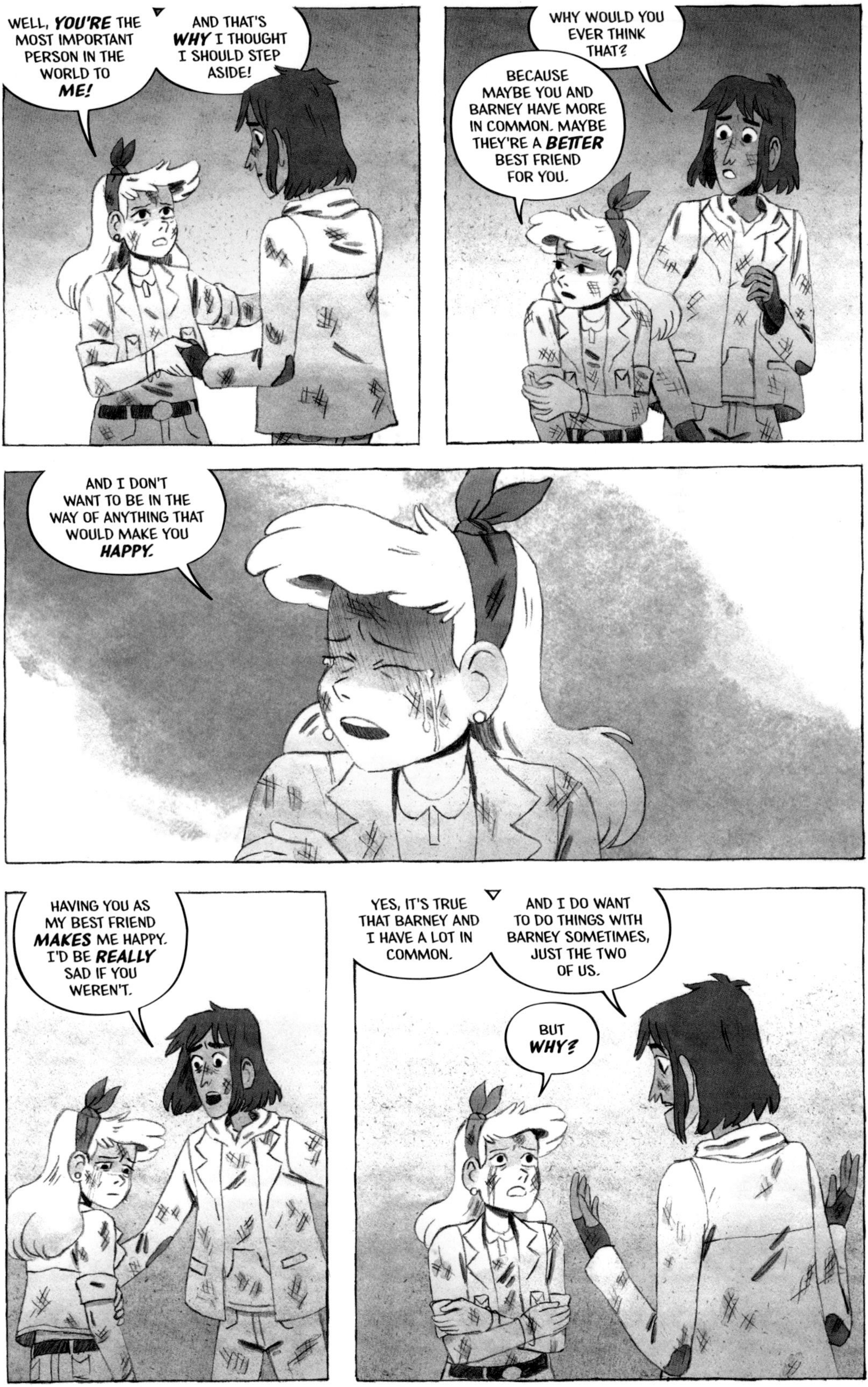
WELL, YOU'RE THE MOST IMPORTANT PERSON IN THE WORLD TO ME!
AND THAT'S WHY I THOUGHT I SHOULD STEP ASIDE!
WHY WOULD YOU EVER THINK THAT?
BECAUSE MAYBE YOU AND BARNEY HAVE MORE IN COMMON. MAYBE THEY'RE A BETTER BEST FRIEND FOR YOU.
AND I DON'T WANT TO BE IN THE WAY OF ANYTHING THAT WOULD MAKE YOU HAPPY.
HAVING YOU AS MY BEST FRIEND MAKES ME HAPPY. I'D BE REALLY SAD IF YOU WEREN'T.
YES, IT'S TRUE THAT BARNEY AND I HAVE A LOT IN COMMON.
AND I DO WANT TO DO THINGS WITH BARNEY SOMETIMES, JUST THE TWO OF US.
BUT WHY?

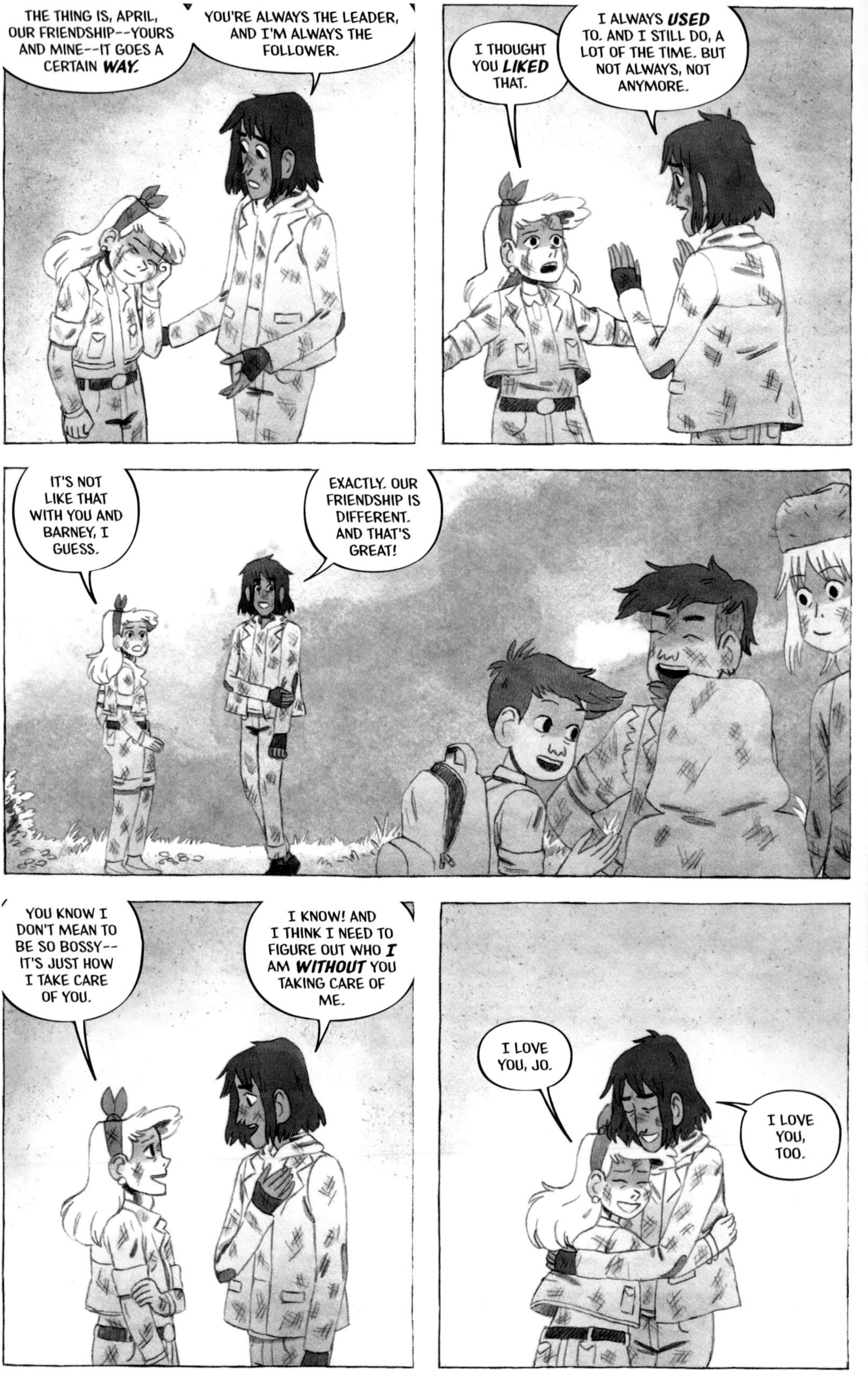
THE THING IS, APRIL, OUR FRIENDSHIP--YOURS AND MINE--IT GOES A CERTAIN WAY.
YOU'RE ALWAYS THE LEADER, AND I'M ALWAYS THE FOLLOWER.
I THOUGHT YOU LIKED THAT.
I ALWAYS USED TO. AND I STILL DO, A LOT OF THE TIME. BUT NOT ALWAYS, NOT ANYMORE.
IT'S NOT LIKE THAT WITH YOU AND BARNEY, I GUESS.
EXACTLY. OUR FRIENDSHIP IS DIFFERENT. AND THAT'S GREAT!
YOU KNOW I DON'T MEAN TO BE SO BOSSY--IT'S JUST HOW I TAKE CARE OF YOU.
I KNOW! AND I THINK I NEED TO FIGURE OUT WHO I AM WITHOUT YOU TAKING CARE OF ME.
I LOVE YOU, JO.
I LOVE YOU, TOO.

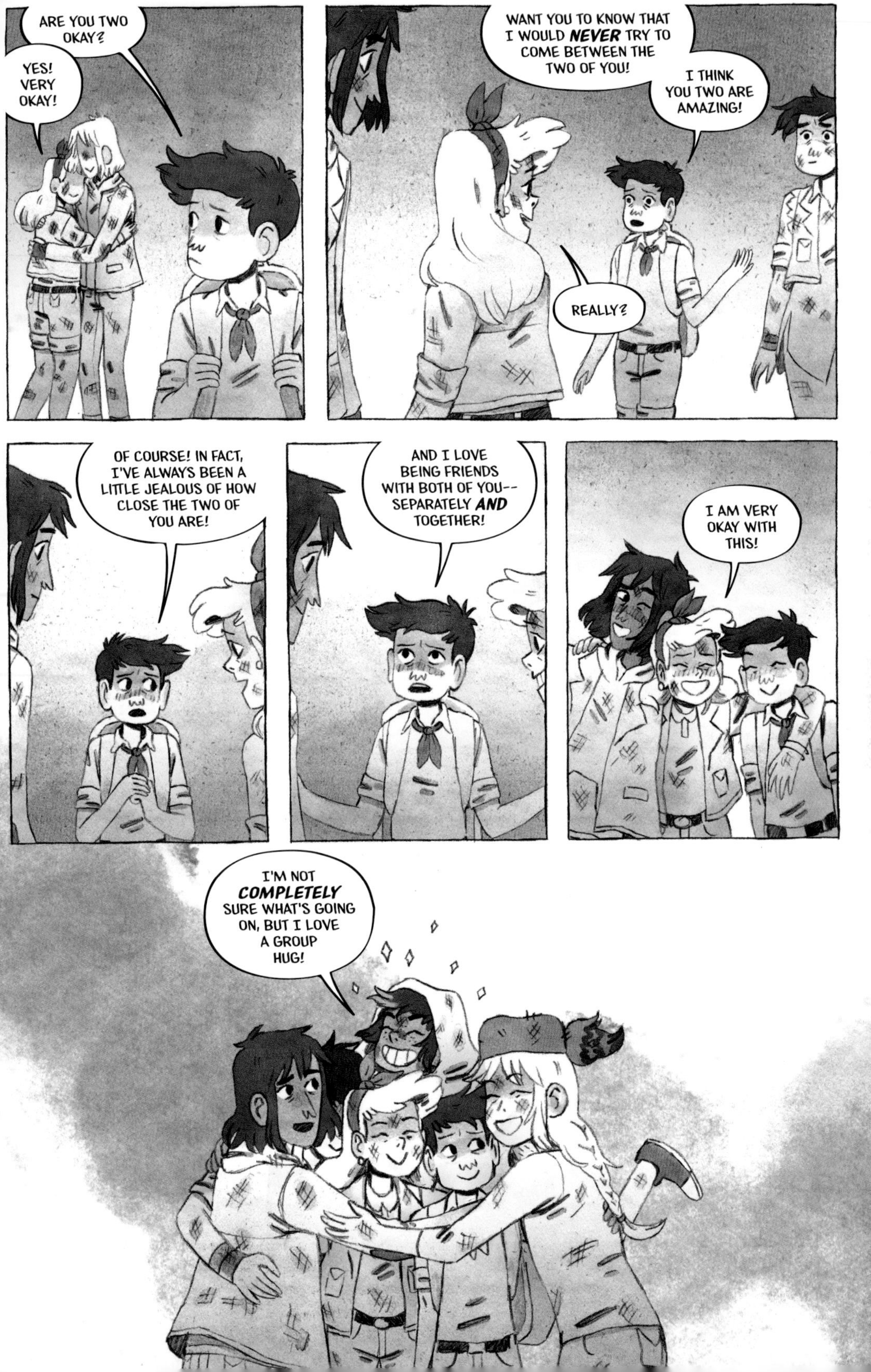

ARE YOU TWO OKAY?
YES! VERY OKAY!
WANT YOU TO KNOW THAT I WOULD **NEVER** TRY TO COME BETWEEN THE TWO OF YOU!
I THINK YOU TWO ARE AMAZING!
REALLY?
OF COURSE! IN FACT, I'VE ALWAYS BEEN A LITTLE JEALOUS OF HOW CLOSE THE TWO OF YOU ARE!
AND I LOVE BEING FRIENDS WITH BOTH OF YOU-- SEPARATELY **AND** TOGETHER!
I AM VERY OKAY WITH THIS!
I'M NOT **COMPLETELY** SURE WHAT'S GOING ON, BUT I LOVE A GROUP HUG!

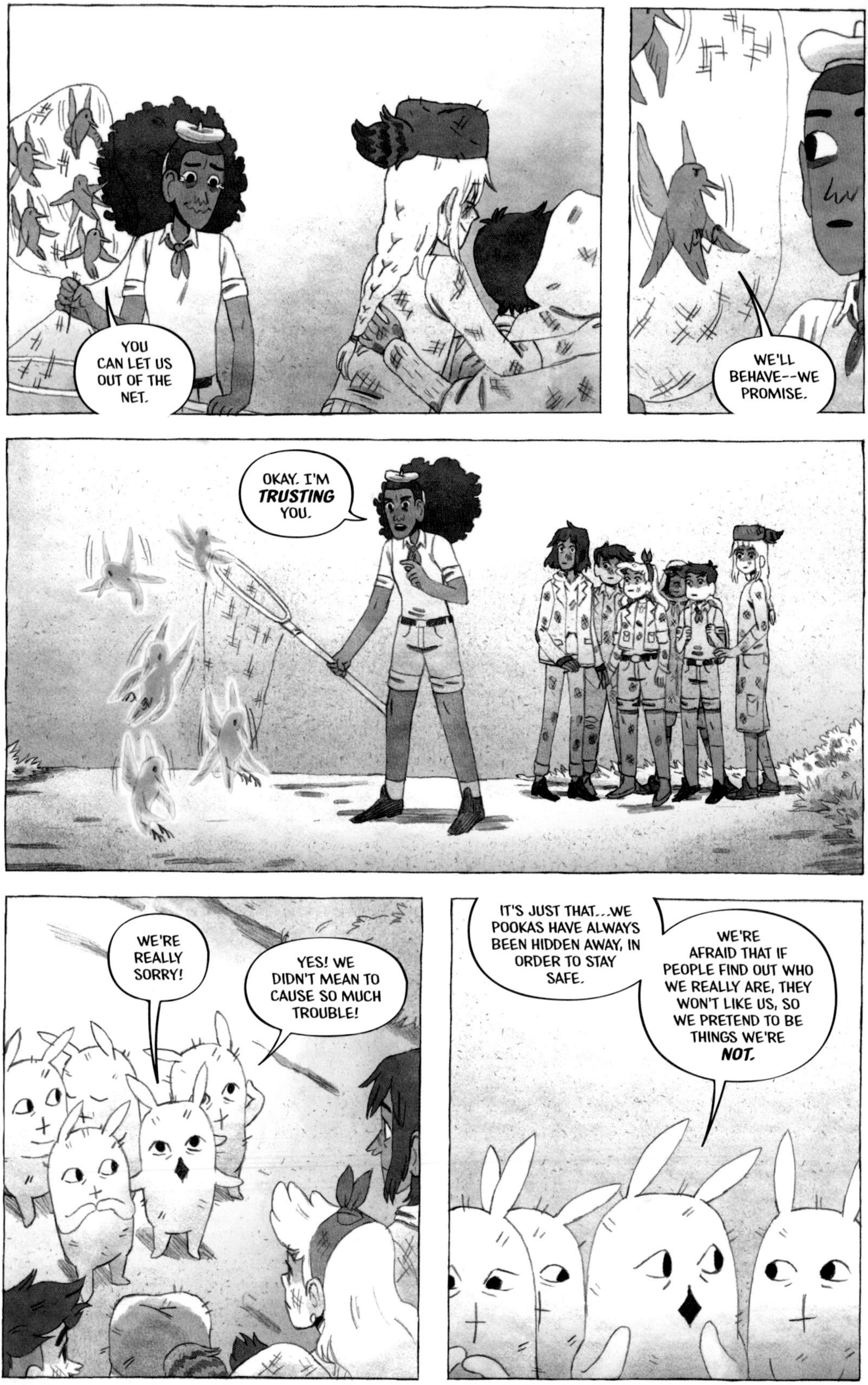
YOU CAN LET US OUT OF THE NET.
WE'LL BEHAVE--WE PROMISE.
OKAY. I'M **TRUSTING** YOU.
WE'RE REALLY SORRY!
YES! WE DIDN'T MEAN TO CAUSE SO MUCH TROUBLE!
IT'S JUST THAT...WE POOKAS HAVE ALWAYS BEEN HIDDEN AWAY, IN ORDER TO STAY SAFE.
WE'RE AFRAID THAT IF PEOPLE FIND OUT WHO WE REALLY ARE, THEY WON'T LIKE US, SO WE PRETEND TO BE THINGS WE'RE **NOT.**

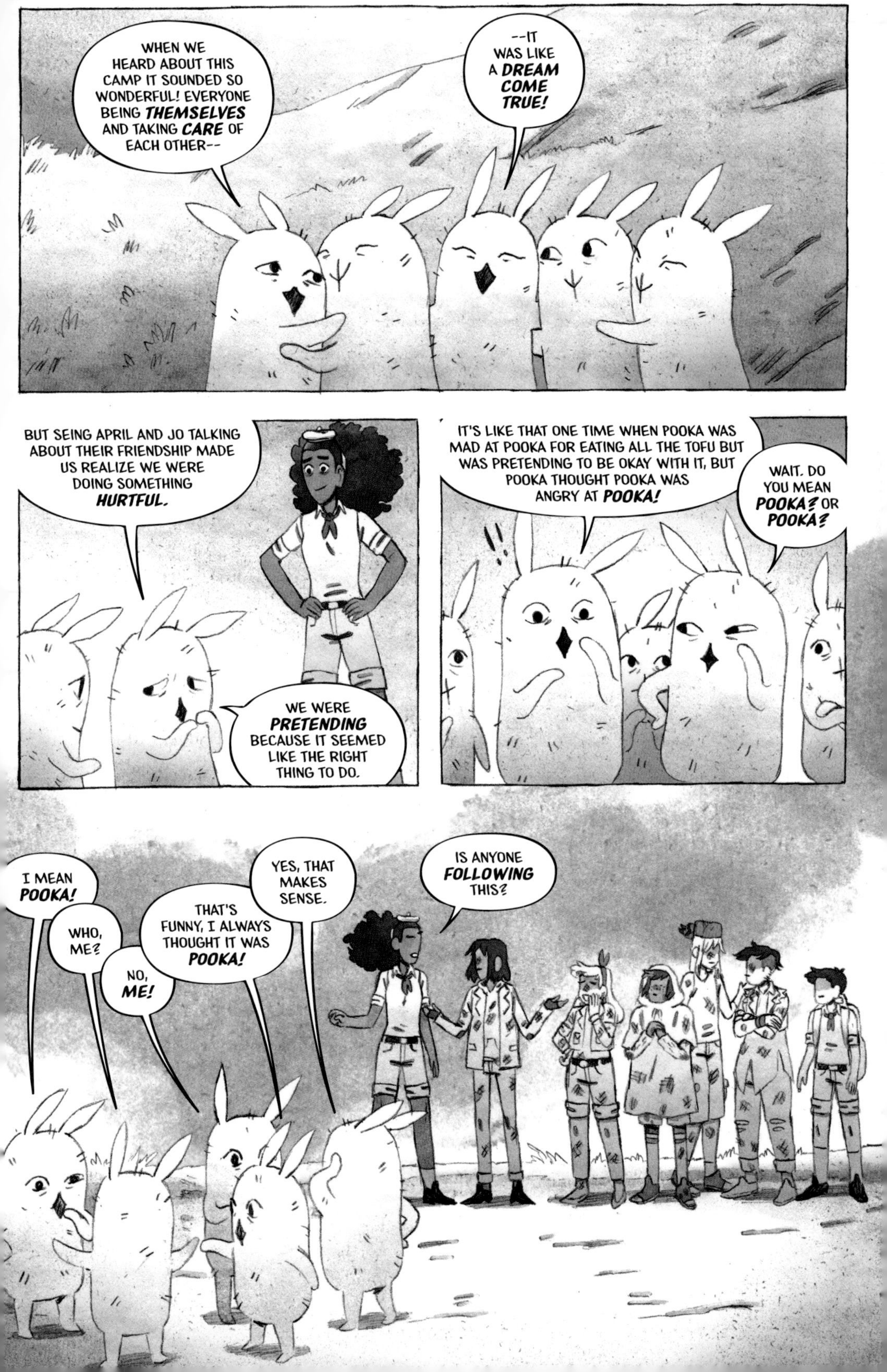
WHEN WE HEARD ABOUT THIS CAMP IT SOUNDED SO WONDERFUL! EVERYONE BEING THEMSELVES AND TAKING CARE OF EACH OTHER--
--IT WAS LIKE A DREAM COME TRUE!
BUT SEING APRIL AND JO TALKING ABOUT THEIR FRIENDSHIP MADE US REALIZE WE WERE DOING SOMETHING HURTFUL.
WE WERE PRETENDING BECAUSE IT SEEMED LIKE THE RIGHT THING TO DO.
IT'S LIKE THAT ONE TIME WHEN POOKA WAS MAD AT POOKA FOR EATING ALL THE TOFU BUT WAS PRETENDING TO BE OKAY WITH IT, BUT POOKA THOUGHT POOKA WAS ANGRY AT POOKA!
WAIT. DO YOU MEAN POOKA? OR POOKA?
I MEAN POOKA!
WHO, ME?
NO, ME!
THAT'S FUNNY, I ALWAYS THOUGHT IT WAS POOKA!
YES, THAT MAKES SENSE.
IS ANYONE FOLLOWING THIS?

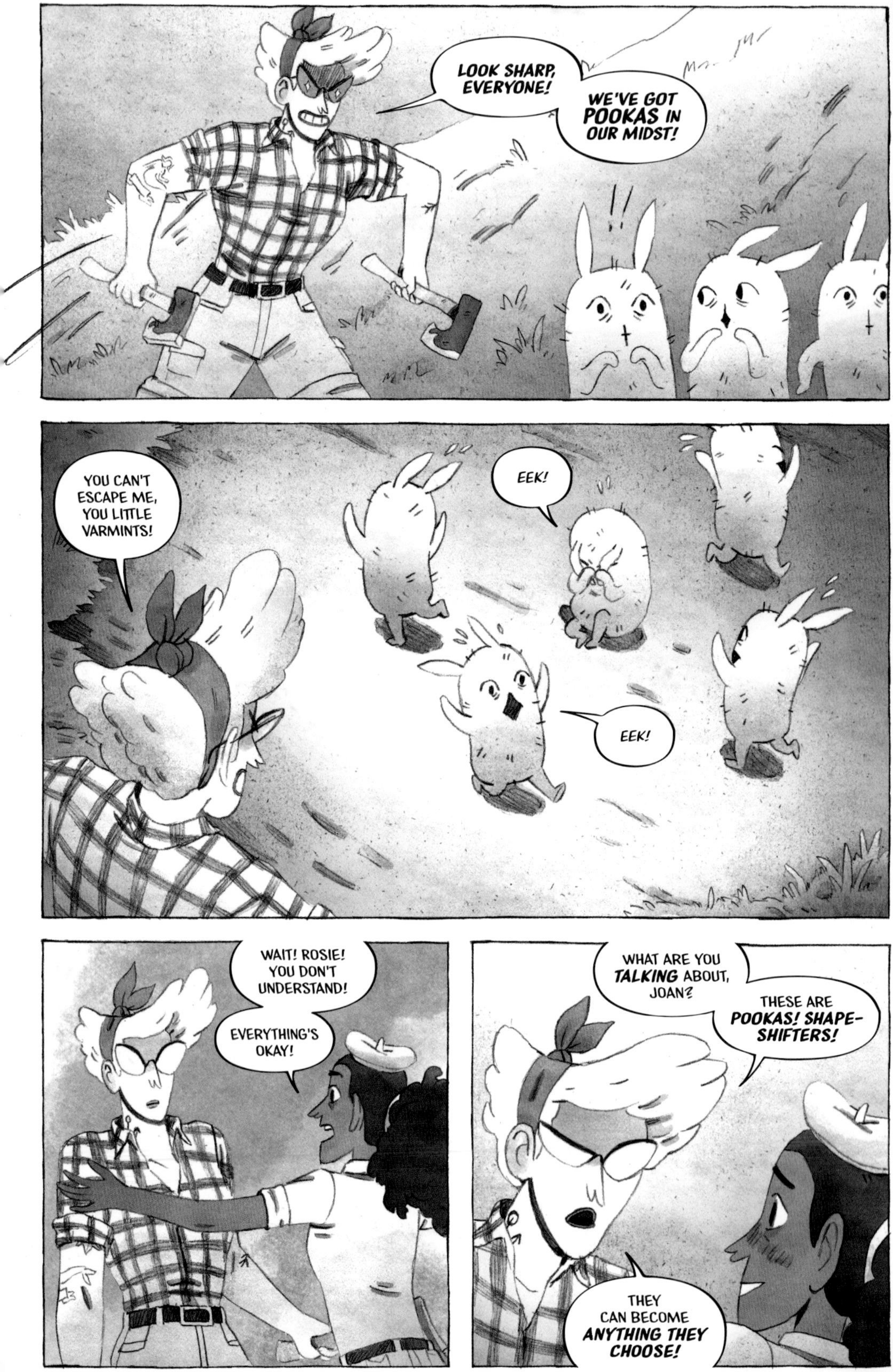
LOOK SHARP, EVERYONE!
WE'VE GOT POOKAS IN OUR MIDST!
YOU CAN'T ESCAPE ME, YOU LITTLE VARMINTS!
EEK!
EEK!
WAIT! ROSIE! YOU DON'T UNDERSTAND!
EVERYTHING'S OKAY!
WHAT ARE YOU TALKING ABOUT, JOAN?
THESE ARE POOKAS! SHAPE-SHIFTERS!
THEY CAN BECOME ANYTHING THEY CHOOSE!

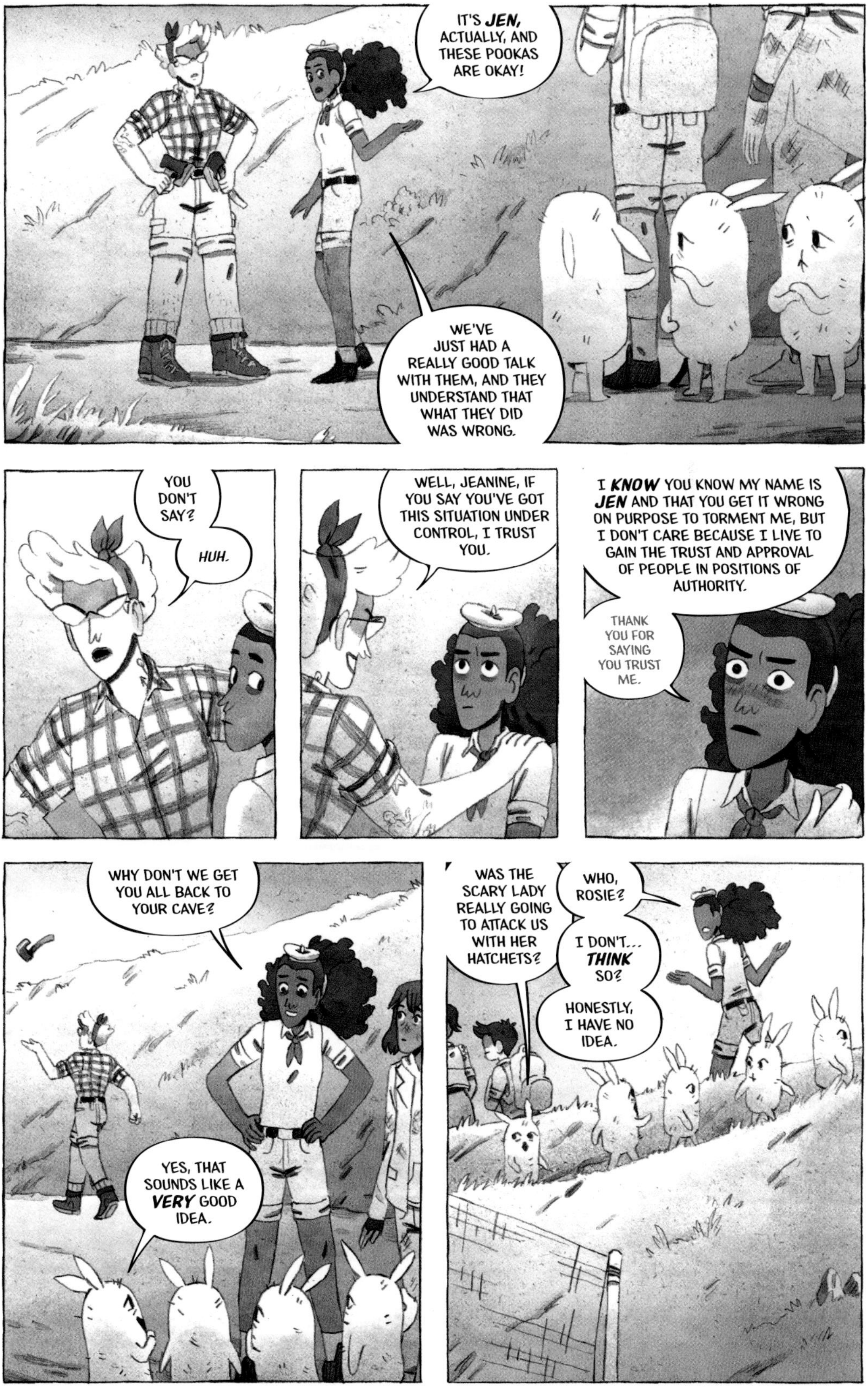
IT'S JEN, ACTUALLY, AND THESE POOKAS ARE OKAY!
WE'VE JUST HAD A REALLY GOOD TALK WITH THEM, AND THEY UNDERSTAND THAT WHAT THEY DID WAS WRONG.
YOU DON'T SAY?
HUH.
WELL, JEANINE, IF YOU SAY YOU'VE GOT THIS SITUATION UNDER CONTROL, I TRUST YOU.
I KNOW YOU KNOW MY NAME IS JEN AND THAT YOU GET IT WRONG ON PURPOSE TO TORMENT ME, BUT I DON'T CARE BECAUSE I LIVE TO GAIN THE TRUST AND APPROVAL OF PEOPLE IN POSITIONS OF AUTHORITY.
THANK YOU FOR SAYING YOU TRUST ME.
WHY DON'T WE GET YOU ALL BACK TO YOUR CAVE?
YES, THAT SOUNDS LIKE A VERY GOOD IDEA.
WAS THE SCARY LADY REALLY GOING TO ATTACK US WITH HER HATCHETS?
WHO, ROSIE?
I DON'T... THINK SO?
HONESTLY, I HAVE NO IDEA.

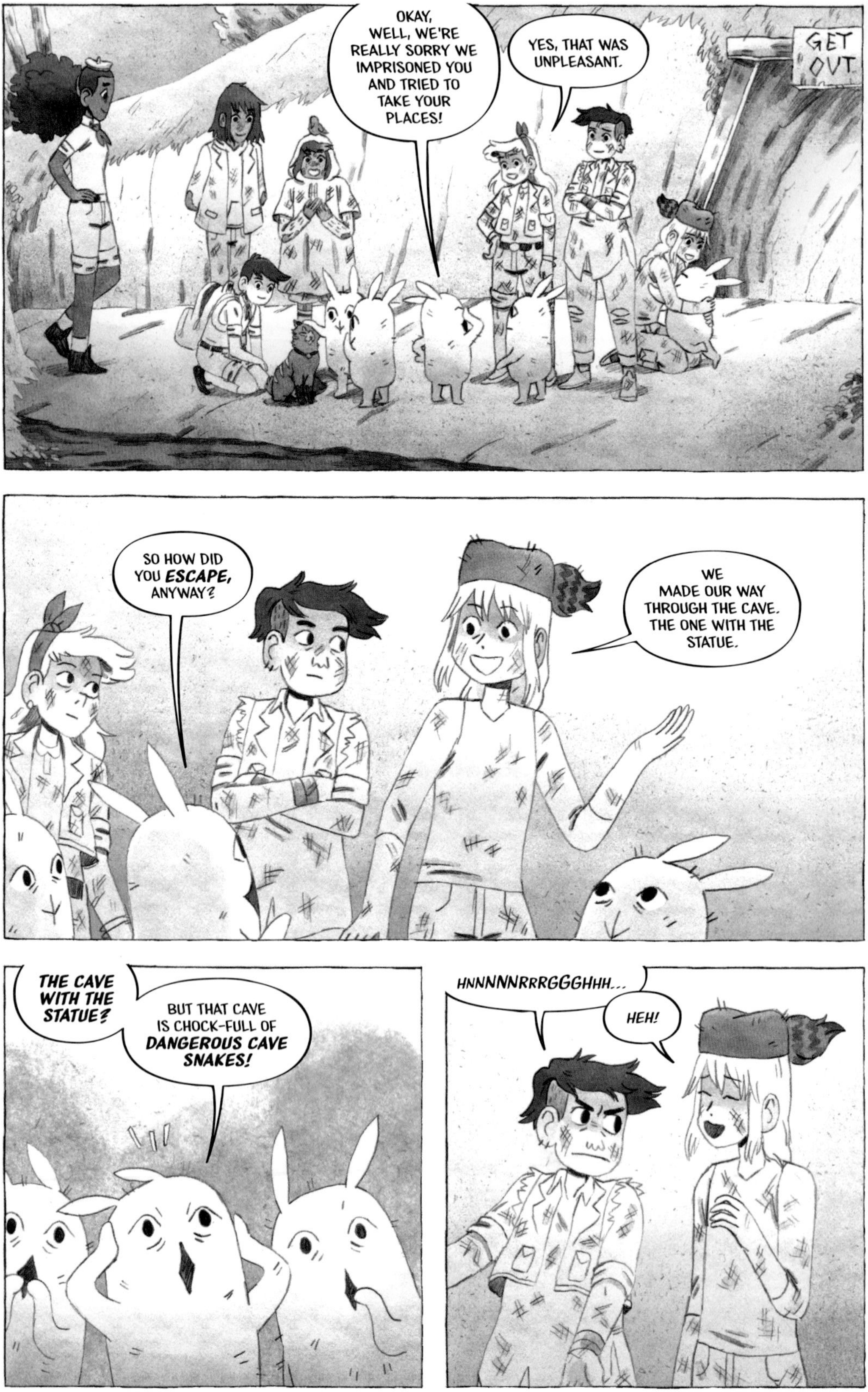
OKAY, WELL, WE'RE REALLY SORRY WE IMPRISONED YOU AND TRIED TO TAKE YOUR PLACES!
YES, THAT WAS UNPLEASANT.
GET OUT
SO HOW DID YOU ESCAPE, ANYWAY?
WE MADE OUR WAY THROUGH THE CAVE. THE ONE WITH THE STATUE.
THE CAVE WITH THE STATUE?
BUT THAT CAVE IS CHOCK-FULL OF DANGEROUS CAVE SNAKES!
HNNNNNRRRGGGHHH...
HEH!

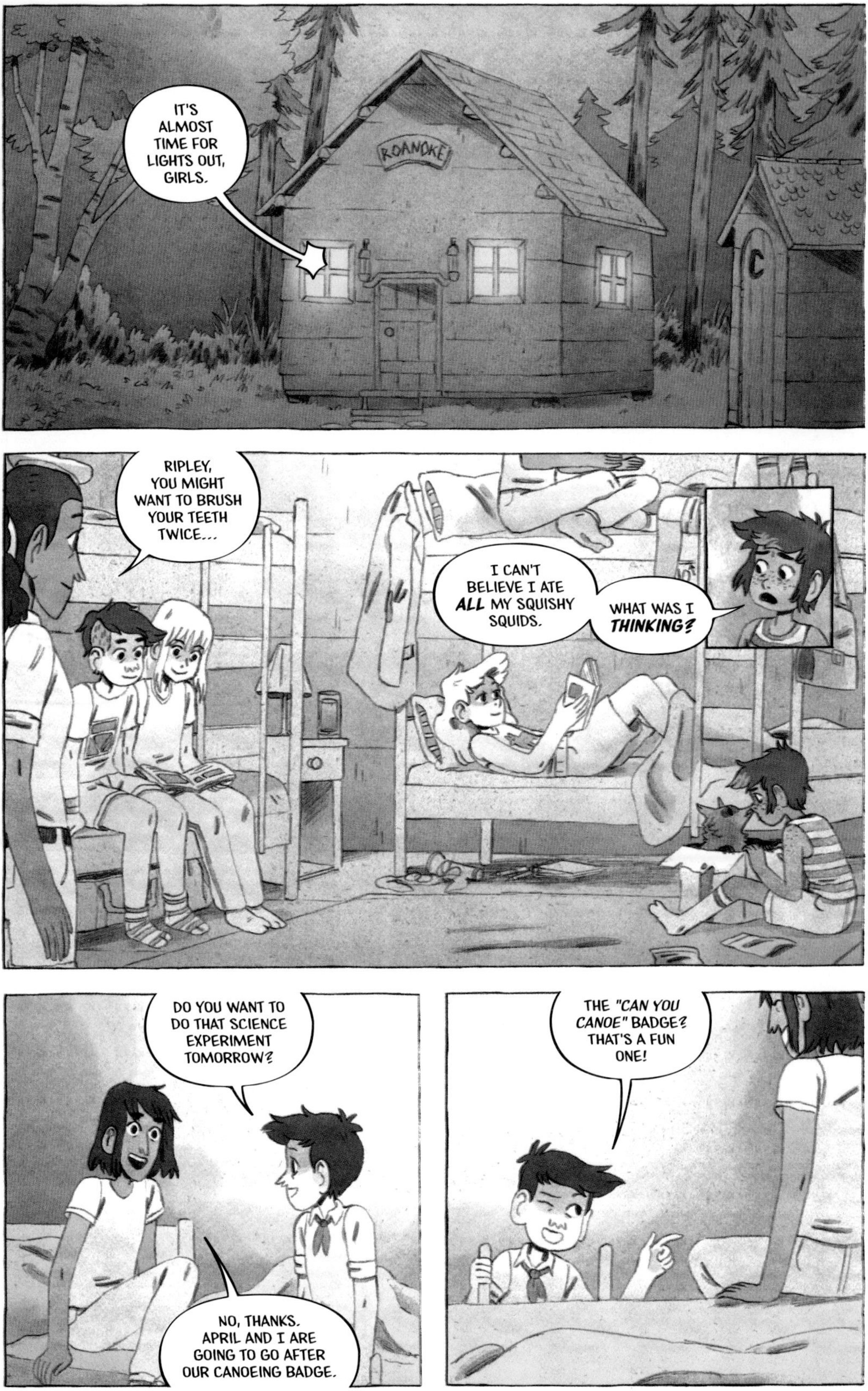
IT'S ALMOST TIME FOR LIGHTS OUT, GIRLS.
ROANOKE
RIPLEY, YOU MIGHT WANT TO BRUSH YOUR TEETH TWICE...
I CAN'T BELIEVE I ATE ALL MY SQUISHY SQUIDS.
WHAT WAS I THINKING?
DO YOU WANT TO DO THAT SCIENCE EXPERIMENT TOMORROW?
NO, THANKS. APRIL AND I ARE GOING TO GO AFTER OUR CANOEING BADGE.
THE "CAN YOU CANOE" BADGE? THAT'S A FUN ONE!

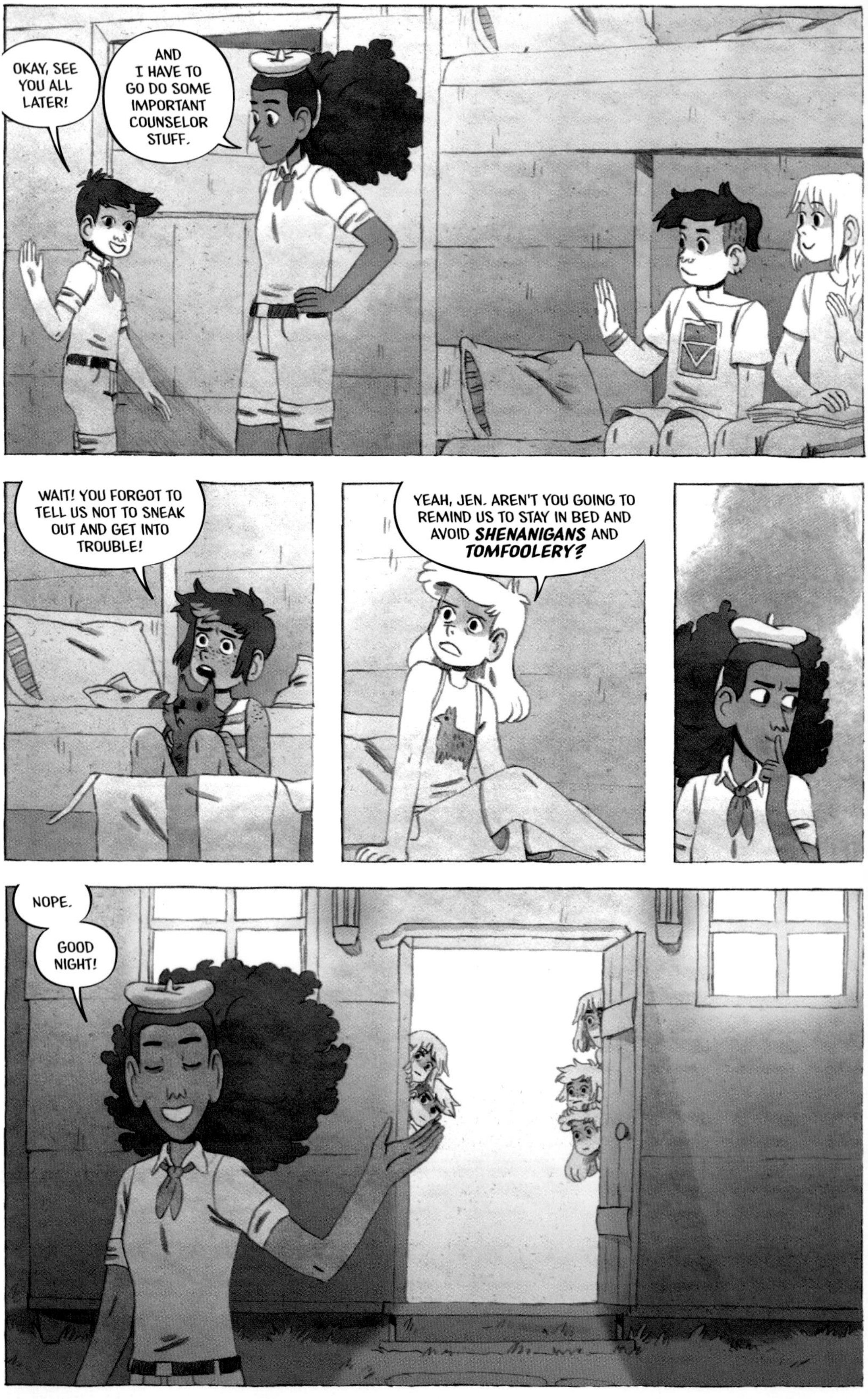
OKAY, SEE YOU ALL LATER!
AND I HAVE TO GO DO SOME IMPORTANT COUNSELOR STUFF.
WAIT! YOU FORGOT TO TELL US NOT TO SNEAK OUT AND GET INTO TROUBLE!
YEAH, JEN. AREN'T YOU GOING TO REMIND US TO STAY IN BED AND AVOID SHENANIGANS AND TOMFOOLERY?
NOPE.
GOOD NIGHT!

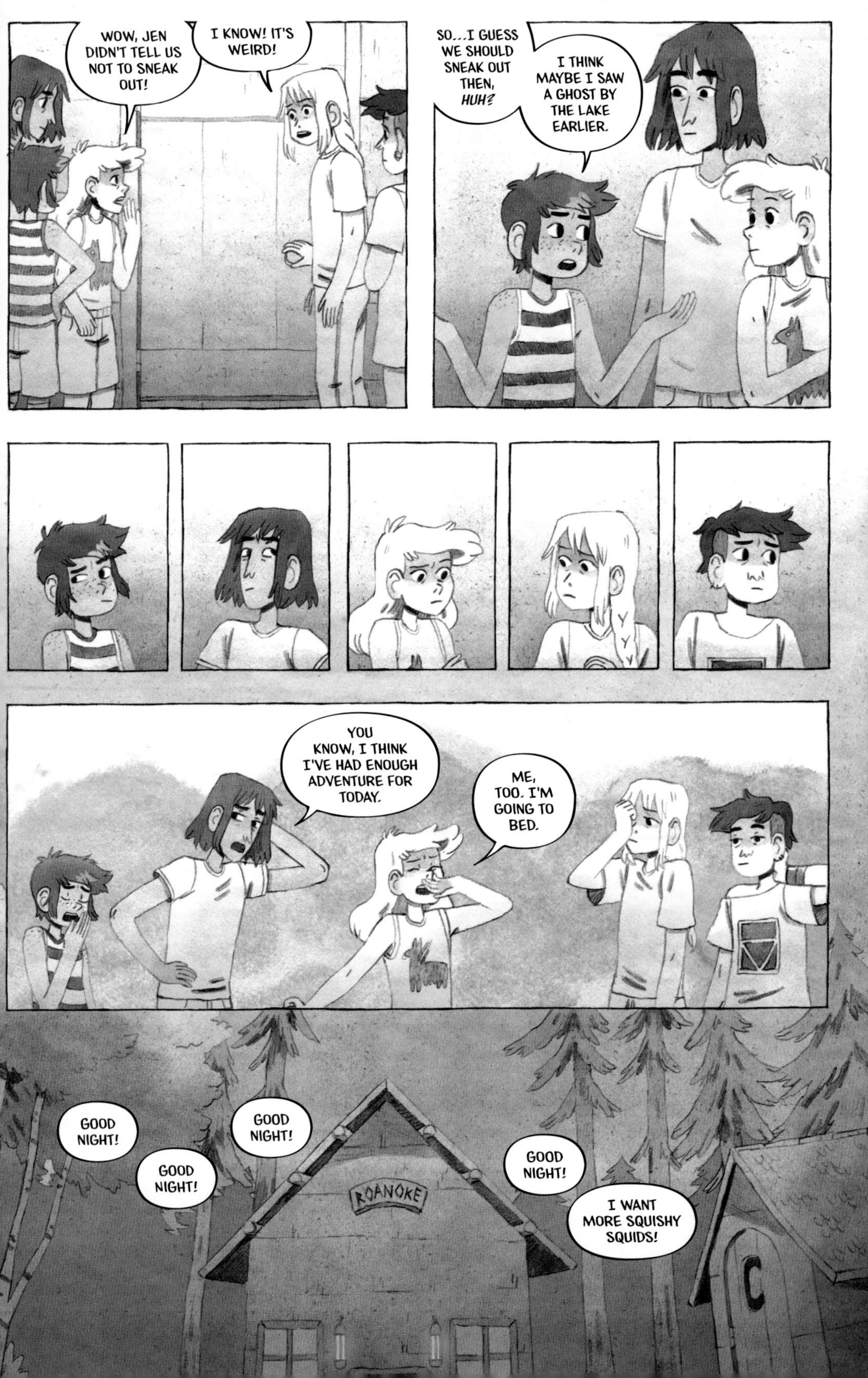
WOW, JEN DIDN'T TELL US NOT TO SNEAK OUT!
I KNOW! IT'S WEIRD!
SO...I GUESS WE SHOULD SNEAK OUT THEN, HUH?
I THINK MAYBE I SAW A GHOST BY THE LAKE EARLIER.
YOU KNOW, I THINK I'VE HAD ENOUGH ADVENTURE FOR TODAY.
ME, TOO. I'M GOING TO BED.
GOOD NIGHT!
GOOD NIGHT!
GOOD NIGHT!
GOOD NIGHT!
I WANT MORE SQUISHY SQUIDS!
ROANOKE
C

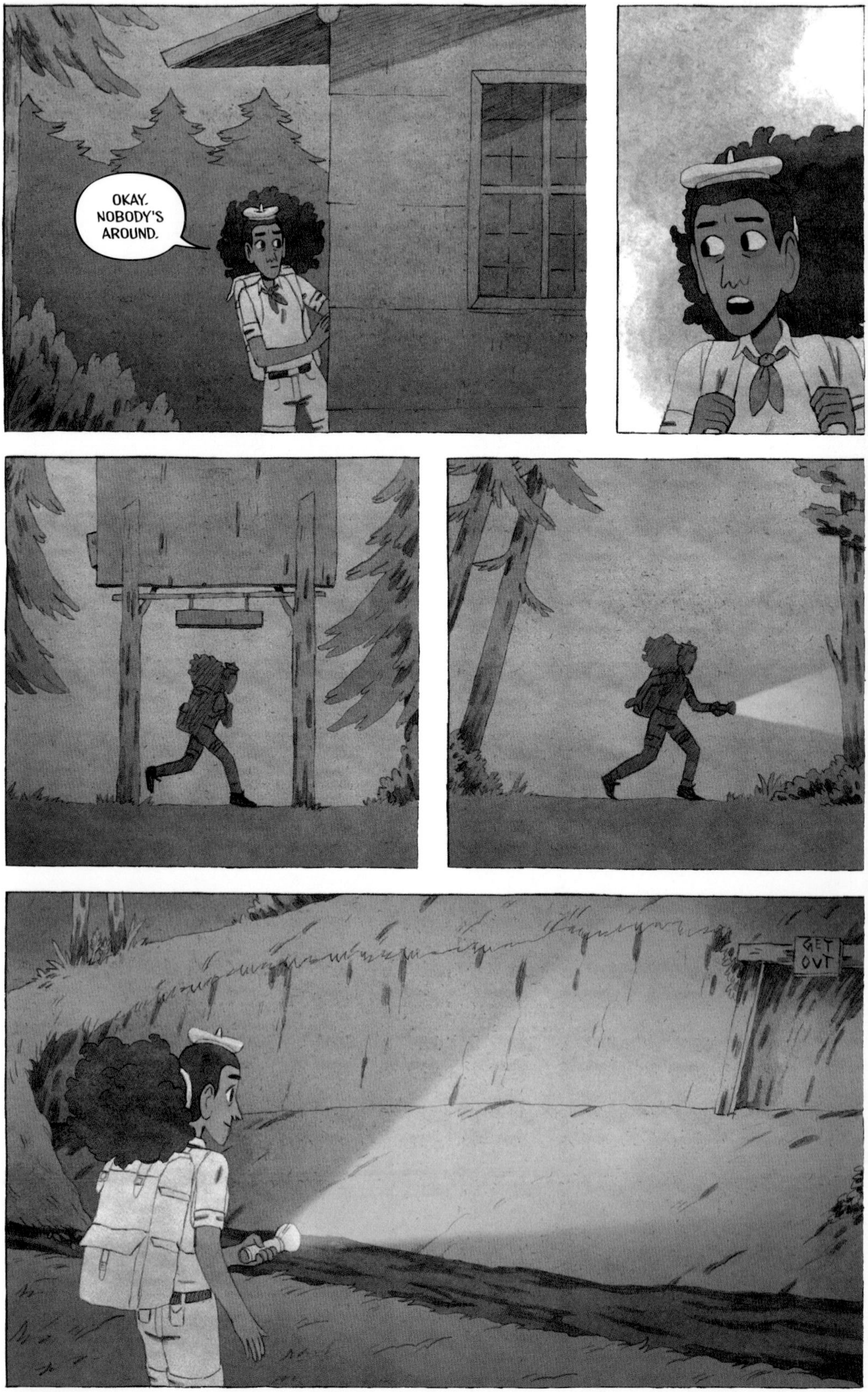
OKAY. NOBODY'S AROUND.
GET OUT

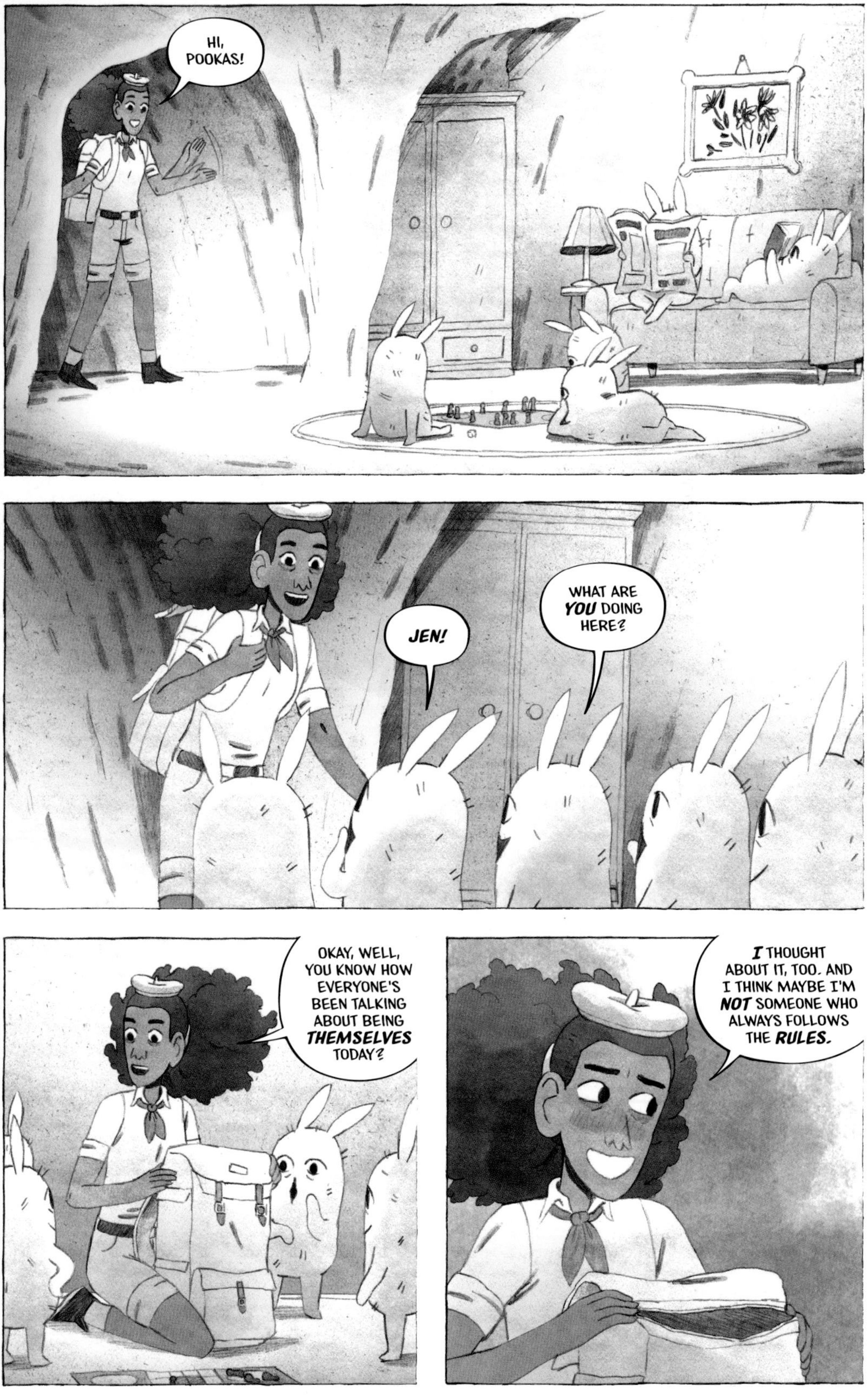
HI, POOKAS!
JEN!
WHAT ARE YOU DOING HERE?
OKAY, WELL, YOU KNOW HOW EVERYONE'S BEEN TALKING ABOUT BEING THEMSELVES TODAY?
I THOUGHT ABOUT IT, TOO. AND I THINK MAYBE I'M NOT SOMEONE WHO ALWAYS FOLLOWS THE RULES.

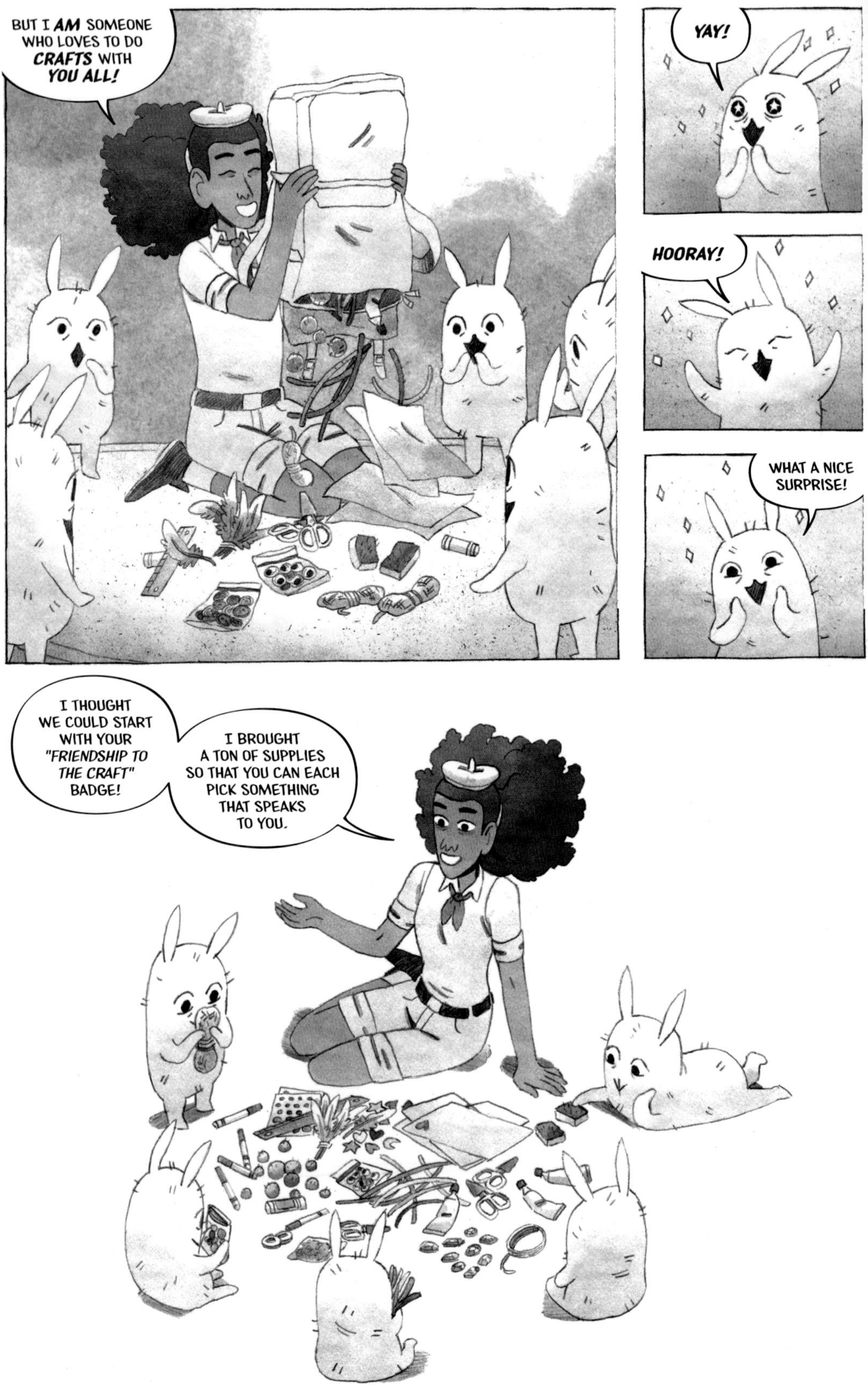
BUT I **AM** SOMEONE WHO LOVES TO DO ***CRAFTS*** WITH ***YOU ALL!***
YAY!
HOORAY!
WHAT A NICE SURPRISE!
I THOUGHT WE COULD START WITH YOUR *"FRIENDSHIP TO THE CRAFT"* BADGE!
I BROUGHT A TON OF SUPPLIES SO THAT YOU CAN EACH PICK SOMETHING THAT SPEAKS TO YOU.

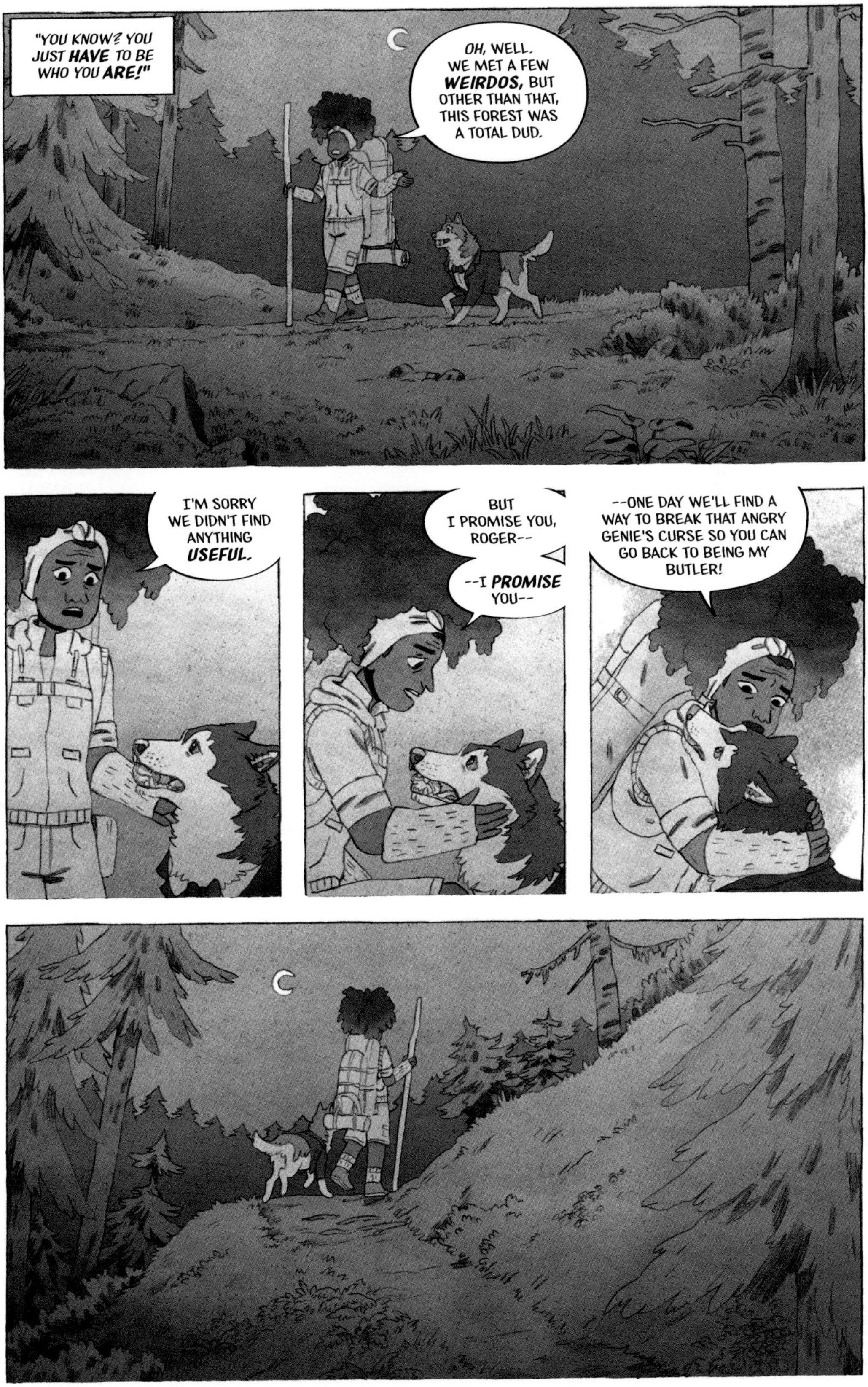
"YOU KNOW? YOU JUST HAVE TO BE WHO YOU ARE!"
OH, WELL. WE MET A FEW WEIRDOS, BUT OTHER THAN THAT, THIS FOREST WAS A TOTAL DUD.
I'M SORRY WE DIDN'T FIND ANYTHING USEFUL.
BUT I PROMISE YOU, ROGER--
--I PROMISE YOU--
--ONE DAY WE'LL FIND A WAY TO BREAK THAT ANGRY GENIE'S CURSE SO YOU CAN GO BACK TO BEING MY BUTLER!

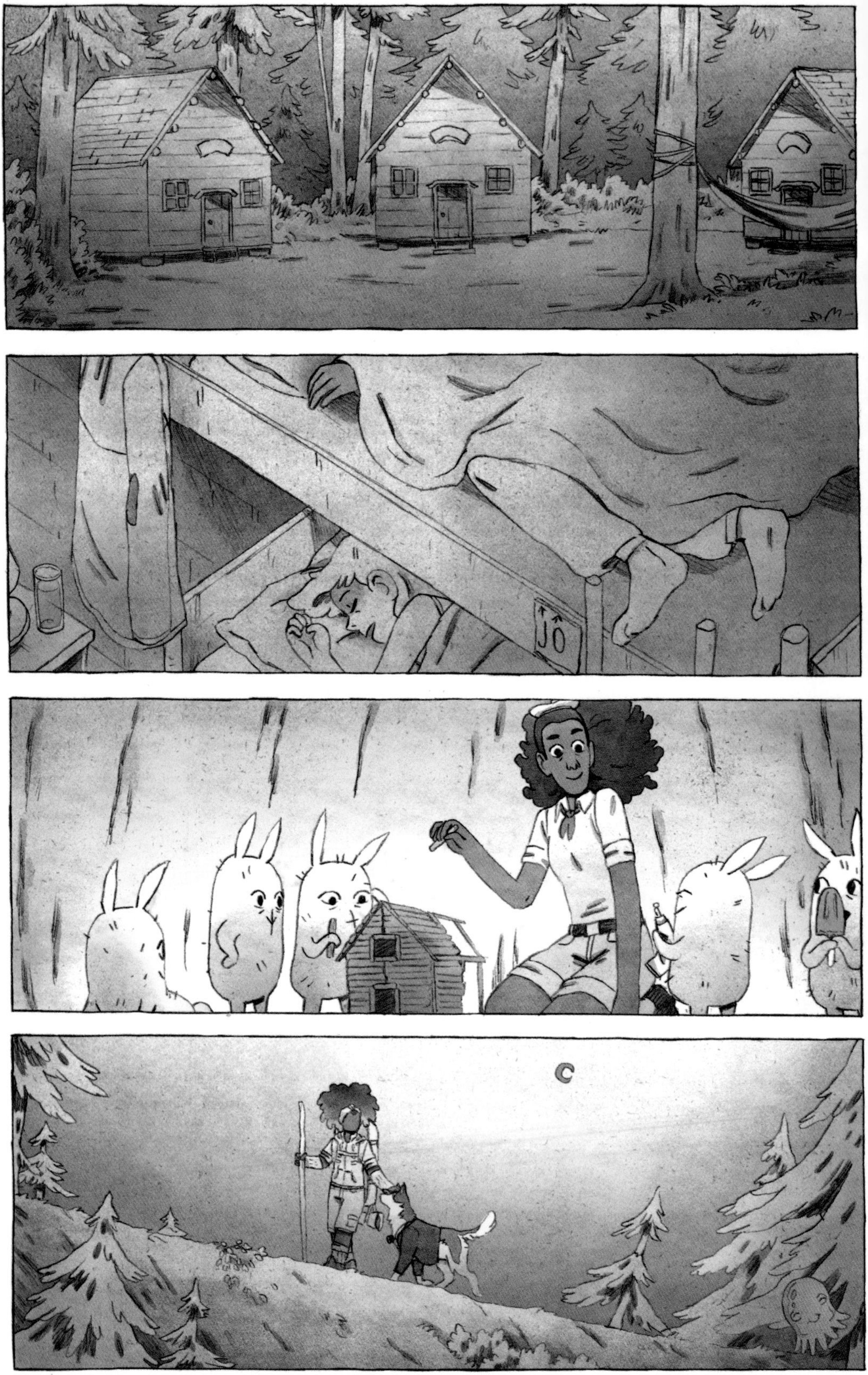
JÔ

Join the Georgia O'Keeffe College of the Arts and Subtle Dramatics basketball team for art, teamwork, and love in

**THE AVANT-GUARDS!**

USDIN ★ HAYES ★ NALTY
THE AVANT-GUARDS
VOLUME ONE
"The Avant-Guards lays up another slam dunk."
—ComicBook.com

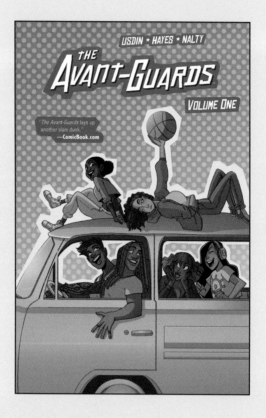

Enroll today with the first volume!

**THE AVANT-GUARDS Issue One**

Written & Created by
**CARLY USDIN**

Illustrated by
**NOAH HAYES**

Colored by
**REBECCA NALTY**

Lettered by
**ED DUKESHIRE**

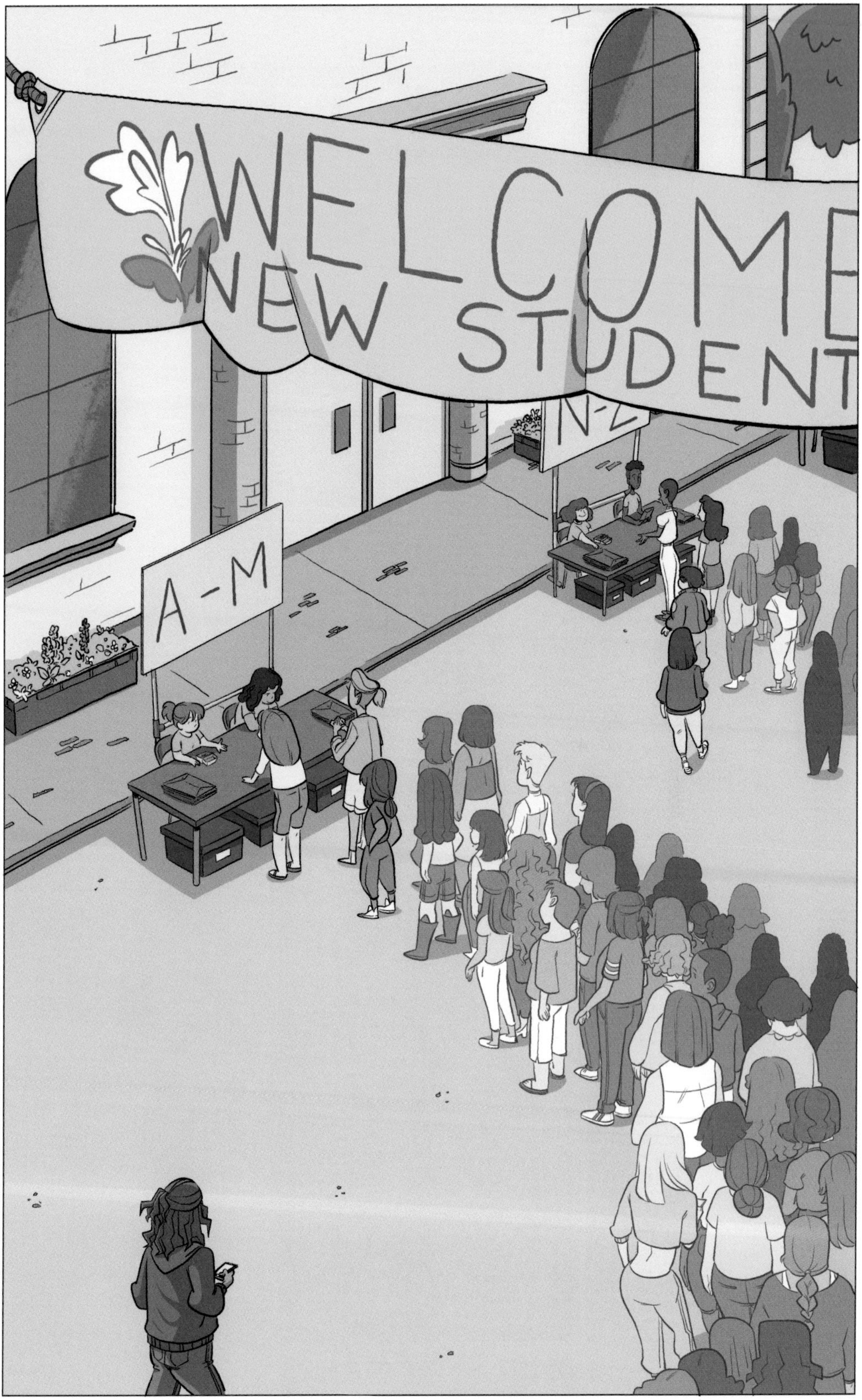
WELCOME
NEW STUDENT
A-M
N-Z

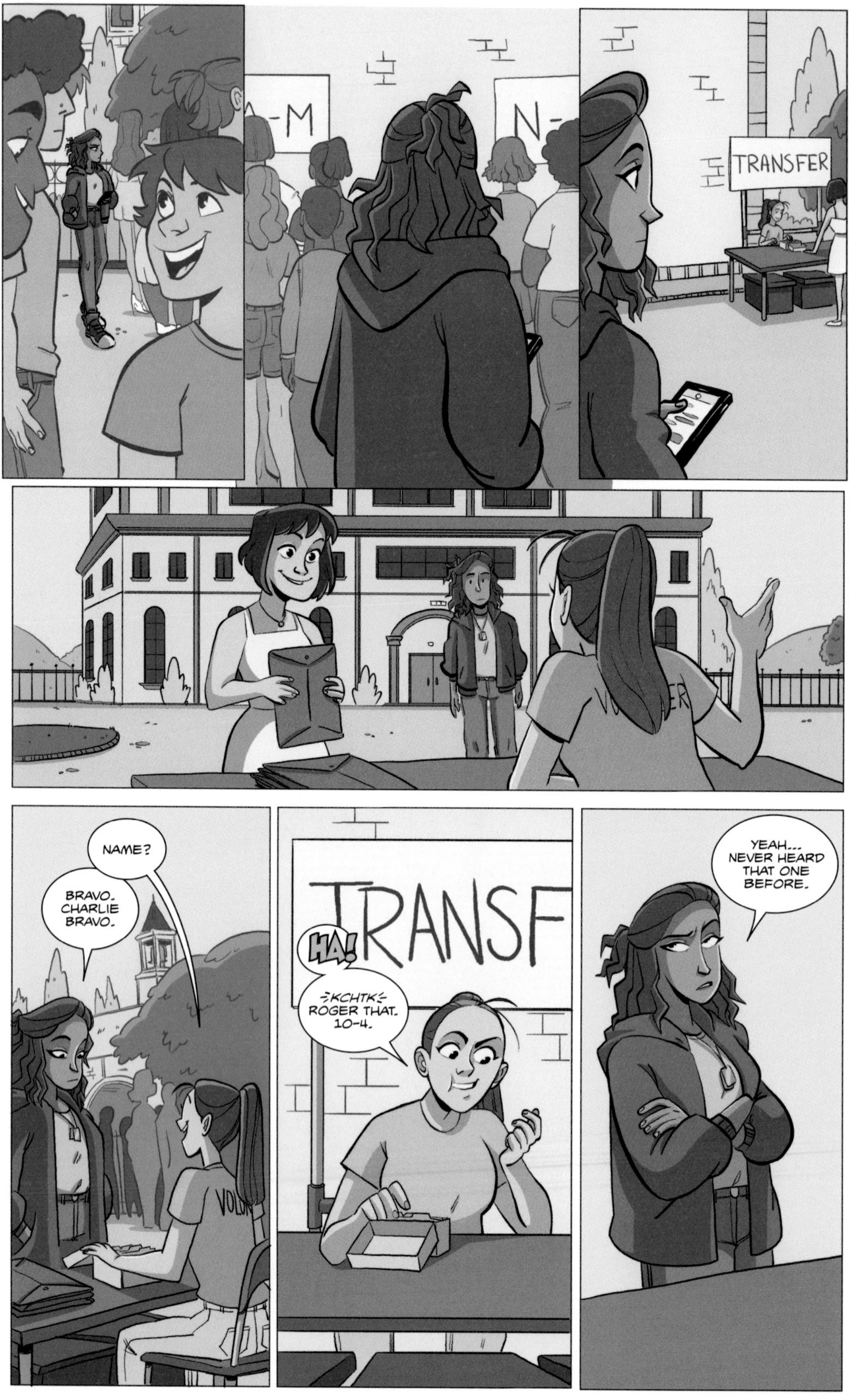
A-M
N-
TRANSFER
NAME?
BRAVO. CHARLIE BRAVO.
TRANSF
HA!
-KCHTK- ROGER THAT. 10-4.
YEAH... NEVER HEARD THAT ONE BEFORE.

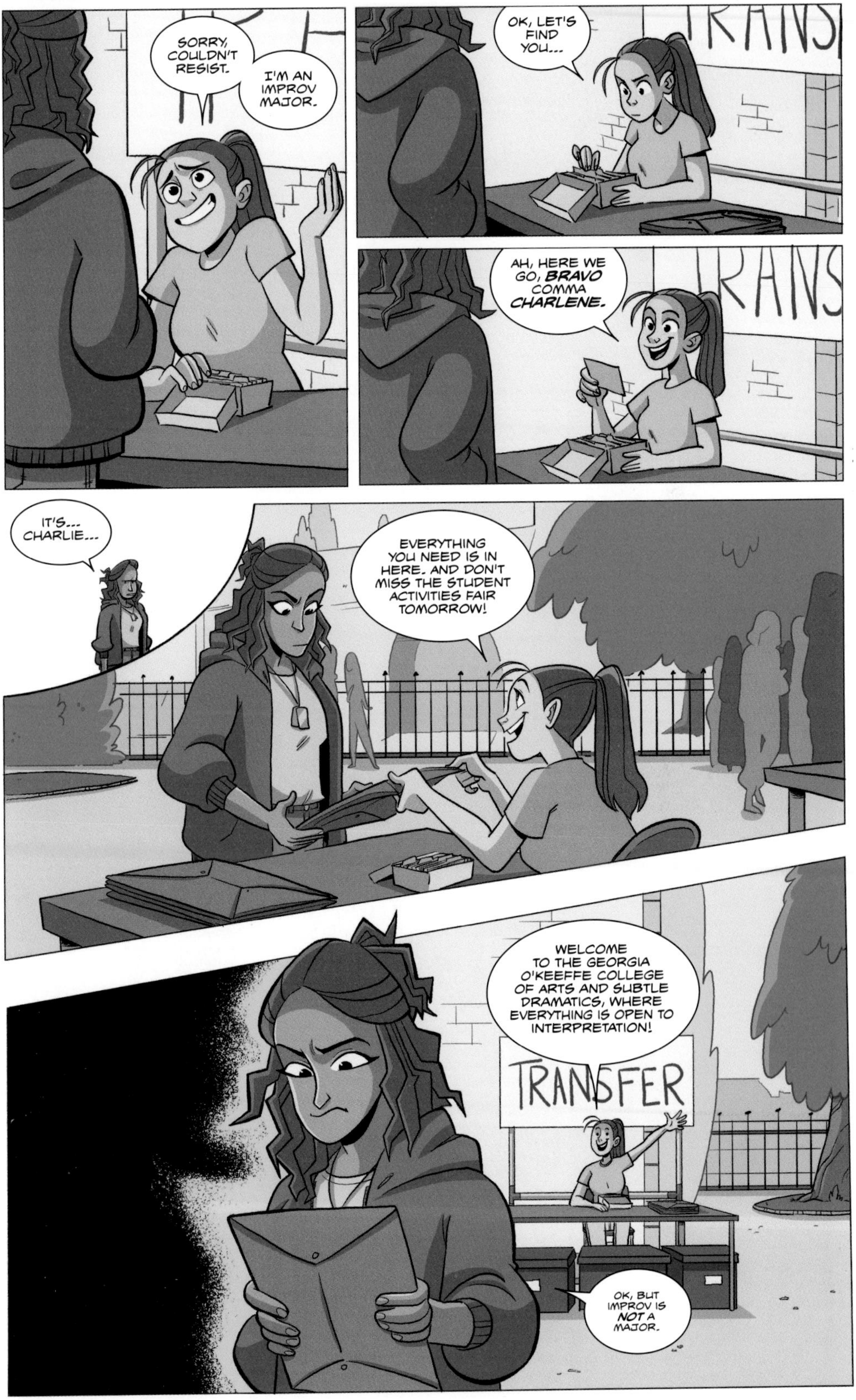
SORRY, COULDN'T RESIST.
I'M AN IMPROV MAJOR.
OK, LET'S FIND YOU...
AH, HERE WE GO, BRAVO COMMA CHARLENE.
IT'S... CHARLIE...
EVERYTHING YOU NEED IS IN HERE. AND DON'T MISS THE STUDENT ACTIVITIES FAIR TOMORROW!
WELCOME TO THE GEORGIA O'KEEFFE COLLEGE OF ARTS AND SUBTLE DRAMATICS, WHERE EVERYTHING IS OPEN TO INTERPRETATION!
TRANSFER
OK, BUT IMPROV IS NOT A MAJOR.

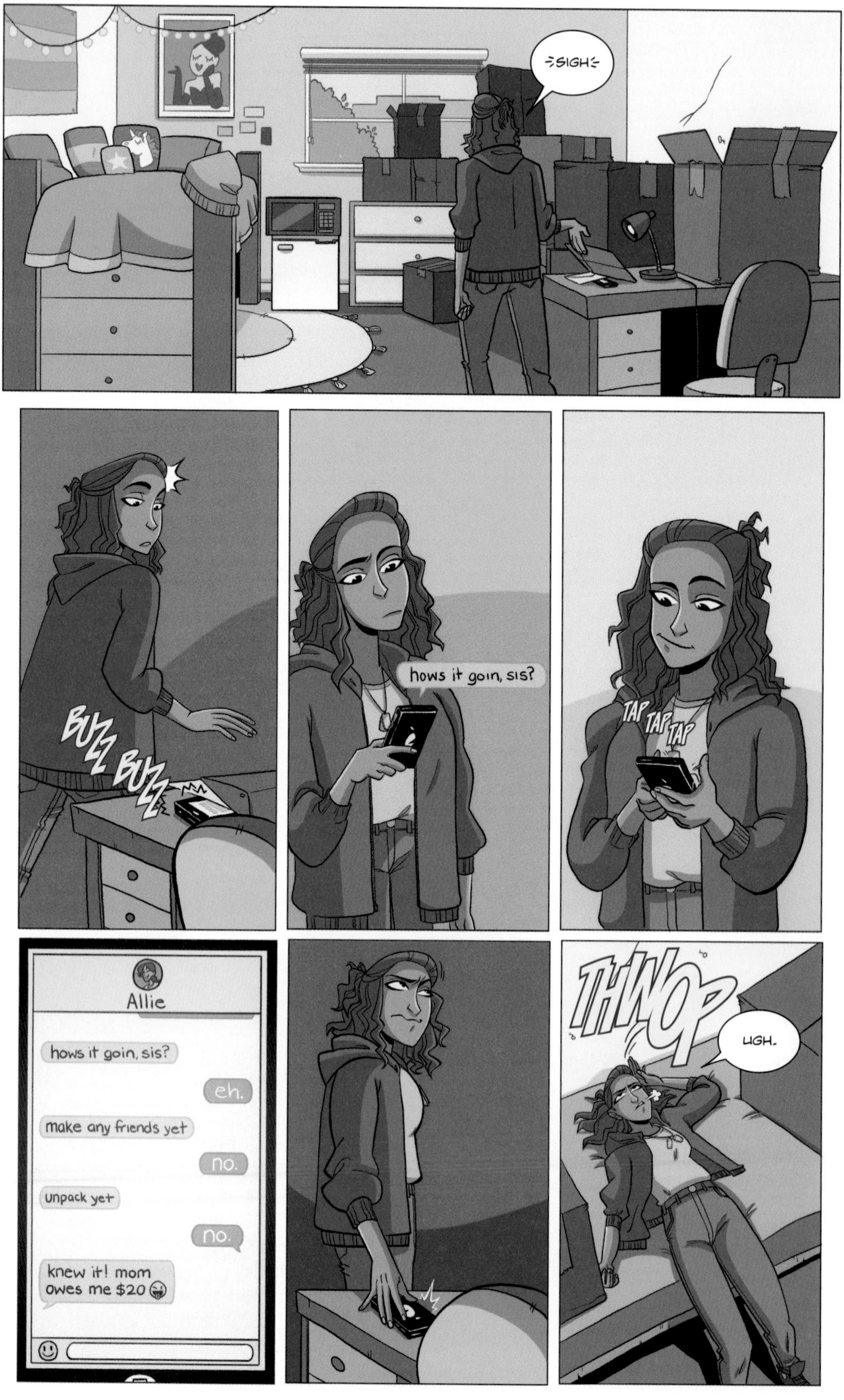

SIGH
BUZZ BUZZ
hows it goin, sis?
TAP TAP TAP
Allie
hows it goin, sis?
eh.
make any friends yet
no.
unpack yet
no.
knew it! mom owes me $20
THWOP
UGH.

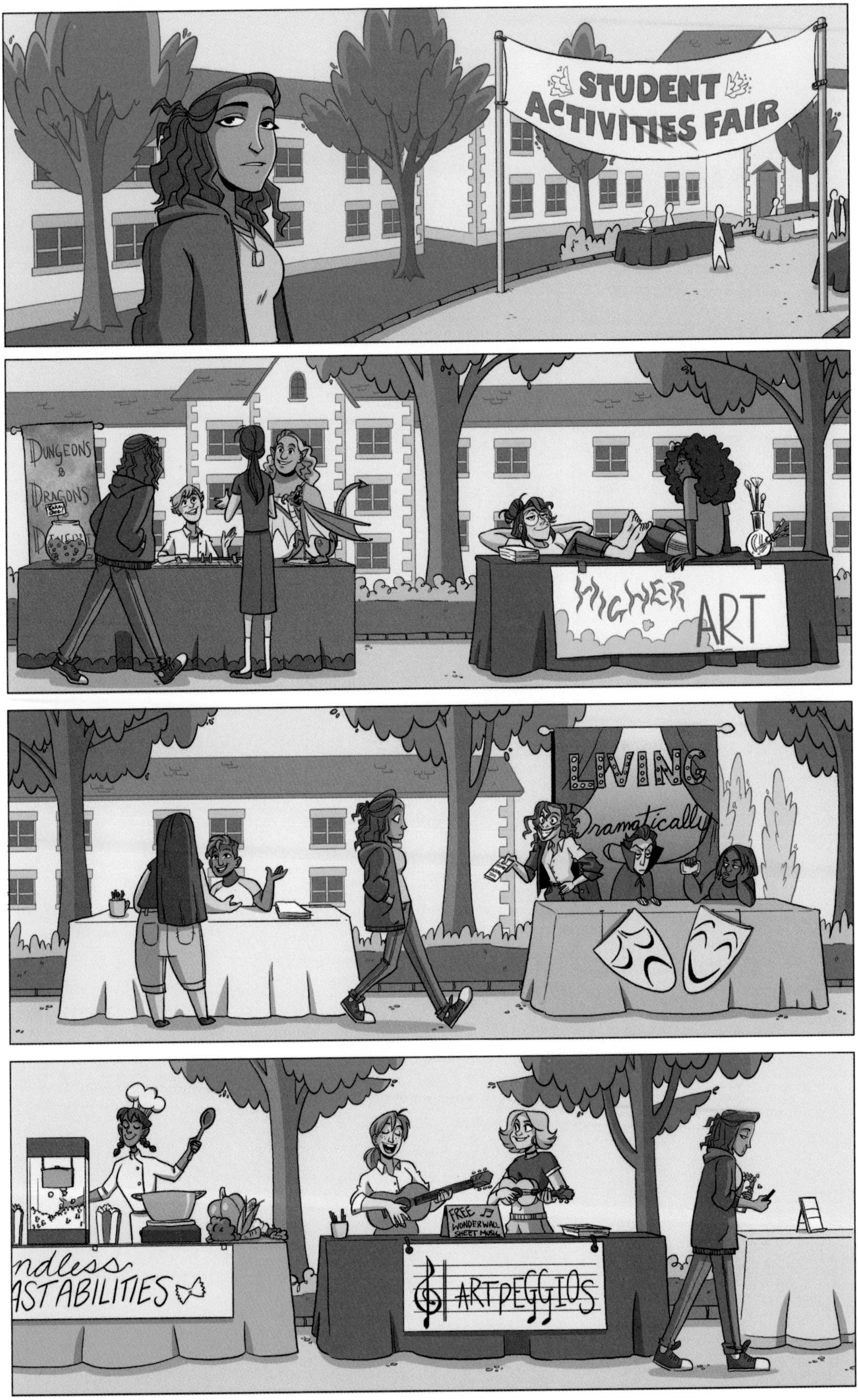
STUDENT ACTIVITIES FAIR
DUNGEONS & DRAGONS
TAKE ONE
HIGHER ART
LIVING
Dramatically
ndless
ASTABILITIES
FREE
WONDERWALL SHEET MUSIC
ARTPEGGIOS

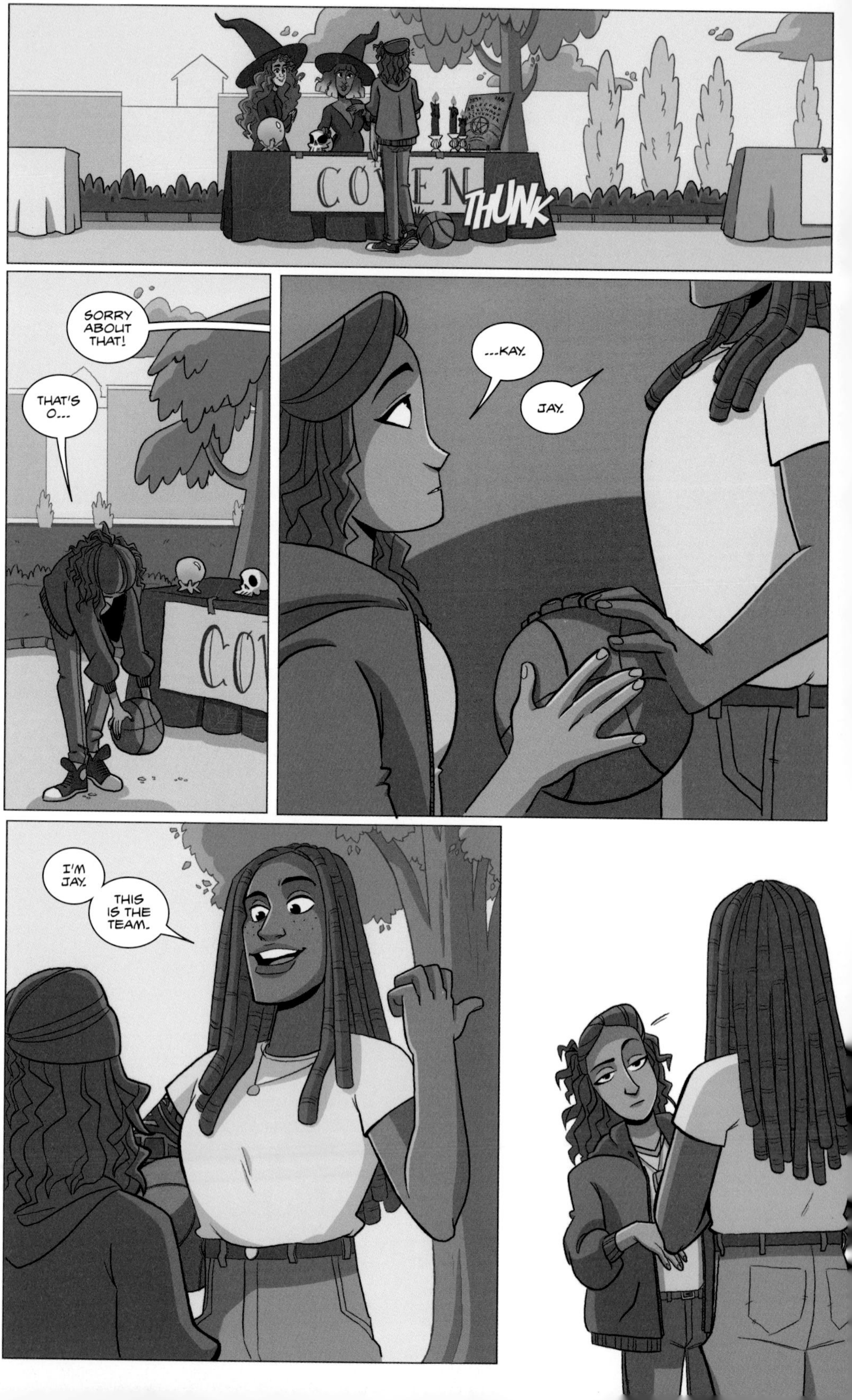
COVEN
THUNK
SORRY ABOUT THAT!
THAT'S O...
COV
...KAY.
JAY.
I'M JAY.
THIS IS THE TEAM.

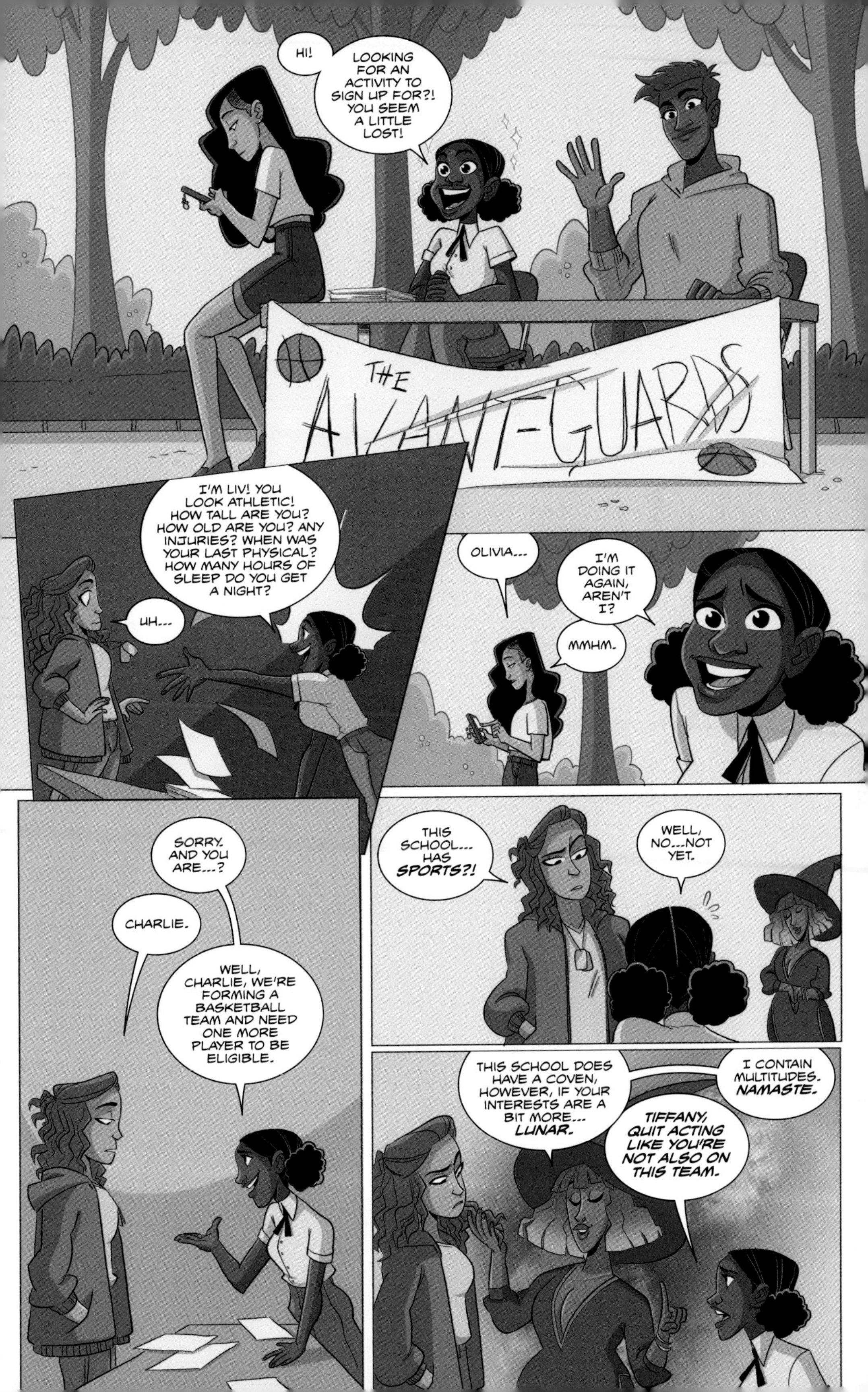

HI!
LOOKING FOR AN ACTIVITY TO SIGN UP FOR?! YOU SEEM A LITTLE LOST!
THE AVANT-GUARDS
I'M LIV! YOU LOOK ATHLETIC! HOW TALL ARE YOU? HOW OLD ARE YOU? ANY INJURIES? WHEN WAS YOUR LAST PHYSICAL? HOW MANY HOURS OF SLEEP DO YOU GET A NIGHT?
UH...
OLIVIA...
I'M DOING IT AGAIN, AREN'T I?
MMHM.
SORRY. AND YOU ARE...?
CHARLIE.
WELL, CHARLIE, WE'RE FORMING A BASKETBALL TEAM AND NEED ONE MORE PLAYER TO BE ELIGIBLE.
THIS SCHOOL... HAS SPORTS?!
WELL, NO...NOT YET.
THIS SCHOOL DOES HAVE A COVEN, HOWEVER, IF YOUR INTERESTS ARE A BIT MORE... LUNAR.
I CONTAIN MULTITUDES. NAMASTE.
TIFFANY, QUIT ACTING LIKE YOU'RE NOT ALSO ON THIS TEAM.

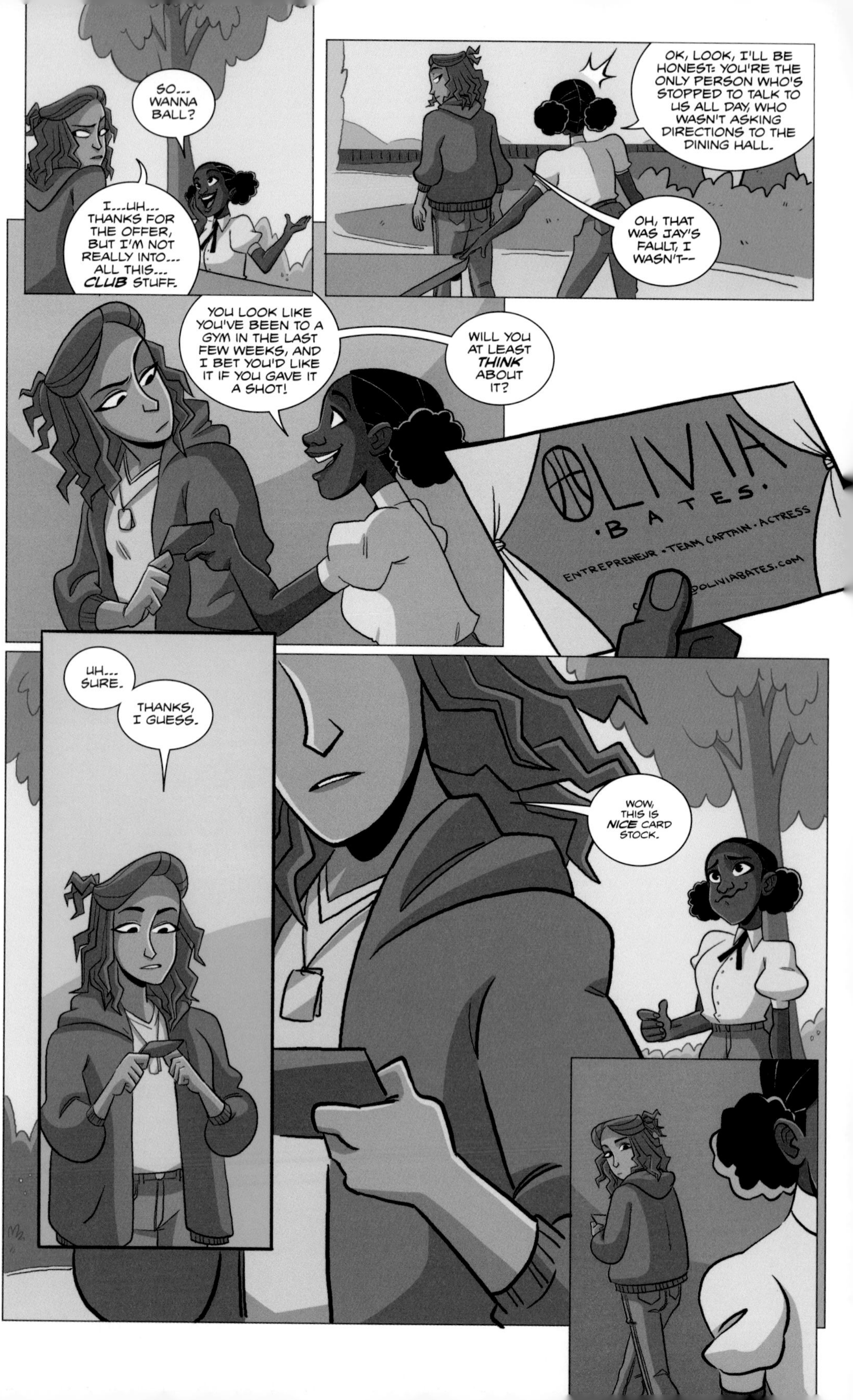
SO... WANNA BALL?
I...UH... THANKS FOR THE OFFER, BUT I'M NOT REALLY INTO... ALL THIS... CLUB STUFF.
OK, LOOK, I'LL BE HONEST: YOU'RE THE ONLY PERSON WHO'S STOPPED TO TALK TO US ALL DAY, WHO WASN'T ASKING DIRECTIONS TO THE DINING HALL.
OH, THAT WAS JAY'S FAULT, I WASN'T--
YOU LOOK LIKE YOU'VE BEEN TO A GYM IN THE LAST FEW WEEKS, AND I BET YOU'D LIKE IT IF YOU GAVE IT A SHOT!
WILL YOU AT LEAST THINK ABOUT IT?
OLIVIA
·BATES·
ENTREPRENEUR · TEAM CAPTAIN · ACTRESS
@OLIVIABATES.COM
UH... SURE.
THANKS, I GUESS.
WOW, THIS IS NICE CARD STOCK.

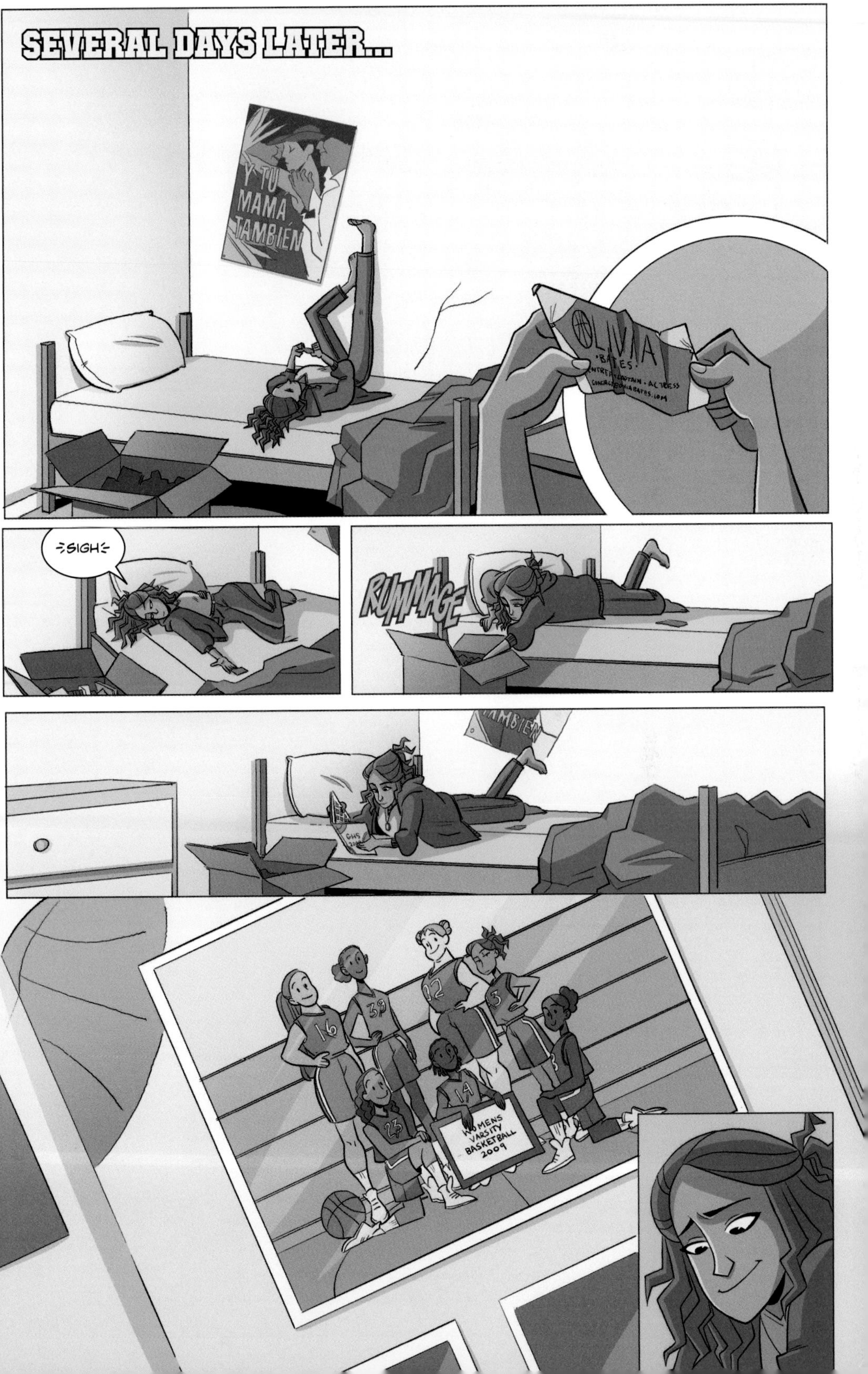
SEVERAL DAYS LATER...
Y TU MAMÁ TAMBIÉN
OLIVIA
BATES
SIGH
RUMMAGE
WOMENS VARSITY BASKETBALL 2009

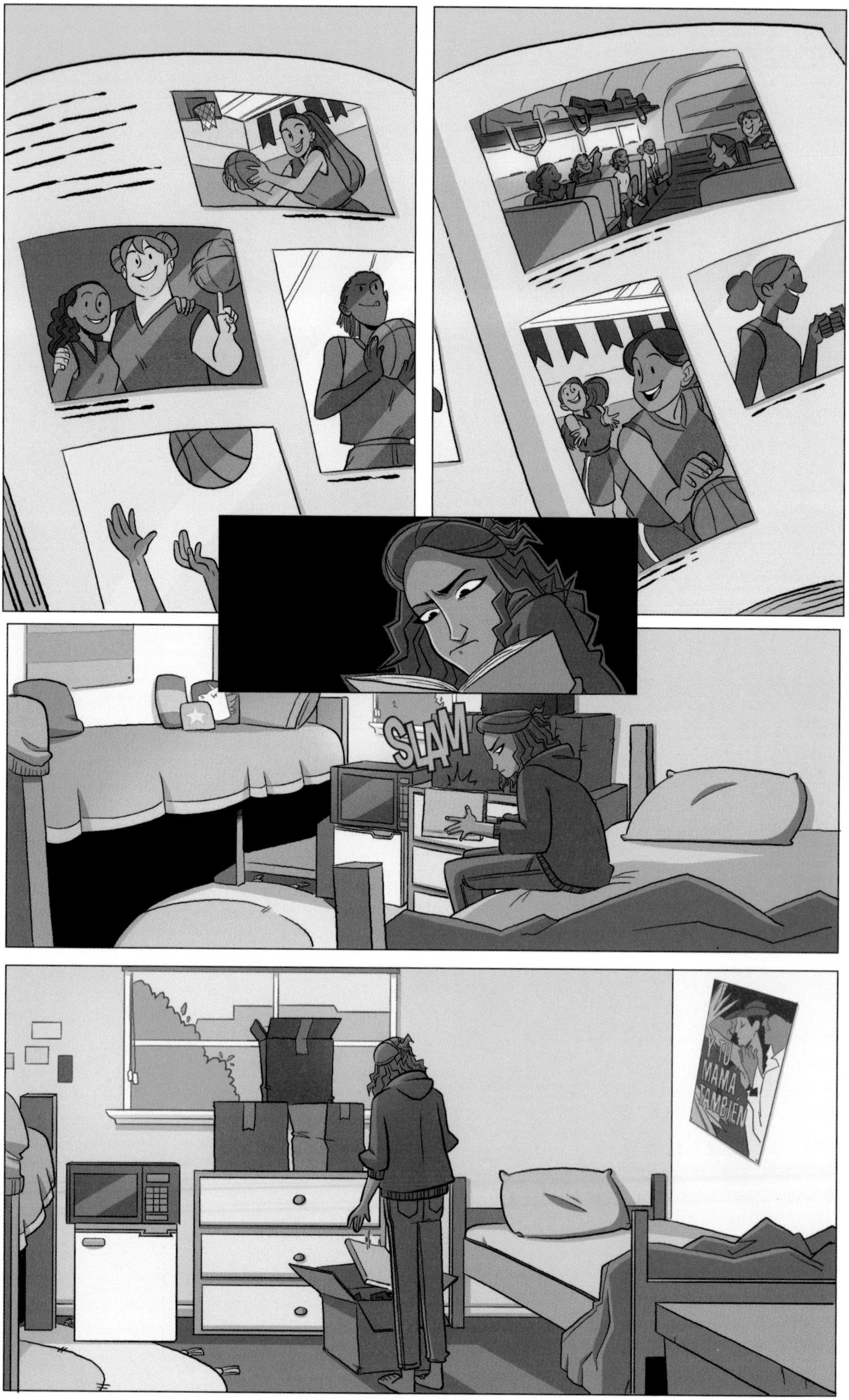
SLAM
Y TU
MAMA
TAMBIÉN

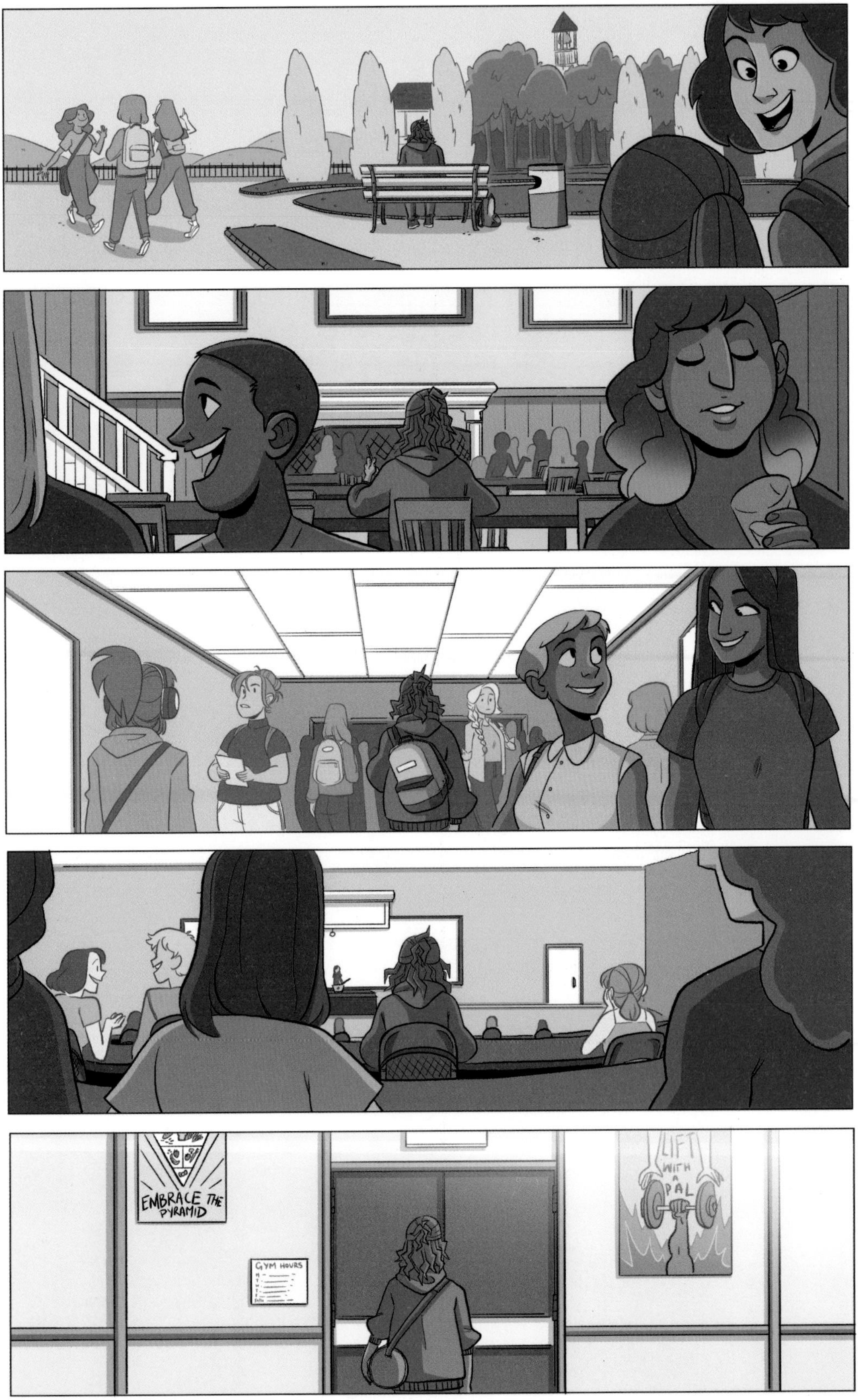
EMBRACE THE PYRAMID
GYM HOURS
LIFT WITH A PAL

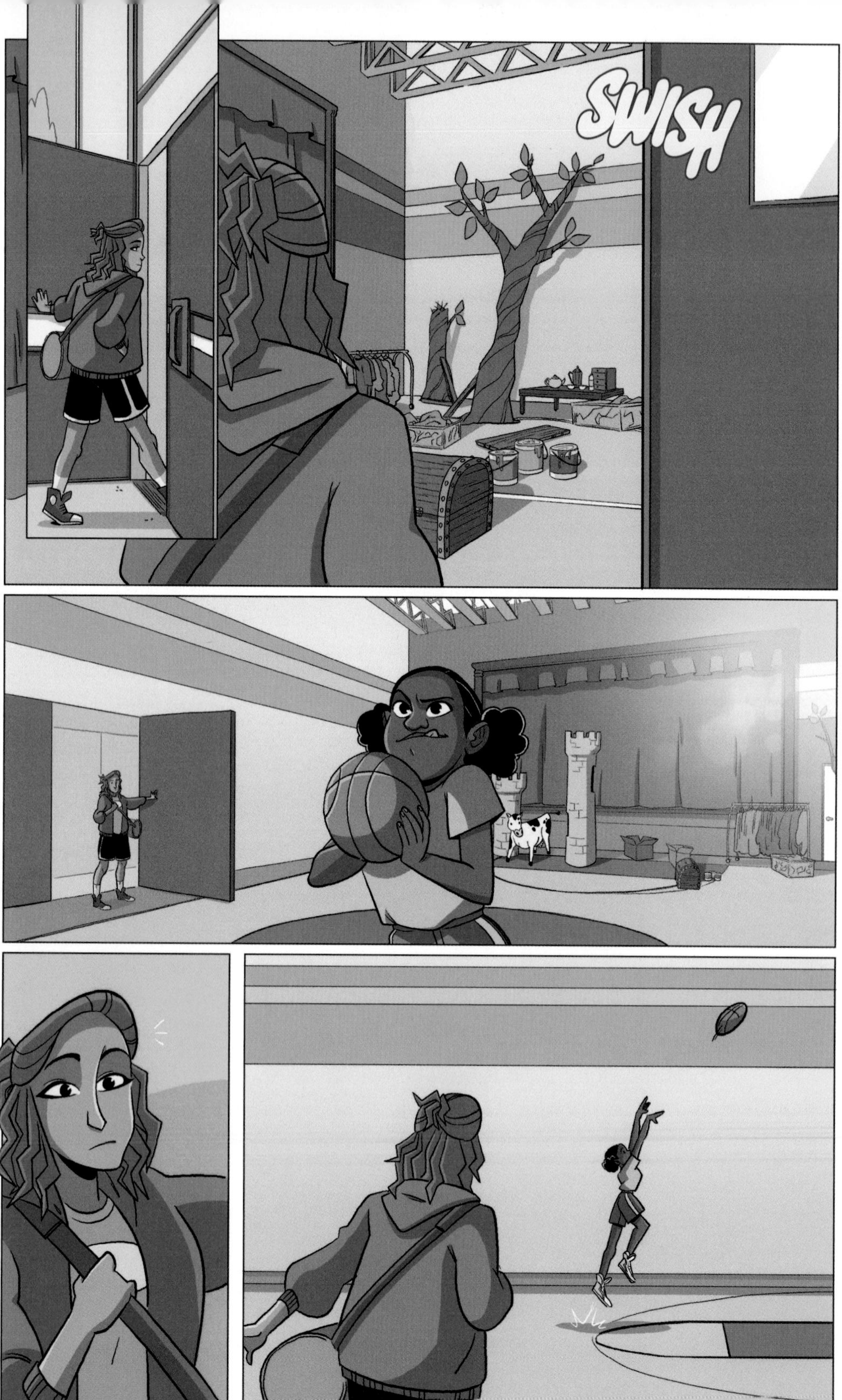
SWISH

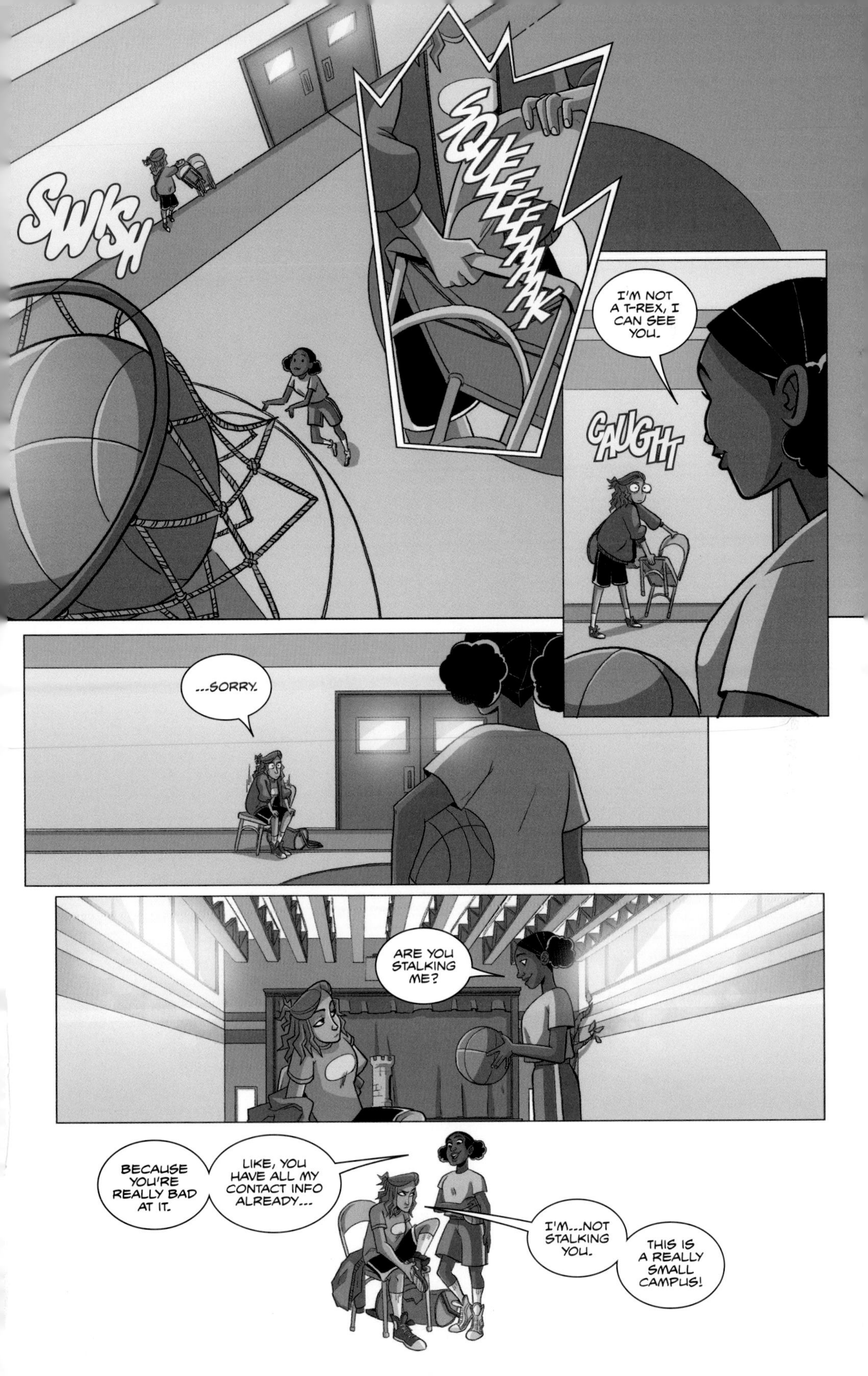
SWISH
SQUEEEEAAK
I'M NOT A T-REX, I CAN SEE YOU.
CAUGHT
...SORRY.
ARE YOU STALKING ME?
LIKE, YOU HAVE ALL MY CONTACT INFO ALREADY...
BECAUSE YOU'RE REALLY BAD AT IT.
I'M...NOT STALKING YOU.
THIS IS A REALLY SMALL CAMPUS!

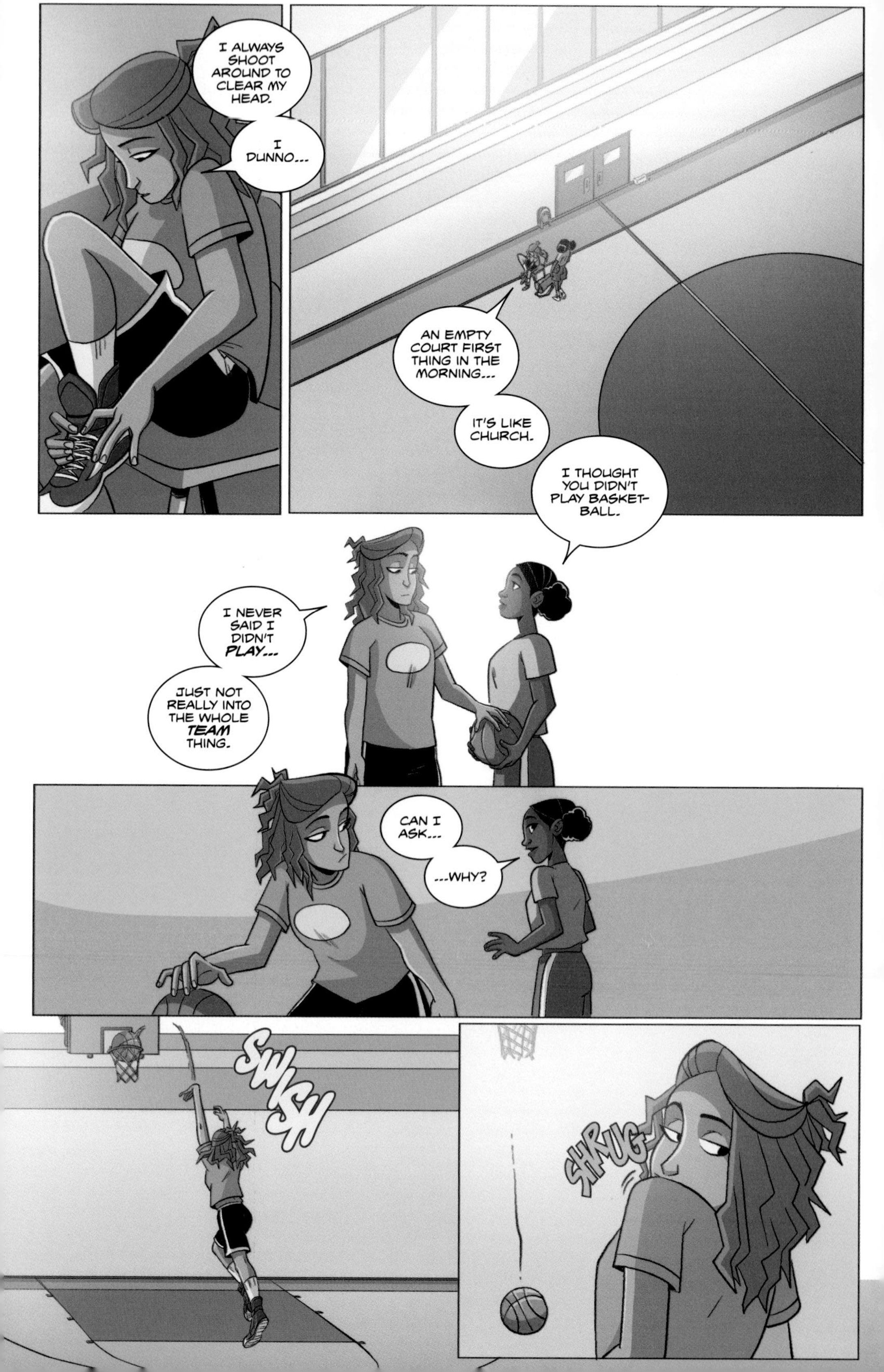
I ALWAYS SHOOT AROUND TO CLEAR MY HEAD.
I DUNNO...
AN EMPTY COURT FIRST THING IN THE MORNING...
IT'S LIKE CHURCH.
I THOUGHT YOU DIDN'T PLAY BASKET-BALL.
I NEVER SAID I DIDN'T PLAY...
JUST NOT REALLY INTO THE WHOLE TEAM THING.
CAN I ASK...
...WHY?
SWISH
SHRUG

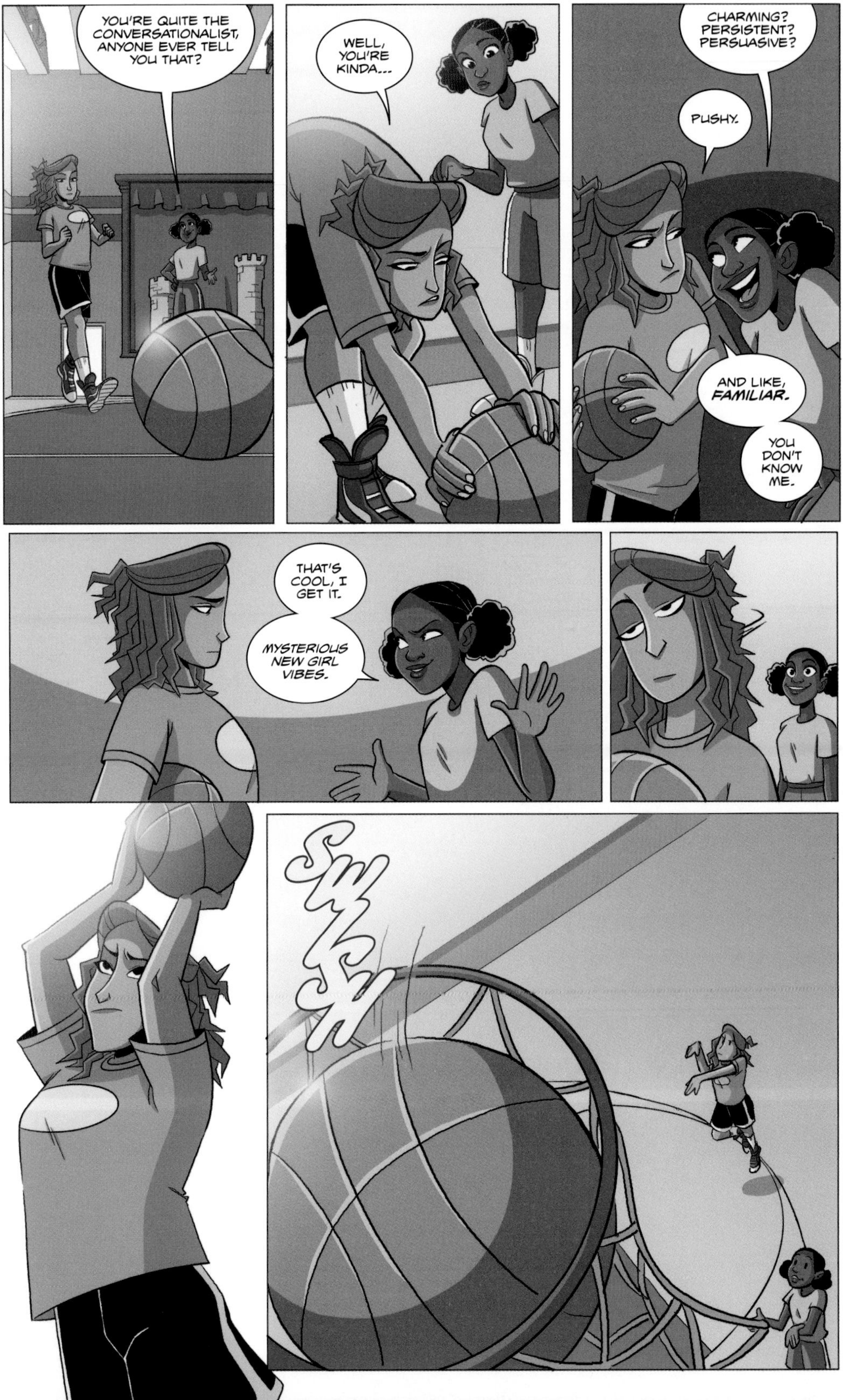
YOU'RE QUITE THE CONVERSATIONALIST, ANYONE EVER TELL YOU THAT?
WELL, YOU'RE KINDA...
CHARMING? PERSISTENT? PERSUASIVE?
PUSHY.
AND LIKE, FAMILIAR.
YOU DON'T KNOW ME.
THAT'S COOL, I GET IT.
MYSTERIOUS NEW GIRL VIBES.
SWISH

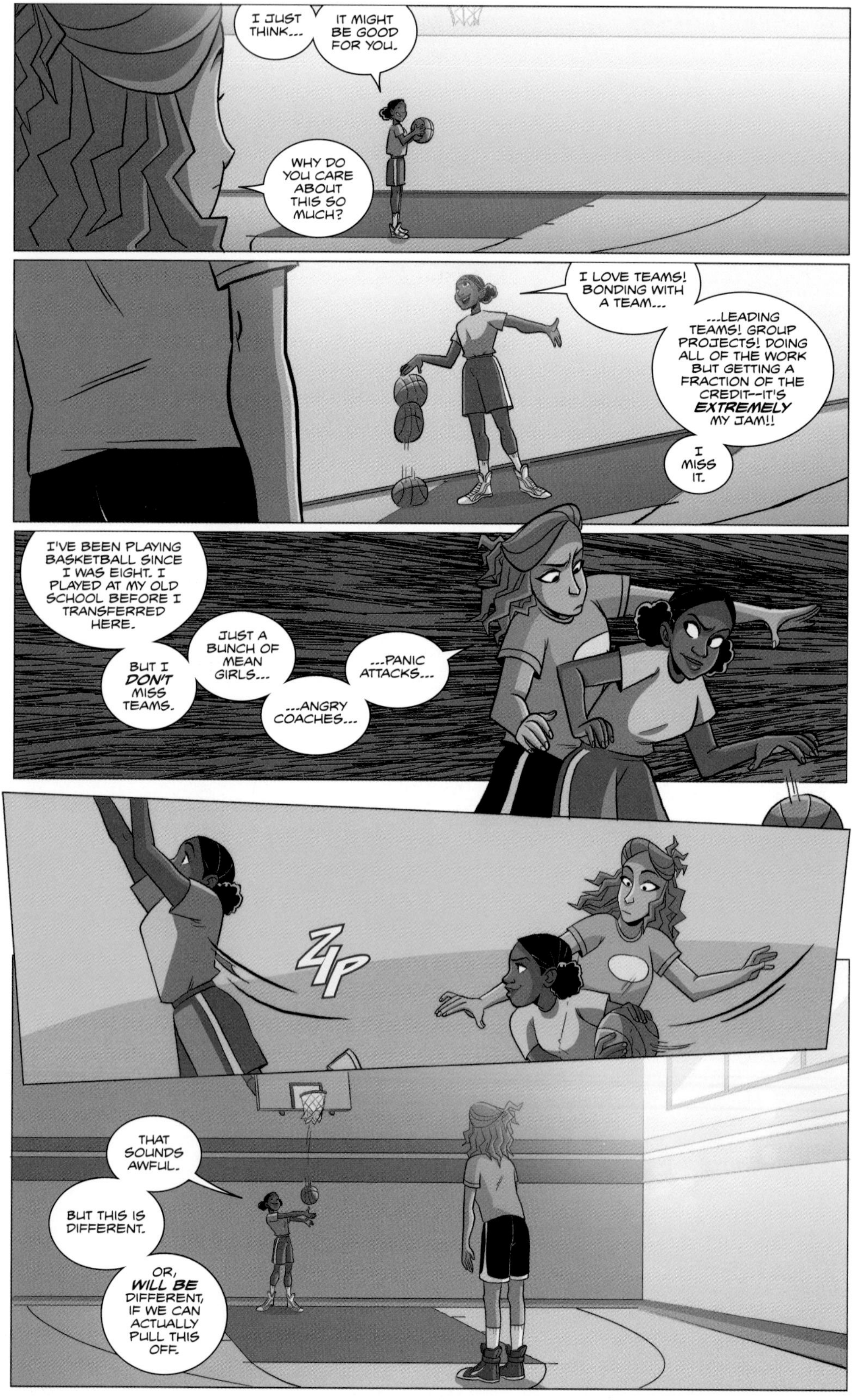
I JUST THINK...
IT MIGHT BE GOOD FOR YOU.
WHY DO YOU CARE ABOUT THIS SO MUCH?
I LOVE TEAMS! BONDING WITH A TEAM...
...LEADING TEAMS! GROUP PROJECTS! DOING ALL OF THE WORK BUT GETTING A FRACTION OF THE CREDIT--IT'S ***EXTREMELY*** MY JAM!!
I MISS IT.
I'VE BEEN PLAYING BASKETBALL SINCE I WAS EIGHT. I PLAYED AT MY OLD SCHOOL BEFORE I TRANSFERRED HERE.
BUT I ***DON'T*** MISS TEAMS.
JUST A BUNCH OF MEAN GIRLS...
...ANGRY COACHES...
...PANIC ATTACKS...
ZIP
THAT SOUNDS AWFUL.
BUT THIS IS DIFFERENT.
OR, ***WILL BE*** DIFFERENT, IF WE CAN ACTUALLY PULL THIS OFF.

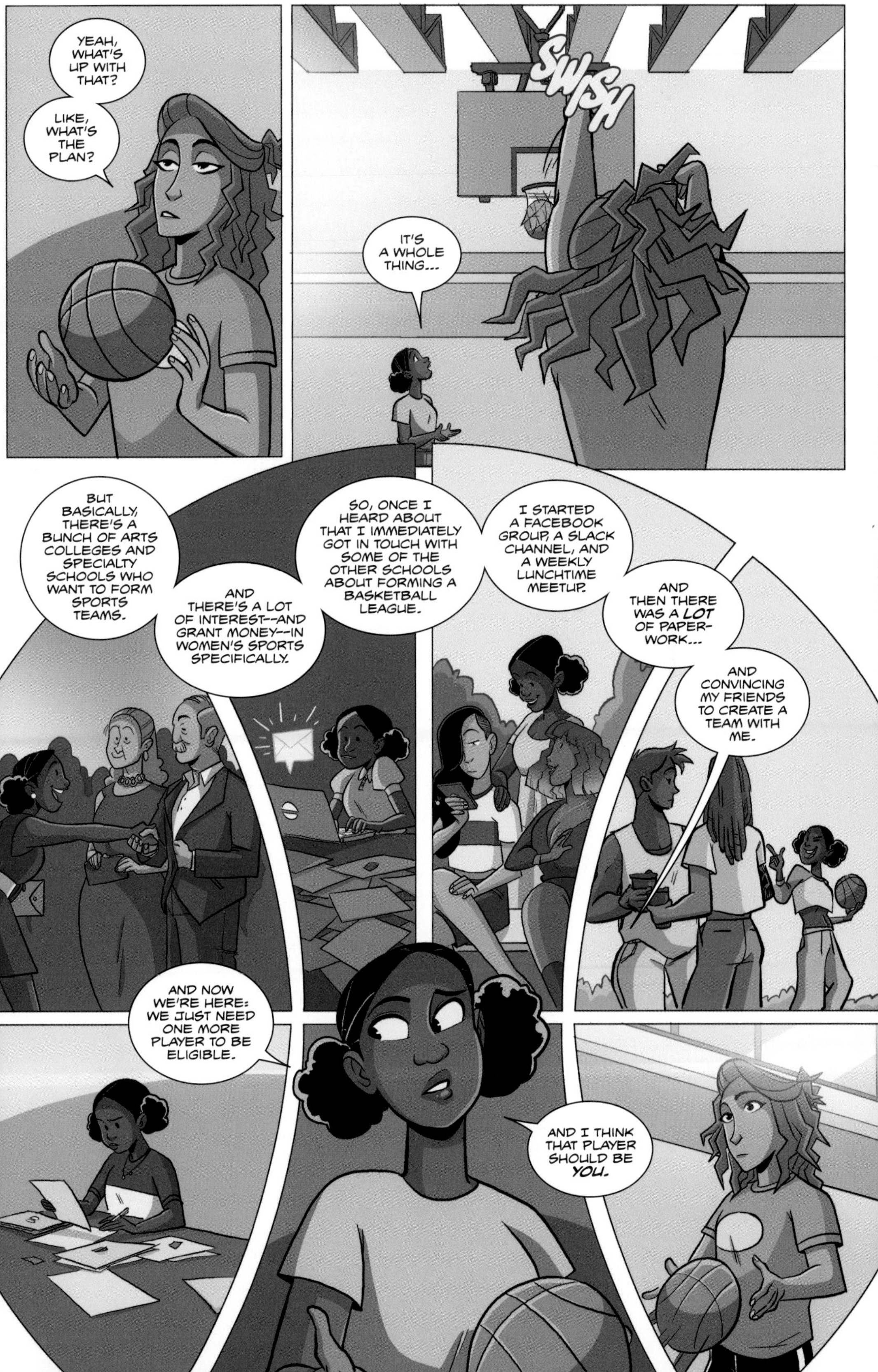
YEAH, WHAT'S UP WITH THAT?
LIKE, WHAT'S THE PLAN?
SWISH
IT'S A WHOLE THING...
BUT BASICALLY, THERE'S A BUNCH OF ARTS COLLEGES AND SPECIALTY SCHOOLS WHO WANT TO FORM SPORTS TEAMS.
AND THERE'S A LOT OF INTEREST--AND GRANT MONEY--IN WOMEN'S SPORTS SPECIFICALLY.
SO, ONCE I HEARD ABOUT THAT I IMMEDIATELY GOT IN TOUCH WITH SOME OF THE OTHER SCHOOLS ABOUT FORMING A BASKETBALL LEAGUE.
I STARTED A FACEBOOK GROUP, A SLACK CHANNEL, AND A WEEKLY LUNCHTIME MEETUP.
AND THEN THERE WAS A *LOT* OF PAPER-WORK...
AND CONVINCING MY FRIENDS TO CREATE A TEAM WITH ME.
AND NOW WE'RE HERE: WE JUST NEED ONE MORE PLAYER TO BE ELIGIBLE.
AND I THINK THAT PLAYER SHOULD BE *YOU*.

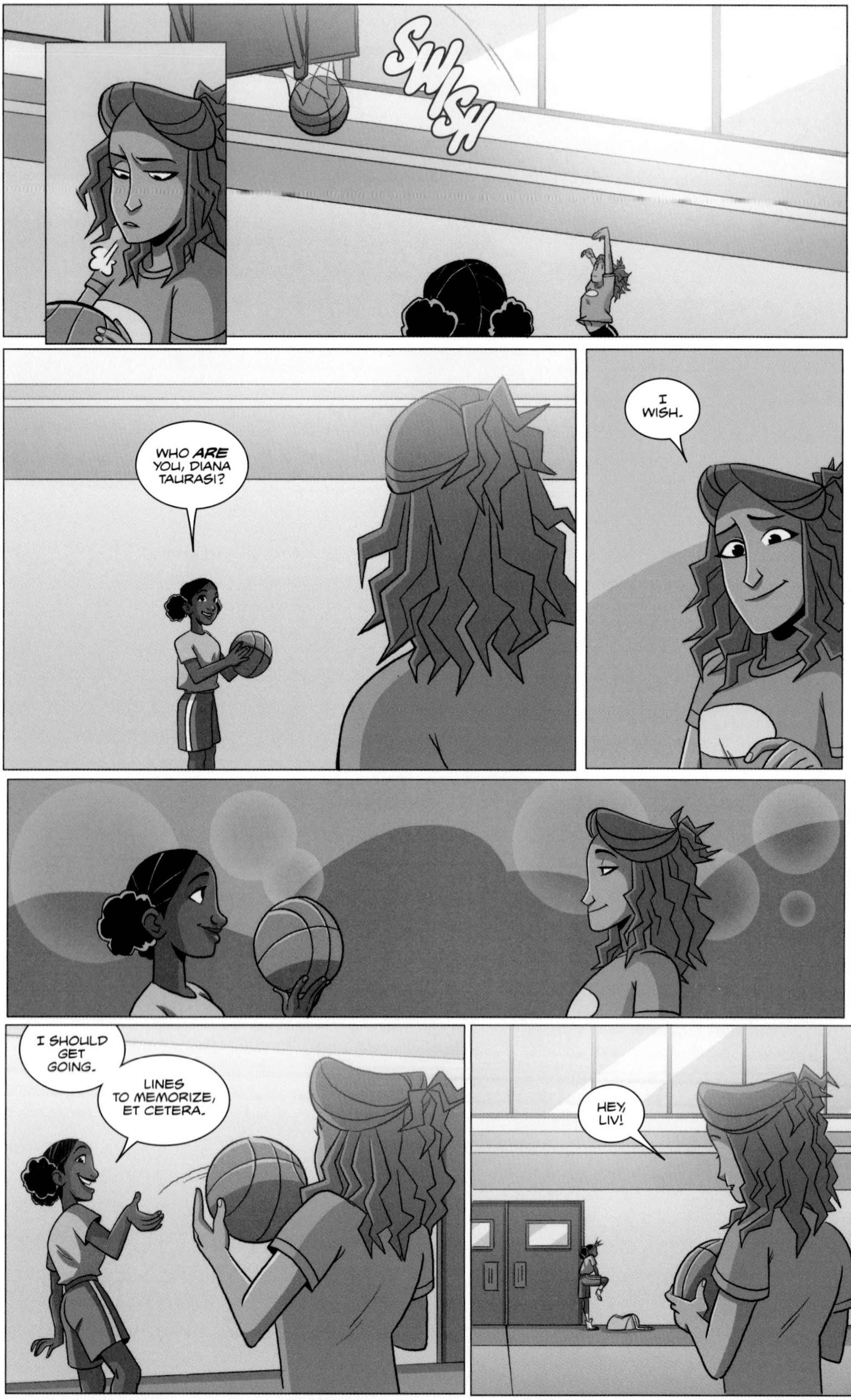
SWISH
WHO ARE YOU, DIANA TAURASI?
I WISH.
I SHOULD GET GOING.
LINES TO MEMORIZE, ET CETERA.
HEY, LIV!

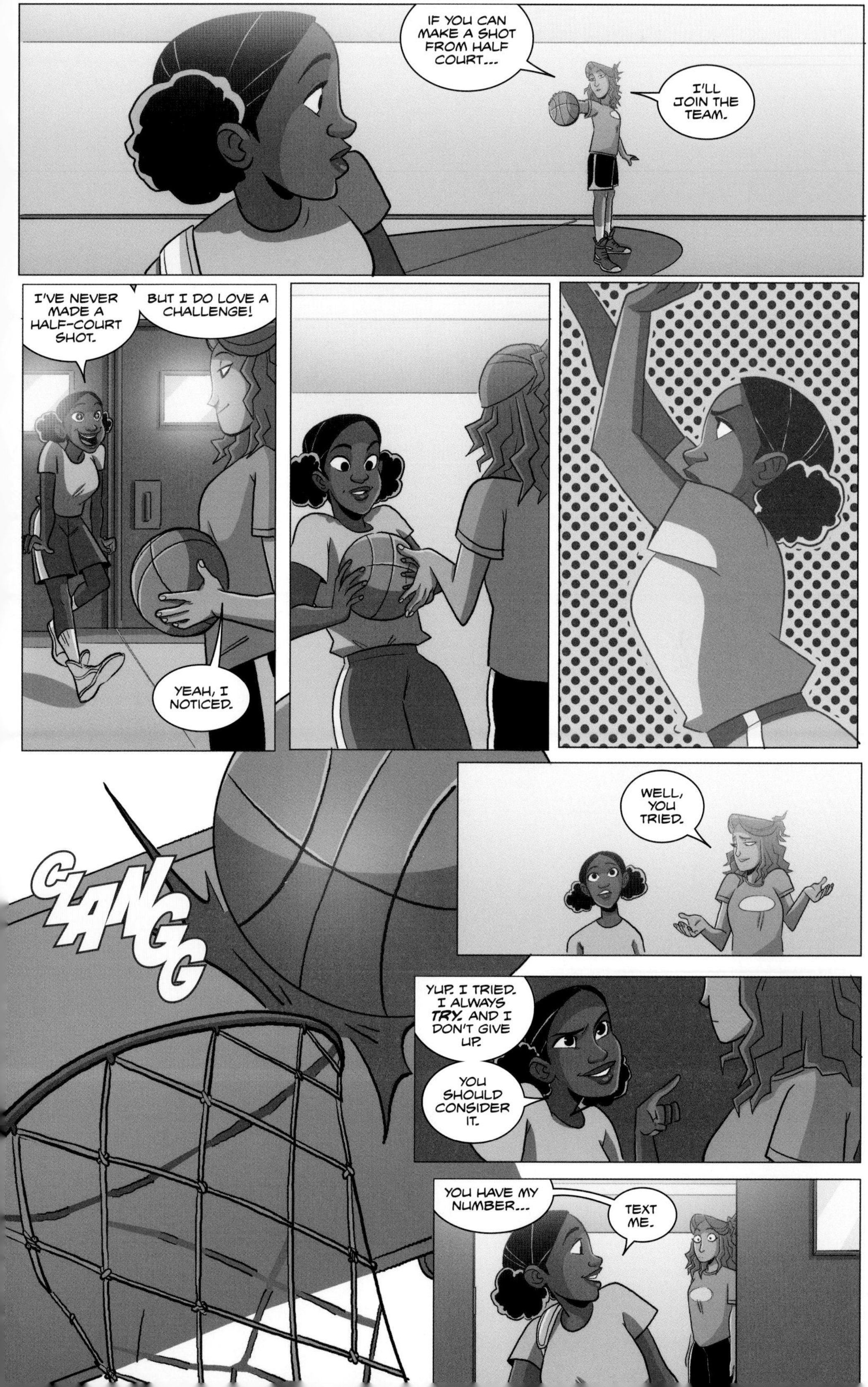
IF YOU CAN MAKE A SHOT FROM HALF COURT...
I'LL JOIN THE TEAM.
I'VE NEVER MADE A HALF-COURT SHOT.
BUT I DO LOVE A CHALLENGE!
YEAH, I NOTICED.
CLANGG
WELL, YOU TRIED.
YUP. I TRIED. I ALWAYS TRY. AND I DON'T GIVE UP.
YOU SHOULD CONSIDER IT.
YOU HAVE MY NUMBER...
TEXT ME.

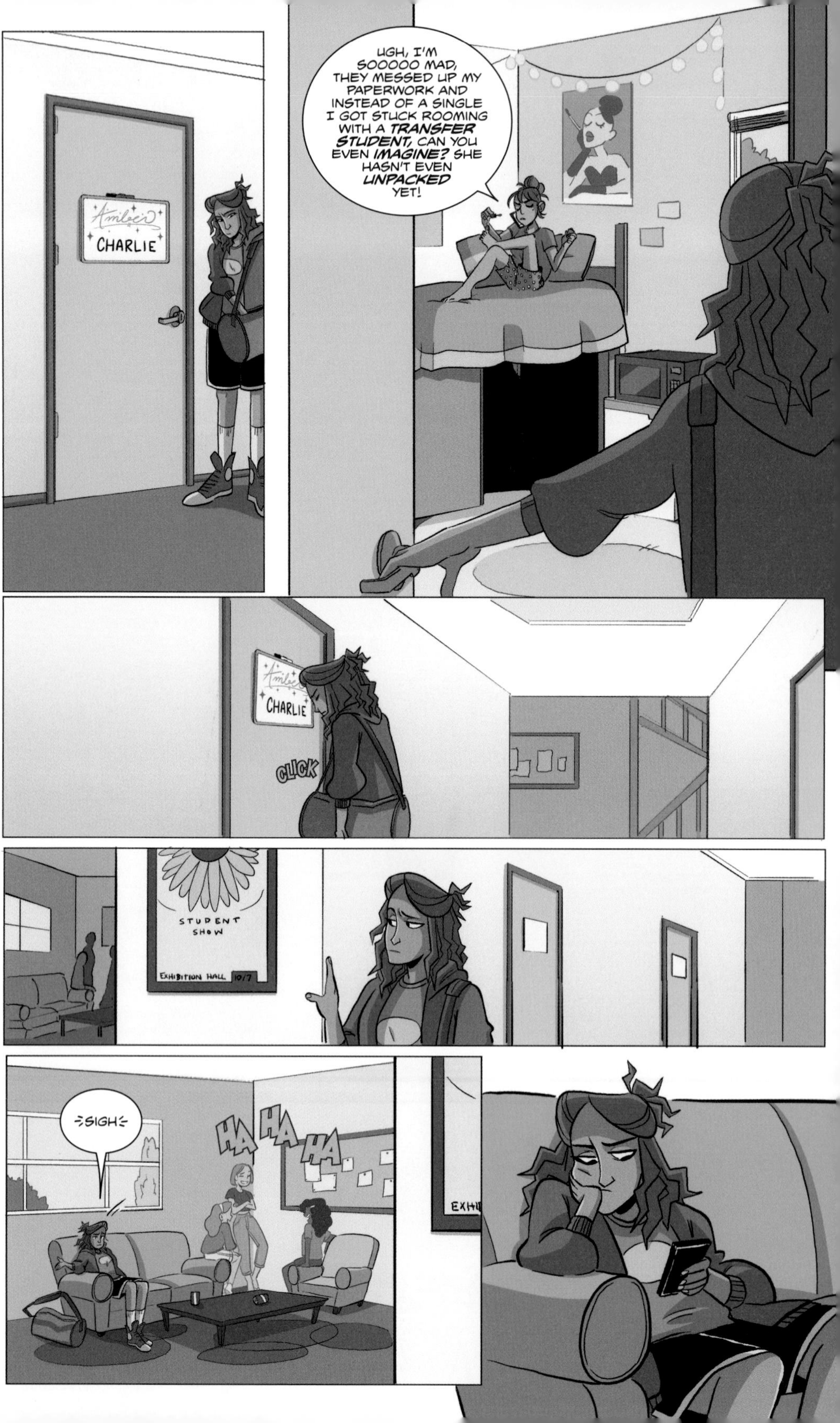
Amber
CHARLIE
UGH, I'M SOOOOO MAD, THEY MESSED UP MY PAPERWORK AND INSTEAD OF A SINGLE I GOT STUCK ROOMING WITH A TRANSFER STUDENT, CAN YOU EVEN IMAGINE? SHE HASN'T EVEN UNPACKED YET!
CHARLIE
CLICK
STUDENT SHOW
EXHIBITION HALL 10/7
-SIGH-
HA HA HA

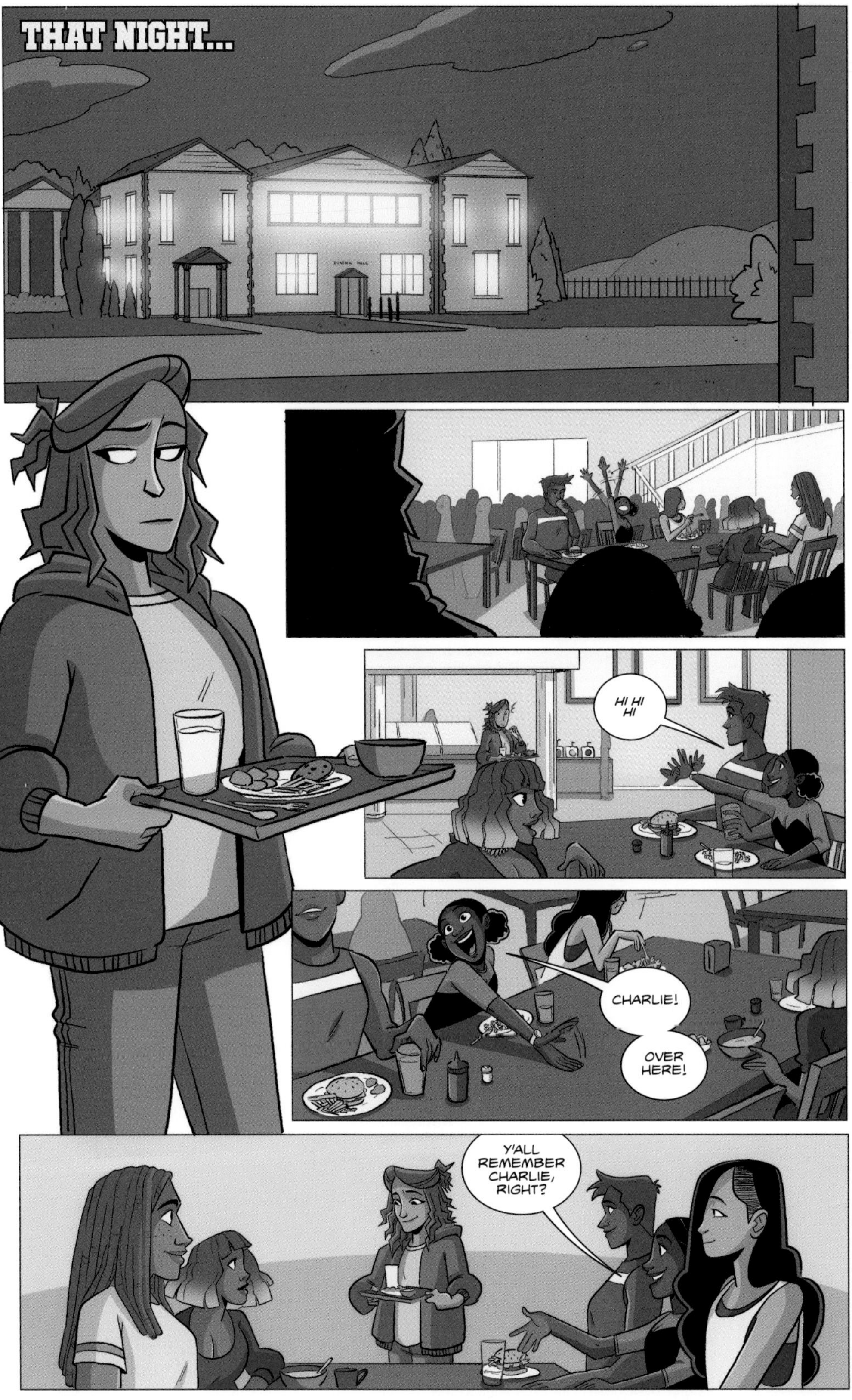
THAT NIGHT...
DINING HALL
HI HI HI
CHARLIE!
OVER HERE!
Y'ALL REMEMBER CHARLIE, RIGHT?

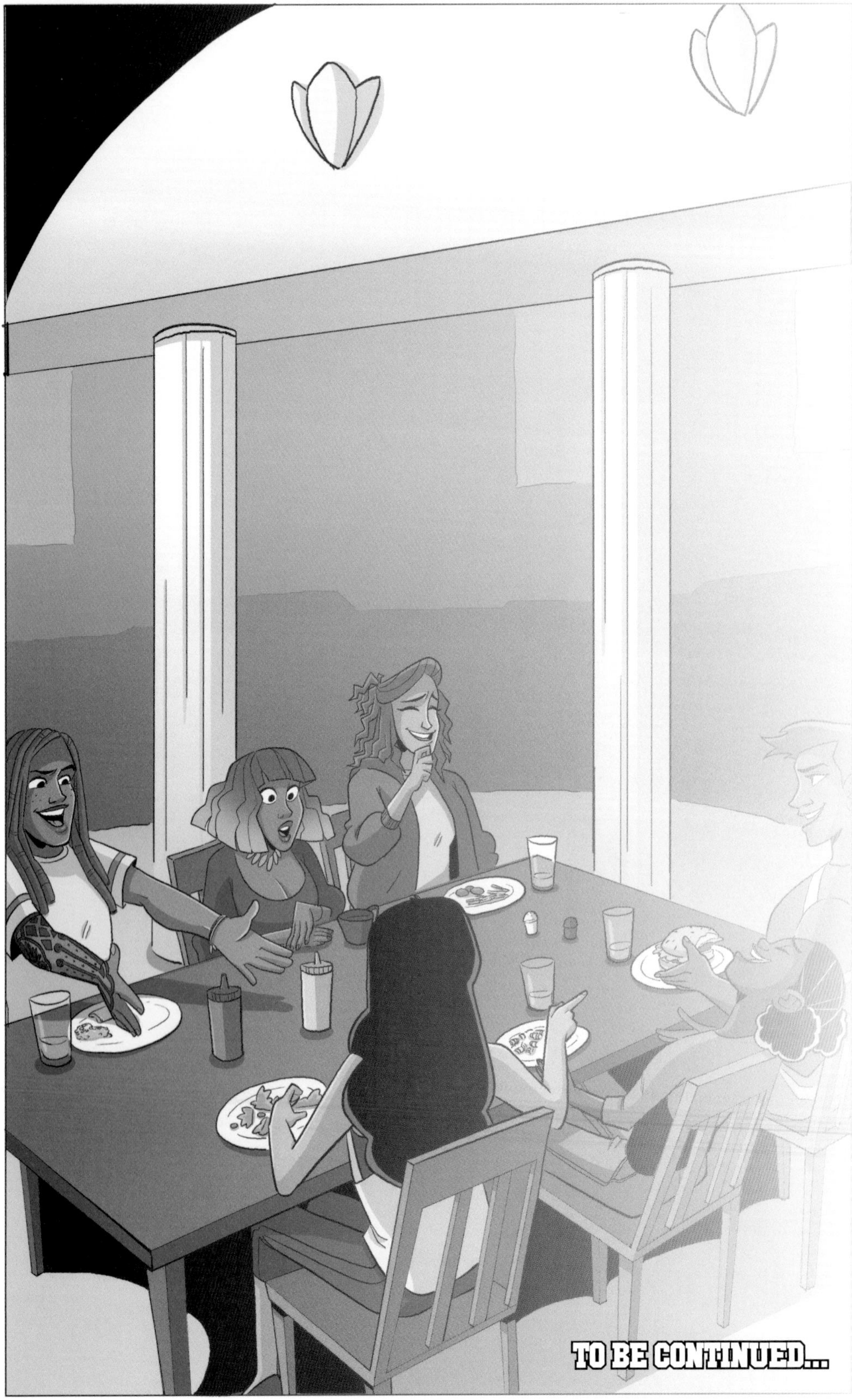
TO BE CONTINUED...

## LILAH STURGES

Lilah Sturges has been writing comics for over a decade and believes she is finally getting the hang of it. She lives in Austin, Texas with her two daughters and a cat named Greg.

## POLTERINK

polterink (also sometimes referred to as Claudia Rinofner) is a freelance artist and professional tea-drinker from Austria. As a kid she really liked spending time in the woods, feeding squirrels and building little homes for fairies out of twigs and moss.

# SHANNON WATTERS

Shannon Watters is an editor lady by day and the co-creator of *Lumberjanes*...also by day. She helped guide KaBOOM!—BOOM! Studios' all-ages imprint—to commercial and critical success, and oversees BOOM! Box, an experimental imprint created "for the love of it." She has a great love for all things indie and comics, which is something she's been passionate about since growing up in the wilds of Arizona. When she's not working on comics she can be found watching classic films and enjoying the local cuisine.

# NOELLE STEVENSON

Noelle Stevenson is the *New York Times* bestselling author of *Nimona*. She's been nominated for Harvey Awards, and was awarded the Slate Cartoonist Studio Prize for Best Web Comic in 2012 for *Nimona*. A graduate of the Maryland Institute College of Art, Noelle has worked on Disney's *Wander Over Yonder* and *She-Ra*, she has written for Marvel and DC Comics. She lives in Los Angeles. In her spare time she can be found drawing superheroes and talking about bad TV.
**www.gingerhaze.com**

# GRACE ELLIS

Grace Ellis is a writer and co-creator of *Lumberjanes*. She is currently writing *Moonstruck*, a comic about lesbian werewolf baristas, as well as scripts for the animated show *Bravest Warriors*. Grace lives in Columbus, Ohio, where she co-parents a preternaturally smart cat, even though she's usually more of a dog person.

# BROOKLYN ALLEN

Brooklyn Allen is a co-creator and original artist for *Lumberjanes* and when he is not drawing, then he will most likely be found with a saw in his hand making something rad. Currently residing in the "for lovers" state of Virginia, he spends most of his time working on comics with his not-so-helpful assistant Linus...his dog.

DISCOVER
# ALL THE HITS

STEVENSON • ELLIS • WATTERS • ALLEN
LUMBERJANES
BEWARE THE KITTEN HOLY
NEW YORK TIMES BESTSELLING SERIES

Allison + Treiman + Cogar
GIANT DAYS
VOLUME ONE

RIBON • FISH • PEER
SLAM!
VOLUME ONE

Hope Larson • Brittney Williams • Sarah Stern
GOLDIE VANCE
Volume One

THE BACKSTAGERS

TYSON HESSE'S
DIESEL
IGNITION

BOOM! BOX

**AVAILABLE AT YOUR LOCAL COMICS SHOP AND BOOKSTORE**
WWW.**BOOM-STUDIOS**.COM



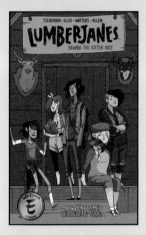

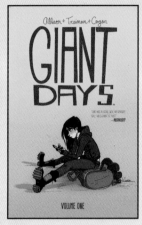

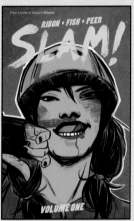

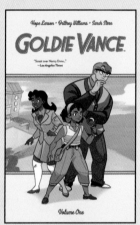

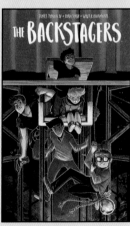

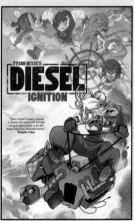

**Lumberjanes**
*Noelle Stevenson, Shannon Watters, Grace Ellis, Brooklyn Allen, and Others*
**Volume 1: Beware the Kitten Holy**
ISBN: 978-1-60886-687-8 | $14.99 US
**Volume 2: Friendship to the Max**
ISBN: 978-1-60886-737-0 | $14.99 US
**Volume 3: A Terrible Plan**
ISBN: 978-1-60886-803-2 | $14.99 US
**Volume 4: Out of Time**
ISBN: 978-1-60886-860-5 | $14.99 US
**Volume 5: Band Together**
ISBN: 978-1-60886-919-0 | $14.99 US

**Giant Days**
*John Allison, Lissa Treiman, Max Sarin*
**Volume 1**
ISBN: 978-1-60886-789-9 | $9.99 US
**Volume 2**
ISBN: 978-1-60886-804-9 | $14.99 US
**Volume 3**
ISBN: 978-1-60886-851-3 | $14.99 US

**Jonesy**
*Sam Humphries, Caitlin Rose Boyle*
**Volume 1**
ISBN: 978-1-60886-883-4 | $9.99 US
**Volume 2**
ISBN: 978-1-60886-999-2 | $14.99 US

**Slam!**
*Pamela Ribon, Veronica Fish, Brittany Peer*
**Volume 1**
ISBN: 978-1-68415-004-5 | $14.99 US

**Goldie Vance**
*Hope Larson, Brittney Williams*
**Volume 1**
ISBN: 978-1-60886-898-8 | $9.99 US
**Volume 2**
ISBN: 978-1-60886-974-9 | $14.99 US

**The Backstagers**
*James Tynion IV, Rian Sygh*
**Volume 1**
ISBN: 978-1-60886-993-0 | $14.99 US

**Tyson Hesse's Diesel: Ignition**
*Tyson Hesse*
ISBN: 978-1-60886-907-7 | $14.99 US

**Coady & The Creepies**
*Liz Prince, Amanda Kirk, Hannah Fisher*
ISBN: 978-1-68415-029-8 | $14.99 US